NIGHT

OF THE

REALTORS

I0611223

David Jenneson

1st WORLD
LIBRARY
Literary Society

Night of the Realtors

David Jenneson

© David Jenneson 2005

Published by 1stWorld Publishing
1100 North 4th St. Suite 131, Fairfield, Iowa 52556
TEL: 641-209-5000 • FAX: 641-209-3001
•WEB: www.1stworldpublishing.com

First Edition

LCCN: 2005904952
SoftCover ISBN: 1-59540-948-3
HardCover ISBN: 1-59540-950-5
eBook ISBN: 1-59540-949-1

This material has been written and published solely for educational purposes. The author and the publisher shall have neither liability or responsibility to any person or entity with respect to any loss, damage or injury caused or alleged to be caused directly or indirectly by the information contained in this book.

The characters and events described in this text are intended to entertain and teach rather than present an exact factual history of real people or events.

To the little
realtor in all of us.

CHAPTER 1

A stiff wet wind blew down from Dog Mountain. The rain from the British Columbia coast storm danced off the dark pavement and ran in moonless rivers down Dempsey Road. Ribbons of fog drifted across the street, blurring Ray Seawee's vision.

The wind picked at Seawee's cuffs. He poked his way up the stairs and spent an agonizing moment on the porch, wanting to run away. A bug lamp twirled at the end of the porch, useless in the rain.

He was afraid to ring the doorbell. When he was released from prison three days ago he was told to straighten up and fly right. When Seawee asked what this meant, his probation officer told him if something felt wrong then it was. "Gut feel," the probation officer jabbed a finger at him.

Praying that what he was about to do was both honest and right, he twisted the rusty doorbell. Amber light glowed deep inside the old house.

Suddenly he wanted to go away and work through this whole question of right and wrong, innocence and guilt. Wrestle the issue to the ground before starting anything fresh. He would get thick square books from the library and read and drink coffee in Starbucks. He would reflect. He would make notes and smoke cigarettes and informed opinions would rise about him like smoke rings. Once and for all he'd get a firm grip on this troublesome matter.

He was about to go and look for a Starbucks when he heard a bump and rustle within the house.

His stomach sank. His first prospect was coming to the door and he had no moral compass to guide him. Would his gut tell him if he said a dishonest thing to these people like his probation officer had said?

The owner of the house opened the door. Ray Seawee realized he knew him. Years earlier he'd ripped off fruit and vegetables from McGregor's back garden for the joy of stealing. Back then Mr. McGregor had been feisty and warlike and he'd come roaring out of the back door waving his arms at Seawee. It was easy for Ray Seawee to outrun him. Seawee added insult to injury by shouting abuse over his shoulder at McGregor as he fled. Mr. McGregor never chased him far. He was overweight, in bad health and as slow as porridge. So now, twenty years later, it was reasonable for Seawee to hope that Mr. McGregor might have become in some way enfeebled and less aggressive.

Mr. McGregor crossed his arms behind the wooden screen door. He seemed to have been in the middle of either getting dressed or getting undressed. He wore only gray flannel dress pants. With dismay, Seawee saw that he was shirtless. Other than the fringe of gray around his head he was the hairiest person Ray Seawee had ever seen. He looked like a retired bear or gorilla. It was like someone had injected a basketball with hair tonic - black curly hair covered him from the neck down. Seawee couldn't help staring at McGregor's stomach. It was so round yet looked so firm, bulging over the narrow black dress belt. Mr. McGregor looked like he'd swallowed a cannonball and was not pleased with it.

"Yes?" Mr. McGregor. It was a strict yes. An impatient yes. A yes that felt more like a no if you were going on gut feel, thought Ray Seawee.

Seawee stared at him through the screen mesh. He realized he'd made a big mistake by coming to this house but now it was too late. He worried that whatever he said would sound dishonest to McGregor and he'd call the police.

Ray Seawee stood tongue-tied.

McGregor frowned in return.

Nothing forthcoming from Seawee.

McGregor slammed the door so hard it knocked the dead bugs off the screen. Seawee flinched. Surely he was on his way to call the police. Of that Seawee was certain. "There's a mute at the door," Mr. McGregor announced to his wife when he went back inside. "I was worried he was an encyclopedia salesman or a Jehovah's Witness. Maybe I was too hard on him. He stood there trying to talk so I closed the door. Well dressed too. In a suit."

"Maybe he's from a local home," said Mrs. McGregor from the back parlor. She sat in an overstuffed chair with her hands resting on the hard wooden arms. "He might be slow. They've probably dressed him up and sent him out for the day. Now he's lost. Go and give him directions."

Mr. McGregor grumbled and started toward the door.

"We have a guide to sign language for the deaf in the encyclopedia," his wife shouted after him. "Take it with you."

At that moment Ray Seawee twisted the doorbell again. It was the only thing he could think of to stop the police being called on his account.

"Listen to that," Mrs. McGregor scolded. "The poor soul doesn't know what to do. Get the encyclopedia and go out and help him."

"What am I, a social worker?"

'And put on a shirt. You must look like a bear to the boy. You'll scare him into wandering the streets all night."

The front door opened a second time. To Seawee's relief, Mr. McGregor now had more clothes on. A white dress shirt now covered his hairy arms and torso. The buttons strained over his hard round stomach. For Ray Seawee's part, this was better than looking at what was underneath. At least now he was dealing with a human and not a bad-tempered grizzly. He noticed that Mr. McGregor was studying a book he held in one hand. In fact, McGregor was ignoring him altogether for the moment.

To Seawee's amazement, Mr. McGregor made a series of strange hand signals at him from behind the screen door.

He then uttered a single word. Very loud. "Are?"

McGregor consulted the book again. Ray Seawee wished he knew what was in there. It was as if Mr. McGregor was learning to speak all over again, aided by hand movements to stimulate his brain. It must be a wonderful book. More hand signals in Seawee's direction now.

"You?" McGregor shouted slowly.

Seawee stood transfixed. McGregor's bald pate gleamed in the porch light as he bent over the book. He seemed to pant with concentration. He looked up and described more signals in the air. His hands looked like fat, hairy birds struggling to stay aloft.

"Lost?" McGregor hollered and beamed with triumph.

This was the strangest greeting Seawee had ever seen. It was far stranger than any of those jive hand routines in prison. He struggled for an answer. Obviously Mr. McGregor was ill. He'd suffered some catastrophic collapse. The man could barely speak. Perhaps he also couldn't hear. That might explain his odd bursts of shouting.

Suddenly Ray Seawee felt guilty. His fruit stealing and abuse-shouting at McGregor must have had a lingering effect. Look what had happened to the poor man.

In reply Seawee spread his hands wide, shook his head from side to side and grinned broadly. It was a silent but cheerful sign language no. He hoped this would make Mr. McGregor feel better after his recent decline.

McGregor seemed stumped. He'd come to the end of the hand-signal road more quickly than expected. Surely this fellow was a wandering idiot. He couldn't imagine either what his next question would be, or how to put it. The idea of putting together long strings of inquiries with laborious hand signals while this fellow gave silent, one-word answers was too much to bear. Why were deaf mutes walking the streets at this hour anyway? What was wrong with the government?

"Humph!' he snorted and slammed the front door for a second time.

He went down the hall to the back parlor. "He's not lost," he informed his wife with an air of finality, as if hoping that would bring an end to it.

On the cold windy porch, Ray Seawee admitted to himself that things weren't really going all that well. His mind swam with consequences. Flashing squad car lights whirled in his head. A jail cell. His one phone call. A numb-nuts legal aid lawyer. He imagined his probation officer clicking his tongue and signing forms booking him back in for a good, long stay at the crowbar hotel. Even if he turned and ran now he'd still have to explain this fiasco to his new boss, Red Devlin.

Devlin was a master realtor. At this moment he waited to hear the results of Seawee's first call. He expected results, not screw-ups. Devlin would surely fire him for this. In a tiny corner of Ray Seawee's mind the prospect of sitting in a Starbuck's and reading up about right and wrong grew smaller and fainter. He turned the doorbell again.

"So you've left him outside!" Mrs. McGregor accused her husband. "Bring him in. We'll be charged with neglect."

The front door opened a third time and now Mr. McGregor motioned Seawee inside. He was happy in the hallway; sheltered from the cold, wet wind on the back of his neck. Mr. McGregor might not be able to talk or hear very well any more, but Seawee thought he could make his pitch to Mrs. McGregor. He remembered her as being slightly less cranky. He knew that as long as *someone* heard him out, the deal was nearly unrefusable. The offer Red Devlin had sent him to peddle sounded almost too good to be true. Red Devlin was a genius. His name would go down in real estate history. The man had invented a way for ordinary people like the McGregors to make money from their home without ever having to sell it. And they wouldn't loose a dime of equity in the process. They could still pass all home and property on to the grandchildren. Ray Seawee hoped it was on the level. He felt lucky to be involved at all.

"He's a Seawee!" Mrs. McGregor recognized him the instant he set his foot into the back parlor. "George, he's a *Seawee*."

To Ray Seawee, what she said sounded like a marine biologist identifying an especially low form of tidal sludge. Worse, if there was a pecking order among tidal sludge, it was obvious that his branch was at the bottom end. She made the name Seawee sound like a bacterial mudworm.

Ray Seawee decided to keep his mouth shut a while longer. If you stood still long enough, said nothing and returned friendly gestures, the way eventually seemed to open. He liked being here. With the warm firelight and overstuffed furniture it was like stepping into a Normal Rockwell painting. As long as he didn't speak, he seemed to be half-accepted. It smelled faintly of wood smoke and good baking. Who cared what they said between themselves? He was supposed to be deaf. So in theory there was no one on hand to hear these insults. *If an insult falls in the forest and there is no one there to hear, is anyone offended?* On balance he was ahead. Besides, he was through the door. If he was going to be a real realtor that's what counted.

"I didn't know there were any deaf Seawees," Mrs. McGregor continued. "I remember that they were all quite bright. Bad, but bright."

"This one's retarded too," Mr. McGregor observed. He pored over the encyclopedia. "I'm thinking of asking him if he wants us to call the police. How can I say that in a few words? This hand spelling hurts my fingers. Seems to get through to him though."

With each word, Ray Seawee sensed himself drifting downward through the social register. He fell layer by layer. Where moments ago he'd been only mute, now he was a half-wit too. On one hand there was safety in silence. On the other, the longer he kept his mouth shut the more he mortgaged his social acceptability.

"We'll call the police." Mr. McGregor muttered from inside the encyclopedia. "Call 911. Tell them we've got a lost retarded deaf-mute stuck in the house. That's an awful long sentence in this sign language. How should I tell him what we're going to do?"

Mrs. McGregor shrugged and patted the wooden arms of her chair in frustration. She looked away. "Just get on with it."

"They'll take him back where he belongs," he reached for the phone.

Seawee felt the shadowy room close in like a jail cell. He scrambled to his feet. "I'm not retarded, I'm a realtor," the words tumbled from his mouth.

Now the McGregors were silent.

"Christ, he's learned to speak," remarked Mr. McGregor. 'We've witnessed a miracle."

Having found his tongue, Ray Seawee knew there was no going back. He plunged forward. All rehearsing and practice went out the window. Only two thoughts remained: be honest and try to look like a busy man.

"This will only take a minute," he added. "I've got more calls tonight. The reason I didn't say anything before is out of respect. I wanted to let you talk first. This is your house. It's only right you talk first. Most people talk too much but I think it's polite to be quiet and let others start. It must be my turn by now. And I'm here to tell you about something important."

Transfixed, the McGregors seemed to have lost their tongues.

"I called on you first because I grew up here. I'm loyal to the neighborhood. Bring the opportunity to those who deserve it most, that's what I say. So just listen to it once. After that it's up to you. I mean, no obligation. No more talking from me."

"Aha!" cried Mr. McGregor to his wife. "You were right. I recognize him now. He's a Seawee all right. Neighborhood thief. Used to chase the little bastard down the lane." Then, turning to Seawee, "Beat it. I don't allow your kind in the house."

Ray Seawee could not let this happen. It was too early in his real estate career. He thought about right and wrong again. Was he right letting Mr. McGregor throw away this opportunity just because he wanted to toss Seawee into the street? But for the wrong reasons? In the dim corners of his mind Ray Seawee searched for the answer. He decided the best thing was to act like a responsible realtor and help Mr. McGregor get past this ornery spell. There was still the possibility that Mr. McGregor was ill and not feeling himself. Yes. That was right. Act in McGregor's best interests even if he didn't know it. Help him out of his wrong-headedness.

"I'm sorry I upset you," Seawee looked at his wet shoes. "I just started at this job."

"You've upset everyone around here," Mr. McGregor shot back. "Robbed and stolen and caused trouble since you could walk. You started off with my fruit trees when you were eight or nine. I finally cut them down because of people like you. I heard they put you away so we'd be safe. By the way, why are you out? What have you done? Escaped?"

Seawee hung his head. He looked like a criminal about to confess. "I don't blame you. I'd be mad too. It's not easy for someone like me."

"You make your own trouble. People like you, no one to blame but themselves," snorted McGregor. "Don't expect pity from us. See the door? In two minutes I call 9-1-1. I'm sure you've escaped, or lied your way out."

Seawee thought hard. Needing a quick, answer he relied on his old standby - the surefire Story of the Mighty Twin. "No sir. I haven't. But if it makes you feel any better there's a Seawee behind bars

DAVID JENNESON

tonight. Safe and sound."

"Half your family in by now I suppose," said McGregor scornfully. "How much is this costing taxpayers? There were a lot of Seawees put away in the end, weren't there?" he asked Mrs. McGregor.

"Just one," Ray Seawee folded his hands. "Victor. My twin brother."

"One? Seems to me the more Seawees behind bars the better. Who cares about one twin Seawee anyway, more or less?"

Seawee narrowed his eyes. "He's the one you chased down the lane. My identical twin. He uses my name. He's got ID proving he's both of us. He's whoever he wants to be. How would you like being me? I try and get ahead and get my own name thrown back in my face. I start a business then find out he's ruined my credit. I can't buy a car. I've tried everything but it all falls flat."

Seawee massaged his forehead, like the memories of Victor hurt his brain.

"He's in and out of jail," his voice broke a little. "He's smarter than me. When he gets out he uses me, I can't help trusting him - we're twins. Promises he'll fly right. We start something together - just some little business. Things go okay for a while. But because he's so smart he gets bored easy so he starts scamming. He's very cunning. Suddenly one day he's gone. No money left. Cops show up. They think I'm him. The bills are a mess. Victor knows how to sign my name. He does both of us in. It takes months to sort things out. Sooner or later he pops up somewhere else."

"Where does he pop up? Around here?"

"Sometimes. Or anywhere. But by then he's run out of names and gets nailed. Everyone makes do with one name for his whole life. These days just one name can be a real headache. But for Victor two aren't enough," Seawee's voiced trailed off into a sob as the injustice of the situation struck home.

"Why not just change your name and get rid of him?" asked Mr. McGregor.

Ray Seawee had become so absorbed in his own tale that this hadn't occurred to him. There had to be a good reason, otherwise he wouldn't have allowed this to happen.

"I've still got pride. Maybe I'll lose everything but I won't lose my name. My mother and father gave it to me when I was born. Sometimes I think it's the only thing I own. If I lose my name I'll be worse than a nothing. No matter how bad it gets I'll hold onto it. Because I know it's a good name and that's what matters."

He stood to leave. Mr. McGregor motioned him to sit back down, but first had to comfort his wife. She pretended to fool with her knitting but quietly sniffed behind it.

DAVID JENNESON

CHAPTER 2

𝔉ingers of mist crept down the creekbeds of Dog Mountain. Sheets of rain swept Dempsey Road. The McGregor house became shrouded in wet darkness as rain thundered down.

Inside, Mr. McGregor was studying the map of Lynn Vale, which was spread out on the coffee table. On it, streets and side roads were marked, and lines, calculations and angles connected a complicated series of red dots. Certain areas were drawn off into polygons and given their own color, with further calculations inside each polygon. It was the map Red Devlin had given Seawee as a primitive sales tool.

"Let's get this map straight," said Mr. McGregor. His bald head reflected a warm yellow glow from the lamp next to Mrs. McGregor. He hunched forward and puzzled over the map. His hard round stomach forced a tuft of coarse chest hair up through his collar. It was as if he were gazing down on a strange and exotic form of pizza, trying to figure out the toppings before buying a slice. Seawee remembered McGregor was some sort of civil engineer and working on this map seemed to ignite a fire in him.

"It sort of explains itself," said Seawee hopefully.

"You're saying this is our house here?" McGregor's finger stubbed a red dot on the map. "1617 Dempsey Road?"

"Um," said Ray Seawee. He didn't understand the map very well either. Red Devlin had explained it to him but gave up when Seawee couldn't grasp the detailed calculations. Some of Ray Seawee's reading material in prison had consisted of old astrological magazines which he had also failed to understand. To Seawee, the magazines and this map seemed much alike. He was secretly hoping that if he and McGregor put their heads together they'd come to some sort of mutual agreement on what the map actually meant.

Ray Seawee had never had a real job. He was now discovering how hard it was to speak in front of a group - even a group of two. It made him nervous.

"You've got us marked down here as holding an open house," McGregor continued. "Okay. So we hold an open house. People come by and look. We go out to a movie. Yet our house is never actually for sale?

Seawee was grateful to Mr. McGregor for asking this particular question. It was one of the few aspects of the complicated transaction, which he understood himself.

"And for that we pay you $100," Seawee said enthusiastically. He was happy to follow Mr. McGregor's lead. McGregor might be irritable and hairy but he was a good map man.

"But what are all these other figures?" McGregor pulled his glasses down his nose.

"Just extra numbers."

"Who puts extra numbers on a map?" McGregor puffed his pipe fiercely.

"My boss."

DAVID JENNESON

"They must mean something."

Seawee smiled nervously.

"I've got the feeling you don't understand this any better than I do."

"Give the boy a chance to explain," Mrs. McGregor cut in. She went out to the kitchen. It overlooked their long back yard, which disappeared into a stand of cedar and Douglas fir, chest-high fern and laurel. To the left, hand-cut log stairs led down to a ravine where a cold creek ran swollen by the rain.

Mrs. McGregor came back with a warm ham, still on the platter from dinner. Soon there was hot fragrant sourdough bread, sweet mustard, cucumber, sliced tomato, and jars of multi-colored homemade pickles. Seeing this, it struck Ray Seawee what a far cry this was from prison food.

Seawee's epicurean experiences left something to be desired. As youngest sibling in the large Seawee clan there was never much left on the table for him. Later on he was/were put in a foster home. Standard fare was saltine crackers and Kraft Dinner. Finally he graduated to prison with its hard-boiled eggs and dry cold toast.

The trauma of his first jailhouse breakfast was still lodged in his mind. On that gray morning a battered tray had been thrust beneath his barred door. The two hard-boiled eggs rolled around on the tray and came to rest against two pieces of rock-hard cold dry toast. A clear plastic container of pinkish juice sat next to watery prison coffee, cold in its thermal mug.

Yet Ray Seawee's despair at his first prison breakfast was nothing compared to the next surprise he had in store. He had thought that with all the prison reform these days, doing a stretch might be turn out to be a holiday behind bars. He regarded the idea of prisoners making license as an old wives' tale.

Ray Seawee made license plates. Thousands of them.

Perversely, Seawee's dysfunctional relationship with food was exactly what had caused he and Red Devlin to meet. The first afternoon of his release from prison he went straight to a convenience store. It was a dorky first move, since it was the same convenience store he'd robbed and been sent to prison for. But Ray Seawee was impatient to exercise his mandate as a free man and get himself a giant sub sandwich. He wanted to taste freedom of choice instantly, and not off some prison menu. He entered the 7-Eleven and stood for a long time before the glass and chrome cooler doors. The choice of sandwiches was bewildering: the Hungry Hungarian, the Brute, the General Cargo, and the Meat Ball Monster. These sandwiches were loaded like large caliber artillery shells onto the top shelf. Beneath them were stacked support sandwiches - the smaller pizza and chili subs; minor burritos and cheese dogs. After prison it was a bewildering array. He finally chose The Hungry Hungarian because it promised 'zesty European flavor.' But it was too late. The nervous clerk, seeing the same trashy whitebread punk who'd robbed the joint three months ago dialed 911.

Ray Seawee was proud to pay for his sandwich with his hard-earned license-plate money. But it by then it was too late. The cops were on their way. In the harsh lights of the 7-Eleven, the twitchy clerk - wanting to buy time until the police came - asked Seawee if he wanted it heated up

"Yeah," agreed Seawee excitedly. "Heated. Heat it up good."

The clerk put Ray Seawee's 'Hungry Hungarian' into the microwave for a full five minutes. When the microwave beeped the clerk used tongs to lift and dump the hot ingot onto a paper plate. Then he served it to Seawee, who walked out into the blustering January night with his first purchase proudly balanced in his left hand. He slit the cellophane. A plume of steam shot into the air. He bit into it, and suddenly hopped about like a man with a hot-foot, trying to chew, swallow and yell all at the same time.

He waited a moment then yanked again at the fabric of the bread with his teeth. It stretched, and then snapped back into its package after he'd clamped down with his teeth and bitten into it. Sub sandwiches, he reflected, had changed since he'd been in jail. Nevertheless stood out in the whipping rain and chewed like a contented donkey. As a free man he would eat what he wanted, even if it was barely digestible.

Then the police showed up. Two white cars with lights whirling roared up through the rain. The cops ran out and spread-eagled Seawee over the fender of the squad car. They could charge him with nothing more than possessing an overheated sub, but they sniffed about him like a pair of Dobermans.

At that moment Red Devlin's Mercury Turnpike Cruiser rolled in, gurgling in the self-serve bay. Clad in white from head to toe, Devlin emerged from the Merc for cigarettes and a large package of Clorets. He spied Ray Seawee's dilemma for what it was - a helpless kid being hassled by bored cops. But most of all Red Devlin was looking for someone just like Seawee. So he got him out of the glue. He strode over and informed the police that Seawee was his employee. Devlin dusted Seawee off and walked him across Mountain Highway to the Starbucks. There for the next hour he described his theory of open houses and maps, how he would sell the White House, and the fortunes that would change hands.

But that was yesterday. This was now. Sitting with the McGregors he struggled to remember the details of what Devlin had told him. His mind was blank. He'd never had to remember anything important. He wasn't afraid of much, but now in the McGregor's cozy parlor he was terrified that he would say something wrong, and then not know the right answer when they caught him.

"What about this map!" Mr. McGregor, interrupted his thoughts. McGregor was still hunched forward in his chair. "Explain these calculations here. These numbers and formulae look interesting. And quit staring at that ham. It's like you're hypnotized."

"He's hungry," explained Mrs. McGregor as if she were talking about a stray pet. For a moment Seawee wondered if she still thought he was deaf or a wet dog. "You're hungry. Aren't you? Of course you are. Eat."

The big pink ham was spellbinding to the starving Seawee. He tried hard to remember the finer sales points of Red Devlin's pitch - the maps and open houses of Open Homes International and the onset of Open House Fever but he couldn't concentrate. Mrs. McGregor passed him two thick slices of ham with dollops of sweet grainy mustard. It made him feel human again and gave him the courage to wing it.

"The thing with the map," said Seawee with his mouth full, "is energy. Open house energy. Buying energy." He poked with his mustard-tipped knife at a carefully mapped-off section of Lynn Vale. "Map any section of a city or town."

"Yes."

"Then count up."

"Count what?"

"The number of houses."

"Okay."

"Then, add up the number of square feet."

"Of the houses?"

"Um, no. Of everything."

"Of the property? Including sun decks? Streets and parks too? Or just what's built on?"

"Uh-huh. Everything."

"I follow you so far."

Seawee concentrated hard. "Then you get buying potential. Then divide."

"Well, we've got two figures here. Number of houses and square feet. Which one do you divide?'

Seawee thought back to the last math class he'd passed, and the fine points of Grade 6 long division. "The big one into the little one," he said

McGregor blinked. As a retired municipal engineer, he had a rough idea of the figures for Lynn Vale. He pulled out a calculator. McGregor punched in the figures with interest. "Lynn Vale has 48,000 houses. We've got 160 million square feet, counting creeks and rivers. So I divide 48,000 by 160,000,000. Gives me .03."

To Seawee, .03 seemed like a fraction of hardly anything. You couldn't build a good plan starting with .03. "Try dividing it the other way around."

"Now I get 333."

"There's your answer. That's the least number of opens houses you need in Lynn Vale," said Seawee hopefully. "Once you get past 333 you start a buying frenzy. People start seeing all these open houses in the neighborhood. More and more every day. They think everyone is selling, and it's a buyer's market. Well, they may be open houses but they're not for sale. Just like yours. But people get interested. They get greedy. They start making offers just trying to get a bargain. Bidding wars start. Pretty soon you have a seller's market, where everyone makes money on their home. If they want to sell. *If* they don't, that's up to them, because it was never for sale in the first place. That's the deal."

"So my house goes up in value, people have already seen it, and yet it's never actually for sale," said Mr. McGregor.

"No obligations," said Seawee quickly.

"Unless I want," said McGregor.

"Unless you want," confirmed Seawee. "And if you get a neighbor to hold an open house, there is an extra $50 in it for you - a finder's fee. If your neighbors get their neighbors to hold an open house, another $50 for you. That's in addition to the $100 you get for holding your own house open in the first place."

"Are you serious?"

"I'm a realtor. I know my job."

"Am I the first one you've talked to?"

"Friends and neighbors first."

"Do you have franchise agreements? "

Seawee paused, unsure. "I'm sorry but I've left them at the office.

"Is there something to sign on this?"

Seawee pulled out an Open Hose contract.

McGregor turned to his wife. "Where's my pen?" he asked. "The good one. The Waterman."

*   *   *

Ray Seawee walked back to the bus stop in the rain. Now he was Seawee the triumphant. Seawee, swayer of minds. Ray Seawee, realtor, full of ham. The ham had energized his mind so he could think better now. He looked up. The mountain fog swept through the radiance of a single streetlight. It brought to mind the glowing end of Red Devlin's cigar through a haze of smoke when they'd first met at Starbucks. Now, his mission accomplished, Seawee was better able to recall in detail how Devlin laid out the plan in full. He started by explaining the open house scheme. Why greedy homeowners would go for it because they'd find the free $100 irresistible.

Yet the open house scheme was just a ruse. Red Devlin had something far greater in mind. Seawee remembered Devlin's childlike delight as he explained the plan. The White House was sitting on private property. He'd discovered this by researching an old estate sale, better still, Devlin knew who the real owner was - an unwitting and minor Washington bureaucrat named Anson Dobell. Devlin revealed to Seawee he'd found an eager buyer for the White House - a 78-year old Japanese billionaire industrialist. The man still had a serious axe to grind with America over Japan's humiliating loss in World War II.

Seawee had been skeptical. He'd heard too much big talk in jail. He gave a cynical one-shouldered shrug. It would take more to convince a connoisseur of bullshit like Ray Seawee.

Devlin lowered his head and became deadly serious. "Look, what I'm about to tell you - its confidential stuff. Can you keep a secret?"

Seawee shrugged again, but in a more positive way.

"My Japanese client, the *Sha Cho*, contributes millions each year to the Democrats and the Republicans. How else does a Japanese exporter stay rich? So don't kid yourself. He's got major influence.

"So," Seawee sniffed. "What's the connection?"

"Open Homes International is based on greed. I've dealt with the public all my life. They are dumb as cattle and ten times as deceitful. But they are greedy. Open House fever will sweep the country like a virus. If I know nothing else I know that. In my bones. Home sales move money through the economy like Ex-Lax. When Open Homes International starts to peak I'll use the Sha Cho's connections to get the U.S. Government involved. They'll want to take credit for it, and I'll make it easy for them.

Seawee was now at sea with this. "Why does the government give a shit about open houses?"

"What if you were a politician? What if you were greedy? Oh dear, I just repeated myself," Devlin laughed at his own joke then launched into a coughing fit, ending in a loud sneeze. He continued: "It's an election year. The economy's in the dumper. They're desperate to take credit for anything good. The Congress and Senate, the Cabinet. Even," Devlin winked, "the President."

"Get out of town,"

Devlin waved the President aside as if he dealt with armies of Presidents every day. "The best part is we're going to do it on national television. I've got it all planned down to the last bribe. Just do what I say and I'll make you rich. Plus I'll throw in your fifteen minutes of fame for free." Devlin spread his arms. "Hell, I'm not even in it for the money."

This was the most well thought-out bullshit Seawee had ever heard. Or it was crazy enough to be true. But there was one element missing.

"If you don't need money what's the point?

What happened next made the deepest impression of all. Devlin spoke with passion about how God made him the greatest realtor of all time. He spoke of himself as Moses marching through the wilderness with an open house sign. But he was getting on in years. He only had a little time left to fulfill his divine destiny. Then

Devlin gazed up. His cigar smoke curled heavenward. He informed Seawee gravely that God and St. Peter were watching his every move with clipboards in hand, ticking off the good points and bad. All his life he'd tried but only come out second best and now this was his last chance. He couldn't afford to screw up.

Seawee was mesmerized. Devlin seemed to stare defiantly into the very eyes of St. Peter, as if daring the celestial sentry to bar him from the Pearly Gates. To Seawee the mundane coffee bistro faded into the background. He felt as if he were in a church instead of a Starbucks. He could have sworn he saw the haloed, bearded faces of the Saints dancing around Red Devlin's head as he spoke. Truly Ray Seawee was in the presence of a great man from another age.

"It's all good, my friend," Devlin concluded.

For Seawee it was a life-changing experience. To him Red Devlin was a cross between Moses and Colonel Sanders - talented, determined, divinely inspired, utterly committed. Ray Seawee had found a hero.

Seawee stood, a solitary figure at the bus stop. He had no idea when the bus would come and there was no one to ask. The store across the street was closed. It was just him, the slanting rain and the towering cedar trees waving in the dark wind. But at least he was off the hot seat at McGregor's house.

Far in the distance he heard the faint *wee-whup* of an ambulance. The sound rose, and then faded through the mist and downpour. It made him think of Red Devlin's mortality. The man didn't have much time.

DAVID JENNESON

CHAPTER 3

Red Devlin didn't look much like Moses as he drummed his fingers on the table at the La Belles on His Toes Lounge. His eyes had suppressed fire in them. This was an exasperating place for a man on a divine mission to cool his heels.

Waiters, tuxed in black and white wafted slowly among the tables. Piano notes floated through the air like tiny toy balloons. Devlin scowled in the direction of the pianist. The musician was on his break. He leaned back, lazily reading a magazine, feet up on the keyboard. Meantime taped piano music filled in the ambience. From where Devlin was sitting it looked like the fop was playing with his feet. An irritating sight. *Bloody tinkle-toes*, Devlin thought. What were lounges coming to?

Devlin rued that he could no longer afford an office, but lounges were the next best thing. They were places of business. Where would real estate and the country be if not for lounges? You only needed to look around. The blue mountainsides of Lynn Vale and Poplar Ridge were pockmarked with new housing developments.

Each one required a complicated series of transactions involving realtors and politicians, lawyers and clients, ink and endless paperwork.

Where did people think where all these ideas germinated? Where were the deals born? In offices? Secretaries worked in offices doing conveyancing and lawyers were office-bound, wrapped up in covenants and fees. The owners of real estate companies grew rich in offices while swarms of realtors worked like ants for them. But deals made in offices? Never.

Red Devlin would tell you that the real deals were made in the lounges of the land. Who needed an office? No office gave you a table, soothing music, a dish of peanuts, and had people waiting on you hand and foot. With cell phones, communication was no problem nowadays. He was even considering giving a cell phone to young Seawee, his first recruit. And no office Red Devlin had ever been in served booze, the vital lubricant that eased the way.

Devlin's bushy ginger brows knit at the thought of Ray Seawee. Talk about your long shot. Yet perversely Seawee had exactly the qualifications Devlin was looking for. He was dumb enough to believe Devlin could turn him into a realtor in an instant, like he'd touched him with a wand. And Seawee was desperate enough to try anything.

Devlin was waiting here to meet Seawee. That would not be for awhile yet. Devlin felt charitable toward Seawee, in a realtor's sort of way. The boy was just out of prison and trying to make a new start. He wasn't the sharpest knife in the drawer but that wasn't his fault. Seawee was out on his own this evening, his first night on the job and it was raining hard. Well, it rained hard in life too, Devlin thought. In fact, Devlin could describe life as a continuous rain broken by cloudbursts of disaster. A dumb kid like Ray Seawee could get into real trouble without a mentor like Red Devlin to guide him.

Devlin fiddled with his Bic and lit a cigarette. He munched a handful of peanuts. He wished he'd had a mentor like himself when he was Seawee's age. As a young realtor he had worked hard. Kept his eye on the ball. *Just get the deal*, the bosses told him. And

DAVID JENNESON

he did. But the houses he sold were high end enough to bring in the big bucks so he switched to downtown condos. Soon that market died so he moved to monster-sized houses on tiny lots. Then they were practically legislated out of existence as eyesores. For all his hard work he had been promised a partnership which never materialized. Fed up, he started his own company. By then he had five houses of his own to keep Devlin Realty afloat.

There were downturns. Deals soured. The bottoms dropped out of the real estate market. On his own hook, Devlin watched his stock of real estate, the ranchers and white Cape Cods he'd spent a lifetime accumulating, dwindle to four houses, then three. Lounges and cars and suits ate up the cash flow. Nowadays they talk about people falling through the cracks. Red Devlin had done so but in a very well dressed way, living the high life all the way down.

Then, having slipped through the bottom of the sump, he sat in a puddle of sipping whiskey and soggy cigar butts and considered his future. Giving up was not an option.

So Red Devlin reached for the biggest deal his imagination could find. The deal that would silence his critics. The deal that would change the course of history. The deal to inspire the losers on the street who were cursed without talent. The deal that would resonate. The one that would put him in the Guinness Book for good. .

For this he needed a headquarters. Nothing fancy. He knew that during his most historic campaigns Napoleon often made do with a temporary headquarters in the village tavern. A tavern was near enough to a lounge for Red Devlin.

He hoped he'd picked the right one. He'd never been to La Belles on His Toes before. It was the only lounge in town where he didn't owe a tab. In the old days Devlin knew if you picked the right lounge the business sidled right up to you. *Lounges remain the engines of democracy*, he thought. He made a mental note to pass this on to Ray Seawee.

A waiter drifted over. He looked handsome and trim, like he worked out a lot. "Anything for you, sir?"

"Whiskey," Devlin answered dismissively, pretending to be caught in the middle of an important thought.

The waiter stood like silently.

"I did say whiskey, didn't I?" Devlin gave him a sharp look after few moments. "You heard me all right?"

"Yes sir. I was waiting to see if there was a particular brand you were interested in."

"Ah, what *kind* of whiskey," Devlin repeated, as if this detail had escaped him. He made a show of going over the various expensive single malt brands but it was all too confusing. "Just bring me bar rye for now," he said, as if intending to move on to the good stuff when he sorted the menu out.

"Bar rye?"

"Bar rye," Devlin confirmed.

"As you wish," the waiter raised an eyebrow as if Devlin had ordered canal water.

Devlin gave him a sour look as he wafted off. This place put on airs. He drummed his fingers on the table again. The pretensions of this place were obstacles to be endured on his way to selling the White House. *If it were easy, everyone would be doing it.*

Meanwhile distinguished looking suits drifted in and greeted one another with the intimacy of some inner circle. Familiar hellos. Lots of hand contact. They looked like lawyers or stockbrokers to Red Devlin - the cream of the crop. Their dark, understated blues or princely gray pinstripes seemed to be the mandatory dress code. It was a little creepy, but Devlin sniffed money.

By contrast Red Devlin was dressed like an ageing Man From Glad with a weight problem. He'd kept his good looks in the way an old bus can be said to still look serviceable near the end of its life. Nicked and dented but still maintaining the original design. Although he'd gone paunchy and his ass had dropped, his wavy auburn hair showed no trace of gray. Some women still went for that. Without meaning to, he created the impression of a

DAVID JENNESON

flamboyant country squire gone to seed. He favored cloud white suits with a blood red or royal blue tie, white belt and shoes. To Red Devlin, the white look still hauled heavy freight. White meant purity. He believed this in-your-face symbolism gave you the edge with a nervous client. The whiter you were the more likely the client would trust you. Anyone could wear dark blue. White took balls. Show them white and look them in the eye. *The more white, the fewer questions*, Red Devlin thought. He made another mental note. He must pass this thought on to Seawee and the rest of his operatives, whenever he managed to recruit more.

He worried again about his first recruit: If Ray Seawee pulled this off, anyone could do it. He'd hire hundreds of Seawees. But he needed Seawee as his experimental white mouse to test his new theory. If it blew up in Seawee's face, so be it. That was the one qualification Ray Seawee had above all others. He was expendable.

He felt someone brush against his knee. "Anyone sitting here?" a voice asked.

Devlin glanced up. One look told him this was no common lawyer. The man was beyond the need to wear suits. Instead he was dressed in understated high fashion casual trim only the rich can afford. He had that permanent light tan big shots get from spending half their lives in the tropics. His closely cropped salt and pepper hair and clipped mustache suggested his roots were in the conservative power structure. Rich, powerful, and didn't give a shit what anyone thought about it. The hum of conversation dropped off around Devlin, as if suddenly people were very nervous.

He shucked off his wet jacket. "Dirty night out. Appreciate you sharing."

Devlin did not recall giving permission to share his table, but this was the way lounges worked. His body was solid as a packing crate.

"Look at this. I'm wet through," he fingered his shirt. "If we were smart we'd be home curled up with a book. Nice fireplace. Little brandy. Ahhh," he gave a resigned sigh,"why do we come here? "

Devlin thought this to be an oddly personal question coming from someone who looked like a drill instructor. Still, he looked like he had dough, and a broke but divinely inspired realtor Devlin couldn't be choosey. He saw his chance. He'd turn this into an exchange between two sophisticated insiders and work it from there. Another axiom came to mind. *When in doubt, be conspiratorial.*

"No rest for the wicked," Devlin winked.

"Mmmm," the man nodded, reaching across and grabbed a handful of nuts.

Devlin's real estate instincts took over. His mind worked hard trying to figure out the man's line of work. He knew if he pegged it first try the man would be seriously impressed. It was a long shot, but his whole life was a long shot now. Yet it never hurt to impress a millionaire. *Impress the rich*, Devlin thought. He made another mental note for the troops.

Devlin now watched him call for big platters of the most expensive hors d'oeuvres in the house. *Wealth*, Devlin mentally confirmed. Another waiter appeared. To Devlin's delight he set down four tumblers of the twenty-buck-a-pop Alberta sipping whiskey. The waiter indicated it was paid by two nearby lawyers. *Power and influence.* The man pushed two tumblers toward Devlin who thought it a public-spirited gesture. In the next instant the equation connected in Red Devlin's brain. *Wealthy, powerful and public spirited.*

"Here's to the night," the man lifted a glass of the silky smooth rye and downed in one swallow.

Like any licensed realtor Devlin did the same.

"To the night before us both," the man finished the toast with a second tumbler poured down the throat.

By instinct Devlin knocked back another shot too. When he sat back his eyes watered. But the clues connected.

Millionaire.

The waiter scurried up with a silver platter of Oysters Florentine. These were not the dainty Blue Point oysters from the East Coast

DAVID JENNESON

but big, raw Pacific oysters five times the size of the human eye. They smelled and tasted like the sea. The millionaire scooped one up. It vanished in one swallow, spinach, cheese, and the works.

Suddenly the story of the poor millionaire's story lay open to Devlin's imagination. As his eyes filled from the straight shots of rye he created in his mind a tortured lifescape for his new partner. The man had raked in money and power on the backs of others. Now it had come back to haunt him. Guilt for the lives he'd ruined. Mortality and St. Peter looked him square in the eye. He needed to ease his conscience by helping others. Devlin had heard about people like this. Trying to buy salvation. Red Devlin was all in favor of buying salvation. He'd sell you as much as you wanted. He knew all about millionaires.

Devlin sensed that this prospect wasn't ready yet. He needed to get eyeball-to-eyeball - go to the mat with this man. This guy had heard a thousand pitches.

Suddenly the pianist finished his break. He thundered to life with an unrecognizable fog of chords. Where the canned music had showed taste, this was loud and clumsy. Devlin winced. He knew all about lounge piano music.

The millionaire's eyes lit up. "This boy's talented," he leaned forward, as if passing on a stock tip. "He takes long breaks but I know him personally and he needs his rest."

Devlin decided to keep his anti-pianist opinions to himself. "Yeah, he's got a big sound for the delicate type."

The lounge filled up - thick with businessmen of all ages in expensive suits. Another waiter brought more food. He set two platters down and backed away like a servant.

"Try some of these scallops. Delicious. And the tiger prawns," the millionaire insisted. He helped himself and pushed a platter toward Devlin. Another glass of Alberta sipping whisky went along with it.

"Now, what's your line of work?" the millionaire swallowed another oyster. Devlin thought the man must have been hard of hearing because he slid closer around on the banquette so as to not to miss his reply.

"Real estate," Devlin began -

"-Here's to real estate!" the millionaire interrupted. He clinked his glass against Devlin's. "No problem with real estate lately. Where would we be without realtors, I ask you? To realtors," he drained his glass. Forced to keep up, Devlin did the same.

The millionaire pushed the next glass forward, twirled his finger in the air and two more whiskies were set down. He seemed constantly wanting glasses at the ready in case he should get the urge to drink to something Devlin might say.

"I'll give you my take on real estate," the millionaire leaned toward Devlin again, as if he was going to whisper another secret. "It's acquired quite a veneer lately. These new people coming up call themselves 'professionals'. But sometimes I think the real professionals are the old guard. The survivors. Spot a deal a mile away and make it on the spot. Men like you."

Devlin coughed self-consciously.

"Do you read history?" the millionaire asked. "Battle of Waterloo, Napoleon's Imperial Guard? Real professionals. They had resplendent uniforms, like you, if I might say. They were tough and expected nothing but blood and duty. In the end they were surrounded by English cannons. They were called upon to surrender the last bulwark. They refused. The English let fly. Afterward there was nothing left. Not even a mustache. That's what I like. I look on you tough veteran realtors as the Imperial Guard of Capitalism. You're what makes this country work," he pushed another whiskey toward Devlin. "I drink to you. You and your kind."

He waved his finger round once again and two more sipping whiskies arrived. Millionaires these days had a thirst for giving.

Devlin felt himself warming up. The heat from the gulps of sipping whiskey rose in his head like an elevator and made him dizzy. He slugged down some raw oysters to reattach his mind to its moorings. He felt like talking. He wondered whether this stuff was Alberta sipping whisky or truth serum.

"I have an appointment here," he began in effort to explain his own presence. "In the meantime, if I can be honest..."

"You couldn't be otherwise," insisted the millionaire. He patted the arm of Devlin's white suit jacket. "No, not you. Not in your nature."

Devlin couldn't believe his ears. This guy would believe anything he said. His mind felt free to range like a chicken, able to say absolutely anything. So he did. "What you see now in real estate is nonsense. Pretense. I know. I started in the 1960's. Back in The Day. Big cars, big lunches, big deals. Back in The Day there was a Golden Age of Real Estate. I was twenty-two. Everyone did business in lounges and wrote it off. Everyone smoked hundreds of cigarettes and wrote them off. Realtors arrived at an open house with a whiff of rye on their breath. I'll let you in on a little secret. In the old days if I couldn't get to a lounge before an appointment, I'd flick a bit of rye on my neck like cologne. It was *expected*."

"Yes, of course. Expected," nodded the millionaire. He seemed transfixed by Devlin's every word. He edged closer. They were almost touching. This was going better than Devlin could have dreamed. He had the man in the palm of his hand. His mind flooded with possibilities. The way made easy by money. But first he had to close the guy.

Devlin slapped down his business card on the table. "See this?" He pointed to the card. "That's the one word I despise most"

The man stared down. "You hate your own name?" he raised his eyebrows.

"No, this word," Devlin prodded at it with his finger. "'*Professionalism.*' There was a time when realtors didn't make any bones about 'professionalism'. People wouldn't have believed it then. They don't believe it now. Back in The Day, professionalism meant getting away with more than the other guy and not getting caught. The more you got away with, the more professional you were. Then some dork added 'professional' to his business card.

Next thing you know, everyone had to do it. After that people expected more. It was a sad bloody day when I had to put it on mine. There it is. You can read it for yourself: 'Red Devlin Realty - *professionalism at its most professional*,' I'm not sure who believes it less - me or my clients."

"Yet you're being completely honest," persisted the millionaire. "What could be more professional than that? You're leveling with me. Man to man. Eye to eye. That puts our relationship on a higher plane. Means you're totally trustworthy. I'm honored to be in the presence of such an ethical man," he said dreamily, pushing another glass of rye toward Devlin.

Devlin blinked. He seemed to have the millionaire under some type of spell. He was totally in command. He could say and do no wrong. "I don't deserve that from someone like you," he said. "But now let me be very honest with you."

"Oh, please do," insisted the millionaire. "I must hear it."

"I want you to think of the single most powerful piece of property on earth."

The millionaire thought. "I don't know. The United Nations Building?"

"And where do the orders come from for the United Nations?"

"Why, the White House."

"There's your answer," said Devlin. "Now tell me this. Who is the lawful owner of the White House?"

"I've never thought about it. I suppose ultimately it must be the American people. Yes. *We, the people.*" But since we're Canadian it would be *They, the people.*

"Now how would you go about selling the White House?" asked Devlin.

"You would have to gain the consent of the American people, or their representative. Someone who qualified as owner by being designated holder of the deed. By law, whoever controls the deed owns the White House. But it may not be even covered under

DAVID JENNESON

existing law. Who would have thought of it?"

"Right on all counts," said Devlin. He lifted his glass.

At this point, the millionaire seemed to be in abject awe.

"As a man like you would know, in a deal like this you can't have loose ends," Devlin hit his stride now, as if he'd spent a lifetime ferreting out loose ends and tying them up. "We have to know the seller. We have to know the buyer. Inside out. Remember when the White House was symbol of American greatness? Now it means broken promises, bloated government and selfish political bickering that has sickened the American people. Do you really think they'd be sad to part with it?"

"When you put it that way, maybe not," admitted the millionaire. "They might see it as a symbol of liberation - a weight off their shoulders"

"Hell, there'd be dancing in the streets," Devlin rattled his ice cubes. "Someone finally got back at the government. Remember the American Dream? Used to be real estate. Buy your own little place and raise a family. Working stiff can't afford that anymore. Nowadays the only American Dream is getting back at the government. That's all the average American has left. Now tell me. Who might be interested in buying the White House?"

"I suppose a lot of people would."

"I'll let you in on a secret. There is a group of ultra conservative right wing Japanese billionaires. They're in their 70's and 80's and still very pissed about America beating them in World War II. And I'm dealing with their main man."

"Of course," gasped the millionaire. "They have the motive. They have means. It would be irresistible. The object would be to humiliate America. Tit for tat."

"I know it sounds a little ambitious," said Devlin, "but I promise you I've never meant anything more in my life. Back in the Day, I burned my guts out working for big shot realtors with big cars making big deals. They got rich by promising me a shot at my own deal. Always the next one down the road. I was the dog chasing the mechanical rabbit. Well, I'll tell you one thing. I'm no dog. And this is no rabbit. This one is mine. And you," Devlin looked him in the eye, "can be part of it. I have a grand diversion set up. A masterpiece. The returns will be enormous."

The millionaire seemed on the verge of tears. Look him in the eye and show him the white, Devlin thought. The man lowered his head, and then came very close to Devlin.

"I will, I will," he whispered. "Tomorrow we'll talk." His hand suddenly clamped down on Devlin's crotch. "But tonight you must stay with me and be my glory!"

A loud and ugly incident erupted. As a result of having his balls grabbed Devlin kicked out. The table was overturned. All platters and glasses went flying with a crash. The millionaire sat back in muzzy shock, suddenly covered with raw oysters. Red Devlin dashed in panic through a forest of gray and blue suits to a far corner of the lounge. Why were there no women here? A flock of athletic-looking waiters wiped and comforted the lustful million-aire who glared in Devlin's direction with the fury of rejection.

Red Devlin stood panting in a corner wishing hard he was invisi-ble. He ordered a whiskey, which he was happy to pay for himself.

"That wasn't very bright, old fellow," a plumy voice came from his left. Devlin looked over. Two lawyers were standing too close to one another, and looking in his direction. Devlin wanted very badly to finish his drink and leave.

"Do you know who that is?" one asked Devlin.

"Some rich pervert," Devlin muttered. "I don't need his kind."

There was restrained laughter. "Rich pervert? We're all rich perverts, old boy. Didn't you see the sign over the door? *La Belles on His Toes*? But that's Judge Mannheim. Trial judge. Likes fraud cases. Business scams. Some people come into the world expecting easy money. When they don't get it they break the rules. Judge Mannheim likes that. Grabs them like he's caught a dog stealing food off the table. You know, scruff of the neck. Throws them into the slammer as hard as he can. Their lawyers slink off and hope they get a fairer judge on the appeal. He's a very bad judge. He's a very bad man. Quite disgusting how we all have to blow smoke up his ass. We're all a little twisted in here but that dirty old bastard makes us look like angels."

"A judge specializing in business scams?" the blood drained from Devlin's face.

"Its an interesting legal concept if you're not the crook."

"I gave the sonuvabitch my business card."

"Better keep your nose clean."

"I haven't done anything yet."

"Judge Mannheim's the one on the bench. He's got the power. Look around you, man. Like it or not, we all need Judge Mannheim. Looks like he wants you too. I hear he adores older dudes. One way or the other he'll get you. Never doubt it."

Red Devlin fainted.

CHAPTER 4

*R*ay Seawee waited at the bus stop. Although raindrops kept falling on his head he stood in triumph.

The bus stop was at the intersection where Dempsey Road turned and then became Lynn Vale Road, leading down the hill. This elbow bend was the highest point houses had been built up Dog Mountain. Beyond this point the pavement gave way to a twisting gravel road through a fir- and cedar-forested watershed, the entrance barred by a big yellow government metal gate.

Across the street from Seawee stood the Upper Lynn Vale Grocery. Although it was closed, he took comfort from the cheery light the food coolers cast from within. His mouth moved as he read the hand-lettered posters taped inside the window. The grocer advertised Mandarin Oranges left over from Christmas for 99 cents a pound and fresh spring salmon steaks for $9.99 a pound.

Seawee scoffed. Who needed cheap oranges or overpriced salmon steaks? Certainly not him. He had ham in his stomach and an

Open House contract in his pocket. He looked up into the rain and rejoiced in the wild free beauty of his surroundings. In the wind the tall hemlocks behind the grocery store seemed to bow down in his honor.

A blurry light appeared at the bottom of the long Lynn Vale Road hill. Seawee rubbed the rain out of his eyes and squinted at it. It was the first sign of life he'd seen in twenty minutes. It was a bus which seemed to take forever to whine up the hill toward him. He waited as the rain pelted down on him. The tires whined on the pavement as it finally pulled to a stop in front of him. The sign read: *'Upper Lynn Vale'*. The wrong bus. Devlin had said to take *'Vancouver Via First Narrows'* to get back down to his lounge head-quarters.

Seawee looked at the bus driver. The driver looked back. Seawee rapped on the bus doors. They opened with a hiss. "What about the Vancouver bus?" he shouted through the rain.

"Behind me." The bus driver closed the doors, put his feet up on the steering wheel, pulled out a magazine and sat cozy. Seawee wondered what was wrong with bus drivers these days that he wasn't offered even a wafer thin slice of hospitality and invited aboard to wait in the dry. Pretty soon the rain would seep through his suit pocket and ruin McGregor's contract. He pulled his jacket closer and stood in the lee of the bus for shelter. After too many minutes a second set of bus headlights appeared. Seawee hurried back to board it.

Suddenly there was the roar of an engine and the squeal of brakes as a large white car shot out from a side street and cut the bus off. The bus driver swerved away and mounted the curb.

The car belonged to Red Devlin. He was woozy from fainting, panicky, drunk and mad.

Down at La Belles on His Toes the medics had been called but quickly determined he'd only fainted. The manager sat him up and dusted him off. Devlin was furious and embarrassed to come to, surrounded by medics and the gawking fop elite. The manager and waiters fanned him. They tried to call him a cab but Devlin staggered out in the rain to his Merc.

Thus he still wasn't quite right in the head when he started looking for Ray Seawee. All he knew was Seawee was somewhere up on Dempsey Road pitching bogus open house contracts. Devlin had spilled the beans to that fire-breathing Judge and spurned his advances. Now Judge Mannheim had every reason to keep a hard eye on the local real estate action. These thoughts had raced through Devlin's frayed mind as he swept the steep side streets of Lynn Vale searching for signs of Seawee.

His mind wasn't exactly on the road as he raced up and down the dark side streets. The harder he searched, the more frenzied he got. Finally he shot out from a side street and cut off the Vancouver bus. When it swerved to avoid him and mounted the curb it rear-ended the waiting Upper Lynn Vale bus, catapulting its inhospitable, magazine-reading driver out of his seat onto the floor. His magazine flew high in the air.

Ray Seawee watched in amazement.

The big white Merc lurched up. Seawee stood gaping it through the space between the two disabled busses. Devlin punched the horn and opened the passenger door. It swung wide. Devlin blasted again. Seawee scrambled between them...

"Move it!" Devlin shouted.

Seawee hopped in. The Turnpike Cruiser roared off with its white door flailing outward. From the passenger seat Seawee watched it swing wide as they took the corner around onto Dempsey Road.

"Grab the door for God's sake," yelled Devlin. He was in no mood to slow down. "Grab the goddam door. People will see us. If they get the plate number I'm done." He roared down Dempsey Road and apparently only saw the stop sign at the last moment.

He rammed down on the brake pedal. Their forward momentum head-butted both of them into the windshield.

After a stunned moment he popped the clutch of the huge Merc. It surged forward, whip-sawing their heads back into the seat. Seawee's door slammed shut on its own. Suddenly it stalled dead, from 30 mph to 0 mph. in one second. Their forward momentum threw their heads into the windshield again. As this happened, time slowed down for Ray Seawee. He became briefly clear-headed. This real estate business is no piece of cake, he thought, as he sailed forward. He watched Red Devlin do the same. Devlin seemed to look back at him in puzzlement, as if he were about to say something but then his head struck the windshield with a crack and his jaw snapped shut.

They both bounced off the windshield back into the seat. Without missing a beat Devlin re-started the car. He dropped the clutch and floored it to get through the intersection, throwing their heads back again.

A black Lincoln SUV roared through the intersection out of nowhere, cutting them off. Devlin punched the brakes instantly. He and Seawee both made a return trip to the windshield. A bit of blood now trickled down Seawee's forehead. He'd been whacked around in prison, but never by a car.

"There's been a screw-up," said Red Devlin once he had the Turnpike Cruiser steady down Dempsey Road again. "I'm re-thinking the plan." His words went unanswered for a moment. Both were seeing stars from his experiment with windshields and the impact of human head.

"The theory works," Seawee tried to clear his mind. He held up the McGregor contract. "Let's stop the car for a minute."

"Ah, calm down," Devlin muttered. He shot the Merc through the dark rain. When they got to the end of Dempsey Road he swerved down Mountain Highway. Lynn Vale Road, Dempsey and Mountain Highway all connected, forming a giant inverted triangle at the base of Dog Mountain. From the top of Mountain Highway you could drive straight back down to the point of the triangle where it met Lynn Vale Road at the 7-Eleven, and the heart of the little community.

Seawee squinted through the windshield. Far down the mountain the 7-Eleven was a blurry red dot. Beyond and below, the forested land tumbled down to the dark harbor. Across the water beaded lights traced Vancouver's streets. They faded over the dark horizon and south toward the U.S border.

"Don't you know how to close a car door?" carped Devlin as the Turnpike Cruiser rattled down Mountain Highway like a great out-of-date spaceship. "What a stinking night. Judges, gay lounges, rain. And now a goddam bus driver who might have my license," Devlin was mad. At the world. At Seawee. At anybody but himself.

"The deal works," Seawee repeated as they shot past the 7-Eleven.

"Shit," said Devlin. A white police cruiser shot past him going in the opposite direction. Lights flashing and siren wee-wupping. "Bet that's for me. One of those bus drivers must've phoned me in." He hunched low over the wheel, maneuvering the Merc down the twisting lower reaches of Mountain Highway as it snaked down toward sea level.

Seawee ducked down in the seat. "I sold a contract."

"Eh?" said Red Devlin.

"They said you're a genius."

"Genius?" Red Devlin raised his eyebrows. The dashboard lights gave an emerald tint to his ruddy face. He seemed surprised, like no one had ever mentioned the word in relation to him. Another police car roared up past them. He accelerated down the hill.

"Let's stop," repeated Seawee. The trees whipped by. He felt like he was riding a round of live ammunition. He braced his hands on the dashboard. "Let's park the car and talk. Or go to your house."

"Not tonight."

"How about your office?"

"I'm moving offices."

"Why are you moving offices?"

"There'll be meetings. People coming. From Washington D.C. Japan. Flying in. Buyers. Sellers. They've got to feel secure. I was thinking of renting someplace with a soundproof boardroom.

Upscale. In a deal like this, *I* have to feel secure. If I don't, the clients will pick up on it. Like they have antennae, like bugs. They get edgy. Ruins everything. Who wants an edgy client? You talk about genius. Putting it together means me feeling secure. That's where the genius comes in. Otherwise you can stick that contract in the shredder. And right now, I'm not feeling so secure."

They hit level road and swerved left. The sickening motion threw Seawee into the passenger window. Through the trees and rain a round yellow sign gloomed.

"There!" Seawee pointed. He was afraid Devlin's aimless, panicky driving would go on all night. He just wanted the car to stop and never to drive with Red Devlin again.

Red Devlin had his own reasons for wanting to stop. He wanted to get the car off the road before the cops started looking for it. It was, after all, a distinctive vehicle. The 1962 Mercury Turnpike Cruiser was twice the size of a normal sedan, with huge double fins above the taillights. Chased by fears of judges and collapsing deals Devlin raced toward the sign. The Merc shot through a cavern of dripping trees and across a highway overpass before pulling up at the Carriage House.

Seawee leapt out onto solid ground and stood, soaked and shivering in the parking lot. Chip bags floated in the puddles. Above him the huge sign flashed, "GOT NOTHING ON FOR LUNCH? NEITHER HAVE WE!" It lit up the wet asphalt every few seconds like a searchlight.

Ray Seawee saw The Carriage House as a glamorous oasis. Red Devlin regarded it as a pathetic dump. He wished this night was over. He wanted to drive the Merc quietly home via the back roads. Alone. Get back to the solitude of his tiny basement suite where he could get his shit together. He worried that the shivering, battered Seawee would collapse from exposure out here and cause more problems.

They crossed the puddled entrance to the Carriage House.

Red Devlin read the name *Carriage House*. It was nothing more than a beer-barn. Back in The Golden Age of Real Estate, the law demanded that hotels have vast beer parlors like windowless airplane hangers. Then the laws changed to allow smaller, cozy neighborhood pubs. Customers deserted the beer barns in flocks, leaving vast uninhabited regions in the dark seas of empty tables. Anguished hotel owners were desperate to bring the patrons back. For that they needed entertainment. A focal point. So the politicians changed the laws again to give them a competitive edge.

Beautiful naked dancers.

To Devlin that was a sad day. It lowered the tone of drinking establishments, and undermined the sedate, loungey behavior he preferred. He viewed the great rambling Carriage House with its loud sign as a sad anachronism. Inside, he expected to see a relic of the 1960's. Badly lit tables full of unshaven longshoremen in plaid jackets and fedoras over ten-cent beer while Patti Page quietly oozed from the jukebox.

He walked through the doors.

In the next instant he was overwhelmed. Flashing lights, tobacco smoke, blaring rock music, cheap perfume and yelling. His eyes stung. Through the haze he saw oily t-shirts, plumbers, bankers in ties, bikers, weasels, punks, drunken husbands, computer geeks, misfits, perverts and rounders standing four deep at the bar and around the stage. They had two things in common. They were all staring at the empty stage. They were all yelling. He had never seen such mass public drunkenness. It was the most unlounge-like spectacle he'd ever seen in his life. He was disgusted.

Seawee became separated from Devlin in the boiling crowd. With the swirling music and lights and excitement he felt like he was in a fun house. Suddenly the disk jockey's baritone boomed over the P.A.

"All right gentlemen, here's what you've been waiting for. Not only Miss Nude Canada, but also this year's Best Chest in the West. Let's put those hands together for *Tasha!*" Loud gypsy rock music chopped in. A tall, blond woman in a sheer black gown stepped demurely up onto the circular stage. Alone up there she seemed vulnerable yet regal and aloof.

DAVID JENNESON

She gave the crowd one glance. That glance said, *if you're stupid enough to sit here and watch, then I will own you while you do it. I'm in control.* It made them press closer with loud whistles. Braying applause. Seawee eyed her up and down. Her black lace skirt split to the hip. A plunging neckline barely held her large, firm breasts. They seemed to Seawee to be as perfect as breasts were ever made by God's own hand. Her legs went on forever. Seawee's eyes ached to follow them up and see just *how* far. He gaped like a fool.

On the opposite side of the stage Devlin shook his head. How could women do this in front of a mob of drooling lowlifes? So it had come to this. Devlin felt sorry that such a beauty had to stoop so low to make a living. In his day she would've been a lounge queen, no an empress. Highballs on the house and fat rich men lined up to give her free apartments.

She gave the crowd a second glance. To Devlin that glance said *deliver me from assholes.* He spied Seawee on the other side of the stage. He fought to turn his mind back to real estate. He went over, put a hand on Seawee's shoulder and guided him into a ringside seat that had just been vacated. Seawee was soaked to the skin and giving involuntary shudders as his wet clothes grew clammy. A bit of blood still trickled from his head butts on the windshield.

"We'll get a beer in you," Devlin waived for the round. "Then let's clear out of this dump."

Seawee watched Tasha. His eyes were beginning to blaze with lust and fever. He couldn't imagine *anyone* wanting to leave here. Seawee decided to use his newfound sales powers. He'd approach Devlin on an angle, crab-like. He spoke with the giddy abandon a rising fever and concussion will give you.

"I think we're onto something big," Seawee shouted at Devlin over the racket. Then he drew his shoulders in and shivered to make the point he was wet. "Really big, I mean. These people I sold the contract to. They want franchises. That Mr. McGregor's not as dumb as he looks. He'll steal the whole idea from you if we don't jump on it."

Devlin pursed his lips. He'd had ideas stolen before. "There's a judge after me. And not for what you think. For unnatural reasons. Imagine. A judge. Remember this, *the higher the position the lower the morals*. I'll bet the creep's out every night. Stalking lounges for older dudes like me. So we need a safe place to do business and entertain clients. Otherwise the deal's off."

Seawee made a face. He'd been screwed by plenty of judges, but the idea of being mounted was painful.

"The man will be thinking about me," Devlin prophesied. "He fell in lust with me on the spot and I rejected him. But then I covered him in oysters too. Rejecting his advances is bad enough. When he gets up tomorrow he'll see the oyster stains he'll get mad all over again. Those were very classy clothes. Tomorrow he'll have to take them to the cleaners. If the cleaner says they're ruined he'll get mad a third time. I'll tell you something, my friend. You get a judge mad at you three times in twenty-four hours and you've got a problem. God help me if the cleaners can't fix it. Oysters stain bad. I've been there," Devlin said gloomily.

"Doesn't sound good," Seawee agreed.

"Judges and real estate don't mix. He has my card."

Tasha whirled by. She eyed them both.

To Seawee she seemed to show a brief flicker of interest. He wondered what she saw that interested her. One old dude and one wet punk? Maybe more. He couldn't tell.

"I'll tell you, that judge has me shittin' pickles."

"Then this place is our only hope," said Seawee, as if the idea had just popped into his mind. "Our new headquarters."

The regulars of gynecology row where they sat, whooped mating calls to Tasha as she undulated near them.

"Woo" called one.

"Yesssss!" shouted another.

"Awwright!" bellowed more.

To Seawee's left, a housepainter in speckled coveralls began to mew

DAVID JENNESON

like a cat. "Aowwwer."

Devlin seemed distracted as Tasha slid down the brass pole three feet away from him and perched, nearly naked, in front of his nose. With great effort he turned his mind back to business. "How do you figure this dump as our new headquarters?" he shot back at Seawee. "How can I possibly bring clients in here? They'd take one look and walk out. Think I'm some lowbrow pervert."

"But that *judge* won't come in here," Seawee sprung his trap. "So yeah he's got your card. Yeah he's hot for your ass. But what homo judge could stand watching this? If he stood here for five minutes he'd puke from the tits and ass and slime balls. And who else will bother us? Who figures we're selling the White House from T*he Carriage House*? All they sell here is flat beer."

Red Devlin drummed his fingers and exhaled a puff of long-tried patience. Unconvinced.

Ray Seawee hung fire. He'd said enough. If he was going to be a good realtor he had to know when to shut up. Once the pitch is made, *he who speaks first loses*. He'd learned that from the McGregors. Have the guts to wait out the silence. His forehead hurt more now. It was bleeding again. The faces around the stage weaved and danced - a wannabe biker, a yappy salesmen, a dissolute banker - even a bored Maytag repairman. In other words, completely normal.

He did notice one insane runt who stood out. Some bum with a bushy, premature snow-white beard and thick white hair, hooked nose and shaggy brows who mouthed things at Tasha in disjointed tongues. To Ray Seawee's fevered mind he looked like an insane prophet who'd wandered in from the desert and needed to be locked up. In fact the more Seawee gazed around the more these types looked familiar. The same sleazy crowd as in prison, only here they had booze and naked women. He realized this was your answer to the crime problem. Turn prisons into huge, 24-hour strip bars and it would keep criminals off the streets forever, because they'd never leave. He wouldn't, anyway.

"Don't be so sure about clients not liking this either,' Seawee's teeth chattered as he hugged his wet clothes. "You said Americans. And Asians. Those guys *gotta* be men. Mano an' macho. Right? Gotta act like they've got the biggest balls in town. This is just what the doctor ordered." he nodded up toward Tasha as she whirled and swept past them. This caused a chorus of loud mating calls and whoops from their seatmates. "All we need to do is mix in with the crowd."

Devlin looked around him, still apparently unimpressed.

Seawee gestured toward the crowd. He leaned close to Devlin. "That's the secret," he whispered. "Blend in."

"How so?"

"Woo!" cried Seawee.

Tasha swung near again. Suddenly she stood in front of them. Dropped her lace skirt dramatically to the ground to reveal those long tanned legs.

"See, it's easy. Try it, woo!" Seawee demonstrated.

"I understand the blending in part," said Devlin, "But we need privacy. Woo! Where do we do the paperwork?"

'Woo! Look around you. Dark tables in every corner. No one's sat there in years. Who'll notice a little table of realtors?"

Watery, flat beer was thunked down in pint mugs but they failed to thaw Red Devlin's resistance. "What about the management? Woo! If we stake out the same table night after night they'll get suspicious. Start asking questions."

"What have *they* got to lose?" asked Seawee flailed an arm toward the dark far reaches of the Carriage House. He took a big swallow. "They'll be grateful. Woo! We might even get more recruits. Half these guys probably don't have jobs or nothing."

"Woo!" conceded Red Devlin. He looked down and saw Seawee's hands were shaking. He frowned.

"Shower! Show-er! Show-ER!" the crowed chanted.

They both looked up. Tasha stood there wearing nothing but little

DAVID JENNESON

black bootie socks and high heeled shoes. Devlin and Seawee had missed the finale. The drunks were worked up. They wanted her to caress her body with water from on-stage showers.

"Blend in," Seawee urged. "Shower! Shower! Show-ER!" he cried.

For the first time Devlin seemed thunderstruck by this sight - a statuesque woman, naked, regal.

"Well guys," the DJ's voice boomed over the speakers, 'Tasha won't stick around unless you want it. Let's hear it. This is your last chance. Do you really want her to get wet?"

"Show-er! Show-ER SHOW-ER!" yelled Red Devlin. He banged his gold ring on the brass rail surrounding the stage. Cling cling cling! Everyone in the row looked at him. The showers, actually a pair of squat fountains, sprang to life from an invisible command.

She moved with soft, fluid movements toward the shower, on tip-toes so her legs were even more sculpted. To the shivering Seawee the shower looked as warm and sweet as baby's bath water.

"The woman has grace," Devlin informed Seawee. "That's rare." Tasha entered the shower. The water fell upon her shoulder gently. Then her hair. Rivulets ran down, slowly caressing her breasts. Droplets hung from the end of her erect nipples. Ray Seawee figured that water was mighty lucky to be doing that. He wished he were that water. The DJ threw her a white towel across the stage from the booth. Seawee and Devlin watched it fly past, turning their heads in unison like a pair of dogs.

The crowd fell silent, spellbound. What would she do next?

She picked the towel up, glanced over and tossed it at Seawee, who was now shivering uncontrollably.

"Here. You need this more than I do. You look cold."

"Wet too," he shuddered. "We had an accident."

The DJ's voice boomed officially, "Will the owner of a white Mercury Turnpike Cruiser, license plate MXA - 176, please come to the booth!"

Devlin choked on his beer. There were now two dripping, bad-tempered cops standing beside the DJ's booth in yellow slickers. One was large and burly with a thick black mustache. The other was reedy with a long thin nose.

Devlin frantically waved Tasha toward him. She picked her way back across the stage and hesitantly bent down.

"For God's sake, come and sit with us a minute." Devlin begged. "I'll buy you drinks; I'll buy you a house. Anything. You'll never regret it. Just say you're with us. Can't explain now. But first go up to the DJ booth and stall those cops for a minute. I'll find us a table in the back."

Tasha regarded him with cold interest. "Why should I? Drunks hit me on a hundred times a day. What makes you so different? And how come you're dressed like Colonel Sanders?"

"I am not a drunk. I'm a realtor."

"We're going to sell the White House," Seawee volunteered dreamily.

"Shut up for God's sake," snapped Devlin. "Boy's got fever," he grinned.

"Did I hear that right?" Tasha leaned down closer. "You're selling the White House?"

"Right from here, from the Carriage House," added Seawee. "It's all set. We'll all make money. And guess what. We're hiring."

"Is he nuts?" she asked Devlin.

"No, delirious."

"It's true," Seawee insisted. "I was the first one hired. Here's the first contract," he pulled it out and passed it over. "Inked and signed. But they wanted to buy franchises. Just wait'll we start selling franchises."

Tasha examined the document.

"This looks real. Maybe he's *not* so nuts," she eyed Devlin.

DAVID JENNESON

"Yeah, it's true," Devlin said ruefully. "I wish he'd keep his mouth shut."

"You're serious." Tasha handed it back. "I can't believe you're serious."

"Ahhh, what's the point in denying it? " Devlin shrugged. "You know now. But keep a lid on it."

"Why do you want me to stall the cops?"

"I had a little accident. With a bus. So they're sniffing around. As you can imagine with a deal like this I can't afford any pre-attention."

"Is that how he hurt his head?"

"Kid head-butted the windshield. Little tap is all. Go and stall them while I get him to a table in the back. Then I'll come and talk to them. Say you've been with us all night. Right here. If they ask how you know me, the name's Red Devlin."

"Tell you what, Red Devlin," said Tasha "It's an hour until my next show. All I've got to do is sit back in the dressing room and read crappy magazines I've already read. Or listen to dancers bitch about their asshole boyfriends. This sounds more interesting. Besides, I'm not crazy about cops either. But there'd better be something up front."

"You mean money," said Devlin.

"No. I mean money up front."

"We'll hire you too," Seawee raised his head.

"Start with the money."

"Fine. You name your price." Devlin dragged Seawee away from the stage. "Just get over there and keep them busy them while I get us squared away."

Tasha pulled on a loose-fitting sheer dress from her bag, the straps of which were designed to keep slipping off her shoulders and down. She glided down the stage stairs and over to the dripping cops.

"Hel-*low,*" she purred. "Here for the show?" The shoulder straps started to do their work. Their eyes followed them. When would they stop? Maybe never.

Moustache and Needle-nose were not on their home turf here. They were victims of The Royal Canadian Mounted Police policy to station recruits far away from home. Both were from rural Saskatchewan.

"Uh, no, ma'am," Mustache managed to get out. "Investigating an accident." He removed his hat as an afterthought.

In the meantime the next dancer made her way toward the DJ's booth from the dressing room behind the bar. There were more cheers. Her name was Cutsie Wu. Asian, she was shorter than Tasha. She had a mischievous way of moving and seemed curious in a sexy, pussycat way as she edged up close to the group. She stood in her little turquoise blue cut-away cowboy outfit and listened to the small talk.

By now Devlin had hidden the ailing Seawee away at a far table and purchased a full tray of drinks from a passing waiter. He now scuttled back toward the booth.

"Excuse me," he asked innocently and he approached the DJ. "Did I hear my license plate number called? Have I left my lights on again?"

The DJ shook his head and hooked a thumb toward the police.

Nether rookie cop had experience dealing with buxom, in-your-face peelers. Staring into the Cutsie Wu's cleavage and following Tasha's falling shoulder strap, the cops' eyes were beginning to glaze over with lust. Possibly the RCMP outposting policy was meant to broaden the scope of new recruits. If so it worked. Each felt his scope being broadened.

It was to this foursome that Red Devlin turned and presented himself as the owner of the Merc.

Cutsie Wu turned and departed for the stage, breaking their trance just a little.

DAVID JENNESON

"We want to ask you some questions," said Mustache.

Devlin nodded and happily motioned them back toward his table like a maitre d'. He offered them a seat which they humourlessley declined. Tasha sat down next to Seawee. Her shoulder strap began its slow southward trip again. The police were obviously finding this investigation difficult yet strangely rewarding.

"There was an accident up on Lynn Vale Road tonight," stated Needle-nose.

"Oh dear, not serious," Red Devlin replied, feigning concern. The cop ignored him. "We have reason to believe you were involved. It was a vehicle exactly like the one we spotted in the parking lot, which you now say is yours. The bus driver got part of your license plate. MXA. Are you saying this car is yours? You're admitting the white Mercury with the MXA plate is your vehicle? Is that what you're saying?" He pulled out a notebook.

Tasha seemed confused. "Hold it. Let me get this straight. I'm thinking of hiring Mr. Devlin here as my manager and now you say he was just in an accident?"

Red Devlin smiled blandly.

"You're hiring *him* as your manager?" Mustache pointed at Devlin in disbelief.

Suddenly Ray Seawee moaned. Tasha's towel drooped over his shoulders and a trickle of blood made its way slowly down his fore-head. From concussion and fever and beer he now watched this from a happy-world of delirium. All this talk of license plates. He kept hearing the prefix MXA. Had he worked on the MXA series in prison? Yes, he thought he had. It seemed to him the MXA series was a springtime vintage. He wanted to go out and check Devlin's plate to see if he recognized his personal touch but felt too weak. Now there were all these people crowded around.

Things were getting dim. He saw the strange man with the bushy white beard and thick white hair standing next to the table. To Ray Seawee he looked like the pictures of the deities he'd seen in the prison astrology magazines. Was it possible that God had become so fed up with the world He'd created that He'd was fed up and had come down the Carriage House to watch peelers and drink flat, watery beer? Quite possible, Seawee thought. Maybe God Himself had come here to check up on Seawee's progress in the honesty department. The idea made his head swim more.

"What's wrong with him?" asked Mustache.

"'Flu," said Tasha quickly.

"Then why is he bleeding?"

"Oh, we had a little misunderstanding in the parking lot earlier," Red Devlin explained. "One of those 'rights to the girl' things." He ran a thumb across the pale, useless knuckles of his right hand as if they were a lethal weapon. Then shrugged toward Tasha. The audacity of this remark seemed to infuriate the cops even more.

"Bullshit," said Mustache.

Devlin stayed calm. "Noblesse oblige."

"That kid could kick the crap out of you," said Needle-nose.

"Him and who's army?" Devlin clenched and unclenched his fist. He casually examined it as if it were a chain mail glove. This gesture drove the cops to distraction.

"I saw the whole thing," *God* interjected from the sidelines, picking up the story. "I had a hell of a time pulling these two apart. They were really duking it out, man. The lady must be worth fighting over."

Tasha got up and stood over Seawee. She leaned over and dabbed his forehead with the towel, treating all to another spectacular vista of cleavage. "He'll be fine," she said. "Leave him to me."

By now it seemed to dawn on the police that their attempt to stick Red Devlin with a dangerous driving rap was fizzling out into a complicated affair where business problems were being compounded by a domestic dispute. Huffily they took their leave, warning Devlin he wasn't out of hot water yet.

For the first time Devlin seemed to relax. He said he needed a rye and went to get one.

Under Tasha's soothing hand, Ray Seawee also relaxed. As well as having concussion and fever, he'd put away enough beer on an empty stomach to be drunk. Yet for all this he lucidly described the plan to sell the White House to her, Cutsie Wu and God. How they would get thousands and thousands of people to hold open houses, all on the same night. It was easy to talk them into it too, he said, producing the contract again as proof. Thousands of open houses and money would be changing hands. All across North America. And people wanted franchises.

There'd be publicity. News stories. With all the free press they'd claim the open house operation was a way to stimulate the economy. That would get Washington into the act. Symbolically of course. As a gesture of leadership they'd get the US government to hold an open house at the White House. The catch was, the White House would *really be for sale.* And when something as big as the White House changes hands, there was a lot of dough to be made, Seawee informed them.

Tasha, Cutsie Wu and *God* listened to this without a word.

"You know, I don't think he's kidding," *God* finally confessed to the dancers. "He's got no reason to impress us. Why would he lie?"

"He's not the one I'm worried about," said Tasha.

"Mr. Devlin has it all arranged," Seawee assured them. "I mean, it's worked out so far, hasn't it? "

The three had to admit that in a distorted sort of way this was true.

"He's a genius."

When Red Devlin returned there was a unity among them.

"We know what you're up to," said Tasha. "We want in. Otherwise we'll get our memories back."

Devlin seemed to be caught completely off guard by this. "What about your careers?" he grinned. "You're professional entertainers. You don't want to just throw that away."

"Yes we do," said Tasha. "You know what being a peeler's like? It sucks. Besides, we can come back to work any time. There's always work. It's like driving taxi."

"Count me in," said *God*. He shook Devlin's hand and introduced himself as Montreal Saunders, unemployed but qualified as a tow truck driver and sometime mechanic.

Red Devlin took a sip of rye and exhaled a long plume of cigar smoke as if it was his soul escaping his body. They had him. He nodded and sat back. A famous realtor once said *the most futile and disastrous day seems well spent when it is reviewed through the blue, fragrant smoke of a cigar.* He accepted this now. He allowed himself a brief reverie back to a better time and a better place. Back to The Day. The Golden Age of Real Estate.

He coughed on the cheap cigar.

That was the trouble with a Golden Age, he reflected. A Dark Age always followed.

"Wait here," he said tiredly. "I have to make a phone call."

CHAPTER 5

*A*nson Dobell sat at the narrow bar of the Tax 'n Spend in Washington, D.C. He carefully sipped a martini. His carry-on luggage was at his feet.

Beside him was a stack of United States government documents. He flapped though them, one page at a time, then on to the next, blankly reading nothing. He sucked on a cold pipe. It gave off a gurgling hiss like a wet tobacco tunnel. Occasionally he sniffed. Beginnings of a cold.

It was snowing outside. He had on his tan duffle coat with wooden peg buttons, the sensible sort of thing his parents used to make him wear. Turned out they were right, Anson thought, fingering one of the varnished pegs. This unremarkable man loved his duffle coat. Anson was as thin as a pen stroke, and large horn rim glasses hung on his beak nose.

He loved his own name. To him it, Anson Dobell rang of a pedigree from a bygone era of American political privilege, when noble-born patricians with odd-sounding names like Franklin and Avril and Estes were driven through Washington streets in the back seats of big dark Packards, and photographed in black and white for the official record.

Anson believed if he'd only been born a few decades earlier, someone with a name like his would have been a shoo-in for the big time. He dreamed of broadsheet headlines: *Anson Dobell Meets with Joint Chiefs. Anson Dobell Denies Affair with Mamie Eisenhower.* And best of all, *Anson Dobell Appointed by the President to Revitalize America.* Think of it. Anson Dobell emerging from a big black Packard sedan waving off reporters with, 'no comment - no time for interviews now.'

Now, isolated at the bar, with tan back toward the world, nose and pipe wet, flipping through a stack of meaningless papers, he gave off a natural bureaucratic rhythm. Flap, gurgle, sniff. Flap, gurgle, sniff. The action of inaction. This was not to be confused with everyday inaction. This was Anson's special inaction. He believed that it saved him for truly important action, which he could be called upon to perform at any moment by the government, but as yet it had not be required.

So Anson was busy looking busy. To him it was second nature - going through the motions of this low-key survival drill he'd practiced for all his working life. Simple as breathing, which he was having some trouble doing through his thin nose. You just had to know the rules:

Rule #1: always have papers in your hand, in front of you, or within arm's reach.

Rule #2: arising from Rule #1, always appear to be deeply absorbed in those papers, or be ready to become absorbed at any moment.

Rule #3: always make sure the papers in which you are absorbed are so detailed and obscure that any superior will be too intimidated to ask about them for fear looking stupid.

Tonight he was ready for anything. All because of a series of phone calls he'd received from, of all people, a Canadian realtor. Anson

DAVID JENNESON

was still curious about precisely what the man wanted. The man's enthusiasm was infectious. After thirty years of his powers and abilities being ignored by the civil service, Anson figured he was due for some comps, perks, freebies or any recognition at all. It was his time.

This Mr. Devlin had somehow burrowed down through the massive United States Federal Government bureaucracy to find Anson Dobell, a low-level functionary of the Pennsylvania Avenue Development Corporation, (PADC). He admired Devlin's effort for what it was - first rate detective work.

Anson's job was shifting bits of real estate here and there for the Pennsylvania Avenue Development Corporation and other even more obscure Federal Agencies.

Years ago large Federal Agencies had expanded to create their own in-house real estate divisions. Smaller agencies with less juice - like the Railroad Retirement Board, (RRB), the Office of Thrift Supervision, (OTS), and the Office of Small and Disadvantaged Business Utilization, (OSDBE), had no such departments. When they wanted to sell or buy a building or piece of land they contacted The Pennsylvania Avenue Development Corporation. They lent Anson out like he was a boring library book.

Anson Dobell was really tired of it.

He sniffed and turned another page. He looked at the green olive in his martini. It had sunk. It had become engorged with vermouth and gin and fallen down like a drunken fat man. Once again Anson had cultivated his drink too long. His olive had gone soft. He tamped aromatic tobacco into his pipe.

The bartender eyed Anson like he'd never seen such a poky drinker. Sounding like he was at the end of his patience, he asked Anson if he would like another.

Anson hesitated, then nodded.

He had to stay. He was waiting for a long distance phone call from Red Devlin. After Devlin's first call to his office Anson Dobell had looked up and given him the number of the Tax 'n Spend in order to give himself cover and deniability.

He'd taken Devlin's second call here, on the bar phone of the Tax 'n Spend. Devlin had described a tantalizing real estate opportunity in Washington D.C. which was short of specifics. But Devlin was a realtor. That said it all.

Anson Dobell feared hidden agendas, special interest groups, lobbyists. They got hardworking public servants in trouble. If something went wrong, the first ones to be sacrificed were the small fish, and Anson Dobell had no illusions about his size in the pond. On top of that, Devlin was a *Canadian*. These days Canadians were sort of second-class citizens, desperate persons, like Mexicans with parkas. They'd try anything. During that second call Devlin had proposed a face-to-face meeting. Anson Dobell's ears shot up like a jackrabbit's. What was the man really after? But then he and Devlin had a long talk about the need to revitalize the American economy. Devlin claimed he knew how to do it without costing the government a cent. And as a Canadian, Devlin couldn't take credit politically. He needed an American. This Dobell had to hear. He decided to play along for a while.

Anson had a bureaucrat's healthy paranoia. He believed the phone company kept detailed lists of every phone call made in America since the beginning of time. *That* was record keeping. So he chose to stick with the safe, anonymous bar phone at the bar.

Devlin had arranged for this final, pivotal phone call. Anson was to wait at the Tax n Spend, bags packed and ready to hail a cab to the airport. The plane tickets would be tourist class only, Devlin warned. Too many government officials like Dobell had been *spotted and recorded* in First Class seats. Why? Because *other* officials, also flying First Class fingered them and told. Figure it out, Devlin said. The secret grid of power is third class air travel. Your ticket will be waiting. To Anson Dobell the man seemed right on the money.

Outside the Tax n' Spend, the Washington, D.C. traffic noise was muffled by a January snowfall. Anson Dobell heard the ghostly sound of the cars and wished he were back in his townhouse. He lived the life of an aesthetic, keeping himself ready for some

DAVID JENNESON

mission. He rose at five, dressed quickly and ate a soft-boiled egg. Then he read the papers, drank black coffee and smoked a pipe. He went to his office and shifted pointless bits of property here and there. For dinner he ate bird-sized bits of the best gourmet food he could find. He made his own desserts. One little man cooking little cakes and sending small sweet smells heavenward. Then he turned in early to read civil service manuals until they put him to sleep. One day was a photocopy of the last.

The bar was heating up from the press of bodies behind him. Anson felt out of place. He might be noticed. He had the bureaucrat's instinctive fear of being noticed.

"Anson Dobell!" roared a voice. "What're you doing here?"

Anson shrunk. Not only had been noticed, but noticed by one of the most powerful loudmouths inside the Beltway. McGeorge Lewis was the high level RICO, (Racketeer Influenced and Corrupt Organizations), point man at the Justice Department. He was loud, patronizing, and drank too much but good at his job, and not the kind of person you wanted to notice you.

Worry furrowed Anson's narrow head. What if the bartender came up and just handed him the phone like last time? It had a long stretchy cord. They knew Anson personally here now. He'd taken calls here before. The bar phone was within easy earshot of that curious McGeorge. Here he would be, talking to some Canadian realtor. It wouldn't do.

The solution was obvious. Anson could not accept Devlin's call. With McGeorge Lewis here, a confidential conversation was out of the question. Anson remembered Devlin's warning - how powerful and devious government officials like McGeorge spied on people like him then used the information when it suited them. What else had Devlin said? The secret grid of power is third class air travel. That had the ring of truth. Devlin seemed to see into the very heart of things.

Anson had no intention of letting McGeorge know about any secret grid. He clapped shut his sheaf of documents.

A moment later the bartender placed his new martini down in

front of him. It was filled to the absolute brim, almost with a vengeance. Anson looked from his glass to the phone behind the bar. He dreaded that it would ring. It could go off at any moment.

"Waiting for someone?" McGeorge pried.

This brought things to a head. There was no way he could take Devlin's call with McGeorge sitting beside him. Only one solution. Leave. Immediately. He downed his martini in one gulp.

Anson Dobell had never chug-a-lugged a martini in his life but now did so. His sudden swallow made McGeorge Lewis raise his eyebrows.

"Leaving so soon, Anson? What, seen a ghost?"

"Yes," Anson said in a constricted voice. "Getting late. Must go."

Anson felt odd. No air in the room.

"Are you all right?" McGeorge now sounded concerned.

"Not feeling well," rasped Anson. "No air." He sounded like a raccoon.

"You're choking on your olive. You're turning blue!"

"Possibly," Anson coughed. Things were getting hazy. His sparrow chest heaved.

"Jesus Christ," McGeorge grabbed Anson from behind. He put him in a Zeus hug and squashed his solar plexus violently.

The first things to go were Anson's glasses. From the recoil of McGeorge's powerful hug they shot off the bridge of his nose like a dragster off the mark. The surprised bartender caught them.

The next crushing hug launched his pipe, trailing sparks, which the bartender one-handed. Then there were a series of violent crunches against Ansons gut, which produced nothing but rattles and wheezes. It felt like someone was hammering him flat.

"You'll kill him," said the alarmed bartender.

"Get ready," cried McGeorge.

A crowd had gathered.

"Ready for what?" asked the bartender, shifting from foot to foot like a linebacker.

"Here she comes!" shouted McGeorge.

The olive popped out of Anson like a cork out of a bottle. Due to Anson's upward tilt against McGeorge's gut it arced up and over like an early space capsule over the moon. The bartender dodged to one side. It struck a whiskey bottle.

Everyone - all the beautiful, powerful people gathered roundabout, cheered. Anson sat froggy-eyed. His glasses and pipe were handed back to him.

"Anson, someone oughta teach you how to drink sometime," said a frazzled McGeorge.

He left the bar. Outside it was snowing. There were no cabs. Anson had horked up an olive and now he had to walk. There was also The Uganda Grocery to get by. The Tax 'n Spend was at the top of a hill. To get to his townhouse, Anson had to go down the hill, pass through a hollow, and then climb up the hill on the other side.

In the pit of this geodemographic depression sat the Uganda. Until recently it had been a decent, family-run grocery store called the Eli Deli. The Greek owner used to order Anson's favorite grocery items specially: smoked Gold Eye from Canada, nutty-tasting preserved confits from the south of France, fine creamy and stiff cheeses. Anson was happy to pay through the nose. But the place had been robbed so many times that the owner had finally thrown up his hands and sold and it had then become the Uganda Grocery.

The Uganda was less a grocery store than an armored booze depot for the dispossessed. The mission statement of the Uganda was not to sell food but to defend itself. Not only was it barred from the outside, it was barred from the inside. Behind the bars of the cashier's booth, bulletproof glass had been installed. Rather than advertise traditional food items like apples and butter and eggs behind the cashier's window, photos of heavy weapons were displayed, plus hospital pictures of injured and convicted armed robbers who had tried and failed.

With no food in his house one night, Anson got up the guts to go down to the Uganda for a bit of cheese. There was none. Only a squeezy orange crayon-colored substance that came with its own crackers. The rest was given over to high-octane booze. The new owner - a large black man with a big skull - eyed him and intimated this was not the safest shopping place for skinny whitebread honkies. Worse, on his way out the thugs and punks hanging outside wanted money. When he didn't come across they threw flour on his duffle coat and whited him out.

Anson's recent experience with McGeorge and the olive left him in no shape for another such encounter now. Two martinis plus repeated thrusts to his solar plexus was a double-whammy. It felt like a water rat was swimming in his stomach.

Gravity seemed to pull him down the hill past the townhouses and rentals and the empty lots toward the Uganda. He felt helpless. He tried to control his feet but they felt like clown's shoes made of floppy rubber.

Shapes shifted and shuffled in front of the Uganda's iron bars. Someone ought to unionize thugs and hoodlums, thought Anson. Then maybe they wouldn't work at night in bad weather.

"It's the wimp," said a voice as they moved toward him.

"Pay the toll," said another voice.

A primitive law and order zone extended in a rough perimeter around the Uganda Grocery. The new owner had never been robbed. Oh, there had been attempts, and lots of woundings of the various participants, although no deaths. Many who'd tried were still recovering in prison hospitals or hopping about in casts. A consensus had formed among local practitioners that robbing the Uganda was too hazardous, as it put them out of work for long periods with disfiguring shotgun injuries.

In return for this, the new owner had extended a kind of no-man's

DAVID JENNESON

land around the Uganda. Panhandling, minor harassment and dope selling was permitted, but muggings and personal injury to potential customers were out of the question. Anyone who broke this unwritten law would be treated as a potential armed robber and shot-gunned at the first opportunity. Local police would be hard-pressed to believe a bunch of teen-age hoods over a local businessman fighting to protect his property. And whatever happened legally, the offender would've already been shot-gunned in any case, rendering all else academic.

Anson Dobell didn't know the ground rules. As far as he was concerned they regarded him as some skinny fuckwimp who had no sane reason for being here other than he might actually like getting beaten up.

He was now at the bottom of the hill, in the hollow and the pool of yellow light given off by the Uganda. He thought of turning to the left or right but gravity and momentum carried him forward. Besides, it was too late. He was surrounded. He clutched his bag.

"Ain't you forgettin' somethin'?" said the biggest gang member. He looked about sixteen but was over six feet tall. Kids are monsters these days, Anson thought feebly.

"Wimps pay the toll. Toll for wimps is twenty bucks. And that's before you give me a blow-job." His last line went down well with the rest of the gang, who laughed and slapped each other on the shoulder.

This was a revolting concept to Anson, and he already wasn't feeling well. It sickened him.

"C'mon, what are you, deaf an' dumb, wimpshit?" shouted the leader. He gripped Anson by the collar, blasting his beery breath into his face.

He poked Anson in the stomach to make his point. One poke per word... "WIMPS... PAY... THE... TOLL."

That's when it happened. It was the sort of defensive mechanism a small, scared lizard might employ in fending off larger predators in the Jurassic age. Anson sprayed him. That is to say, Anson was ill. It was that last poke. The gang leader might as well have been playing with a live bomb. The last hard poke in Anson's midriff touched two live wires and Anson exploded violently. There was a kind of high pressure hissing as Anson covered the gang leader with hot, martini-based vomit. It steamed, then quickly cooled.

The rest of the gang didn't know whether to laugh or be sick. Everyone stood and watched the gang leader as the spray began to freeze on him. He looked down at himself in shock. Then he looked at Anson like he wanted to present him with a dry cleaning bill. It was an expensive leather jacket. Perhaps the puke was corrosive. A sour garlic smell filled the chill air. Anson noted the partially chewed olive from his first martini had also been launched and was now lodged in the man's jacket breast pocket like punk jewelry. It was obvious to everyone the gang leader had caused the explosion himself with all that poking. So far as any gang member knew there was no precedent for this sort of behavior on the part of a victim. This spraying was a new thing.

"God damn," said the leader, backing away to look at the damage in the light of the Uganda's windows. The owner was peering out, judging by his expression, not pleased.

"Pay the toll, wimp," said another gang member weakly.

Anson glared at them, seemingly ready to spray again. They stepped backward.

"Pay the toll -"

"Ah screw you," said Anson and trudged on. A city bus rolled through the intersection, its chains clanking softly through the snow. Actually he felt much better. His head was clear. The winter night air of Washington D.C. smelled clean and fresh from the snow falling through the air. He felt like he'd been relieved of an odious burden, like getting a whole bunch of paperwork off his desk all at once only better.

He suddenly realized he had things to put in order and details to take care of. This Devlin. In his panic Anson had missed his phone call and possibly a third-class plane ticket. Absent-mindedly he fluffed his duffle coat for flour deposits. He hadn't been whited out. But he fretted about his missed connection.

He huffed wearily up the hill toward the townhouse his parents had left him when they passed away. It was a hard walk through the snow but as he gained elevation the standard of living rose again. Gradually the familiar shaped brick townhouses and big street trees came into view. When he got to the door the standard of living was just right for Anson Dobell.

He entered his apartment and realized he was hungry. What he really wanted was a little of that smoked Winnipeg Gold Eye and savory pancakes sewn with wild rice. Out of the question. Since the Uganda had changed ownership his cupboard shelves were bare.

He sighed. He sluffed off his duffle coat and walked into the bedroom. Still muzzy-headed from the experiences of the night it took him a little time to get his pillows in exactly the right order. Once he had it right he stripped off his clothes, jumped into bed and rolled up in his quilt. He opened the window for fresh cold air. Nothing better than being snug and warm in a room full of fresh night air. He could smell the snow, which made him feel even cozier. With that he got down to the business of becoming The Most Comfortable Person in the World. This involved some tossing and turning to get things right.

Finally he got comfortable. He drifted into a soft-edged world of black and white. He was in a starched white shirt being photographed stepping out of a black 1948 Cadillac limousine. Mamie Eisenhower was on his arm. People were instantly respectful of him. He gave them orders. It was yes Anson sir, no Anson sir.

Suddenly there was a fire. Or an air raid. Or a ringing. Yes, there was definitely ringing. Most insistent. Mamie Eisenhower and her friends gave him surprised looks as they began to dissolve. The ringing was making them go away. The ringing persisted above all else. Anson climbed woozily back out of sleep and reached instinctively for the telephone.

"Anson!" shouted a voice from the other end of the line.

"Dobell here," said Anson automatically, as if he were at the office. He blinked in the dark and sniffed. It was freezing in here.

"Devlin here!" cried the voice. He seemed to be trying to make himself heard over some tremendous party. "Anson, are you all right? I phoned the Tax 'n Spend and they paged and paged you. Then someone came on the line and said you were sick."

Damn, thought Anson. That would be McGeorge. The thought of Devlin talking to McGeorge made him feel ill. "I am not sick," corrected Dobell, "just momentarily ill."

"What about our meeting?" cried Devlin over the din at the other end.

"Yes, the meeting....." answered Dobell, trying to gather his thoughts.

"Morning flight booked to Vancouver. Tickets at the airport," Devlin shouted. "Hotel is booked. I'll pick you up at this end myself."

Anson thought about having no privacy from people like McGeorge, and about the prospect of knocking around his apartment for the next week, which he had booked off from work. Besides, he was hungry. Devlin lived in Canada. He thought that maybe he could get his hands on some of that smoked Winnipeg Gold Eye. Canadians must have that sort of thing coming out of their ears.

"Yes," said Anson, "no change in plans at this end. I'll be there."

"How will I know you?" came the voice from the other end. It seemed to be growing fainter. Perhaps a cold front of Canadian air was interfering with the telephone lines.

"Tan coat!" Anson hollered into the phone. "Peg wooden buttons."

"Aaah, good," cried Devlin. "You won't be sorry. I'll see you tomorrow." Just before Devlin hung up, Anson could have sworn he heard the strangest thing. It sounded like a stadium full of rioting soccer hooligans chanting, "Shower! Shower! SHOWER!"

CHAPTER 6

*R*ay Seawee had blacked out but was slowly coming around with Tasha's help. She'd cleaned up the cut on his forehead and he felt like his fever had dropped a few degrees. She'd taken his wet coat and had the bar cook hang it over the hot dog rotisserie to dry it out and warm it up. In all his born days Ray Seawee had never felt so cared for. The physical touching, plus the draping of his dry, comforting coat which now smelled like Oscar Meyer's warm-up jacket across his shoulders made him feel as if he were among angels.

He opened his eyes and saw a circle of interested faces gathered around him. There was Tasha, and Cutsie Wu, and God. He was aware of a huge blob of friendly light in the distance. He vaguely wondered if he was supposed to feel an overpowering love from it. He squinted his eyes and the blob came into focus. The Canuck's game on the big screen. Even that looked peaceful, with millionaire skaters making lazy, arcing curves across the ice to the undulating cheers of the crowd in one more losing game.

"His face is still cold," said Tasha. "He's not right yet."

"Close one," God spat a sunflower seed shell, "thought we lost you."

Seawee wondered what had happened. Had he fainted? Had he died?

"Party's over," Red Devlin strode into their midst. He was all business now, returning from his phone call to Washington, D.C., "call it a night."

"I have another dance," protested Tasha.

"So do I," said Cutsie Wu.

"So what?"

They stared at him sullenly, not moving. Devlin now knew how Moses must have felt leading the Israelites toward the Promised Land. Here was God's mission to be done, deserts to cross, seas to be parted and no time to waste. He imagined Moses trying to prod a bunch of sulky, whiney Israelites to get their asses in gear. What sort of management techniques had Moses used? Caring and sensitive to their needs? Gruff and stern? What did Moses do when he was tired and broke and pissed off? Damn. Perhaps the answer was hidden deep in the scriptures, which he'd been meaning to consult but so far hadn't had time.

"I don't like this change in tone," Tasha eyed him. "We're your staff now. Remember? We don't plan to be sitting here after business hours with no ride home."

"How in hell did you get home before this?" Devlin protested. It was the most Moses-like question he could manage at the moment.

"You ought to just let them finish their dances then give them a ride like they want," said Seawee peacefully. "After all, you hired them. They're your responsibility. And, like, you owe them."

Red Devlin shot Seawee a look that could have peeled bark off a tree. He thrust his hands in his pockets and walked away from the table, calling Seawee after him.

"Look, too much of this deal is going sideways already," he muttered. "My client, Anson Dobell - he didn't sound right. Maybe he's having second thoughts. We need to be fresh and focused to deal with him when he flies in tomorrow morning, and I have to set up a meeting with that little asshole Sheng."

"Who's Sheng?"

"A little asshole, like I said. Never mind. The last thing I need now is to have these bimbos phone the police and change their story. Think of it. Those smashed up, steaming buses. Those cops knew it was me. Dangerous driving is a tough rap. I'll lose my license. A realtor without a driver's license is like a dog with his balls cut off," he brooded.

"All they want is a ride," Seawee spread his hands.

"Well stop helping them," hissed Devlin. "I have never seen a situation where an employer is responsible for people who are still at their previous jobs."

"This is different."

"How so?"

"It's real estate."

Devlin glumly walked back to the table. "Finish your dances. Then we go, and remember who's boss."

The news seemed to breathe new life into Ray Seawee. He perked up and sped back to gynecology row with God hot on his heels. He was going to get a chance to see Tasha dance again. This was twice as good as seeing a regular dancer. After all, Tasha had cared for him and swabbed his brow, just like a nurse in the hospital. Now she was going to get up and slowly take all her clothes off as part of the follow-up treatment. It was too good to be true. Woo, thought Ray Seawee.

Red Devlin slid in beside them and ordered an Alberta sipping whiskey. He relaxed a little. He had the resigned air of a man who, unable to do anything else for the moment, was going to sit back and enjoy the fruits of his labors.

The first dancer came on - tall, dark-haired, with fabulous breasts and long black hair that went down to her well-rounded butt. The disk jockey introduced her as Heaven Leigh. A flurry of mating calls broke out again. Seawee noticed that God had his own method. He shouted in accents and snippets of foreign tongues, "Oi baybee, alley valley voo!"

Ray Seawee gave him a puzzled look the first time he did this.

"What the hell?" God shrugged. "It's different. Sometimes it gets their attention. They think I'm from somewhere else."

It was true. As the night went on, God seemed to attract much more than his fair share of dancers via this method. There were many dancers to attract. Tasha had failed to mention that she and Cutsie Wu were the last of a very long rotation of exotic acts. The wait caused more than a few pints and sipping whiskies to go down.

Finally Tasha came on. She brought the house down. By coincidence her costume this time was that of a hopelessly sexy nurse. Ray Seawee thought he would faint again, but this time from excitement. No one in prison could have imagined he'd end up like this. He was hoarse from woo-ing.

Thus they were a comparatively tight little group when the five of them climbed into the Turnpike Cruiser. It had stopped raining. God bought beer to celebrate the start of his new career. He immediately cracked five, handing them around.

"Where'd you get this dinosaur?" Tasha asked Devlin.

Devlin ignored this insensitive reference to the Turnpike Cruiser.

"Take me home first," God said. "I'm closest. Just up the hill."

"Whatever," sighed Devlin.

He gave Red Devlin detailed instructions how to get to his house, which was situated high up in the backwoods of Lynn Vale.

"Not back up *there*," Devlin complained.

"What's wrong with Lynn Vale?" asked God.

"Ah, never mind," Devlin said, but he sounded worried.

They shot up Mountain Highway. As they passed the 7-Eleven they saw a white police cruiser, which sat in the lot with its engine running.

"Looks like those two cops from the Carriage House," said Seawee casually. "They eyeballed us when we went past."

"Shit," Devlin sounded panicky, "I have open beer in the car. I've had too much whisky. I'll lose my license." He turned the corner and shot up Lynn Vale Road at tremendous speed. If the cops were going to come after him, he apparently wanted a healthy head start.

The sudden acceleration alarmed everyone in the car. "Slow down," shouted God from the back seat. "What's the panic all of a sudden? Turn here. Turn right."

With a long swerving screech Devlin veered right off Lynn Vale Road and up a steep side street. Not wanting to reduce getaway speed he floored it, calling on all the Merc's horsepower. It rocketed over the crest and nearly became airborne. Shrieks rose from the back seat as God and Tasha and Cutsie Wu bounced and clinked.

Up front, Ray Seawee was having his own private deja vu nightmare. Moments ago he had been watching his personal nurse take her clothes off in front of him. Now he was back in the death seat of Red Devlin's getaway car where he'd been brained senseless a few hours ago.

"Not this again!" he cried, burying his head in the seat. "Slow down. Stop. Anything but this!"

"Aw pipe down," muttered Devlin. He was staring straight ahead, concentrating. *Real estate is not for the faint of heart*, he thought.

"Turn left!" shouted God.

This caused another abrupt swerve as Devlin fought to make the turn. It threw Seawee into the passenger window with a thunk. God seemed to purposely wait until the last second before shouting instructions. Seawee wished he would knock it off.

But God did exactly the opposite. In fact he seemed to be making a perverse game of it, shouting directions at the last possible moment, then hollering, "Hidy-HO!" as Devlin went into another suicidal turn.

Each turn took them deeper and deeper into the twisting upper backwoods of Lynn Vale. Finally they were on a gravel road, which snaked and forked. God shouted "left here," or "go right," seemingly when it suited him.

"Can't you tell us before we're on top of the intersection?" asked a rattled Seawee.

"Hard to see," said God, spitting a sunflower seed and taking a swig of beer. His beard hung like a white bathmat over the front seat as he squinted through the windshield.

Finally a shape rose in the headlights. It was an old house which sat on an overgrown lot, its second story rising up from a bramble sea. The roof supported a carpet of moss that appeared to be a foot thick in some places. There was a handmade garage to one side with an ancient tow truck parked on an angle. *Straight Arrow Towing, Montreal Saunders, Prop.* read the sign on its dented door.

"We're here!" said God and hopped out. "Just go back the way you came. Or keep heading straight. That'll get you out too." Then he was gone, vanishing into the wilderness of brambles.

Coming to a halt seemed to restore Devlin's senses. To the others he appeared satisfied to have escaped from whatever phantom police car was chasing him. In fact, he seemed spent and tired. He nudged the gas pedal. The Turnpike Cruiser slowly rolled forward.

They seemed to be driving deeper and deeper into the evergreen forest. "Do you know where you're going?" asked Tasha after a few minutes had passed.

"This way," muttered Devlin, repeating God's instructions, "will get us out..."

"I don't like this," said Tasha to Cutsie Wu. "Here we are in the

DAVID JENNESON

woods with two guys we hardly know - WATCH OUT!"

Devlin had nearly cruised off the road. He took a fork to the left. Now a heavy rain lashed down.

"This is the way," he said sleepily. "A realtor can always find his way to a home. Ha ha."

Seawee doubted that this realtor could. This became more evident as the gravel road climbed and narrowed. It now seemed that they were on the edge of some sort of mountain. To their right the bank went straight up, while on the left it dropped away into nothingness. The Merc began to weave again.

Seawee couldn't stand it any longer. "For Christ's sake, pull over," he cried. "You're too drunk to drive. Rest a minute."

Devlin was happy to comply. He seemed tired of driving for the moment. He carefully pulled the Merc over on the shoulder and shut it off.

"Ah," he sighed with relief as the engine chugged dead.

"Well this is just great," said Tasha from the back seat. "Why don't you drive?" she asked Seawee.

"Give him a minute and he'll be all right," said Seawee. He didn't think this was the right time to admit that his license was suspended.

"So we just sit here in the dark while he has a nap?" Tasha protested.

"Aw, relax," said Devlin. "I'll get us home. Just need to settle my nerves." He took a swig of beer and lit a cigarette. "We've got a big day tomorrow. I'm picking up a very important official from Washington D.C. Got to show him the city. Show him the plan. Show him a good time too."

"What do you mean, good time?" Tasha asked suspiciously.

"Whatever he wants," Devlin spread his hands. "He's a client. Figure it out."

"So I suppose *we're* the good time," said Cutsie Wu with disgust.

"Not necessarily," Devlin leaned back in the seat and blew out a lazy cloud of cigarette smoke. "You're realtors now. Realtors fix deals. We're brokers. Make people happy. Realtors pay *other* people to provide that sort of good time. Unless of course you want to do it yourself, and that's okay too. It's up to you. *To be a realtor is to be free.*"

"Oh," Tasha paused. "Maybe that's not so bad then," she said to Cutsie Wu. "Maybe this thing's on the level after all."

As if to shatter Tasha's fragile confidence, Red Devlin suddenly snapped the key over and powered up the big Merc. He gunned it. As it was angled off the gravel road, it launched in the wrong direction like a poorly docked ship. The Merc shot off the bank and glissaded over green waves of underbrush like a torpedoed liner. It crashed down the steep bank thumping and splintering through the underbrush. As it pounded and turned Devlin fought for control. All the rest could do was hold onto one another and keep their thumbs over their open beers. Clods of ferns were thrown up and pine boughs whipped across windows. Finally with a jolt they came to rest on top of a cedar stump - completely level and upright but facing in the opposite direction.

Five minutes later they finished the steep climb to the road on foot. They were a deflated company. Survivors on a remote mountainside. Seawee and the others stood back, indistinct forms against the backdrop of trees. Suddenly Red Devlin bent over double from the exertion of the climb, coughing and hacking into the dark gravel road.

"Are you going to live?" Tasha bent over and looked at him.

"Gimme a minute," wheezed Devlin and launched into another coughing fit.

"You should quit smoking," Tasha suggested.

"You should quit giving free advice," Devlin hacked on the road and wiped his mouth with the back of his hand.

Seawee went over, pounded him on the back and straightened him up. "We have to get help." Then he brightened as if he'd had a

DAVID JENNESON

thought. "Or we can just leave it there"

"Yeah, let's leave it," chimed in Tasha. "No one will find that hunk of junk for a hundred years. And when they do, it'll be like some perfectly preserved artifact from the past, up on a pedestal. People will think it was some kind of ancient forest god."

"There's no way in hell I'm leaving that car," Devlin exploded. "Nosssir. That Saunders character had a tow truck in his front yard. We'll get him. He has to do it. He's my employee now."

"He's miles back," said Seawee wearily.

"Then we'd better get started," said Devlin. "Let's move it. Hup two," he barked, and started off down the dim strip of gravel. Rain fell steadily. The mists shouldered across the gravel road. Big cedars loomed up on either side. Their boughs swayed heavily in the wet wind.

Ray Seawee soon found himself snuggled in between Tasha and Cutsie Wu as they huddled together for mutual warmth trudging after Devlin. He thought things over. Here he was, soaked to the skin for the second time, marching down some muddy mountain road in the middle of the night, but with two beautiful, shapely women holding him tight. It might be stretching it a bit, but he could say it was better than being in jail. He felt satisfied that he was improving his lot, although it seemed to be painfully slow.

"This is the worst job I ever had," Tasha carped at Red Devlin's back.

"So quit," Devlin shot back. *"Real estate is no walk in the woods."* Devlin seemed utterly determined - possessed by an irrational energy when it came to the Turnpike Cruiser. Tasha piped down and snuggled in closer to Seawee.

"Who does he think he is giving orders like that? God?"

"No. Moses."

"Come on, be serious," she whispered to him. "Is this guy for real?" their feet crunched on the wet gravel. "He's hard to read. Do we need him? I mean, couldn't *you* just do it?"

"Do what?" Seawee whispered back.

"Whatever it is he does. This White House thing."

Seawee thought about this. "The only person who can do what he does," he said after a moment, "is him."

Tasha made a soft, disappointed sound.

"At least until I figure out exactly what it is that he does," Seawee added. That seemed to hold her.

They finally reached a long downhill slope, which meant they were entering the dirt road to God's house. It was a remarkable structure. This was no cabin or shack, but a respectable house one would expect to find on an upscale residential street of the 1930's or 40's, but something had gone wrong. The neighborhood had never developed and the house, like a square of cheese neglected in the back of the fridge, had gone off. Now it was marooned, miles away from any other residential home, on a dirt road, with brambles growing up to the second-story windows.

Leading the way, Red Devlin got the first good look at it. "Real estate can be a hard master," he muttered to himself. He strode up the stairs and hammered on the door. "Saunders!" he cried. "Montreal Saunders! Come out!"

There was a confused bumping from deep within the house.

"This is Red Devlin. Your new employer. I have a job for you."

The porch light clicked on. The front door opened and God appeared in baggy black sweat pants. Sleepily he ran a hand through his thick white hair and beard. Devlin issued marching orders: The queen of the fleet was down and his tow truck would be required - immediately.

God blinked. He put on his coat, ran out into the rain and cranked over the tow truck. They watched from the porch as it coughed and spat smoke and sparks from the stack until it was more or less running. Clouds of exhaust rose high into the night rain. God waved them forward and they stacked themselves into the big cab.

"She's not in the best shape," he said by way of explanation.

"That's why I retired her. She's got heart, but she's got no insurance."

As they chugged uphill Red Devlin gave precise directions as to the route to the Merc. He seemed to have a map in his mind of every turn they had taken. When they arrived on the soggy strip of mountainside road where she'd gone over they realized that there was a problem.

"Where?" asked God.

No one could answer. The rain had washed away all tire tracks. The laurel on the side of the road had sprung back, erasing every sign of the Turnpike Cruiser's final exit into the forest.

"She's gone," said God after several sweeps up and down the road. "Like the Titanic into the deep. You'll never find her."

Devlin's face was made more fearsome by the upward cast of the dashboard lights. "That car," he said evenly, "is a key element to the marketing mix. It has the luxury necessary for big clients. It has big white seats. Not naugahide. Leather. It has size to hold big egos. People with big egos sit in that car and it makes them feel even more important than they already think they are."

"So. Rent one," advised Tasha.

"A car like this cannot be rented!" Devlin erupted. "A 1961 Mercury Turnpike Cruiser isn't an everyday item. Back in The Day she was queen of the road. Find it or that's it!"

He thought about Moses in the desert and calmed himself. He rephrased, "That is to say, or the deal is off. This car is essential to the business." He looked at his watch. Four in the morning.

Seven o'clock in Washington. Anson Dobell would be phoning a cab to go to the airport.

There followed a tedious tracking expedition over a dark mile of mountain road. All concerned paced up and down, peering down the bank for signs of the Merc's demise. An hour later Cutsie Wu made a cry of discovery fifty feet from the tow truck. God ran back, fired it up and drove to the spot.

"This is the place," cried Cutsie Wu. "Here's where we went into an alternate reality. I sense it."

Seawee ran the tow cable down, hooked the car to it then God hopped into the cab and activated the winches. There was a grinding, wrenching sound as rusted gear teeth meshed. The tow truck's front lifted off the road. As they watched, it was dragged backward with a scraping of gravel toward the edge of the bank due to the weight of the lodged Merc.

God ran a hand through his white mane. "We need counterbalance," he said. "Climb on the hood."

They all climbed on. Red Devlin, draped across the hood like a shot moose, carefully pulled back his white cuff and glanced at his watch. Right about now Anson Dobell would be eating a free light breakfast in third class, high over the American heartland.

"Try 'er again," said God from the cab. He seemed to be enjoying this. "Block the wheels." Seawee jumped off the hood and crammed muddy boulders behind the tires then climbed back on.

"Hi-dee-ho!" shouted God.

On the fifth attempt the Merc gave way. They could feel, rather than hear a barely audible moan of movement deep within the forest. God laughed and gunned the engine. Through the noise they could hear sounds of crackling underbrush and snapping tree limbs. Heavy objects were being plowed aside as the Merc came up the hill, turning over and over like big hooked whale. Finally it emerged through the laurel bushes and up onto the road.

It was covered in so much mud and debris it barely looked like an automobile at all. Devlin jumped in and started it up. The Merc hummed like a baby. God ran around and inspected it, and said it seemed fine except for the noticeable sag in the left rear. This made it look like it had a bad hip.

"Spring's shot," said God.

"Fix it by ten and I'll pay you a bonus." said Devlin.

"Don't have the tools," said God. "I'll tow it to the Chevron. I

DAVID JENNESON

know the guy there. "

As a gray winter dawn broke over Lynn Vale, God's tow truck emerged from a side road hauling a strange cargo. The two policemen from the Carriage House were just going off shift. It passed them heading in the opposite direction down Lynn Vale Road.

They rubbed their eyes. "What was that?" asked Mustache. "Should we stop it?"

"It looks like a float for a parade," said Needle-nose. "or a replica of some early military vehicle or tank camouflaged with boughs and undergrowth and mud."

"Very authentic," agreed Mustache.

"Probably those Legion guys," decided Needle-nose. "They're always putting floats and exhibits together like this to educate kids about the war. Most impressive."

CHAPTER 7

*A*nson Dobell sat stuck in the middle row of a stubby Boeing 727. His only luggage, a carry-on bag, was crammed in above him. He would have been more at home in a long, elegantly thin Boeing Constellation. With its distinctive three-tipped silver tail and dolphin-shaped body, the four-prop Constellation had been queen of the skies in 1948. It was an aircraft in which postwar rules applied. Pipe smoking was allowed. Cigarettes were encouraged. Second hand smoke was sought after. Whiskey was free. Steaks were rare and business was well done. He recalled stories from his father who had taken these long slow flights across Truman's America. He said that a man felt like a Rockefeller by the end of the day. Meanwhile, below, a powerful America moved, growing and rustling, lit by the headlights of farm trucks and powered by strong coffee.

In order to blend in with the third class passengers ordering low priced drinks, Anson asked for a glass of red wine. Stuck in the middle seat he found it hard to drink. His elbows were wedged into fat passengers on either side. Earlier, he'd attempted to have the same kind of important-sounding conversation with them that

DAVID JENNESON

he imagined his father had done in the days of slow planes and fast trains.

He had been rudely ignored.

Perhaps, Anson thought miserably, he should have traveled by train. He remembered the ads he'd seen in the National Geographics, about the *Empire Builder* and the *El Capitan* and the *California Zephyr*. He sat back and briefly imagined those steel-fluted tubes of power, where influential people in double-breasted gabardine stretched out after dinner, smoking a pipe in the dome lounge while the red and tan *Olympian Hiawatha* roared westward on seven-foot wheels through the American night.

Anson sometimes wondered in softhearted, or softheaded moments, if by meditating on stacks of old magazines he could mystically launch himself back into that era, become famous and take his rightful place alongside the great names of the age.

The fat man next to him snuffled and jerked and made him spill a bit of his red wine. It left a small dark spot on the sleeve of his tan duffle coat. Anson sighed and sank back into the middle seat of third class air travel. At least his head cold was clearing up. He realized the sheaf of documents he had brought was useless. No one noticed or cared. There was no point in pretending to study them. He wished he could throw his cheap red wine out the window. It made him drowsy and lightheaded.

He remembered a National Enquirer headline he'd glanced at recently while passing the Uganda Grocery. It shouted the discovery of a DC-3 passenger plane lost in 1947, which had just been found in the woods of upstate New York, perfectly preserved and intact. *Skeletons in the seats. Old Golds still smoldering in the ashtrays.* He wished his seatmates on that plane instead of this.

He wondered briefly about his destination - Vancouver, Canada. Anson had never been to Canada. Anson had never actually been anywhere more than twenty miles out of Washington, D.C. His parents had never taken holidays, so when Anson grew up and went into government service, neither did he. Plenty for him to do and see in the capitol of the most powerful nation on earth.

He spent his happiest holidays in the Library of Congress. Few Americans could call the Library of Congress their neighborhood library, but Anson Dobell could. He'd read the dozen volumes of *The Unabridged History of the American Civil Service.* He read archived issues of *American Mercury.* When he'd felt drowsy he had sneaked over to the travel section and pulled out old volumes of National Geographics. There he read the ads and looked for stories featuring naked African women, which seemed to wake him up.

This armchair travel was the extent of Anson's worldliness. He had heard about Canada, and learned a lot about it from the ads in the old National Geographics. He knew that Canadians hunted a lot. And fished. They were always pulling big silvery fish out of sky blue waters. Perhaps these were the sought-after Winnipeg Gold Eye. Canadians dressed sensibly, in red-checked hunting shirts that would probably last for years. Must get himself one while he was up there. Go splendidly with his duffel coat. He'd get Red Devlin to pay for it.

He wondered what sort of accommodation Devlin had waiting for him. He knew most Canadian hotels were made of logs. This made sense, with ninety-nine percent of the country covered in trees. But these weren't just regular log hotels. According to his information they were grand, baronial log chateaus, imbedded into high mountainsides with spectacular views. Anson could envision the Canadian Super Continental with its silver vista-dome passing a mile or more away through the valley below.

With so much land and so few people, he wondered how Canadians ever managed to get enough people together to have a city at all. Perhaps they weren't really cities, but just convenient reference points on the map for airline pilots to aim at. You'd land at Vancouver Airport and take the vista-dome to the nearest mountainside log chateau. Where did regular Canadians live? The image of igloos with television antenna suggested itself.

What about cars? Well, yes, he thought, they would have to have cars, but not as good as American cars, nor as new. Quite possibly it was like Mexico or Cuba, where old American cars migrated like elephants before they died. Suddenly Anson realized he felt sorry for Canadians. They probably dressed in period traditional costumes because they had to put on shows for tourists. He was thankful to be an American with a good education. This Devlin was probably a hopeless rustic. He was probably the owner of a hunting lodge, with money in his pocket, a real estate license and some big ideas. Anson decided he'd have to be patient and gentle and guide the man.

He finished his red wine and drifted into sleep, dreaming of slim Indian maidens waving at him from behind towering cedars.

*   *   *

There was ant-like activity around the Lynn Vale Chevron for such an early hour. The mechanics weren't on the job yet, but it seemed that God knew the owner. He was in a serious discussion with him. God was poking the fellow in the chest and pointing to the foliage-and mud-covered apparition sitting in the Chevron lot. From his behavior it looked like God was owed some sort of favor by the Chevron owner and now he was collecting.

Devlin had everyone clean the branches and clods of moss and mud from the Merc until it slowly began to take on the aspect of an automobile again. God worked the owner over with his negotiations while Devlin nervously glanced at his watch. Finally God walked over to Devlin.

"Here's the deal," he said to Devlin. "He'll let me fix it, and he'll rent you the garage and tools for one hour so I can do it. He wants payment in advance. He wants you to get that wreck into the garage now before some cop sees it."

"Feh," huffed Devlin. He thrust a check at the garage owner. God backed her into the garage and raised her on the hoist.

"Well?" asked Devlin as God raised her on the garage hoist.

God clicked his tongue as he stood under the great vehicle and spat a sunflower seed. It landed on Devlin's white tie and stuck. Devlin frowned and stared down at it. Authentic branches and twigs stuck to swatches of moss and mud all over his expensive white suit. He now looked like some mad retired colonel decked out in formal camouflage. It was an interesting multi-purpose concept - a well-tailored camouflage suit you could wear on combat missions then go straight to a fancy dress ball featuring politicians and generals without having to change. Silently Devlin flicked the offending sunflower seed from his tie.

"Rear springs are shot, it looks like," said God. "Big job. I'd think about renting something for today."

"Impossible," said Devlin. "I drive this car and no other. End of discussion."

"How long do I have?" asked God.

Devlin rolled his eyes. "One hour. And that only gives me half an hour to get to the airport."

"Impossible," said God.

Devlin was about to explode again but caught himself. He tried to be more Moses-like. "My friend," he laid a hand on God's shoulder, "that's what real estate is all about."

*   *   *

The butty woman passenger on Anson's right snuffed out his Indian princess dreams with her rear end as she maneuvered out of her seat and past him. He blinked open his eyes to stare at the expanse of her broad *ass*.

They had not reached Vancouver, but were in Seattle, Washington. Almost all passengers disembarked except Anson, and very few people boarded. *Very well*, thought Anson, *I'll go north on my own*. He wondered why no one else was going to Vancouver. Canada must be a primitive place indeed, he conc-luded. Probably the only Americans who ever went up there regularly were anthropologists who studied Canadian hunting and fishing rituals.

A few minutes later the engines whined and the runway dropped away. The jet nosed up into low cloud. Anson relaxed in the anonymous whiteness. He was surprised when the plane began to descend again almost immediately. He thought any city in Canada would have to be an immense distance from any large American city. The plane dropped out of the clouds and Anson peered down to see if he could spot the border. He was almost certain the white line of snow where Canada started would be clearly visible.

Instead he saw a city contained between blue mountains and the sea. A vast bay lead to a narrow passage, then into a long, sheltered inlet around which the city rose. It seemed mythical in the drifting cloud. It reminded him of pictures of Rio de Janeiro in National Geographics. Concerned, Anson Dobell checked his ticket just to make sure he hadn't flown to Rio by mistake. Nope. The ticket was stamped "Vancouver".

The jet eased down onto a pristine runway.

His bewilderment continued as he walked through the airport. No one wore plaid hunting jackets. There were tight crowds of silk-suited Oriental businessmen anxious to be off and away to the great Asian markets across the Pacific. Whole families of East Indians in bright flowing robes and turbans met and embraced.

Anson felt alone and dazed in his duffel coat. He quietly fingered his varnished peg buttons and frowned at the stain on his sleeve. Then he remembered that Red Devlin would be watching for his tan duffle coat. He scuttled past International Arrivals and out into the bright daylight. Still he saw nothing recognizably Canadian. No igloo nor hunting lodge. There was a long rank of cabs and airport buses, and a parking lot gleaming with what appeared to be thousands of late model cars. Beyond that there were wet green fields, and beyond, the blue mountains.

Then a beautifully restored Mercury Turnpike Cruiser drew up to the high curb. Sparkling white. The door opened and a man, also in white, swarmed up the steps.

"Anson Dobell," the man hollered, "paging Anson Dobell!" He anxiously scanned the crowd.

Anson meekly raised his hand.

"Anson!" cried the figure. He advanced pointing fingers like two six guns then shook his hand warmly. "Red Devlin. My staff is dying to meet you."

Anson was hugely relieved. Everything was suddenly falling into place. He'd been right about Canadians all along. They *did* dress in special costumes. He'd read old Life Magazines about legendary realtors of the postwar era who'd built thousands of homes for returning WWII vets. And made millions. *Millions.*

Now Anson was looking at the real thing. He thought that he had actually never seen someone dressed like this. Like a tribal chief. He'd dealt with plenty of American realtors, but they were anonymous drudges compared to Red Devlin. These Canadian realtors had respect for their roots. Like Ukrainian dancers they dressed traditionally. They wore the white real estate attire for which realtors everywhere were famous. He noticed streaks of gray in Devlin's ginger hair. They didn't look natural. They looked like mud. Mud daubing. Perhaps another rite.

"Welcome to Canada and Open Homes International. It's all here - what you've been waiting for," Devlin guided him by the arm. He led Anson down the stairs toward the Turnpike Cruiser.

The allowable stopping time was about thirty seconds at this busy passenger pick-up location. Two big brass-buttoned Canadian Commissionaires approached. They looked like overweight stationmasters. They threatened to have the car towed but Seawee held them off like a guard dog.

Seawee's suit was clean but soaking wet. He had had to clean himself up as well as he could in the Chevron washroom, while Devlin changed into a fresh suit he had stored in the trunk of the Merc. Tasha and Cutsie switched into more conservative costumes from their peeler garment bags.

"My associate and vice-president," gestured Devlin as he hustled Anson Dobell into the back of the Merc, "Mr. Ramon Seawee."

Seawee's head swung around at the sound of Ra-*mon*. He gave Anson a curt nod. "My staff," Devlin said grandly from the front seat.

Tasha and Cutsie Wu sat demurely on the white leather upholstery.

DAVID JENNESON

Anson sat beside them and felt a sudden thrill at being close to two clearly sexy women. ."My driver, Mr. Saunders," Devlin continued his introductions. God nodded. He had found a chauffeur's cap. "And my sales associates - this is Miss Tasha, my assistant and Miss Wu

"I'm very pleased to make your acquaintances," said Anson Dobell politely, "and I must say, this car is beautifully restored. I've never ridden in such a splendid antique. It feels like a limousine. And it smells so fresh," he sniffed. "Pine-scented. Even pine needles on the floor. How very thoughtful of you."

"Nothing's too good for an associate of Open Homes International," said Devlin over his shoulder. He winked happily at Seawee.

Anson Dobell failed to notice an exhausted relief which fell over the others. They pulled onto a Canadian highway. It had hardly any cars on it he observed, and right in the middle of the day. Maybe he'd been right after all - most Canadians were out hunting and fishing. Anyone who could afford a new car must have parked it at the airport.

"Could I ask a question?" ventured Anson after some time.

"Surely," said Devlin, "that's why you've come."

"When is winter here?"

"Eh? " Devlin half turned. "I'm not sure I get you."

"Winter," repeated Anson. "In Washington we have ours in December, January and February. You're obviously ahead of us in some way. You must have your winter in September and October because now it's January and you've got spring. It must be something like time zones. I thought the seasons only changed from north to south, but obviously they change east to west too."

The car was stunned to silence. Even Red Devlin was at a loss for words. Next to him, Ray Seawee looked like he was trying to mentally swallow a whole boiled egg.

In the back seat, Tasha stared across at Anson Dobell in

blank disbelief.

"Mr. Dobell," she placed her hand gently on his sleeve, as if wishing not to embarrass him, "this is our winter."

Anson was unperturbed. Far from it. What he was seeing was better than any book or magazine. "If this is winter, then it must be snowing in July," he said cheerfully. "It's like the seasons are reversed. Like Australia. This place is the best-kept secret I've ever seen."

The others looked at each other with blank expressions. "No one knows about Vancouver," said Seawee. "We like it that way."

They now approached the city itself, which was protected by mountain battlements rising from the sea. Unseen from here, Lynn Vale was tucked up between them.

"Vancouver is a helluva nice place," Devlin pointed out.

"Like Rio," Anson agreed. "I'm afraid it won't be so secret once Open Homes International gets rolling," he sounded mockingly regretful.

"Oh yes. Open Homes International," Dobell repeated absently as they crossed the long arc of the Oak Street Bridge. He saw tugs pulling log booms down the muddy Fraser River. "How does that work exactly?"

Devlin leaned over the back seat and explained the theory: Paying people to hold open houses created a buyer's market, which really became a seller's market. Homes would be bought and sold. Billions would change hands and the economy would get a massive jump-start. The government would want to be involved, he added, because it would make them look good.

Anson Dobell frowned. He peered at Devlin, as if trying to determine if he was really a real estate genius on the level of the legendary Bill Levitt. "That's the most wrong-headed idea I ever heard," he said after a moment. "The public will never go for it. Too much inconvenience. How long has this program been under way? Is it doing well?"

"Er, yes. Took off like a rocket. You could say my staff and I are batting a thousand."

"How many contracts do you have?" asked Dobell .

"One," said Ray Seawee from the front without turning around. "I think it's in the trunk. But we just started last night." Red Devlin looked at Seawee like he could cheerfully have murdered him at that moment.

"Mr. Devlin," Anson said officiously, "your theory is clearly untested. From what you tell me I cannot in all conscience act as a consultant in any capacity on this project. I know a bit about real estate on the government side, but I can't see what possible use I can be to you. I hate to say it, but you might as well turn the car around and take me back to the airport."

Again Devlin wondered what Moses would do if faced with this situation. Here was another mule-headed Israelite wanting to bail out before the trek began. Devlin brooded in the front seat. This was unthinkable. Anson was the linchpin to his entire plan. Devlin needed to insert the hook. Early. Have Anson in up to his neck.

Anson sniffed and wiped his nose.

"Whoa, slow down a minute," Devlin's mind worked desperately. "I've got people working on Phase Two as we speak. As for my staff, we've only begun recruiting. Soon we'll have hundreds, no, *thousands* of agents in the field. We are expanding. Mapping out territories for franchises. Daily." He nudged Ray Seawee with his knee for some help but none was forthcoming.

"No. Turn around," said Dobell sadly, watching the dream-like city slide by. "This will amount to nothing. It won't do."

Devlin's cell phone warbled

"Aha, probably my staff now," he said, relieved for the chance to think. "Devlin here," he woofed impatiently.

"Give me Ray Seawee," said an angry voice. "Seawee I said. Is he there? This is the number he gave me."

Red Devlin suddenly felt sick at heart. This was probably some irate probation officer Seawee had lied to and now they were going to publicly haul him in by the scruff of the neck. If things kept going like this Devlin felt he'd be dead by the end of the day.

"It"s for you, *Ramon*." Devlin innocently handed the phone to him.

Seawee frowned and put his ear to it.

"Ray Seawee?" shouted a hot voice.

"Yeah, it's me," Seawee sounded a little scared.

"McGregor here. I have some questions about this deal we made."

Now Seawee felt queasy. Things were definitely falling apart. What the hell had Devlin got him into? "Shoot," he said, hoping McGregor wouldn't.

"This is some deal you got me into. I've been reading this contract. It's mighty short on specifics. I want to go over it with you now. In person. Immediately."

"Immediately," repeated Seawee without blinking.

'Then get over here now or the deal is off! If I don't see your face in half an hour I'll be taking action of my own," said McGregor. "Do you read, Mister Cell Phone Seawee?"

"Yes, sir," said Seawee quietly. "I read."

"Well good," shouted McGregor. "Over and out!" The line went dead.

Ray Seawee turned around for the first time. "I'm sorry, Mr. Dobell. This is a real emergency. Just stick with us we'll get you back to the airport right away.

Anson Dobell shrugged. He'd made his position clear. He was off the hook. He didn't even need to pretend to look at the stack of documents in his briefcase. If these Canadians wanted to drive him around in the back of a vintage limousine through some kind of evergreen city where winter was spring, so much the better.

Ray Seawee whispered the address in God's ear and the Merc

picked up speed. Red Devlin kept nudging Seawee's knee and asking for some kind of explanation with his eyes. Seawee looked stoically ahead as they crossed the Oak Street Bridge into Vancouver.

Devlin crossed his arms. He looked hijacked, betrayed, ignored, and mad. He hadn't slept. He had probably forgotten that no one else had slept. Gritty flakes of dried mud fell from his hair into his eyes. The convict Seawee, whom he'd saved, was now going to turn himself in to the authorities in front of his pivotal client, or worse, go on the lam. Devlin was besieged by halfwits. He rolled down the window and threw his cigar out where it bounced and sparked around on the bridge deck.

God swung the Merc smoothly onto Pacific Boulevard. It skirted False Creek, a small saltwater inlet that formed the southern edge of the Vancouver's core. They sped through Vancouver's downtrodden Downtown Eastside and came to a broad span crossing to the North Shore and Lynn Vale where houses were stacked up the mountainside. This was the Canada more in keeping with Anson Dobell's expectations. No sign of log chateaus or vista-domes, but there were plenty of trees. The car shot up Mountain Highway, past the Chevron and the 7-11, and on to Dempsey Road. God eased the Merc into a parking spot in front of a house where there seemed to be a traffic jam.

"This might take a bit. I think we'd better all go in," said Ray Seawee somberly.

Red Devlin seemed relieved. At least they weren't in front of a police station. But they were at the house where Seawee had sold the Open House contract. It looked like they were holding an open house now. This was wrong. People were supposed to wait, and then hold them all at once, on a pre-arranged signal. They needed Open House signs. They needed a realtor for God's sake. Obviously Seawee had ballsed the thing up. Never should have been hired. *Too many realtors spoil the broth.*

They got out of the car. Ray Seawee felt the pocket of his wet jacket. "I need a new contract," he said sadly. "I think mine's in the restroom of the Chevron."

Devlin had a box of them in the trunk, but the Merc's earlier tumble had scattered them everywhere. Seawee opened the trunk and plucked one from under the spare tire. He adjusted his tie and approached the house warily as it seemed to be filled with shouting people. The rest of them followed, Anson Dobell shuffling up at the rear in his duffel coat.

Seawee walked slowly up the stairs. He looked like a man going to his execution. What kind of fraud had Red Devlin caused him to perpetrate?

He rang the doorbell. The front door swung open and there stood Mr. McGregor, grizzly-like as ever. A tuft of gray hair poked out of the top of his sweat suit. "Get in here, Seawee. You've got a hell of a lot of explaining to do."

DAVID JENNESON

CHAPTER 8

*A*fter the spectacle at *La Belles on His Toes*, Judge Mannheim sat alone at his table and brooded. His night of tomcatting had gone for a shit.

That flamboyant realtor had pitched oysters on him and then fainted. Paramedics were called. As far as Judge Mannheim was concerned, having anyone in uniform show up at *La Belles on His Toes* while he was on the prowl - even paramedics - was far too risky.

Worse, covered in soggy oysters, he was now rendered a less-than-desirable object to those around him, which made him drink more Alberta sipping whiskies. He would need the extra courage to try and collar a bright young lounge partner for the night, but time passed and it came to nothing. Covered in smeared oysters bits Judge Mannheim looked like a bi-sexual toad. The other patrons of *La Belles on His Toes* - Crown Prosecutors and lawyers over whom he had so much power - used the opportunity to gain brownie points. They took turns sending over drink after drink so there was never any question of the Judge having to pay, but at the same time they kept their distance.

So the Judge drowned his sorrows alone. When the lounge closed he left in a drunken funk. His car was an oversized white brute like Red Devlin's, but newer and sleeker. While the Turnpike Cruiser looked like an early finned rocket striving to become airborne, Judge Mannheim's Olds was a designer spaceship. As he squeezed and contorted to get into the low-slung driver's seat his wallet rode up and out of his back pocket and plopped unnoticed gently out onto the wet parking lot.

Once he got himself squared away behind the wheel, Judge Mannheim narrowed his eyes to slits and concentrated on his driving. He cruised past the spotless Saab and Mercedes Benz dealerships, now closed. The drive gave his brain time to work. The Judge was a unique individual. His lust crossed gender like the short-circuited wires of an old toaster. Who cared what sex a person was so long as they were warm and still breathing? If he'd been a normal womanizer it would've been easy. He was rich. He was married. He was a judge. If the media caught him fooling around with some flooze, big deal. It would have the news impact of a mosquito hitting a bus. But this sneaking into *La Belles on His Toes* and cruising for lads was a thing that had to stop, he told himself.

By now the lights were going out all over his mind. The last thing he wanted to do was go home at 3 AM and cobble together a story to satisfy his wife. He cruised around several long blocks of the old industrial area, past derelict buses and yowling stray cats. The wind was utterly gone from his sails. Before another two minutes had passed he sneaked into an alley and went to sleep in the car.

But that was last night and this was today. He wanted to forget the whole episode. He'd been home and changed his shirt and jacket and he now pulled his car up in front of the Zum-O-Zar Dry Cleaners. He ran his hand down his face. It felt leathery and ragged. He entered the dry cleaners and gave the sodden garments to Aziz, the young Iranian boy at the Zum-O-Zar. He wasn't happy about having anyone see his creepy clothes from the night before, even this Iranian kid, but at least he had fresh shirts to pick up.

DAVID JENNESON

The Judge watched the boy take his clothes. Remarkable race, these Iranians, the Judge stroked his chin. So well formed. Standing in the warm, brightly lit dry cleaning shop with the January sun pouring in, his mind softened and drifted to Central Asian poetry.

> *There is a boy across the river,*
> *With an ass like a peach,*
> *But alas, I cannot swim...*

He stopped himself. Was he mad? His close call at *La Belles on His Toes* last night was like a good hard spanking. He bewailed his inability to suppress his own nature.

"Your shirts, Mister Judge Sir," said the boy proudly, handing them across the counter. "Medium starch on hanger."

"And these others by tomorrow," Judge Mannheim said tiredly. He was still wearing his pants from the night before. He hoped he still had money in his wallet.

"As you weesh, Mr. Judge sir."

Despite his mood the Judge couldn't help feeling kindly toward cute, hardworking little Aziz. "Here, I've got a tip for you," he reached into his back pocket. He felt nothing but his hard butt. No wallet. He grabbed his jacket back from Aziz but found nothing. He thought of the table at *La Belles on His Toes* and instantly knew that was the last place he had seen it. That realtor must have picked it up. The wallet didn't worry him. It was the little address book inside. Pages of high profile male sexual partners from *La Belles on His Toes*. Names and numbers. And notes. Oh yes, the Judge was good at making notes. His address book was full of them. There were notes regarding the person's performance. And deviances. That kind of information could ruin a prosecutor. Hang a judge.

"I'll pay you when I come back," the Judge smiled weakly as he backed out.

"Mister Judge Sir, you looking sick," said the young Aziz. "There is McDonald's across the street. Maybe you sit drink coffee there for a while."

This seemed like good advice to Judge Mannheim. He felt rising panic. His silent wife had taken the kids off to Saturday morning hockey and swimming so he had a little spare time. He wanted to park in the calm, dripping Lynn Vale forests and just think - but McDonald's was closer on this cold January morning. He felt bitterly short-changed. Not even a hand job last night and now nothing but trouble to show for it.

He tossed his pockets for change as he walked into McDonald's. Enough for a coffee, but just. He sat down and brooded over his thin brew. Anxiety percolated up inside him. A stolen wallet. He had to think. Make mental notes. A list. What phone calls to make. Cancel all credit cards? Or maybe not.

Would the realtor use stolen credit cards?

No.

Would the realtor return his wallet?

No. The Judge had spooked him off forever.

Would the realtor go through the wallet?

Of course.

He was a realtor. You couldn't fight Mother Nature. Dogs pissed on lampposts. Realtors investigated wallets. Couldn't help themselves. If the Pope were a realtor, he'd zip your wallet quicker than anyone.

What would the realtor do when he found the Judge's list? Would he put two and two together? That this book of prominent male citizens was also a list of the Judge's sex partners? What about the notes in the margins? Was the realtor a detail man? Would he read them? Would he get it?

Yes, the Judge winced.

His secret was out, and with it enough ruination to bring his life down around his ears.

He gulped his coffee and tottered back for more. Reached for his change. A nickel short. The McDonald's kid let it go. He thanked him and felt like a broke old bum as he shuffled back to his seat. He barely noticed the two off-shift cops come in and sit two tables away. He turned his back to them when he sat down so they wouldn't recognize him. He was in no mood for them. Gloomily he eavesdropped.

"Wasn't that the damnedest thing you've ever seen?" remarked Mustache as he gnawed like a beaver at a panel of hash browns.

"What's that?" asked Needle-nose, sniffing his McMuffin.

"That camouflaged float. Totally unique. Like nothing I've ever seen. It sort of looked like a First War tank, and sort of like an armored personnel carrier, but with that camouflage made out of all natural materials, it seemed to embody the spirit of the war in an organic way."

"That's the dedication of those Legion people," replied Needle-nose. "They'll do anything. Go to any lengths to teach our children what the war was like and keep the memory alive."

"So we don't have to fight another one," Mustache pointed out.

"Exactly right. They don't think about themselves. I'll bet that project took hundreds of hours of volunteer labor, and for what? One parade. Those Legion people stand for all the right things," Needle-nose counted off on his fingers. "Patriotism, comradeship and family values. I'm thinking of joining."

"Me too," agreed Mustache. "I'm for family values. And anyone who isn't, better stay out of my way."

The Judge sighed. Family values. Who knew about family values better than he did at this moment? He valued his family. He would do anything to keep them from harm. Now a realtor had the power in his hands to destroy his family. So the Judge would have to annihilate him first. Simple. It was a destroy-or-be-destroyed world.

The Judge still felt muzzy-headed. What was the realtor's name? Revlon? Or some other kind of lipstick? Revlon? It wouldnt come to him.

What was it the realtor had said? Something about selling the White House? That had to be illegal. There were laws in this country. He could be charged. There had to be something on the books. Unauthorized sale of a foreign capital. Maybe holding open houses with undue care and attention. Had to be a hundred laws the realtor had broken already. Judge Mannheim would keep the realtor skipping so fast he wouldn't have time to go through wallets. He warmed to the task.

He walked over, "Hello boys, just off shift?"

Mustache and Needle-nose practically fell over themselves pulling a chair up for the Judge. Mustache offered to buy him a refill. Needle-nose offered breakfast. Let them do it if it makes them happy thought the Judge. After that he needed sleep. He reminded himself tiredly that he must still cancel his credit cards.

*   *   *

Ray Seawee approached the front door, which McGregor had left open. In an effort to cheer himself up for what he knew was coming, he mentally counted off the days he'd been a realtor.

"One," he mouthed silently.

Then more tentatively, "two."

Three? he wondered. He had to think about it. He decided that technically-speaking he was still on day two.

As a bonus, the two days felt like five to him because he'd barely slept or eaten. It was now clear to Seawee that whatever scam Devlin had duped him into committing had caused catastrophic consequences in the McGregor household. It would surely violate the conditions of his parole. He would be back in his cell by day three.

He had been through this kind of parole-breaking trauma before. He dreaded what was waiting for him behind McGregor's screen door. McGregor would have him back in jail in an hour. He'd have good stories to tell the other prisoners though. About Tasha. How she nursed him like a midnight angel then the next minute had taken off her clothes. This would be appreciated.

DAVID JENNESON

The more he thought about it, the more downhearted he became about losing his freedom so soon. Despite what anyone said, Ray Seawee knew he wasn't a congenital crook. And he wasn't one of those twisted fucks who proudly paraded themselves around in prison after committing some startlingly stupid crime. No. He wanted to go straight. Be among the innocent for once. He briefly considered his earlier vision - sitting in coffee houses and reading about honesty, truth and innocence, then achieving renown as a famous honest realtor. Maybe next time. He wondered what his dishonest twin brother Victor would do in a situation like this. He gulped as he raised his eyes to meet the furious McGregor.

Too late. McGregor reached out and gripped the lapel of Seawee's damp suit. "Where's my contract?" demanded Mr. McGregor.

There was a small riot going on in the McGregor living room.

"Your what?" shouted Seawee. It was hard to hear over the racket pouring out the front door.

"My contact, twit! Where is it?"

"In the Chevron washroom," said Seawee quietly, mortified at how dumb it must sound to Tasha.

"Eh?" cried McGregor through the racket. Apparently he couldn't hear either. "Speak up for Christ sake. Ah, this is no good. Follow me."

Seawee, Devlin and the others trickled in behind McGregor's squat form, but there was not enough room to maneuver. The McGregor home was filled with hostile neighbors hollering about who had gotten there first, who had the rights to what, and arguing other obscure issues of precedence. Some waved pieces of paper with a date and time scrawled, signed by McGregor, like chits from a butcher's shop. The phone rang constantly. He fought through the crowd, waving his hairy arms. To Seawee, Mr. McGregor's arms looked like mossy logs. They reminded him of being marooned with the Turnpike Cruiser in the dark rain forest only a few hours before.

"Keep your shirts on," McGregor shouted at the crowd as he

plowed toward the bathroom. "In here," he said to Seawee over his shoulder "only safe place. Lock the door behind you."

They fought their way through. Anson Dobell squeezed in last.

"Those people have gone mad, and they're my *neighbors*," muttered McGregor once they were inside. He swabbed his bald head. The neighbors were now beating on the bathroom door like they were after some hard-to-get drug at a party. The sound made McGregor sag.

"Lemme rest a minute," he sighed.

Tasha, Cutsie Wu and Anson Dobell perched primly on the edge of the bathtub. Seawee leaned against the sink and Devlin stood with his back against the door, muffling the pounding sounds. McGregor collapsed on the toilet seat. There was a respectful silence while he gathered his wits.

"Nice washroom," Tasha piped up politely. It echoed off the little black and white tiles.

"My contract. Where is it?" McGregor demanded after a minute

"I left it at a gas station," Seawee said. "I swear. But I have a new one here. A contract I mean. We can rewrite it. On the spot. Or tear it up," he added hopefully.

McGregor seemed to be coming apart over the bowl. "I've never seen anything like this," he sobbed, "these people have caught some fever." He coughed like a man in a crowded TB ward. His story came out like a confession.

"After you left last night I got interested in this open house theory. So I phoned my neighbor Alf. It was late. I only wanted to have a phone conversation. But when Alf heard he wanted to come over. He got excited. Wouldn't leave. What about franchises, he asked me? Franchises? What do I know about franchises? He said if I didn't come to a joint franchise agreement with him right there on the spot he'd do it himself and to hell with me. We had a fight. I threw him out. Then I got worried. Couldn't sleep. So first thing this morning I phoned another neighbor and they were interested too. Then I went out and visited three or four more. They *all* wanted to sign up. Wanted their own franchises too. That was at ten o'clock. Word must've spread. Now I've got this…" he waved a hand then coughed again. Tasha squeezed past Seawee and filled a glass which was by the sink with water. She handed it to McGregor.

"Thank you," he took a swallow. It seemed to compose him.

"I'm a retired man," he glared at Seawee. "You never warned me about this. You never said anything about this … fever. You, Seawee. You come into my house with a scheme and I sign up for it. I give you another chance in life. Benefit of the doubt. Then you merrily go off with the contract and the fine print in hand, in some limousine no doubt, leaving me with nothing in writing. Just your word."

"Based on your advice I make a few phone calls. All hell breaks loose. And I don't have a goddam nibbit of documentation or instruction on how to deal with the consequences. I thought you realtors were supposed to be professionals. You call that professional? You never even *mentioned* franchises. How dare you leave me with so little backup, knowing what would happen? I'm not well. I ought to sue the lot of you for endangering my health."

McGregor coughed again. Tasha patted him on the back.

Ray Seawee was still trying to figure out the long and the short of things here. He hoped McGregor would see a bright side somewhere.

"Other than that everything's great, right?" he said hopefully. He leaned on the sink and held the empty contract in his hand. "We'll just fill out this paperwork again and initial it . . . "

McGregor snatched the contract out of Seawee's hand, crushed it into a ball and threw it into the toilet beneath him. Then he flushed it. All politely waited while the toilet gave a throaty cough like it was choking. It gurgled to silence.

"Look here, Seawee," said McGregor finally, "don't try and piece me off with some pissant contract. I know what I'm sitting on. Not a gold mine. Not a diamond mine. It's a Goddamned platinum mine. I want five hundred of these contracts for myself to sign other people up so I can get the fifty-dollar finder's fee. Because you know what? People are happy, no, *delighted*, to hold an open house for one hundred bucks cash, no strings attached."

McGregor took a long slug of water. It seemed to add steam to his argument.

"That's the first thing they think of," he continued. Then they figure out that if *they* want to do it, everyone else will too. So they want in on the ground floor. They demand a pile of blank open house contracts for themselves. Get the fifty-dollar finder's fee by signing others up. About two minutes after that, they figure out that they can get a network of people working for them, signing others up so they'll get a piece of every finder's fee. Then they want their own territory. A franchise. It's horrible. Like some virus. They're like ants swarming to the nest."

The racket on the other side of the door caused Anson Dobell to pull his head back into his duffle coat like a turtle.

Red Devlin cleared his throat. "If I might clarify things here…" he began.

"I'm dealing with *him*," McGregor snapped. He pointed at Seawee. "He got me into this. He'll get me out."

Ray Seawee struggled to do the right thing. *A realtor's first loyalty is to the client*, Devlin had told him. That meant he couldn't be happy until McGregor was happy.

"I can't be happy until you're happy," said Seawee. "What can I do for you that I'm not doing now?" he added. To Seawee, his words were freighted with sincerity. He thought it came off sounding pretty good.

"Ah, screw you and that salesman's bullshit," McGregor frowned and coughed. "Give me five hundred open house contracts. Give me five hundred franchise agreements too. And leave 'em blank. I'll do the rest."

Anson Dobell clinked his pipe against the edge of the tub again and shook his head from side to side as a signal. *No* in business sign language.

"Five hundred franchises?" asked Seawee.

"For starters," said McGregor.

"If that's what it takes." Seawee shrugged. He thought hard, trying to apply Red Devlin's complicated formula of property size, population potential plus factoring in date of application. He felt that he was beginning to master it.

McGregor watched him suspiciously.

"Actually we might owe you more," Seawee suggested. "Offhand, I'd say you're entitled to more like seven hundred and fifty franchises. But I'd have to do the calculations first."

"Deal," cried McGregor. He stuck his hand out to shake on it.

"Check the paperwork first," Anson Dobell muttered over his pipe. He seemed floored by what was transpiring.

"Who the hell's he?" McGregor cried in exasperation.

At this point Red Devlin intervened. He removed himself from his position at the door and swept toward McGregor like a great calming wind. In his white suit he was like an overweight and aged Elvis, serene and all-knowing.

"I'm afraid there aren't any franchise agreements ready right now," Devlin said. As he spoke the muffling effect of his body on the bathroom door was lost and the hammering became even louder. Loud music was evident from some point in the house. Someone's kid had found McGregor's Guy Lombardo collection.

"I'm Red Devlin," he said softly. He shook McGregor's hand. "I suppose you could call me the President and CEO of Open Homes International. This," he nodded toward Anson, "is Mr. Dobell, our valued consultant. These beautiful ladies are part of my staff."

McGregor frowned. Suddenly he was surrounded.

"Due to a printer's error," continued Red Devlin, "our franchise agreements are late in arriving. But when you see them, tomorrow at the latest, you'll find that you are only entitled to market five franchises. Not five hundred."

McGregor started coughing again. It ended it with a violent sneeze. "I want four hundred," he wiped his nose with toilet paper, "or I'll sue. For false pretenses. Endangerment to my health. Then I'll call the newspapers. We've got a new one here too. The Poplar Press. They eat up scandal like this. They'll hunt you down like a rabbit."

Devlin paused. *Discretion is the better part of real estate.* "I'm sorry Mr. McGregor, but you'll have to deal with my Franchise Manager on this. I always go with my staff. This is Tasha, Mr. McGregor. You two come to an agreement, then she'll clear it with me."

"And what about that mob out there?" McGregor jerked a thumb toward the bathroom door.

"Not to worry. My Recruitment Director, Mr. Seawee and his assistant, will be happy to take care of that for you right away."

"And by the way, you owe me four thousand bucks," said McGregor, removing a baseball-sized crumpled mass of paper out of his pants pocket and thrusting it forward. "These are the closest I could come to contracts on my own. Designed 'em myself."

"Tell you what," said Devlin without missing a beat. "We'll get some proper contracts for you from the car, fill them all out, and give you a stack of blank ones too. Then, tomorrow, I'll personally bring a check by for every open house you've signed up as of midnight tonight. And remember, should any offers of sale result from these open houses, the listings go to Open Homes International - *Professionalism at It's Most Professional.*"

McGregor gave a silent nod.

Thus, if anyone had been taking minutes, the first board meeting of Open Homes International had just concluded. To escape their watercloset boardroom they had to form into a human wedge with Ray Seawee, newly appointed Director of Recruitment, at the sharp end. He opened the door to a tangle of arms and legs and

DAVID JENNESON

faces which were red from yelling. Seawee realized now this scene looked very familiar to him. He'd seen it all before when the food got too rotten in the joint. Typical prison mess hall riot. Suddenly he felt right at home. With a surge of happiness he realized that now, for once, the shoe was on the other foot. He was in charge and he knew exactly what to do. He'd seen the guards do it a hundred times.

"FREEZE!" he shouted.

The neighbors froze. As instructed. Startled out of their wits. Some thought it was a police raid. They were stunned to silence. The only noise was a Guy Lombardo LP quietly riffing away on the old phonograph.

"Stay where you are!" Seawee waded out among them. "Remain silent! If you can find a seat, do it now."

They stared back at him, stupid with shock.

"I said NOW!"

There was a frantic game of musical chairs.

Seawee stood out in the middle of the McGregor front parlor carpet. There were still far too many people. "Those who can't find seats line up on the right! Let's move it, people!"

A queue formed.

"But I was here first," whined a sappy looking hulk with glasses, "By rights I should be at the front of the line."

Seawee spun and stared. His eyes were filled with fury like he was ready to cold cock this fool, just like he'd seen prison guards do. Lay the big sniveling wimp out with one of McGregor's kitchen stools. He was having the time of his life.

He was one inch away from the man's face. "You," he whispered and poked him in the chest, "shut up. Everyone gets taken care of. If you can't find a seat, stand in line. You follow?"

The man slouched to the back of the line.

Seawee got Cutsie Wu organized at the dining room table. She was flanked by Devlin and Dobell who were to keep things orderly and businesslike. McGregor sat like a bad-tempered bullfrog making sure he got his cut. McGregor was also necessary to adjudicate the various claims of priority for the dozens of chits he had issued.

Rather than sort things out piecemeal, Seawee elected to take the first person standing in the front room parlor and have them plead their case before the dining room tribunal. All documents would be examined and judgments levied. Those in chairs could wait. The first person was a thin man with a pinched face. He was wearing a curling team jacket. Seawee sent him through to the dining room.

"Keep it short," Seawee warned.

Then he realized he needed some blank open house contracts. With the line of applicants running smoothly he dashed out to fetch them from the trunk of the Turnpike Cruiser.

There he saw a terrible scene unfolding. Apparently when he had grabbed the blank contract for McGregor, several more had fallen onto the lawn. This created an evidence trail back to the trunk of the Turnpike Cruiser. As neighbors arrived they had spotted the contracts. They had formed up as a mob, demanding more from God who was guarding the car. Handling the shaft of an open house sign like a thrusting spear, he had been holding them back. He looked like the last surviving pike man of an army from the Dark Ages, holding off a tribe of barbarians. It was a picture as old as the twilight of history, as old as mankind itself.

The crowd had obviously been repelled once. Now they were regrouping. As Seawee watched, they formed up for a frontal assault. Suddenly a fat man burst out from behind a big laurel hedge. Seawee was transfixed. The man looked like an insane pig. God dropped to a low-to-the-ground stance. At the last possible moment he thrust the open house sign straight ahead. It plunged against the attacker's plumb-shaped gut.

"Erf!" he cried.

Still, his momentum carried him forward.

DAVID JENNESON

There was a moment of silence. Everyone stopped. The open house sign gave. It slowly bent like a bow. God shifted backwards to absorb the impact. Suddenly it snapped with a bright crack. Splinters flew. The man fell to the side and rolled onto the grass holding himself like a trussed ham.

A cry went up and the mob surged toward the now defenseless God.

From the porch, Seawee didn't figure the mere order to freeze would work.

"STOP OR I'LL SHOOT!" he hollered in his best prison guard voice.

This had the desired and instant effect. Not only did they stop in their tracks - many dropped to McGregor's soggy lawn. Seawee ran forward and took the high ground beside the embattled God. A few neighbors lay face down in the driveway, hugging the gravel. Others had their fingers digging into the lawn. Slowly they raised their heads. In the waning January light they looked like refugees about to be marched into dark woods for special measures.

"Ladies and gentlemen!" Seawee shouted. "We're here to do business. This is not the way we do business. You're endangering private property, plus this Mercury automobile and an employee of Open Homes International. Do what I say and everyone will get their fair share. On my command, get up slowly. Form a line. File into the house. Orderly like."

They gathered themselves up slowly. Wives reached out to retrieve handbags thrown aside. A man put his shoe back on. From the McGregor door a pleasant, semi-organized babble invited them inside. The line wound up the stairs.

Seawee went over to God, who leaned against the hip of the Turnpike Cruiser. He inspected the splintered shaft of the open house sign with some interest. "I can't believe an adult charged into this thing like a berserk animal," God said, "I've never seen customers like this, even in the towing business. And it's famous for hostile customers."

"This real estate takes some catching onto," agreed Seawee.

Inside, Tasha touched McGregor on the arm and drew him away for a private meeting. The setting winter sun came through the front window and fell on her. Tweed suit. Gold glasses. Blond hair up. Fabulous body. McGregor looked rueful. Like he had thrown away forty good years in business by not hiring a secretary like this. How could he have been so stupid?

"I want fifty-percent of everything," he began in a nettled voice.

"No, you can't have that."

"Yes I can. Why not?"

"Because I'm worried about your health. Mr. McGregor, listen to me," she laid a hand on his knee. "I'm a health expert. I work out every day and keep myself trim. See?" She held open her jacket, exposing the spectacular proof

By McGregor's expression he could see. Boy could he see.

"What you want," continued Tasha, "is in and out of this thing quick. Nothing long term. It's too stressful." The incident they'd both witnessed through the living room window, of Seawee and God quelling the front yard riot, gave weight to her statement.

"Don't underestimate my health," muttered McGregor.

"Right now on paper you have zero percent," Tasha poked his knee with her finger to make her point. "Zero percent and you're a nervous wreck. If zero percent does this to you in one morning, fifty percent will kill you by nightfall. You want to enjoy the time you have left with your wife, don't you?"

From the look on McGregor's face, he wasn't so sure he did. "You're talking like I'm already in the ground," he said miserably.

"I'm looking out for you," said Tasha, caressing his furry arm. "What good is fifty percent if you're only around for a month to enjoy it? I think ten percent would keep you busy. You'd last a long time on ten percent. We could work something out where all you do is collect money. No work. Lots of holidays."

"Forty percent," woofed McGregor.

More people filed in.

"No," sighed Tasha, "Ten."

"Thirty and that's it."

"Ten.'

"Okay, twenty-five," McGregor demanded, loosing patience.

"Five," Tasha countered.

"Five? Wait a minute. You're supposed to come up to meet my offer!"

"Who says?'

"Everybody knows that," cried McGregor in an exasperated voice. "This is diabolical."

"Show me where it says that"

McGregor looked befuddled, as if his mind was working at cross-purposes. On one hand he seemed to want to drive a hard bargain. On the other he wanted to drive Tasha into the sack. Throughout his business career McGregor's main negotiating tool had been bad-tempered bluff. Now his Grizzly Bear temper went lame on him. How do you get mad at a pretty woman? One you've just met? Someone you might be working with? Rubbing shoulders, so to speak? Why screw it up now? "Hmmmm," McGregor said.

"Okay, ten." Tasha agreed brightly. "I have second thoughts about your health, but I'll take a chance."

"McGregor, you're needed." It was Devlin's voice. He was awash in the crowd at the dining room table.

Tasha shook McGregor's hand with a firm grip as he stood up. "Thanks, sweetie. I'm so happy, aren't you? Now we can work together. Maybe I'll see you a lot more."

Stirred, McGregor rumbled back to the dining room. A neighbor in a green sweat suit and the fat man who'd been speared were waving conflicting chits in Devlin's face.

"These guys both say you promised them the entire territory west of Mountain Highway. And they've both got notes signed by you. Both are marked 10 AM today. What gives?"

McGregor dragged the glasses out of his shirt pocket and examined the evidence. "There's been some mistake. It's impossible. I'm usually more careful."

"So who was first?" asked Devlin impatiently.

"Me," they said together.

"C'mon, move it," came a grumble from down the line. "Yeah," came another, "this is taking forever."

Seawee marched off down the ranks. More bad tempered shouting. McGregor fiddled and dropped his glasses. Everyone became tense.

"Anyone gets attitude on me goes to the back of the line!" hollered Seawee. Again he cowed them.

So it was that Red Devlin and Open Homes International did a landrush business that January afternoon. The dining room table became littered with contracts. Luckily Cutsie Wu had taken a high school accounting course and she kept a running account. After awhile Red Devlin lit a cigar and called for an ashtray, which was provided by a sniffish Mrs. McGregor. The ashes soon salt-and-peppered the table. McGregor hollered for coffee. The aroma of strong percolated coffee combined with Devlin's cigar and the McGregor's wood-paneled parlor lent a clubby atmosphere to the proceedings. All applicants came in and stated their case before the impaneled court. They were judged, thus or thus, and sent on their way with an open house contract and sometimes a promissory note for a franchise.

The role of scribe fell to Anson Dobell in the recording of promissory notes. He removed his duffel coat, revealing a charcoal Guernsey sweater he had purchased at Burberry's on Washington's Dupont Circle. The sweater was worth more than the average business suit. Anson seemed glad he had worn it. This far north, the January day was shedding light already. In fact a wet marine weather front was rolling across the North Pacific from Japan.

Anson's attitude seemed to have changed completely. No longer sour and negative, he seemed almost as happy as if he'd been at home in his Washington townhouse. This was better. Wood-paneled room. Cigars and coffee. Petitioners bowing and scraping. It was like being a member of a powerful Senate sub-committee. And Anson was at his best with his Mont Blanc fountain pen, inscribing important documents in this distinguished setting. He imagined the image as a black and white photograph in a thick square history book. He tamped his pipe and rolled up his Burberry sleeves. Who needed Harry Truman?

Rain flicked against the January window.

The throng got a late lunch. Mrs. McGregor fretted in the kitchen. All these uninvited guests. Finally hospitality got the better of her. She came out with platters of hot baking powder biscuits, butter, cheddar and jam, and with mugs of hot tea for the foot soldiers of Open Homes International.

She slid a warm biscuit on a plate close to Devlins elbow and leaned close.

"You're just giving away money," she whispered. It was less an observation than an accusation.

Devlin turned. "No ma'am. Speculative investment. Essence of real estate," he grinned like a cat.

"Anyone can give away money," she got up stiffly and walked away.

Ah to hell with her, Devlin thought. Finally he had his lost tribe following nicely along to the Promised Land. He sat back and took long, satisfied puffs on his cigar. *This*, he decided, *is what Moses would have done.*

CHAPTER 9

*G*od had retrenched to a more defensible position in the driver's seat of the Turnpike Cruiser. There he fell asleep. A sudden flurry of hard cold raindrops plicked against the windshield like a handful of gravel. That woke him up.

By the time he wandered into the house the tea was gone and Red Devlin's debt to the new inductees of Open Homes International was $5,000 and rising fast.

Most were simple hundred-dollar open house contracts. In an effort to collect the extra fifty-dollar finder's fee, some neighbors claimed to have recruited other neighbors, who naturally claimed the opposite. This created a kind of compound accumulating interest on the original amounts as unfathomable as a seaman's knot. In the end Devlin could only stare at the knot's exterior and wonder about the financial twists and turns within. McGregor could not help arbitrate these disputes. They had occurred between second and third parties of the real estate tidal wave McGregor himself had helped create. Finally Devlin gave up and accepted all claims at face value. He told himself he would sort it out later.

Cutsie Wu toted up $6,050. McGregor, keeping a running tab, happily watched this from his chair at the far end of the dining room table. He added his commission of $705, plus the $300 Devlin already owed him, and slid a handwritten invoice across to Devlin for $1,005, payable upon it being slid across the table. Devlin stared blankly at the invoice. His eyes hooded with worry and fatigue. "You'll probably be selling more tonight," he said in a threadbare voice. "Add it all up. Everything you've sold by midnight. I'll pay you tomorrow."

"A thousand bucks is a good enough day's work for me," said McGregor. "I'm not a greedy man, and I'm tired. I won't be selling another thing until tomorrow. So you can pay me for today right now."

"This is incorrect," said Cutsie Wu, peering at the document over Devlin's shoulder.

"How so?" demanded McGregor. "In what way? You saying I can't add?"

"I'm saying you're paying yourself commission on your own fees," replied Cutsie Wu curtly. "See. Here," she pointed to the mass of scribbles, "and here again. This total is incorrect."

"Prove it," said McGregor.

"Get me a calculator," said Cutsie Wu.

Curiously, no member of Open Homes International had a pocket calculator with them, nor could McGregor produce one. Finally he brought an old black Remington manual adding machine up from the basement, the Sherman tank of early finance. Cutsie Wu mastered it quickly.

"This thing's cool," she said.

She punched the Remington. It rattled like a skeleton happy to be shaking its bones again.

"You're proper fee is $610," she ripped off the tape.

"Right by my count," Anson Dobell piped in.

McGregor's face darkened, "You're robbing me," he muttered.

Ms. Wu was short and pert and very pretty. She was wearing a tight black business suit but there seemed to be no blouse beneath it. McGregor appeared to be checking to make sure of this. Since when had oriental women become this shapely? Apparently he was running into the same problem he'd had with Tasha. Hard to fight with a beautiful woman. Twice in one afternoon. He concentrated, gathered his explosive bad temper into one spot and tried to focus it on Cutsie Wu. Again it spluttered on him.

"What's with you people?" he grumbled doggedly, "What are you, a mob accountant or something?"

"No," Cutsie Wu paused. "A realtor."

She whittled the numbers down again on the Remington. It sounded like castanets. McGregor gave up - couldn't follow it.

"Okay, okay," he surrendered. "Doesn't matter anyway. I've still made enough for one day. I'm going to make reservations for a big dinner out tonight. Roast lamb with a crust on it. Best red wine. Bottles of it. I'll be thinking about how rich you're going to make me."

The idea of such a dinner clearly struck a resonant pang in Ray Seawee's stomach. "Dinner sounds like a real good idea to me," he shouted over his shoulder at Red Devlin.

Devlin seemed deaf to Seawee's dinner request.

"Whaddayou say, chief?" Seawee repeated. "If we can't sleep at least we can eat."

"Yes, we definitely need a meeting," agreed Devlin, gathering papers and stuffing them into his pockets. Where was his briefcase? In the trunk? In the forest? He instinctively felt for his wallet, causing papers and contracts to cascade out of his pockets.

"I'll keep these for you," Cutsie Wu intervened. She organized them neatly and folded them into her large handbag. "You look like you're ready to lose something."

DAVID JENNESON

"I'll drop your check 'round first thing," said Devlin to McGregor. "Best I can do. Got another meeting now. Very important, as you can see."

McGregor's eyes narrowed. He knew he could do nothing. Check in the mail. It was the realtor's way.

As the staff of Open Homes International filed back into the Turnpike Cruiser, the sun broke briefly over the trees like a watery spotlight.

"I'm out of cigarettes," Devlin told God wearily as he climbed into the passenger seat. "There's a store at the end of the block." The Merc rumbled to life and God nosed her away from the curb.

"Mr. Devlin," Anson Dobell cleared his throat from the back seat. "Permit me to say that I was wrong, and to be the first to congratulate you. Open Homes International is a stroke of brilliance. Just what the economy needs. You have got a tiger by the tail, Mr. Devlin. In my modest view you may be the Henry Ford of real estate. The next Bill Levitt. However I can be of service..."

"You can and will, my friend."

God pulled up in front of the Upper Lynn Vale Grocery. "Wait here," coughed Devlin. "I've got to go and talk to the asshole inside. Imagine. I've got the deal of the century going down and have to screw around with some cockeyed little prick in a pissant grocery store."

To Anson Dobell, the Upper Lynn Vale Grocery did not look like a pissant grocery store at all. The bars of fading winter sunlight fell through tall hemlocks and made it look like a small Canadian chateau. He studied it from the back seat. It was surrounded on three sides by tall evergreens the color of dark emeralds. Lynn Vale Road was the only street he had ever seen where seventy-foot fir and spruce trees towered in every front yard, down and away as far as the eye could see. Beneath the rain dripping from the awning the signs read: AVAILABLE FRESH FRUITS - VEGETABLES - MEATS - SEAFOOD IN SEASON. It looked to Dobell like a grocery for a prosperous mountain resort.

In his limited travels, the only other grocery store Anson had really experienced was the Uganda in its foggy depression. In his own aging Capitol Hill neighborhood back in Washington, no one who was really sane shopped at the Uganda. He scanned the landscape for the gang of thugs which he felt sure were a part of every neighborhood grocery store. All he could see was an elderly couple walking a Golden Lab. But, he thought, who knew what happened after dark? Possibly monster Canadian teenagers came out of the woods drinking beer.

"Excuse me," he turned to Tasha, "this seems like a very prosperous grocery store, but I wonder why the owner isn't advertising a liquor special?

"Grocery stores can't sell liquor in Canada," Tasha explained patiently. "Except in Quebec. I think they can sell beer and wine there. Maybe that's why they want to separate. But that's two thousand miles east. Strongest thing you can get here is extra caffeine cola."

Even though Anson was a thin person he was perpetually hungry. Always looking for bits of this or that. He watched Red Devlin disappear into the store and then asked another question.

"Is the food here fresh?"

"How would I know?" answered Tasha. She looked at Anson Dobell as if he was her retarded little brother. "The grocer's probably Chinese. Ask an expert," she jerked a thumb toward Cutsie Wu.

Cutsie Wu seemed tired of this American's dumb questions. "See for yourself," she said.

Anson turned his head again. The posters in the window were being changed. Inside, a pretty Chinese teenager in a scarlet apron balanced on the counter and taped new ads to the window. FRESH SEAFOOD SALE STARTS TOMORROW! MUSSELS! HALIBUT! FRESH HERRING ROE!

Anson couldn't believe his eyes. "*Frozen* herring roe is priceless in Washington, if you can buy it at all," he said. "This is fresh. Where on earth do they get it?"

Tasha groaned a little. "In case you failed to notice this is the West Coast. Surrounded by salt water. You know, the sea?"

Anson took this in. More signs went up. SALMON! SMOKED WINTER SPRING. BLACK COD JUST IN! FRESH PRAWNS BY THE BUCKET. Anson watched dreamily and went into a kind of altered seafood consciousness.

*   *   *

Red Devlin saw the Upper Lynn Vale Grocery as a pain in the ass. Kang Sheng, the owner, was a major part of that pain. Former owner, to be more accurate.

Devlin stood before the unoccupied cash register. Teenage daughters chattered in Mandarin, putting up signs. This was odd for second-generation Chinese kids. Usually their first language was English, and they spoke it better than most Canadian Prime Ministers.

Typical Sheng, Devlin thought. The little dictator had probably laid down the law that only Mandarin could be spoken among the family. Doing his personal best to make sure his precious Chinese culture lived on in the land of the white man. In Devlin's opinion Sheng was far too tightly wound for his own good. But then, working for Matsumoto, Devlin's Japanese financier, Sheng had a good excuse.

The Japanese and Chinese didn't like or trust one another to start with. They were different animals. The Chinese were emotional. Quick to blow up. By contrast the Japanese were formal and polite, slower to anger but more deadly in revenge. The Chinese called the Japanese 'the Germans of Asia'. The Japanese referred to the Chinese as something racially inferior, even though they were from the same rootstock. The most recent episode in this thousand-year long racial feud was the atrocities the Japanese inflicted on the Chinese in Manchuria during World War II. It left a bitter cud in the throats of the Chinese. The Japanese had yet to apologize. The Chinese had yet to forget. It was a matter of face.

Not the best groundwork for a joint venture, Devlin sighed.

If that was not enough, Sheng and Matsumoto's relationship was further poisoned by the perverse way it had come about. Devlin had heard all about it from Sheng's tirades.

Sheng considered himself much more than a mere grocer. He was an ambitious Hong Kong businessman. When he immigrated to Canada he bought the Upper Lynn Vale Grocery and immediately saw its potential. It was the only store for miles in any direction, an island in the middle of streets full of suburban executive homes. He immediately sought to transform it from a remote grocery outpost to a high-end seafood deli. He needed money, so he found a financial backer and went into partnership with the Kwee family. The Kwees were Taiwanese.

When the Kwees got involved the store doubled in size. Suppliers who had put Sheng on the waiting list suddenly became available to Sheng. Now he could bring in the best seafood; squid, prawns, geoducs, even herring roe, and produce. Sheng now stocked rare sweet melons, hard to find even in the Chinatown bins. They sat like juicy shrunken heads.

His store was remodeled. The Kwees added a second story apartment as a revenue center. All the sod was skinned off the property surrounding the store and blacktop was slapped down. Sheng found himself to be a minority owner of his own business, but he worked hard to pay the debt off from his percentage of profits.

Then, as part of a real estate swap, the Taiwanese Kwees sold their interest to the Japanese Matsumotos. This, according to Sheng, proved that Taiwanese Chinese were no better than half-Japanese anyway.

But too late. Now the Miamata Matsumoto, the son, used the apartment upstairs for trysts or for entertaining. A dozen guests would pull up and a drinking party would begin. Matsumoto would send his arrogant chef down to Sheng's superbly stocked store for dinner supplies. He took what he wanted. And cigarettes! These Japanese smoked like fiends, and never paid for anything. Sheng complained bitterly that they robbed him blind.

DAVID JENNESON

Unable to bear it, Sheng renegotiated the mortgage so he could pay it off more quickly. Part of Matsumoto's price for this was to have Sheng act as message-taker and go-between for people whom, for whatever reason, Matsumoto did not want contacting him directly. Sheng felt like he was an indentured servant.

Devlin privately bewailed the fact that the biggest real estate deal in history was complicated by an Asian cultural racial feud. The two parties he had to deal with not only hated each other, but hated white men too. Matsumoto was especially racist, and came from a small but powerful extremely right wing, traditionalist segment of Japanese society. The one redeeming fact was that they held their violent arguments in English so Devlin could follow along.

Devlin was fed up with them both. He was tired of Matsumoto's childish insistence on using a middleman, as if direct contact with Devlin would dirty him. He was sick of both of their obsessions with gaining and saving face. Devlin didn't give a shit about face. He wanted money. This face business just got in the way, and since they both hated white men, Devlin had developed an attitude toward both of them. He wasn't sure which one pissed him off more.

"Gimme cigarettes, and where's your father?" Devlin asked one of the daughters as he paid for the cigarettes with the last change from his pocket.

The daughter seemed apprehensive. "Out. Buying fish now," she giggled nervously. "We are closing now. Getting ready for big seafood sale tomorrow."

Bullshit, Devlin thought.

He turned and shouted toward the back of the store. "What sort of father hides behind his daughter's skirts?" A well-aimed insult never failed to get the hot-tempered Sheng's attention.

This produced one angry grocer from the back. If Kang Sheng made a lot of compromises in life, apparently losing face in front of his family wasn't one of them. He had been cleaning expensive fish in the back and had instructed his daughters not to disturb him. Devlin's brutish voice insulting him in his own store again was more than he could bear.

Sheng stormed down the aisle like a fierce little dragon. He wore a vermilion apron. His bright yellow gloves still clutched the fish-gutting knife.

"Out. Get out or I slit you throat. You won't disgrace my name again." By now he was waving the knife under Devlin's throat. The daughters froze.

"Sheng, calm down," Devlin grinned nervously. "Just trying to have a little fun. Only a joke. Ha ha. My apologies if I offended you."

"You'd better apologize to my daughters too," said Sheng hotly.

Devlin apologized, steepling his hands and making an exaggerated bow as he did. "How's that?" he asked as he rose up. His face flushed bright red from bending over.

Sheng grated his teeth, clearly detesting this fat white buffoon who had infiltrated his life.

For his part, Devlin got under Sheng's skin whenever he found it necessary; it was a useful way to get his attention. After all the trouble he'd had with both of them, he sort of enjoyed it. Like poking a stick at a Chinese wolverine in a cage.

The grocer faced Devlin in the aisle like a sulky fireplug. "So what do you want? A meeting with Matsumoto I suppose."

"In one hour. Tell him it's an emergency."

"I'm busy. Call him yourself."

"Not allowed. The main man doesn't want me calling him direct. You know that. Matsumoto's rules. You're his middleman. It's your job."

"No. Too busy now," snapped Sheng. He looked away. The fishing knife turned in his hand.

Devlin sighed. "Fine, then don't. Matsumoto will find out you denied him this opportunity. Because you were cutting fish. You're

DAVID JENNESON

saying a fish is more important than your boss?"

Sheng said nothing. His daughters had vanished, apparently not wanting to witness any more face-losing.

Devlin let the remark sit, and then bent forward and hissed, "he'll snip your little dick off."

Sheng erupted into a rapid-fire series of Mandarin expletives and personal insults Devlin couldn't follow. Devlin then grabbed a couple of packs of Pall Mall plain ends from behind the till and stalked off down the aisle. "Put these on account," Devlin said over his shoulder. "On account of I don't have any change right now. Ha ha."

Sheng spat on the floor.

At least the message would be delivered. This was vital as Miamata Matsumoto had access to vast funds at a moments notice and Red Devlin was stone-broke. Or, as a more contemporary-minded realtor might put it, resource-challenged. Devlin had run this venture on his own ticket so far. Now all accounts were depleted. All credit cards maxed. Matsumoto had promised money. In fact, Matsumoto's father had promised Devlin money, so as the son he was honor-bound to provide it. He had yet to deliver. If Matsumoto chose to ignore Devlin's call for a meeting, or to suddenly become unavailable as he had in the past, things were going to get embarrassing and ugly. Quickly.

Devlin looked out the window at his waiting car. He distractedly peered into his empty wallet. Patted his empty pockets. He had to keep the hungry, frazzled members of OPEN HOMES INTERNATIONAL on ice for a few hours until Matsumoto came up with some cash.

Real estate is the mother of invention, he thought.

            *   *   *

Red Devlin slid into the front seat of the Turnpike Cruiser and told God to drive. Then he swung round to face Anson Dobell.

"I don't know how to thank you for coming all this way on your own time." he reached back and warmly shook Anson's hand. "You've seen the explosive power of Open Homes International. I'm sure you have plenty of ideas. Here at Open Homes International we work hard, and we play hard. So I've planned a bit of a treat for you."

Ansons eyes brightened.

"You see," Devlin leaned further over the seat, "we want to try and avoid the sort of, ah, uncontrolled economic activity you saw back there at the McGregor house. But it happens. When it does, it attracts the copy cats," he gave a sharp glance out the window as if on guard for an army of greedy realtors.

Anson leaned forward, absorbing every word.

Devlin was almost whispering now, "So we must be alert. Keep things to ourselves. Mr. Seawee has found the perfect place. The last place they'd look for this sort of top-level activity to be going on. Do you follow me, Anson?"

"Precisely. That's the way we do it at PDAC on the QT and PDQ, but only if we have repurposing issues."

Once more Dobell succeeded in silencing the loquacious Devlin with a streak of meaningless conversation, this time in bureaucratic shorthand. Devlin shook his head. He had never met someone like Anson Dobell who could mesmerize him yet leave him completely in the dark. He lit a cigarette and turned to God, "Carriage House," he said.

God stroked the Turnpike Cruiser smoothly down Mountain Highway. Rays of slackening sunlight poked down between the pines, turning wet patches of blacktop into puddles of bright yellow. They crossed the bridge over the Lynn Creek and pulled into the littered parking lot.

The Carriage House did not flatter itself even during these waning hours of daylight. It was a fat square box wrapped in a wrought iron balcony like a face guard. The new local newspaper, the Poplar Press, had recently named it the number one eyesore of the community. The Carriage House was an outpost of bad taste.

DAVID JENNESON

Devlin escorted Anson Dobell by the arm through the wet parking lot, "You must be aware this is a special place," he whispered. "Safe. I've arranged with management to give us space in the back. Having seen what you've seen, and *knowing what you now know*," he squeezed Anson's arm, "this is the best place we can be. We have ourselves a secure environment, as we say in the trade."

He smoothed and patted the back of Anson's duffel coat, easing him through the swinging doors.

Devlin had timed Anson's entrance either dead right or dead wrong, depending on your point of view. They'd hit the late afternoon Sex-stravaganza. That meant that three of the last four afternoon shift dancers got onstage to do a final show together.

Ray Seawee brightened like an angel walking into heaven. Three babes on stage at once. If he could get a cold beer and hot chicken wings it would be paradise.

Red Devlin held up his arms as if to ward off the blast of smoke and noise and lights. The music thumped around him like helicopter rotors.

God rubbed his hands together.

A pack of bodyshop mechanics swarmed in like a herd of barbarians. Their ponytails hung out beneath the bills of reversed baseball hats, dipped in transmission grease. They cut Anson off and swept him along in their wake.

To Anson they represented yet another tribal group. "And what clan are you fellows with?"

"Suck my dick, fuckwad," sneered one of them.

Red Devlin eased up behind Anson, collared him and guided him to safety.

"What a touchy fellow," observed Anson as Devlin led him toward a table. "Very un-Canadian."

"Forget it. Enjoy yourself," soothed Devlin. "Everything's arranged. Relax. Sit. Eat and drink. Meet the staff. Watch the show. Could be your lucky night." Devlin nudged him. He sat

Anson down with the others at a round table near the stage.

"Order whatever you want," said Devlin. I have to make a call."

Devlin then took Seawee aside. "Keep them busy. You're in charge. I've got a quick meeting. Back soon."

Seawee looked at him suspiciously.

"Hey, I've got to meet with the two biggest assholes in the universe," said Devlin. "Be thankful you can stay put here. It's going to be ugly. Money always is." Devlin rubbed his thumb and forefinger together and winked, then slipped out of the Carriage House.

CHAPTER 10

*W*hen he received the grocer Sheng's message, Miamata Matsumoto had no intention of driving to meet anyone late on a dirty Saturday afternoon in January. Least of all Red Devlin.

Then he thought better of it. These were his emotions speaking. This Devlin was a Westerner, and a particularly low form, the one they called a realtor. But that didn't mean the man was stupid.

Matsumoto, raised in the elite, closed society of wealthy right wing, ultra-traditional Japanese industrialists, supposed realtors were something like the Japanese *eta* caste. They even sounded the same. The *eta* were those who touched unclean objects. Among their numbers were gravediggers, butchers, leather workers, prostitutes, and beggars. They were the Japanese counterparts to India's untouchables. The *eta* were little known outside of Japan. The word was not mentioned in polite Japanese society. But membership in the caste did not preclude actual intelligence.

Miamata Matsumoto was enough of a liberal thinker to accept

this. He had no doubt that his father, the owner and President or *Sha Cho* of the Matsumoto Corporation - a massive manufacturing and trading company, still regarded the Western realtor-*eta* caste as sub-human. Miamata was willing to give them credit for at least possessing guile.

He suspected this Devlin was trying to provoke his anger by demanding a meeting on such short notice. The thought made Matsumoto agitated. It was important that he remain free from this realtor's manipulations. If he let Devlin get under his skin, it would cloud his judgment. Matsumoto concentrated on detaching himself from his own emotions. He refused to bow to Devlin's goading and become the victim of his own temper. Any aggravation would come from this end, from Miamata Matsumoto, North American Director for Matsumoto Corporation and the only child of the President.

Matsumoto was in his office. It was Saturday but he worked every day of the week. Matsumoto Corporation owned the top three floors of the Canada Place office tower. They overlooked the changing moods of Vancouver's Burrard Inlet. Below him, a starched white cruise ship sailed on ribbons of foam, outbound for Alaska. Waiting freighters dotted the gray-green sea. Some were emblazoned with the huge white MATSUMOTO LINE letters, in port from Japan. Miamata liked seeing those freighters hard at work, bringing in Matsumoto goods for the Westerners to spend money on.

Things were going so well but now this phone call. He wished his father hadn't left him in charge of dealing with the realtor-*eta*. But his father had given this Devlin his word. That meant Miamata was honor-bound to follow through. *How* he did it was up to him. He could make it as easy or as painful as he wished. He still smarted from Devlin's provocation.

He gazed out across the Inlet. The wind whistled off the dark mountains and blew up angry whitecaps. A sudden squall lashed the Inlet with rain. The next moment hard shafts of sunlight broke through the clouds. Miamata frowned. Even the weather was troublesome. Perhaps if he wrote a haiku his anger would subside. He picked up his fountain pen, engraved with the Matsumoto

DAVID JENNESON

Corporation logo. The pen had heft. Every movement of his hand seemed guided by a greater power. He paused, then wrote:

My companion
on this windy winter road?
A tap-dancing leaf.

He stared at the words on the vellum in the slackening afternoon light. Smiled. Satisfied. He leaned back and flicked open a battered Zippo, the kind Japanese tourists bought in Vietnam as the lost property of an unknown American soldier. His thumb fanned the wheel. He watched the brief shower of sparks and then the flame ignited the end of his cigarette. He blew a slow blue plume into the silent, expensive office air. He looked around him, wishing he had the liquor of strong black coffee in his throat to go with this most excellent cigarette. He suppressed the wish, then flicked the ash and inhaled deeply on the Old Gold, just to hear the lit tobacco crackle. He thought that at least the Americans made good cigarettes. In the end, this was all about the Americans.

But first he had to deal with this Canadian realtor.

He decided to seek counsel in the *Bing-Fa*. Oriental philosophers and generals had laid out these thirty-six strategies over the past two thousand years. He analyzed the situation. All strategies were available to him yet he must take care in choosing. Be calm as water. Teach this Devlin to obey the rules. Soon a course of action became clear. He tapped the pen's butt end down on the desk with a steady beat.

Kill the rooster to scare the monkey. If you have a monkey that's misbehaving, you strangle a rooster in front of it. The monkey sees this, is terrified, and you get no more trouble.

Sighing, he picked up the phone and called Sheng the grocer.

"I told you no meetings without twenty-four hours notice," he said in his gruff mumble. "Who's your boss? Me? Or this realtor? You're a mouse. You listen to anyone who tells you what to do. I will be there. So will you, but you'll wish you weren't. Bring your bandages."

Matsumoto slammed down the phone as hard as he could. Keeping a beholden Chinese middleman in line was easy. By comparison there was no helping backward Westerners like Devlin. They were guided by ignorant trust and blinded by greed. In such a country even a one-eyed man could rule armies of the greedy.

*   *   *

Red Devlin slipped out of the Carriage House at sunset, a red-eyed bankrupt. He quietly drove off in the Turnpike Cruiser, leaving the staff of Open Homes International on the hook. When he arrived at the Upper Lynn Vale Grocery he burst through the doors. The grocer Sheng angrily walked toward him.

Sheng regarded Devlin with disgust. Because Devlin's frantic maneuverings had left him sleepless for nearly forty-eight hours, Devlin looked like Colonel Sanders stoned on junk. Sheng watched Devlin shamble over and stand somnolent in the produce section. Waiting for Matsumoto, Devlin lit his last cigar, fouling the quartered melons.

With the giant seafood sale in the morning Sheng was run off his feet. Everything was in peak season. Word would spread fast around Upper Lynn Vale. Tomorrow Jeep Cherokees with kids stuffed in the back would rumble up on oversized wheels. The mothers would run in. You never saw the husbands. They were probably off lapping up beer at the Legion Hall down Lynn Vale Road. Sheng felt sorry for the hard-working mothers. They were just like him. Legalized slaves.

In the meantime his concern was Devlin. The realtor now appeared to be asleep on his feet in front of the Durien melons. He imagined with horror what his customers would think, skirting around the sleeping Devlin like small pleasure craft around the Statue of Liberty. At least the Statue of Liberty held up a torch of freedom. All the snoozing Devlin had to offer was the tip of his smelly cigar. Sheng became alarmed as the ash grew. Devlin snuffled pleasurably. The man seemed to be sucking in sleep from the very air. The snore sent a nasal, vibrating resonance down to the tip of the cigar, causing the long ash to shimmy but not fall.

DAVID JENNESON

Sheng's daughters tittered. He hissed them into silence.

He stalked toward the sleeping realtor with a saucer. His theory was to poke Devlin once in the stomach, producing an upward motion, which would vibrate down to the tip of his cigar and cause the ash to drop into the saucer. Once he got up close to Devlin he was revolted at how stale beer and smoke smell permeated the man's suit. Nevertheless, he prodded once, experimentally, and held the saucer out.

Nothing.

He poked again more firmly into the lower regions of Red Devlin's white paunch.

Devlin's eyes opened. "Bugger off, I'm sleeping." Devlin was clearly bad-tempered on being awoken. "I haven't rested in days. I oughta kick your ass for waking me."

Sheng was ready for a confrontation but not this kind. He knew he was no match for Devlin physically. He realized that the realtor was twice his size, yet the man was challenging him to fight. In his own store. In front of his daughters. Sheng stood helpless in the middle of the floor. Losing face by the second.

"I should throw you out." He said.

"Yeah. Then Matsumoto will kick your ass too," Devlin grumbled. The ash tumbled from his cigar and dropped on a sweet white melon like bird shit.

That did it.

Shamed beyond belief, Sheng muttered, "White pig." Then he marched red-faced to the back of the store. He couldn't take another minute. One way or another he was going to end this for good. Now.

Devlin decided to let Sheng have the last word. He leaned against the counter and drifted off again. Even Moses had to sleep sometime.

*   *   *

The door banged open and woke Red Devlin up. He opened his eyes to see Miamata Matsumoto enter, looking angry. And he was wet.

Sheng emerged from the back with a sour look.

Matsumoto barked something in Japanese and jerked his thumb toward the apartment upstairs.

Sheng held his palms up, not understanding.

Devlin snuffled, still waking up. Another cigar ash fell silently to the perfectly clean floor. Sheng swore in Chinese and went over to scoop it up.

Devlin saw Matsumoto's face harden. He clearly did not like being ignored by Sheng. The Japanese concept of their own racial purity puts them, in their own eyes, high above all other Asian peoples, not to mention Westerners. Matsumoto had a particularly bad case of pure-bloodedness. To be ignored by a Chinese worm was infuriating. Loss of face. He marched over to the crouched Sheng.

"I said go upstairs now. Are you deaf?" He spat on Sheng in anger.

This opened Devlin's eyes for sure. Little Sheng rose up, white-faced. He wiped the spittle. His daughters looked away in embarrassment. Matsumoto dismissed them all with a snort. He strode regally out of the door. Devlin figured Matsumoto expected that he and Sheng would follow like serfs, which they did.

The entrance to the apartment over the Upper Lynn Vale Grocery was an anonymous exterior door. When Matsumoto unlocked it, Devlin climbed the stairs like the oldest dog on earth. Half asleep. Head bowed. Plodding. He reached for his cigar that had inexplicably gone out. The stairway was dark and smelled of dust and new paint. He could feel Sheng dogging his heels. He fought to gather his wits. His realtor's sense was slowly returning.

He vaguely wondered how to give Matsumoto his yin/yang combo of good news/bad news. The good news was that Open Homes International was out of the gate and down the track faster than anyone had imagined. The bad news was that the plan was going to take a lot of money. Now. Up front. Fast.

DAVID JENNESON

They entered the upstairs apartment. The place always jarred Devlin. There was the ten thousand dollar Italian butter-soft leather blue couch, the teak panels and wainscoting, the vintage 1950's turquoise Formica bar counter. Behind the bar a window looking down onto dark, deserted Lynn Vale Road. There was a solid marble backgammon table. This room alone was loaded with enough expensive booze, electronic entertainment equipment and art to take up a year's salary for the average person. A sumptuous little clubhouse in the middle of nowhere. Yet Devlin knew that it didn't work. Wealth meets bad taste.

"Mr. Matsumoto," Devlin bowed in the East Indian style, hands raised, prayer-like, instead of the proper Japanese bow showing respect with hands held at the sides. It seemed to irritate Matsumoto, and instead of returning the bow he thrust a heavy cut crystal ashtray at Devlin, an invitation to butt out his smelly cigar. Sheng glowered in the corner.

"How thoughtful of you," said Devlin humbly, bowing to the ashtray for extra humility.

Matsumoto winced and shook his head like Devlin was trying to drive him mad.

Kill the rooster to scare the monkey.

He strode past Devlin and confronted Sheng.

"You stupid, common shopkeeper," he shouted. "I said no meetings on Saturdays. No meetings without proper notice. You are the connection. This is your only responsibility yet you can't get it right. Do I have to beat it into you?" He slapped Sheng across the face.

Sheng stared back hard at the taller Matsumoto. He didn't flinch.

"This client does not know our rules yet," Matsumoto pointed at Devlin. "You do. Yet you ignore them. Over and over!" He slapped Sheng again.

Devlin cringed. He wanted to look away but couldn't take his eyes off Sheng.

Sheng seemed to quiver. As if his life were passing before his eyes. To Devlin he looked strangely unfocused as he stared at Matsumoto's tie.

"Next time it will be your daughters!" A third blow from Matsumoto reddened the grocer's cheek.

With a sudden roar the little grocer revealed his fish knife and plunged for the gut.

Matsumoto yelled and leapt to one side in what the astonished Devlin supposed was a Samurai maneuver. He grabbed Sheng's wrist and they struggled.

"Whoa, hold on you two," Devlin moved forward to intervene but they were locked in combat, fighting for their lives.

Matsumoto jerked and heaved. The knife was suddenly thrust upward. The Finnish Fiskars stainless steel blade was seven inches long; narrow at the hilt and needle-sharp at the tip. There was a gasp and a choking sound.

Matsumoto pulled his hands away from Sheng and stepped back. The knife had penetrated beneath Sheng's chin and it had been driven upward to the hilt. Devlin caught the grocer as he fell, and lay him on his side.

"This is unfortunate," a rattled Matsumoto spoke quickly. "This man attacked me. I had to defend myself. You saw. You will deal with it. We have lost our intermediary. You and I will now deal directly. Here is my card. Do not call for six weeks. The reason should be obvious to even you."

"This man's dying for Christ sake," Devlin felt sick. He kneeled down. "Get the ambulance. Call 911. Get his family up here. Jesus God, what have you done?"

"You will be compensated for any trouble," muttered Matsumoto. "I meant only to teach you a lesson. Kill the rooster to scare the monkey. Innocent parable. It got out of hand. Only meant to be symbolic. I must go now."

"Don't run out now you barbaric little prick. He's bleeding

everywhere. Do something."

Matsumoto did do something. He bent down and withdrew the knife from beneath Sheng's chin. It came out as soundlessly as it had gone in. Blood beaded up on the stainless steel blade. From the look in Sheng's eyes, the grocer seemed glad to have it out of him. His throat gurgled like a baby. Devlin thought he was going to faint.

"There has been no crime," Matsumoto's voice seemed far away. "This was self defense. Still, I prefer not to be involved. I wasn't here. If I wasn't here, there is no witness. Without a witness there can be no charges. If you wish to continue our relationship, you will deal with the details. Call me," said Matsumoto. He dropped the knife, gave a shallow bow and fled down the stairs.

Devlin held the grocer's head up in the crook of his arm.

"Jesus I'm sorry for anything I said to you," he murmured to Sheng. He was shaking. He couldn't comfort the man and reach for the phone at the same time. "Talk to me. Say your name. Stay awake!"

The grocer gave him a peaceful look, as if he'd just got his first glimpse of a Chinese heaven with special Ming Dynasty angels. Sheng was climbing that mountain to walk up there among them clouds. Where the rice is high and there are melons growing and there ain't no fields to plow.

Sheng looked up once more as if Devlin was a forgivable fool, doomed to blunder about the known universe for all time, eternally missing the point.

"God man - don't die," pleaded Devlin.

Sheng was finally able to ignore him.

Devlin didn't know whether to cry or be ill. This was the worst real estate meeting he'd ever been to. Talk about unprofessional. He couldn't take his eyes off the dead Chinese grocer. Devlin had stabbed people in the back over real estate. He'd been stabbed in the back himself too. But this was ridiculous.

Stunned, he sank down on the leather couch and tried to think. He counted the pros and cons off on his fingers. One dead grocer on his hands, one judge with an ax to grind, a rapidly accumulating debt, and a half-assed staff currently eating and drinking on a maxed-out credit card that he had slipped to the manager of the Carriage House. On the plus side of the ledger he had lit the spark of Open Homes International. It now burned brightly. The fuse led all the way to the White House. Somewhere down the line was a shaky promise of money from Matsumoto.

So Red Devlin did what any realtor would do in a situation like this. He quietly slipped out, and sold his house.

*   *   *

Anson Dobell was working hard on his blending-in lessons at the Carriage House. Seawee and God spelled each other off in this respect. One would sit back at the table with Tasha and Cutsie Wu while the other got his eyeful in the front row with Anson. Seawee took his turn at the seat at stage level.

By six in the evening the front row had become a collection of all of the reasons bars make trouble for women. All the excuses men find to stay were there.

Young men who were expected to meet dates and would never make it, and if they did there would be trouble because they were so damn late. Older men who were expected home by their wives hours ago knew they were already in trouble so they stayed on longer. They figured they couldn't get into any more trouble than they were in already, so what was the loss? They all sat around the stage with two things in common. They had all been there too long and not one of them would admit it.

The music cut out suddenly in mid-beat. "Let's put those hands together for Sweeeet SER-EN-IT-Y!" boomed the disk jockey's voice.

The crowd seemed to have briefly died, a single organism turned stupid by beer. The only sound was two mechanics arguing drunkenly about the boiling point of oil.

DAVID JENNESON

"C'mon guys, let's hear it!" the disk jockey demanded. His scolding seemed to jolt the crowd and clear their heads. There was clattering applause and a few tentative mating calls.

"Woo!" cried Ray Seawee.

He looked over at Anson Dobell, waiting for him to follow suit. To his dismay Anson was sleeve-deep in a big platter of chicken wings.

Seawee was torn and confused. Since he believed Tasha had danced *just for him* the night before, he felt this made him boss of the row. That meant he had to enforce standards and set examples. In Seawee's mind, rule number one was that you didn't eat in front of a woman who was trying to erotically arouse you. Even the license plate stampers in prison knew that much.

Seawee noticed Anson's formerly fastidious nature had gone to the dogs. He had crimson wing sauce up around the cuffs of his tan duffel coat. There was a fresh pint of beer in front of him with an empty off to the left. He didn't seem to have a care in the world.

Seawee gave him a sidelong glance. "Woo!" he repeated more sternly. This was a hint for Anson to get with the program and stop lowering the tone. The vinegary tartness of the chicken wings made Seawee's eyes water. It shot up his nose, invaded his brain then down to his gut. Suddenly Ray Seawee was very hungry.

Anson blinked over at him. "Pardon me? What was that?"

"WOO!" cried Seawee in exasperation. "Remember? We lay low. Act like the rest of them. We *blend* in. You never know who's watching. Where did you get that chicken? Woo!" He wanted to reach into the pile of vermilion wings but stopped himself. Someone had to set an example.

"I don't know where you're going with this woo business," Anson skinned a bone neatly. "Your friend with the beard, Mr. Saunders, gave me entirely different instructions. However, I'll try. He looked up at the stage. "Hoo!"

"Can't you just say it?" Seawee cried, exasperated. "Woo! WOO!" The demonstration inadvertently sparked a flurry of competing woo's around the row accompanied by piercing whistles. Someone yelled *purrrrfect!*

"My God," gasped Anson as the dancer tiptoed to the center of the circular stage. "Do you allow children be tattooed in Canada?"

Ray Seawee looked up at Sweet Serenity. The name fit - sweet as a child, serene as a slow flowing river. She had the innocent aura of a 14 year-old princess who had just walked out of a village deep in the forest. She blinked like a bambi, this young and stunning native Indian girl. A mane of shimmering black hair down to her butt. Sure enough, there was a tiny tattoo on her ankle.

"She's not a kid. She's a *peeler*," said Seawee as if the two were mutually exclusive. "Besides, they all have little tattoos these days. It's like some badge."

From the look in Anson's eye, Seawee could tell his mind was drifting off the tracks. He had a dreamy, faraway look.

"This is just like Canada in the National Geographics," Anson informed him. "Trees everywhere. Mountains and forests and sea. Grocery stores without barred windows, filled with fresh seafood. Backpackers instead of thugs. "

Seawee nodded, earnestly trying to follow what Anson was talking about. He knew Anson was important to the White House deal but wasn't sure why. He figured it was better to agree with him.

"And this Open Homes International." Anson continued. "Exploding out of the very earth like this. Astonishing."

Seawee had the thread. "Yup. She's gonna go big."

"And now this," Anson looked up at Sweet Serenity.

More cheers rose.

"She looks like a genuine Canadian native Indian princess! Why, back up there in the forest I'll bet there's village after village filled with these magnificent people. Hunting. Fishing. Red flannel shirts and crackling bacon. Wood smoke and maple syrup. Her village is probably just up and over the next hill. Imagine her staring silently down at the Vista Dome from her high mountain passes."

DAVID JENNESON

Seawee was bewildered again. And a little worried. Anson had an irrationally romantic look in his eye. Seawee had seen it before.

"Maybe I'll steal her away," Anson leaned close to Seawee and muttered conspiratorially. "Make her my own. I'll defect to Canada."

Seawee gave Anson a helpless look.

"Ho, baby, baby, bay-beeee," Anson shouted in his best foreign-sounding accent, just the way God had taught him. He sounded like an Italian speaking Cockney.

Sweet Serenity glanced his way.

"Prettee bay-bee, bay-bee, ovah heah!" Anson shouted. It didn't matter that it sounded like he had come from some terrible place with an awful language. It got her attention. That was all that mattered.

She smiled and began her dance, then glided toward Anson, curious.

"Oh yes, yes, ovah heah, prettee bay-bee simply mahvellous!" Anson chanted as she approached.

Seawee looked away, embarrassed at the spectacle.

Not so Serenity. She knelt in front of Anson on slender legs. She smiled warmly and seemed inexplicably charmed. "Where abouts are you from?" she asked, clearly intrigued.

This angle had apparently never occurred to Anson. "India," he said in the next breath.

"India. Cool."

She then drew herself up the brass pole and slipped across to the other side of the stage where they were hooting charges of favoritism. Anson's eyes followed her. He seemed in awe. She had spoken to him. Him alone and no one else. He'd been chosen from the pack. This made Anson rev up his Eurotrash chant with more energy than ever.

Ray Seawee sadly shook his head. Anson was falling prey to a syndrome common to even veterans of gynecology row. This was the predisposition to fall head over heels in love for fifteen minutes. The chief symptom was the victim's sudden suspension of disbelief. Dumb, ordinary men momentarily believed that one of these beautiful, incredibly sexy women gave a flying fuck for them. Common sense went out the window. In Anson's case, the more he chattered, the more Sweet Serenity arced back toward him. Seawee glanced over again. Anson looked like he thought something was in the cards all right.

He became so inspired using *The Voice* as God had taught him that he out-shouted all other mating calls on the row. Men fell silent. Anson was stealing the show, but Ms. Serenity was laid back enough to let it go.

Her performance reached a crescendo in sensual blue jazz. Wide eyes and white teeth flashed as she slid down the brass pole, undulating softly, inches in front of Anson like a willowy whip. She seemed plugged in to a current of exotic electricity.

"What part of India did you say you were from?" she asked him as she drew close.

Anson screwed up his courage again. "I'll tell you if you tell me what you want to drink afterward," he jabbered back, scoring his second point for quick thinking that day. Actually, it wasn't quick thinking at all. God had told him to always utter the first thing that came into his head and not worry about anything else.

Suddenly Anson's head was jerked back. It was the shaven-headed manager, grabbing him by the scruff of his duffel coat.

"Hold on, Casanova. Who's paying for all this?"

"Eh?" asked Anson, startled back to his regular Washington DC voice. "I don't understand."

"Humph. Some Indian," said Sweet Serenity and left for greener pastures on the far side of the stage.

"You too pal," the cook poked Seawee. "And them over there too," he jerked his thumb back at the table where Tasha, Cutsie Wu and God were eating. "That old guy left a bum credit card. Who pays

DAVID JENNESON

the tab?"

Seawee felt his jacket but had left his wallet in another life. "Give me a minute," he muttered. He left the confused Anson to sort out his love life and went to Tasha's table. Everyone had just finished a large if not splendid dinner. God sat before a mound of chicken bones and a ring of empty pints. Tasha and Cutsie Wu had platters of fish and big carafes of cold white wine.

"There's no money," said Seawee, hangdog. "Devlin's credit card is bogus."

"Par for the course," said God with his mouth full.

"What's with this guy?" cried Tasha. "Is he nuts or something? This is a bad joke."

"No," said Seawee. "I think he's caught short. I'm broke too. But he owes me."

"He owes everybody," said Tasha peevishly.

"I think he's fixing that now," said Seawee. "He's gone to get money."

"Yeah, well who's going to fix this?" Tasha pointed at the empty plates. "I'm broke. I just paid my rent."

"I'm bust too," God shrugged.

"And me," said Cutsie Wu.

"What about your Barney Fife friend down there?" Tasha pointed toward Anson. "He's from Washington, DC. He must have money."

"I don't think we can do that," said Seawee slowly. "He's a client. We're realtors now. The client never pays. That's the realtor's way"

"What are you suggesting?"

"Well, I was thinking. You're a realtor, but you're a dancer too. And for this one time if you were to dance, maybe they'd pay you. Then maybe you could pay this. And get paid back of course."

"Forget it," said Tasha.

"Just this one time. Think what we've got to gain in the long run."

Tasha sighed and rolled her eyes. "I don't believe I'm doing this."

"It's better to dance as a realtor than dance as a dancer," said Seawee. "Realtors only dance when they want to. Dancers have to dance every day."

Shaking her head she picked up her purse and walked toward the disk jockey's booth to make arrangements. "This never ends," she said to the disk jockey.

Meanwhile the lovelorn Anson Dobell wiped his fingers on a napkin and lit his pipe. Sweet Serenity had shot him down bad. Seawee slipped in beside him.

"Sorry about the little misunderstanding," he said. "These bar managers are pretty uppity these days."

Anson seemed happy to hear the anti-manager sentiment.

"At Open Homes International we have a tradition." Seawee continued. "When we close a successful deal, we celebrate. We eat. We drink. And we dance. So now we're going to dance."

Tasha put a high-heeled shoe out onto the stage. She glanced to the left, to the right, and then did a bolero turn. Wild gypsy music played. Fast violins and passion. Black skirts whirled. It was as if some beautiful receptionist had gone wild and was tearing off her clothes. The row first fell silent then exploded. No one had seen anything like it. Anson's pipe remained hanging unlit from his mouth,

"Our tribute to you," Seawee whispered to Anson. "Do us right. We'll do you right. It"s the realtor's way."

So it was that Open Homes International managed to pay the bill. They tucked Anson Dobell into a room upstairs, and arranged for his cab to the airport the next morning. Then they all made their separate ways home. As they did each privately wondered if Red Devlin was mentally unstable or financially challenged. Or both.

DAVID JENNESON

CHAPTER 11

Dawn seeped through the tattered curtains of the dirty basement suite window.

Red Devlin snuffled awake. Finding himself sprawled out in an overstuffed chair, he realized with a start he must have dropped off to sleep in mid-getaway. To him this proved he was no criminal. What sort of criminal goes home after a murder and has a nap?

It didn't matter. He knew he had to get rid of the evidence. A few minutes later he watched his balled-up, bloodstained white suit melt in the fireplace. *I love the smell of burning polyester in the morning*, he thought with bitter sarcasm. In an effort to give the suit a decent sendoff he had rolled it up like a log and doused it with a tot of his best brandy. Then he had placed it like a corpse on the pyre of his butt-filled fireplace.

Involuntarily he took in deep gulps of air but it was hard. Maybe the emphysema was coming back. His love of the rum-tipped cigar and the plain-end cigarette coming back to roost.

Clinically, Red Devlin was in shock. Having Sheng, the grocer, die in his arms and then fleeing the scene of the crime was not his cup of tea. He had broken plenty of laws in his time - real estate laws. But not this. Never this. He kept seeing the grocer's eyes turn to flat, lifeless objects in the passing of a moment. Death rattled his realtor's bones.

His mind was hounded by questions. Had he been recognized? Would Sheng's daughters finger him? Who could place him at the crime scene? Who couldn't? There were no witnesses in the apartment, he thought with relief. Then he became angry. Why should he feel relieved because there were no witnesses? He hadn't done anything wrong for anyone to witness. If there had been a witness then they could testify to the fact that he had tried to stop the killing. There was a witness, for Chrissake. Matsumoto was a witness. Yet he claimed not to be. And, under the bizarre circumstances of their arrangement, he wasn't. It didn't make sense. Crime and punishment and real estate were a bad mix where nothing came out right.

Devlin wiped his brow. His white suit blazed in the fireplace. Worried thoughts raced through his mind like snakes and ladders. He decided to slow down with a tot of brandy.

He tried to relax. His hand shook and the brandy sloshed in the snifter. A few drops slopped onto his hand. Sitting before a fire, watching his favorite suit burn into gooey cinders in a stinking basement suite was not how Red Devlin had pictured spending his golden years as a master realtor. He looked at his miserable situation and gave a fatalistic shrug. At least he had brandy.

This was the reality of realty. Lifestyles of the Broke and Anonymous. Furniture worn and chipped. A room long and narrow with a high window at one end that permitted a thin shaft of pale, watery dawn light. The view, from tiptoes, consisted of one green garden hose rolled up like a snake which was stiff in winter on a frozen patch of mud..

Devlin looked gloomily about him. The room stank. The refrigerator was always empty, ashtrays always full. He shifted his butt in the damp overstuffed chair. He was wearing only his underwear.

DAVID JENNESON

This was the sorriest picture of all. He had attempted to econo-mize by making a bulk purchase of underwear several years ago at a bankruptcy sale. They came in only one color and size; black and small, but they were an excellent value. As a result Red Devlin had walked around for the past two years feeling like he was wearing a slingshot. Now, nearly naked, he was squeezed into them and looked like a blotchy hippo in black bikini spandex. It was almost as bad as seeing a pink elephant. He was however, unaware of his spectacular appearance

Then Red Devlin decided to get his act together. He searched out his old phone under a cushion and with elbows on his knees he stared at the receiver and contemplated his first call. He knew the president of a successful real estate company for which he had once worked. Devlin had made the man rich, then he had set out on his own and eventually he owned five houses. But later there had been expenses and market corrections. Devlin watched his precious stock of real estate, the little residential empire he had spent a life-time accumulating, dwindle from five to four houses, then three, then one. His constant wheeling and dealing and lounges and cars and suits were like water trickling through a grate. And now this. In fatter days Devlin had added this basement suite to generate extra rent. As his stock of houses dwindled he had first moved in upstairs, and then further cut his expenses by moving downstairs and renting out the upper floor. Now, with the sale of his last house to his ex-boss, he was suddenly a renter in his own dump. He looked around with disgust. He had a sudden urge to complain to the landlord.

Instead he dialed the president of the real estate company and got him out of bed.

"Devlin here. I need to sell the house. I need the money today."

"The old one up on Dempsey?"

"Yes," Devlin looked around him sadly. "The one with the in-law suite."

"I'll give you market price. There'll be a personal check waiting at my office at ten this morning. I'll leave it with the weekend receptionist."

"Thank you. I appreciate this."

"It's not like I don't owe you," the president hung up.

He looked up at the frumpy swag lamp hanging over his chair. Dust balls clung to its chain. As he stared up at the hideous thing he panted like a cornered animal. It was all too much.

To hell with it all, he thought. He decided to have a nervous breakdown.

He had never had one, but from what Devlin had heard, people who had nervous breakdowns were put in comfortable hospital suites with clean white sheets for months on end. He was sure there were less stressed-out people than himself in there right now enjoying nervous breakdowns. They would come out of the hospital perfectly relaxed, well fed and with a better outlook. Devlin became depressed. He could see a bad end to this miserable life of his. He would end up as a crazy old man, his mission unfulfilled.

Nevertheless, he believed that what he'd been through entitled him to a nervous breakdown. He wondered how you went about it. The problem was he had never seen one so he didn't know how bring them on. How hard could it be?

He closed his eyes and inhaled deeply. He held his breath tight. This expanded his stomach like a puffer fish over his black jockey shorts, like it was some special realtor's organ. His gut turned red and mottled like the surface of Mars. He hoped to come out of it weeping and muttering mad things. He quickly realized he couldn't hold this breathless pose long enough to achieve nervous breakdown critical mass, or lift-off, or whatever it was called. Catching his breath, he concentrated on the most depressing images he could think of. He imagined Moses having a nervous breakdown in the middle of the desert.

It didn't work. It was not a thing Moses would do.

Of course there was the other kind of nervous breakdown. He had heard about people who just went to sleep normal one night and woke up crazy the next morning, but he didn't have time for that.

DAVID JENNESON

Maybe a heart attack or stroke. Devlin had never had one of these either but felt that, due to all his efforts, he was owed some kind of health-related excuse to escape this latest turn of events. It would be so much easier than running away to Washington, DC and living on the lam. A mild heart attack would do. He imagined the sympathetic headline: *Innocent realtor found clinging to life in affordable suite.* He gazed down over his protruding gut, down to his chicken legs. He became impatient. It was 5 AM. In lounges all over the world, in London and New York and Tokyo, realtors were having their first drink of the day. Time was wasting.

Then he thought of how he had abandoned Seawee and the rest. It cast him into another appalling fit of depression. It passed over him like a dark wave.

He thought about his bleak prospects and bit fiercely into left his arm in the hope that it would make him insane. Instead it made him wish he had enough spare change to buy a sub sandwich down at the 7-Eleven.

He stopped trying to have a nervous breakdown. Instead he went into the kitchen and fried up some baloney in a black cast iron skillet. There were two hard-boiled eggs left too. They rolled around on top of the stove while he fried the baloney. When he ate them they put his feet back on the ground some.

*   *   *

Sheng would have been happy. His Super Seafood Sale was receiving priceless free publicity as television lights bathed the windows of the Upper Lynn Vale Grocery. The news cameras were gathering background shots for the developing murder story while waiting for the police to bring the body out. Although Sheng might have complained about the unflattering glare of the TV lights, everyone in town would know about his Super Seafood Sale.

The police had only arrived recently because Sheng's family had taken so long to call. Out of respect and fear for the little tyrant they had all waited downstairs. As hours passed they become uneasy. They searched for but could not find a key to the upstairs suite. Suddenly his wife broke into spontaneous wailing. Nothing would comfort her. In order to calm her down the daughters urged her to call 9-1-1. It took the 9-1-1 operator a long time to figure out her grief-stricken shrieking in broken English.

The police came with whirling lights, kicked in the door, crept upstairs and found Sheng's body. Immediately the police tied the yellow ribbons. Then the media arrived. Then the neighbors. Wrapped under the ambulance blankets Sheng looked thin as a pizza slice, as he had in life. Except now death seemed to flatten him, letting his steam out, like a pizza delivered cold and late.

"Poor little runt," said Mustache to Needle-nose as they performed crowd control in the pre-dawn rain. Inside, Mountie detectives combed for DNA and fiber evidence while waiting for a Chinese-speaking interpreter to take the family's statements.

Needle-nose blinked out into the glare of television lights. By now there were knots of alarmed bystanders. He was looking at the black skid mark the bus tire had left on the curb the previous night. It was clearly visible. He frowned in a pointy-nosed way.

"You know," he said, "it seems like there's been a regular crime wave going on around this store."

"How do you mean?" asked Moustache.

"First the bus. Now this."

"Lighting strikes twice," shrugged Mustache. He shivered deeper into his RCMP slicker. They looked like sentries on some dark, wet front during the Great War. Gusts of wind rushed down the mountains and blew squalls of rain in their faces, paused, then delivered another blow. "You don't listen so good," said Needle-nose. "Remember what Judge Mannheim said? That a bunch of realtors here in town were up to no good. He said keep an eye out. So what have we got here? We've got a serious bus accident and a dangerous driving incident last night. That old snake down at the Carriage House did it too. I know he did, and he sure looked like a realtor to me. Now what do we have? A murder. Right in the same place. I tell you, I've got a funny feeling about this."

Mustache raised his eyes skyward and shook his head. He looked long-suffering. "That's the stupidest theory I ever heard." He lit a cigarette.

"Oh yeah? So what are you saying? That you know more than Judge Mannheim? And there's no smoking on duty."

"Then I'm on my break."

"Maybe you ought to listen to your betters. You might pick up a few tips on police work."

"Maybe you oughta butt out."

"Well maybe I'll take my theory to Judge Mannheim. At least someone around here appreciates a probing mind. You ought to get some initiative. You'll be calling me sergeant before you know it."

Mustache gritted his teeth. He looked like he wanted to throw a punch.

"Pardon me," he said, "but I've got more important things to do. Like take a leak. Can you handle this alone?"

Mustache walked off in disgust in search of the bushes. Inside the store, frazzled Mountie detectives were doing their best to take notes from the family's torrent of bereaved and broken English A cop, fluent in Mandarin Chinese, who was called from the Vancouver City Police, was still miles and hours away.

*   *   *

The fried baloney and hard-boiled eggs had brought Red Devlin back to down to earth. He scooped up the ashes of his white suit and flushed them down the toilet. Then he took a fast shower. He threw on his best casual clothes and packed the only bag he had in the house, a small red tartan suitcase.

He dashed out, hid the Turnpike Cruiser in the garage, left the key inside her and closed the door. This made him a little sentimental. It was like locking a faithful hound in the doghouse. He quietly hummed a few bars of "Old Shep" and made a silent promise to return, thinking: *real estate is loyalty to the loyal.* He was about to call a cab but then thought no, they'll trace it back to the house. Nowadays they could trace anything.

So Red Devlin just walked away. Like speeded-up film he cut down Dempsey Road on foot. He had much to arrange and no time to do it. He knew he had to go to Washington DC but would prefer to do it on his own schedule, and without a murder hanging over his head. He silently cursed at fate for dealing him another black card. He didn't feel very Moses-like as he turned the corner and hustled down Mountain Highway trying not to look furtive. He wondered what had possessed him to buy a cheap tartan bag. He was grateful when he moused into the 7-Eleven lot and found a dozing cabbie.

Devlin barked orders to the cab driver. Minutes later they were down in Poplar Ridge and had pulled up outside Devlin's former employer's real estate office. Devlin paid the driver with his last pocketful of change, and picked up a personal check for two hundred thousand dollars in the real estate office.

Then it hit him. Sunday. Damn. Not one bank open in the whole province. He paced up toward 15th Street and Lord Grey Avenue, the main nerve center of Poplar Ridge. Closed banks flanked the intersection foursquare on all corners. The early brunch crowd streamed past him smiling like animated dummies. He felt his back touch the cold bank wall. Envelope in his pocket. He felt like a dope dealer.

Realtors and bankers are deadly enemies. Realtors lie to bankers and the bankers get mad. Realtors swear they will never lie again and bankers swear never to believe them. Yet six months later they are at it again, dancing close and breathing hard. Red Devlin looked around. At this moment the four closed banks seemed like stern church deacons on this Sunday morning. Each bank had its own reason to be wary of an account in the name of Red Devlin. To Devlin, the buildings looked like they were scowling at him. His past enterprises had caused him to share his banking business among them all. Too often he had deposited large checks at one or the other, only to have the amount diminish or vanish altogether, absorbed by some previous debt to which he considered himself personally disconnected.

He pursed his lips in thought. The weight of the past forty-eight hours pressed hard on him like an overdue mortgage. The baloney and boiled eggs now made him feel drowsy. He dozed like a bull-frog in the cold morning sun.

There were four banks: The Toronto Dominion, the Bank of Montreal, the Imperial Bank of Commerce and the Hong Kong Bank of Canada. He tried to remember which bank was currently most fed up with him and which was about ready to kiss and make up. It was hopeless. He slipped into the nearest instant teller room.

Devlin knew nothing in the known universe traveled faster than a bad check. He now squared off against the bank machine as if it was some squat robot intent on eating his money. It was hateful. Like sacrificing cash to a pagan God. He punched in the massive deposit and watched gloomily as it ate the envelope with the check. He half expected the machine to burp from its big meal.

Nothing.

In the next ten minutes he kited his money through three more bank machines, taking a ten thousand dollar withdrawal each time. The rest he dumped on his credit cards.

Bank machines were never designed to be abused like this. But come Monday morning, the bankers wouldn't be able to deny the check was there, despite the unorthodox way it had gotten into the system. By the time they had their fit he would be long gone.

Besides, it was Devlin's money in the first place.

His final cash take was forty thousand dollars. Come Monday morning the bankers would be howling on the phone to one another like kicked dogs. All that money chasing all those checks in circles, and for what? The bulk had ended up on Devlin's own credit cards. They would curse Devlin out. Swear to do this and that. But they wouldn't.

It was the same old story. Bankers and realtors.

When he emerged, Devlin felt like a professional wrestler who has just left four hulking bank machines senseless in the ring. This would make it harder for Seawee on Monday morning. The bankers would be in a foaming snit but they would sort it out. Besides, it was the bankers' faults for keeping such out-of-date hours. These days businessmen did business on Sundays just like any other day. And since when did business stop just because a banker wanted a day off?

He hailed a cab.

Minutes later he pulled up outside Seawee's rooming house. He knocked on the door, cocked an ear and heard a braying snore inside. Seawee was sleeping off his first forty-eight hours of realtor-dom. He tried the knob and it opened. Apparently Seawee, fresh out of the penal system, expected every door to lock behind him when he closed it.

Devlin stood in the center of the sparsely furnished room. He noted no whiskey bottles nor drug paraphernalia. He shuffled and stamped his foot. Still no response. Seawee was dead out. Devlin approached. He sat on the edge of the bed and then pulled out an envelope containing a perfectly good ten thousand dollar check made out to Ray Seawee. He shook Seawee's shoulder.

"*Ramon*," he whispered.

"Huh? Woo?" Seawee cried out from a deep sleep. He opened his eyes. and blinked in disbelief, like he was seeing kindly old Saint Nick who had stopped by on his sleigh.

"You're the boss up here now," Devlin said softly. "I'm counting on you. And this is your money." He placed the ten thousand dollar check onto Seawee's chest.

"Ten thousand dollars," Seawee stammered, "for me?"

"You're a realtor now. Every realtor needs operating funds. I took forty thousand out of the bank and I'm giving you ten. And here's a standard franchise form. Just fill in the blanks and get it printed up. These are operating funds, my son. "

"For what? Operating on what?"

"Business is booming. You're the chief representative for Open Homes International in Canada now. A Director. Deals to make, books to keep, and miles to go before you sleep. You'll do it with this," he tapped the envelope, "and these," he flipped him two credit cards.

"What about you?"

"I've been called away to Washington. Urgent."

"You never mentioned going to Washington so soon."

"Never mind. Things are moving fast," Devlin hissed. "I don't have much time. Here's what you do. You pay all those Open House people first - McGregor and the rest. Then pay the women and Saunders. Then pay yourself. You must pay yourself too. Get franchise forms printed up. Sell the franchises for whatever you can get. Find a realtor with a license. If a house gets sold, it goes through him. You can do this. Just keep your ducks in a row. Put the extra money into this bank account."

Devlin tossed a card with a bank number onto the bedspread. "Don't spend a dime you don't have to. I'll send more money as you need it. Check for messages from me at the front desk of The Carriage House. That's where I'll leave them. Get those women out there selling the franchises. Those two broads are the best things that ever happened to real estate. Give them standard commission. Wish I'd thought of it myself. Treat those bimbos like goddam queens, *Ramon*. This is your chance to go straight to the top. Your grub stake. Your new start. You follow?"

Seawee nodded.

"Good, Ramon. Listen to me. The train is pulling out of the station. Is it going to New York? No. Is it going to London? No! Is it going to Paris, France? NO! The conductor is shouting. 'All aboard. All Aboard! ABOARD!' Can your hear him, *Ramon?*"

"Yes," Seawee whispered.

Devlin looked around Seawee's cheap room. "Don't be left behind on the station platform. Are you coming?"

"Yes!"

"Last chance. ABOARD!" Devlin's voice rose.

"YES!" Seawee shouted.

"GOOD, Ramon! Because we're on our way to the Promised Land!" Devlin's eyes blazed with evangelical fever. He then gave Seawee's hand a quick pump and slipped out like a wily old trout into the deep water.

CHAPTER 12

Red Devlin watched the lights of Washington from a DC 9 at night.

He flew from Vancouver to Seattle and dozed on the plane in Seattle as additional Washington, DC-bound passengers boarded. To cheer himself up he'd bought a carton of Pall Mall plain ends from the duty-free. When he finally got to his seat he was floored to find that since he had last flown in a jet, all flights had been reduced to non-smoking. Now he rolled the plain-end anxiously between his lips and studied the terrain below.

To Devlin, the night view of Washington, DC through the jet's window looked like a great mandala of fortune. It was a glittering wheel, the spokes of which radiated grandly but had become bent and twisted over time. To a normal person it would not have looked like a wheel at all, but Red Devlin had special vision and knowledge.

Beneath the pattern of bright streets and high monuments he

could still see the original design of Pierre L'Enfant - architect of the city. The footprint of this genius was visible only from thirty thousand feet - still deep and clear after two hundred years - it would never fade from view.

Devlin had become a fan of L'Enfant. He was a French Major who had been commissioned by George Washington to design Washington, DC. Washington also appointed three local squires as commissioners to oversee the work. He assumed the commissioners would give L'Enfant step-by-step instructions. The commissioners assumed Washington would deal with it. As a result L'Enfant did what he pleased. He designed Washington, DC based on The Three Pillars of Real Estate Wisdom: *Location! Location! Location!* He who dies with the best view wins. In his design L'Enfant also ignored the detail of who owned the land in the first place.

When Red Devlin discovered this it led him down the dark road into America's past. Even though he was a realtor, Devlin was dismayed to discover the level of fraud, incompetence and general cussedness that accompanied the founding and building of the nation's capitol. It broke his heart. If only he could have been there to do it first.

It confirmed his General Theory of Real Estate: *Golden Ages repeat themselves through history.* If what he had experienced in the late 1960's, back in The Day, with big cars and smoky lounges, whiskey-soiled suits and missed appointments was The Golden Age, then the buying and building of the US Capitol and the White House was the Mother of Days. President Washington and early masters of the craft, ethically on a par with Devlin, had set up office in the tobacco swamps and forests of Virginia and Maryland. They were Real Estate Leonardos.

Devlin was also developing a separate General Theory of Golden Ages. It was part of his General Theory of Real Estate. Ironically, his close study of the cycles of Golden Ages down through history caused him to think of realtors as a parallel to the vampiric legends. Both seemed to rise and fall with the passage of centuries. Throughout history the public tried to rid themselves of both plagues - realtors and vampires - through various burnings, stakings and lawsuits. It didn't work. Vampires and realtors came back like dandelions, or cancer. This caused Devlin to mentally reassess his own vocation in more contemporary terms: *Real estate is an opportunistic disease.*

The plane shuddered. A veil of dark cloud obscured his view of Washington. Pellets of icy rain riddled the window. The *fasten seat belt* signs blinked on.

"We're experiencing a minor weather problem and we'll be circling above Washington National for a few minutes," announced the pilot's muzak voice. "Relax and enjoy your flight."

Devlin waited for the No Smoking sign to blip on, then realized you didn't need no smoking signs going on and off on a smokeless flight. Gloomily Devlin regarded his unlit Pall Mall. He had distracted himself with his strategies and hadn't thought about smoking, but now he wanted a drag. "Bah," he said in frustration and flung the thing into his lap. His mind was haunted by cares and delays.

"You know," came a husky, tobacco-darkened voice from two seats over, "I've been circling this city since 1947 and I still don't understand it."

Red Devlin raised his eyebrows. He had been so absorbed in brooding over his own plans he had failed to notice the tiny form on the aisle. He turned. From the sound of the voice he half-expected to see a skeleton puffing on an Old Gold.

A leathery woman in her mid-seventies eyed him back. "Yup. Used to come in and out of here on the DC 3's. Same thing. Weather troubles. Flying in circles. Only thing then you could smoke. And drink." She rattled her plastic cup full of half-melted cubes and shot it a rueful look. To Devlin it looked wishfully like Alberta sipping whisky. This wasn't the first time some old broad had hit on him.

"Before my time," replied Devlin obsequiously, hoping that would hold her.

"You look like you're on the lam," she shot back.

Devlin was stunned. She'd nailed him cold. He might as well have 'fugitive' stamped on his forehead. "What would make you say that?" he laughed feebly.

"That suitcase. Is it just your carry-on? Or is that it?"

"Why, er, carry-on," Devlin was unsure of his ground, "but I travel light. Travel light and right. Or travel light and travel tight. Isn't that what they say? Ha ha." He pressed his knees together trying to obscure the tartan bag full of cash.

"No one travels with a cheap grip like that unless they're moving fast. You must've got caught with your pants down. Seen a lot of cheap bags like that coming into this town. Seen a lot of expensive Italian leather suitcases going out. Except the ones who get caught. They go out in the back of a sheriff's van. Looks to me like you packed up and left quick. Couldn't wait for the bus so you took a plane."

The jet whined in lower.

Devlin puffed himself up. "Madam I don't know what you're implying but . . . "

She held up the flat of her hand. "No matter. She stretched out her hand in greeting. To Devlin it looked like shark cartilage covered with turkey skin. "Dilt. Gloris Dilt. Didn't mean to be rude. You talk funny. Where're you from, Ireland?"

"God no. Canada."

"Jesus we get a lot of Canadian weather down here. Canadian fronts. Canadian cold air masses. Do you people ever warm up?" she smiled, rattled her glass and patted his knee.

Devlin silently bewailed this development.

"I fly right through it." she carried on. "Fly everywhere. Have since the early days. I work for STAT. Short for United States Statutes at Large. Who do you work for?"

"I am self-employed," said Devlin with as much credibility as he could muster.

"Well, you might think I'm old but they still need me. I'm a national resource. Know every law and statute Congress ever made. In the early days they used to fly me out because some of our less co-operative states were slow in enacting certain Federal laws. You probably could name them yourself. So I fly out and personally make them do it. Lots of old ex-Governors still want to shoot me, sweetie." She rattled her cubes again.

Just then the soft and enigmatic *bing, bing, bing, bing, bing* floated through the jet's intercom.

"Never heard that on a DC 3," remarked Gloris Dilt. "Nothing but little round windows. Big steaks. Whiskey. And power." Then she paused, "Am I talking too much? I'm sorry. Excuse me," she leaned across and patted Devlin's knee again, "I adore quiet men."

She was right. For once Red Devlin *was* quiet. He looked down balefully at the thin white little plain end cigarette sitting in his lap as the jet whined through the cold Canadian air over Washington.

She smiled again and winked.

That wink made Red Devlin decide to be circumspect in his dealings with Gloris Dilt. She knew too much about laws and statutes. Who knew what American laws he'd be breaking in the days ahead? She still had a powerful streak of man-hunger coursing through her too. Blue-veined lightening at seventy-five years. Why were so many older women walking about in a horny funk these days? Didn't they just *run down*? Hadn''t he read that somewhere? And why did he attract them like blue bottle flies? Troubles upon troubles.

"So, Mr. Self-Employed," Gloris Dilt's rasp whined out like a fishing reel. "What line of work did you say you were in?"

"Real estate," Devlin said shortly. He did his best to look preoccupied. This was hard. There was nothing else to preoccupy him except the unlit Pall Mall rolling around in his crotch.

"Been my experience that you self-employed types need decent digs at a good price. Especially a man like you - traveling light. I've got a townhouse in Georgetown. Take in boarders when I want.

Big bedroom. Office with a view and phone. Even a library. All the privacy you want. Meals too. And cheap."

This appealed to Devlin's judicious side. He had to accomplish a lot with very little money. Paying a fat bill to an acquisitive Washington hotel every week was heavy on his mind. So was sitting in an expensive and empty Washington apartment. Yet now he saw visions of Gloris Dilt with a whiskey glass in one hand chasing him round the townhouse like he was some elderly male bimbo while she hurt herself on the sharp bits of furniture. The prospect was still too good to pass up.

He turned. "Privacy, you say?" he raised his eyebrows.

"I'm a busy woman. You won't see me. Unless, of course, you want to," she added with a wink. That winking again. Why did older women persist in winking at him? It was terrible.

"Well I'm a busy man," he emphasized. "Very busy and very private. It's hard to say which describes me more, busy or private."

"Then we've got a deal," Gloris stuck out a bony hand. Red Devlin shook it then withdrew his hand quickly.

"Of course, I'll still have to buy sweaters and an overcoat," mused Devlin, looking for a little negotiating room. "Can't bear chilly rooms."

"Just got state of the art heat and air conditioning last year but you go ahead if it suits you. Nothing worse than chilly rooms. What did you say your name was again?"

"Devlin. As in Red Devlin."

By answering that question, Red Devlin made a bad tactical error. He traded cheap accommodation for a crippling lack of privacy from one of Washington's premier dowager scrutinizers. In his divine mission to sell the White House he would shoulder a second cross. This was answering Gloris Dilt's endless questions until the jet finally touched down. It wasn't so much in the way of an organized cross-examination, where the questioner has a destination in mind, and where the answer to one question aids the questioner in narrowing the focus on the next. No. The Dilt

Method was more open-ended, like broad beam radar scouring land and sea for any clue of data.

She repeated his name, as if chewing on the information.

Nodding in a courtly manner he repeated it: "Yes, Devlin. As in Red Devlin.

"Red Devlin, realtor. And what kind of a name is that?"

"Scottish," Devlin said nervously.

"And from where?"

Devin's mouth was dry. "Br'ish Coumbia."

"Again please."

"*Bird*-ish Columbia," he emphasized in his West Coast patois.

"Ah. You mean *Brit*-ish Columbia. In Canada, you say?"

"Yes."

"Born and raised?"

"Totally."

"What happened next?"

"Business school.'

"After that?"

"Dropped out to support my family."

'And then?"

Devlin sighed. He could see a trend emerging here. He had hoped that the brevity of his answers might cause Gloris Dilt to lose the scent of the information trail, since he was only revealing tiny bits of information. Nevertheless she seemed perfectly happy to ingest the tidbits one at a time, like a feeding crab. In fact, she seemed to enjoy it. She fell into a hypnotic rhythm of questions, which advanced Devlin''s life story by agonizingly small increments.

"I got a job selling."

"Selling what?"

"Encyclopedia."

"Britannica?"

"World Book."

Devlin wished she would ask broader, more philosophical questions that would allow him to pontificate and digress. Either that or something more specific that he could get his teeth into and divert her from the true chronological path, since pretty soon he was going to have to start lying. Yet perversely, it was in his interest to play his life out to Gloris Dilt in these micro-sized pieces. When the DC 9's tires barked on the tarmac he was at the stage where his wife had left him and taken the kids because of his real estate shenanigans. By then he felt like he had been married to Gloris Dilt for forty years.

Some people arrive for the first time in Washington, DC with either a sense of purpose, or of wonder, or both. Red Devlin stepped into the Washington National Airport concourse feeling like a whitebread weevil about to secretly eat out the heart of America. Which he was. Each nerve in his body was a tiny paranoid radar dish, jangling and sensitive to the most obscure stimuli. Every fiber of his realtor's being told him to get into Washington and get out. Fast.

"Hope you're not carrying cash in that thing," Gloris poked her nose in the direction of the tartan bag as they passed a security guard. "Anything ten thousand dollars or over and you're supposed to fill out Form 4790. Declare every cent. Same with electronic transfer. Send anything over ten thousand dollars either way across and the bank has to fill out Form 4789. Tough rap too. They catch you right now with cash and with no Form 4790 they can seize the money."

"Really?" asked Devlin matter-of-factly, feigning academic interest.

"Five hundred thousand dollar penalty. And five years in jail. They only do spot checks for it now. Foreign and domestic. Departures and arrivals. It's the coming thing. Money laundering. The profile is what they look for."

Devlin said nothing but his eyes bulged like a hunted stag. They approached two plainclothes airport dicks with radios, who were giving Devlin's tartan bag a hard look. Devlin sucked in his stomach to improve his profile. The security men stepped out and approached.

"Hello boys," said Gloris Dilt, neatly stepping in front of Devlin.

"Mrs. Dilt," said one. "Didn't see you there. Where you in from?"

"Seattle. Got a new boarder in the bargain too. Meet Mr. Devlin. Realtor."

"This guy's with *you*?" asked the other.

"Sure is. Say, I don't suppose you boys could help out an old lady and a new man? These cab line-ups are murder. How about you show us through to the VIP stand?"

The two airport dicks fell over themselves to accommodate. "That Mrs. Dilt," said one as he fell into step beside Devlin. "She's a real regular. And she's still got a lot of juice."

"Juice?" Devlin feared the worst. He hoped he didn't mean eye-winking knee-patting juice.

"Influence, man. Power. She knows what's in everybody's closet. Every skin and bone. Mind like a steel trap. Don't cross her. Nossir."

"And how would a fellow cross her?" Devlin tugged at his coat sleeve cuffs. "You know, in which way."

"Business I guess. But," the man dropped back half a pace, "I hear it's sex, man." He shook his head as if Gloris Dilt's appetite was the bane of Washington, DC, something to be endured and fed but never cured.

Devlin did his best to recover his sangfroid as the limo drove through Washington and the cold Canadian front. The tires were silent through the new snow. Still it was tough, since Gloris Dilt was nibbling on information again by asking more questions.

Devlin gave the one-word answers she seemed to savor like pop-corn chicken. While doing so he managed a glimpse through the tinted windows of the limousine. He was secretly thrilled to be on the very streets the genius Pierre L'Enfant had laid out almost exactly two hundred years ago in his brilliant but fatally flawed plan.

What he saw was a grand, expansive, deliberate city, filled with imperial architecture. The Americans had done a hell of a lot of work down here in the last two hundred years. They made it look and feel like what it was - the most powerful city on earth.

Jesus they're going to be pissed when I pull this off, Devlin shuddered.

Gloris Dilt paid the limo driver and had him bear all bags into the house. Although it was dark and he was tired, Devlin was amazed at the structure. The brick Victorian townhouse was on a corner lot, so looked twice as big as its neighbors. Her three-story turreted tower commanded the intersection. Through the flakes of swirling snow it seemed to twist upward like an ancient cedar. Charming.

"It's not designated heritage if that's what you're wondering." Gloris Dilt seemed to read his mind. "Oh, those wimps at the Pennsylvania Avenue Development Corporation tried to make it heritage. I stopped 'em cold. The joint's all mine and worth a mint. Your room's in the tower, honey. Follow me."

Again Devlin became cautious. Towers could be locked. People could be imprisoned in them. They had been. Damsels in distress. He'd read about how they had to grow their hair into long braids before they got out. For a fleeting moment he had a vision of him-self locked in some upper tower room desperately trying to grow his hair into long frazzled ginger-and-grey braids like Rapunzel. Gloris Dilt would be outside his locked bedroom door in a negli-gee, hollering at him to declare he would be hers and hers alone.

She took him to the third floor and opened the door to the top level of the tower. "Here's the bedroom. Bathroom off. That stair-well by the window leads down to the office."

DAVID JENNESON

Devlin viewed the digs with a realtor's eye. *Opulent charm.* He had trouble squeezing down the narrow curving stairwell into the office below, but when Gloris clicked on the light he saw it was worth the effort. Antique oak desk, wooden filing cabinets, a phone and fax machine. Pen and paper at the ready. There was even an archaic computer, although Red Devlin didn't care. He hated them. On one wall there was a signed black and white photo of Dwight and Mamie Eisenhower stepping off a Lockheed Constellation.. Even Devlin could tell it was no standard White House public relations photograph. It was candid. It had caught them both off-guard. The President had a brooding, concerned expression and Mamie was whispering something in his ear. In its own way it was intimate. Whoever had taken it had somehow managed to get it signed by the President and First Lady.

"Stairwell leads down to the study. My ex-ex-ex loved this office," said Gloris. "So did my ex-ex and my ex."

"Eh," asked Devlin, not understanding.

"Buried three husbands in this place. Wore 'em out I guess. So I figured to hell with it and set up the place for borders. Not that I need the money." She named the price. Devlin nearly swooned with joy. The monthly rent was the price of a king-size executive suite at the Jefferson for a single night. Devlin fought to suppress his excitement at this stroke of luck.

"But none of that God damn basement suite stuff here," warned Gloris Dilt.

"How's that?" asked Devlin innocently.

"You have use of the kitchen, living room, whatever you want. I'll cook when I have time, or you can fix something for yourself. But keep it clean. I don't want to see underwear hanging off chairs. I do and I'll wrap 'em around your neck and throw you out in the snow."

Devlin took this seriously. He wondered if Gloris Dilt's various ex-husbands had been hung by their own underwear. He didn't fancy being garroted by his black jockey shorts. They were tight enough already.

"You might wonder why I'm being so generous," said Gloris Dilt sweetly. "Fact is, I like a man about the house. That's it. Okay honey, now you get a good sleep," she patted him kindly on the butt. "I sleep upstairs, in the back, in case you were wondering."

This was another statement that made Red Devlin shudder. "I was wondering if I could just kind of sneak downstairs and have a look at the study," he said when he recovered a bit.

"Suit yourself. Rent's in advance. Leave it on the kitchen table."

Devlin crept down the narrow, curving stairwell and into the first floor study at the base of the turret. He clicked on the light and gasped. It was as if he'd stepped into some parallel Red Devlin universe where everything had gone right. Burled walnut walls curved away from the three large windows. Books lined the walls from floor to ceiling on both sides. Before the windows sat an oval desk, with a pair of antique banker's green reading lamps. A vintage sepia globe stood at hand, but sadly, no brandy.

Then Devlin spied the phone. Even that was antique. He eased himself carefully and quietly into an overstuffed leather chair and felt it sigh as it gave way to his tired bulk. Gingerly he picked up the receiver. The ancient device had a dial tone. Whatever God realtors thank, Red Devlin now thanked profusely as he carefully inserted his finger and heard the staccato *ricka-ticka-ticka-ticka-tick* of the rotary dialer in his ear.

DAVID JENNESON

CHAPTER 13

*H*alf an hour's cold dark walk southeast of Devlin's turreted study, across the Rock Creek Parkway, down in Foggy Bottom, Anson Dobell was suffering from Post-Canada-Depression.

His little townhouse was his whole world again, but now it felt like a short blanket. His parents had willed him this place just after they'd bought it in WW II with the last heel of the family fortune. He remembered growing up in Foggy Bottom, which was full of Germans. Italians. Mosquitoes. Irish. Bullies and stinking factories. Who had named it Foggy Bottom? It described his life.

He had more troubling thoughts. That Devlin character. He had vanished at the critical moment like a vampire fleeing the sunrise. Devlin's Open Homes International was obviously working, but Anson now had serious doubts about his own importance to it. He was supposed to be a consultant. He hadn't consulted on anything at all aside from taking a few notes at that hairy Mr. McGregor's dining room table. He could think of no useful purpose he could serve. Devlin's reasons for wanting him had to be suspect. The man wasn't to be trusted. Best to rid himself of Devlin.

In an effort to cheer himself up, Anson imagined that maybe he would take his savings and mount expeditions into Canada on his own, free of realtors. Then maybe he'd find what he was looking for: a chateau grocery store on a mountain top with an Indian maiden for a wife, where the Vista Domes coursed up the river valleys like big silver salmon. He sighed in his bed. Some knuckle of truth in his gut told him it would never happen. He'd never escape this little house. It was hard drifting off to sleep. Perhaps he never would again. He was torn to pieces by his troubles.

Suddenly the phone jangled him out of slumber. It rang many times before he could get out of his bed, point his toes into his slippers and shuffle to the phone.

"Dobell here," he said irritably.

"Anson," whispered the voice. "It's me, Devlin. I'm in town. All set up and established. We must meet."

"I don't think so," sniffed Anson sadly. "I have no part to play in this. I'm of no value to Open Homes International. And I think you should be ashamed for leaving your employees in the lurch like that. They were, by the way, very helpful in getting me back to the airport. So no. Sorry. Call someone else."

There was a choking sound on the other end of the line. "Anson. You must understand your importance. I was called away suddenly. Surely that happens to you sometimes."

"I've never been called away suddenly for anything," Anson replied hollowly.

"Well I was. For business. Money. I apologize. But I'm here now."

"Prove it."

"That I'm here?"

"That's right. You could be anywhere. Canada. Seattle. Even Winnipeg."

"Winnipeg?" Devlin spluttered. "Why would I be in that

DAVID JENNESON

godforsaken place?"

"Exactly my question."

"Why would I lie about being in Washington?"

"Lots of people do."

"How can I prove it over the phone?"

"I'm going to hang up."

"NO! I mean please, no. Anson, how about this? We'll meet tomorrow and I'll show you *exactly* how important you are to Open Homes International. And if you don't like it, I'll give you $10,000 in cash. In *Canadian funds*. That means you can fly back to Canada at any time and spend it to your heart's desire. Works like a golden maple syrup up there. Canadians love Canadian money."

An image flashed across Anson's mind: himself, flush with Canadian funds, taking a free trip into the green and blue mountains to find his dream.

"Dinner's on me," added Devlin. "Anywhere you want."

A second image flashed across Anson's mind. Not some fancy restaurant, but his own kitchen, once again brimming with all of his favorite foods and delicacies. He could force Devlin to stock him up. He never imagined himself such a wily negotiator. Imagine $10,000 in Canadian funds plus all his favorite foods just for meeting with a realtor.

"If this meeting is so important then we should have it here," declared the famished Anson. "We'll make it ourselves. Dinner, I mean. Here. I'll give you a list." He heard the bedeviled Devlin fumbling around for a pen and pad. With that, Anson reeled off all of his favorite foods like a sleepy child on the line to Santa Claus. Devlin scribbled, cursing the 1924 vintage fountain pen he'd plucked from the desk, which was leaking genuine 1924 ink. The list grew.

"Hold on," Devlin cried, "I need more paper."

Anson paused, got his breath, then went on for another minute or so.

"That's it?" Devlin concealed his vexation. "Right, I'll see you tomorrow at seven."

"Aren't you forgetting something?" asked Anson peevishly.

Devlin sighed. What did Anson want now? A kiss goodnight? "Forgetting what?"

"My address. Don't you want my address?"

"Or course I want your address, Anson," he said soothingly. "How forgetful of me."

"2410 M Street. Take 19th down from Dupont Circle and turn left. There I am!"

"Thank you for such clear directions. We'll see you tomorrow. Good-bye now." Devlin sighed and placed the black Lucite receiver in its cradle. He sat back and sighed like he was never so happy to get off the line in his life. He peered about the dim study, looking for a humidor full of one of Gloris Dilt's dead husband's cigars. There was a tiny noise by the door. Or was there? He became alert. Nothing. He shook his head. Probably just overtired. He took the list and marched up the spiral stairs toward his assigned room. He flopped down spread-eagled. Then he thought better of it and turned on his side so he wouldn't snore. Snoring might rattle the panes and make Gloris Dilt strangle him with his own tight black underwear.

*   *   *

Devlin got up early and showered in his little private bathroom. He found his way downstairs to the kitchen and poked a hopeful finger on the button of the coffee maker. Sure enough, it was primed and began to hiss coffee straightaway. Gloris Dilt's kitchen looked like the cover photo of a 1948 issue of Modern Homes, but it was all new to Devlin. He was nosing about here and there when a voice from behind startled him.

"Hi honey," Gloris Dilt winked. "Coffee on the run for me, but we'll talk later," she dashed out the front door.

Devlin gulped his breakfast and coffee, grabbed his tartan bag, stuck a Pall Mall in the corner of his mouth and struck a match. Then he hailed a cab. The first stop was the nearest bank machine. Here he said a little prayer, punched in his numbers and after an intolerable delay of whirrings and beepings, watched a thousand dollars of American money flop into the tray.

When Devlin stepped out of the cab he was surprised to see people ice skating in front of the National Archives building. They ought to have more respect for America's national filing cabinet, he thought. He certainly did. As he approached the shimmering white marble structure and climbed the stairs toward the marching rows of Corinthian columns he saw the letters carved in stone: ARCHIVES OF THE UNITED STATES OF AMERICA.

To Devlin this seemed inaccurate. If it were up to him he would replace it with: POSSESSION IS NINE-TENTHS OF THE LAW, which was in his mind nearer the mark. These capricious thoughts vanished as he passed through the six and half ton bronze doors. *Christ. These people are anal about record keeping.*

Devlin now did his best to appear the awestruck tourist. He climbed the stairs inside to the rotunda and peeped into the helium-filled glass and bronze cases. Yup, there they were, the pillars of American democracy on paper: the Declaration of Independence, the Constitution, the Bill of Rights, the Charters of Freedom, through the layers of laminated glass. All in an eerie, green-tinted light created by the helium gas. Devlin stood before them briefly, his tartan suitcase clutched in front of him with both hands, like a peasant at a roadside shrine.

Devlin was impressed but not satisfied. All the laws ever enacted by Congress were here. All Federal Government legal papers. A billion official documents were housed in this joint, even the embarrassing ones like Gerald Ford's pardon of Richard Nixon. Devlin figured the government ought to put a few more of the good ones out here on display, especially the ones an enterprising realtor might be interested in viewing. After all, realtors were people too. They had interests. Realtors were even tourists sometimes. Besides, he just wanted an innocent peek at the fine print of a certain document. He kept searching the displays until he came to a temporary display of political cartoons and knew he had come to the end of the line.

Jeesus, a guy has to do everything around here himself, thought Devlin. His arm was starting to ache from carrying the tartan suitcase, loaded with Canadian money. Even though it had just over half the value of American money it was still heavy. He worked his way back to the research rooms of the Genealogy Department. Here dozens of people sat intent, heads bowed, tracing their family histories. Like everything else about the Archives, it was an imposing and splendid room. Devlin was interested in finally seeing this place first hand. The Genealogy Department had been extremely helpful to him over the past few months.

He padded on quietly to the General Research Department. When he saw a big sign that said "Inquiries" he became nervous. At this delicate point he hesitated to alert a government official on any level by asking for any sort of document. He kind of hummed and strolled around in front of the Inquiries Desk for a while. Soon the Archivist could not help but notice him.

Suddenly he stopped in his tracks, as though a thought had just struck him. "Excuse me, but I was wondering if you could help me," he turned to the Archivist behind the desk. "A good friend of mine is dying. He's a little delirious. A Mr. Burnes. He's a realtor. Have you heard of him?"

"No sir," said the Archivist. "Although I'm sorry to hear about him."

Devlin shook his head like a funeral director. "Too late for words. But he keeps crying out to see a certain document as he suffers. God knows why. Last wish. I came here thinking maybe you could help."

"Yes sir," said the archivist. "You just fill out this request form and we'll get right on with the search."

Devlin filled out the form. He was still using the 1924 Waterman fountain pen he had snatched from Gloris Dilt's desk. It still wrote badly. He glanced up and noticed the Archivist's nameplate. Kenneth Batter. He was small, young and keen and in splendid physical condition. Looked like he worked out a lot.

"Kenneth, I've never done a document search before. This is somewhat of an emergency. How long would it take?"

"We'll have it done in two weeks, sir. To the day. I'll put it through right now."

Devlin waved his hands in front of him dismissively. "Kenneth, *Kenneth*. Mr. Burnes may not have till the end of the *day*. He's been very good to me. I don't think he'd object to my donating at least a hundred dollars toward the betterment and well being of the National Archives. Could I just put this through you? Or maybe you could find a use for it yourself," Devlin winked.

Kenneth Batter adjusted his wire-rimmed glasses, looked to the left and right. "Well, my gym fees run out next Tuesday," he said after a thoughtful moment. "It's tough to afford on the salary of an Assistant Archivist."

"Well there you are," said Devlin soothingly. "If you become unhealthy, then the National Archives will suffer too. And there are important government documents pouring through the door every day."

"Like the marching Chinese," agreed Kenneth Batter.

"Well who wants that?" Devlin held out his hands.

"By the end of the day, sir," Kenneth Batter accepted the request form and the donation. "And sir, if you don't mind me saying, you really are a caring person."

"Just a photocopy or any sort of reproduction will do," said Devlin. "My friend Mr. Burnes just wants to lay eyes on it. If he can still see by tonight, poor soul."

"We close at four. By the way sir, if I could ask something?"

Devlin tensed, "Ask away."

"Are you Scottish? You sound Scottish."

"No," Devlin answered sadly, "but Mr. Burnes is."

Red Devlin skipped on gleeful white shoes out of the Research Department of the Archives of the United States of America. He found himself on Pennsylvania Avenue. Standing on the legendary street made him feel as if he was closing in on the White House as indeed he was. He plunked himself down on a bus bench and lit a smoke. The number of limousines whipping up and down Pennsylvania Avenue through the dim winter morning light astounded him. It was like pictures he had seen of Moscow. He looked down at his tartan bag. Must get a new one, he thought. His gut rumbled. He had not eaten enough Northern Italian sausage to see him through. He puffed on his Pall Mall and stamped his feet in the cold. The plumes of smoke and steam he gave off were sucked down Pennsylvania Avenue toward the White House by the wind of passing limousines.

He shivered and pulled out Anson Dobell's hateful list. He stared balefully at the two pages of inky scrawl. Hailed a cab. He slid onto the front seat. The driver smiled broadly at him. He was a big man, wearing a turban and he had a thick black beard. Devlin stuck the list under the cabby's nose.

"Where can I get this stuff?" he asked irritably.

The driver leaned forward and squinted. "Sorry sir. I am reading Asian languages but I am not reading this one. Maybe trying Islamic Center? I take you there?"

"I can read it, for Chrissake. I want to know where to buy it."

"Of course sir. What are we buying?"

Devlin rattled off the first half dozen items.

The driver stroked his thick black beard. "This is tall order. But we shall try. I am Mohan, your driver," he reached across and shook Devlin's hand. "Together we shall succeed, insha'allah."

Mohan eased the cab onto snowy Pennsylvania Avenue and fell in with the ranks of Yellow Cabs and black limousines. He seemed to be driving aimlessly, stroking his beard.

"Are you sure you know where you're going?" asked Devlin, fidgety after a few minutes. He tapped the crystal of his watch.

"I am thinking."

"I'm not paying you to think, I'm paying you to drive."

"I am thinking you should be giving me list," said Mohan as he pulled up in front of a gourmet seafood store.

"I thought you couldn't read it."

"Oh no," he wagged an index finger. "If this is English, I am reading with your help. Then while you are buying I am planning. Thinking ahead," he tapped his skull. Then he brightened. "We are having teamwork."

"Jesus Christ, this is America. Don't they have one place that sells all this stuff?"

"Sir," Mohan placed his hand on his heart, "if they were having, we would be. Now I am needing list. For planning."

"Feh," said Devlin. He knew when he was beaten. He handed it over.

Mohan scanned down the list and whistled. "Hoh boy! You are having big dinner tonight. Making big deal." He winked. "You are making big date?"

"Something like that," muttered Devlin.

Mohan pulled up in front of a high-end deli. "Here we are getting first item," he instructed.

Devlin hopped out. Five minutes later he emerged with an armful of parcels, which he chucked over his shoulder into the back seat. "Okay, where to next?" he asked Mohan.

Mohan turned around. He peered at the pile in the back seat and frowned. "But you are not sticking to list."

"Screw the list. This is fun."

Mohan clicked his tongue and pulled out into traffic.

"Wait a minute," Devlin cried. "Find a gentleman's clothing store first."

Thus Red Devlin began adding his own wish list to Anson Dobell's. Time and again he hollered at Mohan to stop and ran into a store. This distressed Mohan, who stoically promoted adherence to the list. His back seat and trunk were filling up. The rear springs sagged ominously. Mohan weakly waved the list at him.

"Screw the list," said Devlin dismissively, "I'm having fun again for the first time I can remember." Indeed, for Red Devlin this was like being back in The Day when he had money to burn. He stood on the snowy sidewalk and dumped packages through the rear window. "Listen here, Mohan. Time's wasting." He tapped his watch again to emphasize the point. "I've got a better way to do this. Park the cab and you come in too. Then you can help carry. My arms are getting tired." At this Mohan appeared to give up altogether.

At the last stop Devlin dashed into an upscale liquor store. He came out with an armful of clinking bottles, two of them being Alberta Sipping Whiskey. He leapt into the front seat, twisted the top off a bottle and lit a cigar with an air of immense satisfaction.

"Hah! Mission accomplished. Here, have a snort."

"Alas, I cannot," Mohan placed his hand over his heart again. "It is against the religion."

Devlin glanced at his watch. It was only two-thirty. The January snows and strands of lights still up made it feel Christmassy. He had time left. Business of a higher order to attend to. He took another pull of sipping whiskey. "Mohan," he burped, "National Shrine of the Immaculate Conception. Step on it."

Red Devlin adhered to no organized religion. If a client asked if he had a religion, he would say yes, then wait for clues to the client's own. After that he would agree with the client's religious beliefs as much as he could, given his limited knowledge.

Yet on a deeper level Devlin believed in letting minor saints and deities feed at the trough now and again. Not as bribes. As *offerings*. Devlin figured saints were unbribable or they wouldn't be saints. Yet he had a hunch that *offerings* to saints might carry some influence. If saints existed at all, then Devlin was sure it was in some unimaginably distant heavenly head office, where they sat on comfy, cloudy office chairs and made decisions about people like him.

No harm in getting them on side now. Gain some spiritual Air Miles. This deal was his main shot. He needed things to work. He needed the Archives to produce the document he had requested. He needed Anson Dobell to say yes. He needed all the help he could get.

So he brought flowers in a vase. As he stepped into the National Shrine of the Immaculate Conception he was mindful that every American Catholic who had ever lived had personally contributed to this place. He felt watched. He looked up and saw the vast mosaic of Christ in Majesty staring down at him from above. At first he felt like a dissolute, evil bug crawling up the aisle between the rows of pews. Had Moses ever felt like a bug in church? Not bloody likely. He straightened up and made his way proudly toward the looming marble canopy. The scale of everything in Washington was so exaggerated. It took awhile for a man to get his size back.

He quietly attached a note to the vase explaining to Catholic authorities that this was intended for Saint Homobonus, the patron saint of realtors. Devlin knew Saint Homobonus had been a highly successful early Italian businessman who was canonized in 1197. The dude had staying power.

Devlin reached furtively into his pocket and pulled out a fifth of gin. He needed to give this some extra spiritual juice. After spending nine hundred years on Heaven's board of directors, Saint Homobonus might be thirsty. As quietly as he could Devlin drained the water from the flower vase. It made a gentle splashing sound and a puddle spread beside the marble stairs leading up to the alter. It looked like a plough horse had pissed on the floor. Then he poured the gin into the vase and stuffed the flowers back in. He raised his hands prayer-like and bowed from the waist down. Then he backed away; hoping no priest would break his neck himself by stepping in the spreading slippery puddle.

It crossed Devlin's mind he might throw a little extra prayer in to boot. He settled down in a pew. Quietly he formulated the prayer in his mind. The peaceful atmosphere of the Shrine began to soothe him. It was like he was in the most relaxing, mellow lounge in the world. He drifted off, then dropped off. It seemed like only a moment had passed when he awoke and looked up at the stained glass windows. Total darkness outside. He looked at his watch - 3:35 PM. He had fallen asleep and his stinking cheap watch had stopped. The last few days had caught up with him.

"Shit PISS!" he cried, and fought his way between the rows of pews. It crossed his mind that this wasn't the greatest thing to shout in a cathedral, but it had a wonderful echo. Red Devlin fled down the center aisle. "You'd oughta change your religious affiliations, buddy!" shouted a kneeling fat man in a tight suit.

He cut down the snowy cathedral steps. Into the cab. "Archives. ARCHIVES! When do they close? What time is it? Mohan! Why didn't you wake me?"

"I am praying. If you are inside praying then I am praying also outside. Out of respect."

Mohan sped toward the Archives. Devlin dashed in. It was seven o'clock. Deserted. He skidded on wet shoes toward the desk and asked the night receptionist for Kenneth Batter, Assistant Archivist. Gone. Research Department closed. He asked if there was a document left in his name. The bureaucrat shuffled around and drew an envelope out, "Devlin?"

"Yes, yes DEVLIN!" his voice bounced off the walls.

Without another word he grabbed it, stuffed it in his jacket and fled back to the cab, about to perform the greatest sales pitch of his life, an hour late, with a cab full of the most expensive thawing groceries money could buy.

CHAPTER 14

*A*nson Dobell restlessly waited for Devlin. Seated alone in his kitchen he peeled off his comfy slippers revealing a pair of bright red woolly socks. Out of boredom, he tentatively slid one foot back and forth across the highly polished hardwood kitchen floor. The surface was as smooth as polished glass. He stood and found that after a little practice, with a running start, he could slide quite a long way. Right across the floor in fact. Anson puffed on his pipe and slid. He had found something new to do on a lonely night. Sliding made him feel free.

He made himself a cup of instant coffee. He walked through the swinging doors into the dining room and sat down at the table. He tamped down another pipe of aromatic *Amphora* tobacco but soon he became fretful again. This Devlin was playing tricks with his mind. First abandoning him at that wonderful cabaret with its gorgeous dancing naked realtors, and now phoning very late last night, pretending to be in Washington.

It was obvious Devlin had lied about being here in Washington.

Otherwise he would have arrived here over an hour ago, wouldn't he? Anson resolved to have no more dealings with realtors. He was about to switch off all the lights in the Dobell household and retire for another dinner-less night when the doorbell rang.

Anson wondered who this could be. He knew it couldn't be Red Devlin because he did not believe that Devlin was in Washington. Perhaps it was thugs, or home invaders. Had to be. Regular people never rang his doorbell. He crept down the hardwood hallway in his woolly socks and came nervously to a halt at the front door.

"Who is it?"

"Me," answered a muffled voice. "Devlin. Sorry I'm late."

"Prove it," said Anson suspiciously.

"What do you mean prove it?"

"This could be anybody. The streets aren't safe. Prove it."

"How can I do that from here? Who else would I be?"

"You could be anybody. A thug. Ever hear of home invasions?"

"Open the door for God's sake. See for yourself."

"Too dangerous."

"Anson," said Devlin as calmly as he could. "If it's not me then why would I be standing out here with all this food for Chrissake? See for yourself."

The mention of food made Anson more curious and bold. He snicked the chain lock and opened the door a crack. A large flat oblong can poked through.

"See here. Winnipeg Gold Eye. Smoked. Now open the door. I'm freezing out here."

Anson opened the door to reveal a spectacular sight. Red Devlin in a tweed fedora and a vast fur-collared overcoat with a burning cigar in his teeth. His arms were filled with packages. Behind him on the stairs, a bearded man staggered like an overworked bearer beneath a mound of parcels. Devlin swept through the door. Behind him

DAVID JENNESON

the mound of parcels groaned and plodded forward.

"Mohan," Devlin ordered. "That first load goes in the kitchen. Then bring the rest."

"I am not seeing kitchen," said the mound.

"Kitchen?" Anson brightened. "Follow me," he joyfully sped down the hall clutching the Winnipeg Gold Eye. Mohan staggered behind and deposited his burden in the middle of the kitchen floor. It rattled and clinked as he set it down. Devlin tugged off his coat and let it drop on the floor as Mohan coolied in the rest. The pile on the kitchen floor grew ever larger.

"This is much more than I asked for," said an awed Anson.

"Not sticking to list," rebuked Mohan as he labored past beneath another pile.

"Hell, what are friends for?" Devlin clapped Anson on the shoulder and led him into the dining room. He settled into a chair. Its four V-shaped wrought iron legs splayed out beneath his bulk. "I thought we'd have a good old sit-down. Good friends, good food, good drink," he plunked a bottle of sipping whisky on the table. "Sit thee doon, sit thee doon. Aw Christ, don't tell me I forgot ice."

"You are forgetting but I am getting," said Mohan wearily. "Then I am going home and having the mother of all dinners." He trod out.

Anson was like a kid on Christmas morning. Opening one package after another, he would carefully extract the desired item from a bag, inspect it, and then slide it to a spot on the table like he was building a collection.

"Washington is an impressive city," Devlin began conversationally.

"Impressive, but unsafe," Anson replied.

"I drove by the White House today. Now tell me, why is it barricaded up like that? Looks like some hated American compound in the Middle East. Didn't expect it. Shocking in fact."

"People keep attacking it. Flying private airplanes at it. Shooting guns at it. Not to mention 9/11. What's this?" Anson examined a package. "Oysters in leeks and pine nuts. And mussels stuffed with basil." "That'll do for starters. Set 'em down here. Where's Mohan with the ice? Shooting guns at the White House, you say? What on earth for?"

"Mad at the government, I suppose. Everyone seems to be these days."

"But why do they pick on the White House?"

"Symbol I guess."

"Well it must be a helluva symbol if people are shooting at it. Pass those down here." Devlin bit into a ripe red cherry. "Maybe America needs a new symbol. Maybe after two hundred odd years there's been too much water under the bridge here in Washington. Americans are fed up to the teeth. In fact, maybe a new symbol is exactly what America needs."

Anson thought about this and chewed contemplatively on a cherry. "A new symbol? It's a possibility."

"I agree with you," said Devlin quickly. "America needs a rebirth. A battery recharge. You've seen what Open Homes International can do in Canada. Imagine the power it will have to renew America." He spat his cherry pit into the ashtray with a ping. The doorbell rang. Anson raced off to get it.

"I want nothing to do with Open Homes International," he cried over his shoulder as he disappeared down the hallway. "There's no part in it for someone like me."

Devlin became alarmed. He ran after him. "No! You're wrong! You're more important than you ever dreamed. You must listen."

A bedraggled, wan Mohan stood at the door with several bags of ice. "Finding ice in winter is not so easy," he said miserably. "Ice is everywhere," he nodded his head at the snow on the ground, "so no one is selling."

Devlin lapped off a few bills from his roll of hundreds. "Here. Go buy yourself a dinner. You've earned it."

Mohan looked down at the money and placed his hand on his chest. "I am thanking from heart. Salaam alakum." He handed Devlin his card, bowed deeply and was gone.

Devlin grabbed the ice and hurried after Anson as he raced back down the hall toward the kitchen.

"Sit still for a minute," Devlin cried. "Here," he dumped ice into two tumblers and sluiced large tots of whisky into them. "Try this stuff. A fine aftertaste with brie and grapes and a pipe of your favorite tobacco. I don't care what order you have them in. Just stay put."

Anson settled warily into the chair as Devlin reached into his tartan bag.

"The reason it seems like you have no part in Open Homes International," began Devlin, "is that you're too important to worry about such details. I'll be taking care of them myself. Starting tomorrow. You have more important work to do."

While Devlin fumbled in the tartan bag Anson slipped out of his chair and scurried into the kitchen for another package. Devlin cleared his throat. He pulled out what appeared to be an old document box but left it closed.

"How long have you lived here?"

"Since I was born."

"Parents?"

"They lived here."

"And grandparents?"

"Lived in Washington, but not in this house."

"And *their* parents?"

"Them too. I've always wondered about that. I think at some point one part of the family migrated west. Pacific Northwest maybe. Another part stayed here in Washington, but I've always wondered how far back we go. I'm afraid I've lost track."

"You can stop wondering. I've got proof here that the Dobell family goes back to the 1750's in this area. Since before the Revolution. Since before it was Washington, DC."

"Really?" Anson sounded thrilled. His heart swelled with pride. "I've always felt like I had Washington blue blood in my veins but nothing like this."

Devlin nodded in affirmation.

Suddenly Anson became suspicious. "How do you know all this?"

"I had it traced in the genealogy department of National Archives several months ago. They are really very thorough. See here. The papers."

Anson puffed on his pipe. "I've never seen genealogy traced before," he said after a moment, "but it looks official."

"All the way back to Dobson Dobell, resident and minor land-owner in a place called Beall's Levels," Devlin confirmed.

"Good heavens," said Anson. "My full name is Anson Beall Dobell.

"Well there you go," Devlin wiped cigar juice from his lips.

"This is certainly appreciated," said Anson. "But why have you gone to so much trouble? What does this have to do with Open Homes International?"

"Open Homes International is real estate. Correct?"

"It seems so."

"Then I'm going to tell you a story. A real estate story. Your Congress voted to build Washington, DC on the Potomac in 1789. When George Washington came down here in 1791 to start construction, do you think he bothered to see who owned the land first? Nooo. He started surveying and cutting down trees right off the bat. In fact, there was supposed to be a ceremony to lay the first stone marker that was to be the beginning and heart of the city. George Washington laid the marker and had the ceremony all right. But it was a *secret* ceremony."

"That sounds un-American," Anson frowned.

"Maybe so, but here's the father of your country, acting like some common..."

"Realtor?" Anson volunteered.

"I suppose that's one way to put it," huffed Devlin. "Only after he started hacking and cutting did George Washington appoint three commissioners to find the owners of the land. In the meantime he hired an insane genius, the French architect Major Pierre L'Enfant."

At this Devlin bowed his head and raised his glass. "To Major L'Enfant." he said. Anson did likewise. "L'Enfant designed the plans," Devlin continued after a moment's silence. "Problem was, George assumed that the Commissioners were giving instructions to L'Enfant while the Commissioners assumed George was. So here we have the founding of government mismanagement in America." He raised his glass again.

Anson frowned and pouted. He poked petulantly at the aromatic tobacco in his pipe.

"Present company excluded of course," added Devlin quickly. "Always a few good apples in the barrel. And in some cases," he winked, "bound for great things."

This seemed to restore Anson's spirits. He became thoughtful. "I can't believe George Washington would mismanage anything."

"Not his fault. He was just too busy. Poor man was off founding cities and towns all over the country. Didn't matter anyway. It was L'Enfant's nature to ignore all instructions. It's the way of geniuses. L'Enfant got his great vision for Washington DC's design stuck in his mind like a chicken bone. That was when the trouble started."

"There was trouble?" Anson leaned forward.

"Hell yes, there was trouble. George was called away to go and found something else. Maybe a railroad or a stock exchange, I forget which. In the meantime he told his Commissioners to get ahold of the tobacco farmers who owned the land Washington DC was going to be built on and make a deal. When the Commissioners finally located the landowners, they told them The Father of the Country needed their land to build the capitol of America. The landowners were getting rich from growing tobacco. They thought about the offer. Considered it on a patriotic level you might say. Then they told the Commissioners what they could do with the capitol city of America."

"And what was that?"

"The founding middle finger," Devlin guzzled an oyster. "God these are good. Have one. I stopped at the Found Fathers' Oyster Bar - these are the specialty of the house." He thrust the plate forward. An oyster on its half shell slid off the plate toward Anson's lap. Anson caught the shell in both hands.

"Oh bravo!" Devlin took another swallow of whiskey. "Good catch."

Anson gulped the oyster down.

Red Devlin was on a roll. "Now there's a perfect example. That oyster came flying off the table at you out of nowhere and bingo! You caught it. *You* were successful. Poor busy George Washington tried to catch the critical situation with the nation's capital and those landowners at the last minute. He wasn't successful."

Anson frowned at this and shot off into the kitchen to rummage through the grocery pile. "According to you George Washington couldn't do *anything* right," he called back.

Devlin found this aggravating. It seemed each time this man took issue with something he shot off into the kitchen to look for more goodies. Devlin peeked over the swinging doors. There was Anson sliding around the table in his woolly red socks looking for a tempting package. He shook his head. He realized he would have to watch every single word he said, or soon he would not be able to establish eye contact with Anson over the growing pile of food in the middle of the table. Anson returned with smoked chicken. Devlin regarded this package with passing interest. Momentarily he wondered if there was such a thing as smoked bologna, and what it would taste like once you had fried it up.

"You must remember George Washington was terribly over-worked," soothed Devlin. "Every country can have only one founder. The man had to do practically everything himself, otherwise he wouldn't be called the founder. That's the way it was with George. In my view his strategy was first rate. He gathered the landowners at a place called Sutter's Tavern. I believe there's now a plaque marking the spot somewhere in downtown Washington. George opened negotiations with a round of ale. Then more ale. Then Madeira. Then port wine. Soon he had the landowners drinking out of the palm of his hand. It was here that George Washington, the father of your country, made what is in my humble opinion the greatest real estate deal since the pharaohs did the groundbreaking promo for the pyramids. Everyone staggered home happy."

"So he got it right after all," Anson said smugly. He popped a stuffed mushroom into his mouth as if it were a period at the end of a sentence.

Devlin had to pick his words for fear Anson would go skating off for more provisions. "Sadly, no. Such is the fickleness of clients. When the landowners sobered up the next day they realized they'd been diddled. So when the Commissioners showed up to sign the deal, the landowners told them again what they could do with the capitol city of America."

"Which was?" Anson frowned.

"To go fuck themselves, I'm afraid," said Devlin sadly.

"That doesn't make sense at all," argued Anson. "How could anyone go back on their personal word with the President of the United States? Especially the *very first President?*"

"Because George Washington got them so drunk they agreed to sell their land for a criminally low price."

"How much?"

"Sixty-six dollars an acre."

"What's wrong with that?"

"The only payment was for land that would actually have a building sitting on it. The rest of the land - eighty-percent - streets, plazas, parks, monuments and so on to be sold at no charge. Free. Absolutely brilliant." Devlin raised his glass. "To George Washington, the father of American realtors."

Anson did the same, like he actually need a stiff drink by now. He seemed troubled by this news. George Washington, the father of the country, a *realtor*.

Devlin tossed ice in the tumblers and poured big refills as he continued. "It got worse. George was finally forced to meet them again at Sutter's Tavern. This time he tried a different tack. Took the high road. Fixed them with that arresting presidential stare. For the landowners it must've been like having Mount Rushmore pissed at you. Still didn't work. Finally George sweetened the pie. Gave them a cut of the sale of commercial property plus timber rights. They all signed except one. David Burnes. He is recorded as owning Beall's Levels, where the White House now stands. He and George left hurling abuse at each other."

"Beall's Levels again," nodded Anson.

"Exactly."

Anson paused, about to bite into a slurpy pear. "Appalling. Poor George Washington was only trying to found America's capitol and what did he get for it? Abuse."

"Heartaches," echoed Devlin, "and his suffering went on. He ordered L'Enfant to redesign Washington excluding David Burne's land, but did L'Enfant follow his orders? Nope. Then the landowners demanded to see L'Enfant's design. L'Enfant refused that too. The man lived in a world of his own. Finally George Washington personally forced L'Enfant to reveal his design. Big mistake. The landowners were floored when they saw L'Enfant only planned to put buildings on five hundred acres. The rest, three thousand acres, were for parks and plazas. And by their agreement, free land. Yet through some miracle George Washington kept the deal from going sideways."

"Sideways?"

"Deals go sideways. Deals go south. Same diff," Devlin took another swallow. "While all this is going on L'Enfant tears down someone's mansion. It was in the way of his planned route for New Jersey Avenue. Turned out to be the mansion of one of the Commissioner's uncles."

"Good God."

"George Washington paid for the damage but he was running short on cash. He decided to sell some of the lots to the public but L'Enfant was opposed. L'Enfant again refused to provide the maps. So George shit-canned him."

"So that was the end of him," Anson seemed relieved.

"Hell no. It didn't bother L'Enfant. He immediately found work designing and building a mansion for a very wealthy man in Pennsylvania. The man ended up in debtor's prison paying for it."

"So what happened with the tobacco farmer? David Burnes? Did he ever sign?"

Devlin sat back and lit a cigar. "We're not sure," he said slowly. "Some say he did. Some say he didn't. I believe he did. Doesn't matter anyway."

"It most certainly does," Anson raised his chin defiantly. "If Burnes didn't sign, the White House would be sitting on private property."

"It is."

Anson swooned. The heady mixture of real estate, sipping whisky and White Houses sitting on private property was getting too stratospheric. He seemed engulfed.

"Hold on, are you all right?" Devlin reached out. "You look pale. Take a bit of whisky. Here. Steadies the nerves."

"I can't imagine George Washington making such an oversight. It's beyond belief."

"No, no George Washington was right on the money. He nailed

the deal down tight. But why do you think David Burnes held out? Makes no sense after Washington sweetened the pot. Burnes must have known he was going to get rich from it. Why not just sign and get on with it?"

"Maybe he wanted more money?" suggested Anson hopefully. Where Devlin seemed to have all the answers, his bureaucratic mind was desperately trying to make sense of this mess, which seemed to be getting worse with each passing minute.

"No. David Burnes didn't own *all* of Beall's Levels. He was negotiating to buy it from your ancestor, Dobson Dobell. See here." Devlin opened the battered wooden storage box. "I spend my holidays in Seattle every year. Rummage through auctions and the second-hand stores around Pike Street Market.

One day I found this box full of old papers and real estate documents at an estate sale. I've studied American real estate. Got my Washington and California State realtor's licenses. So these old papers were of interest. I bought the whole lot for a few bucks and I went to a Chinese restaurant and sorted through them. It appeared to be some sort of unfinished transaction. Here. I'll show you. But be careful. They're fragile."

Devlin cautiously withdrew the documents and explained the meaning of each one to Anson, who was by now both alarmed and transfixed. "The deal between Dobson Dobell and David Burnes was never signed," Devlin concluded. "They were breathing hard but they weren't dancing. So David Burnes sold land he didn't own. These documents prove it."

"No ancestor of mine in his right mind would allow that to happen." Anson smacked his palm on the table.

Devlin privately questioned that any Dobell, living or dead, was in his right mind. He drew on his cigar. "I figure Dobson Dobell was holding out. His acres were lumped in with the two hundred and twenty-five that Burnes owned. Burnes wouldn''t have mentioned it to George Washington, as it would have weakened his position. I figure Dobson Dobell had a plan of his own. He was going to let the sale go through, then hold the government to ransom for his

DAVID JENNESON

little bit, which is where the White House sits. Get ten times the value. Very sharp. Exactly what I would've done."

Anson gingerly took a sip of his whiskey. He seemed stunned and angry. "Why didn't he follow through? All these years the Dobells have been scraping by when we could have been...."

"Rich?" Devlin filled in the blank.

"Like owning a gold mine," said Anson.

"No, like owning a diamond mine," Devlin snorted as he sifted through the Dobell genealogy report. "But see here. According to the National Archives, Dobson Dobell was killed in a canal boat accident on June 28, 1791. That's the day Burnes signed. Shit. Maybe it was no accident. Maybe he was pushed. I never thought of that. Dobson had other small holdings, which his family was able to live off. The Beall's Levels land must have been his little secret. Maybe he had a mistress."

Anson's face fell. Devlin bit his tongue. He'd said the wrong thing again. The mention of an unfaithful, womanizing Dobell ancestor was enough to send Anson shooting off into the kitchen and burrowing into the groceries again. Devlin cursed his big mouth. *Dang.* He tried to recover. "Or maybe he was thinking about his descendants. Maybe he was thinking about *you.*"

It was too late. The spell had been broken. "Why should I believe any of this?" Anson returned with dessert, a pathetic little squashed cheesecake. "You could be making it up. You've gone to all this work. What's in it for you?"

"You have a legitimate claim on the White House. You own it. All we have to do is get a deed drawn up. Then you can list it. And I can sell it."

"*Sell* the White House?"

"Yes," Devlin said passionately. "With me. God gave me this talent. He *made* me the greatest realtor in history. I've known it since the day I was born. I'm getting on in years. My health isn't what it should be. I know in my bones that if I don't do this now, God will be very angry with me when I die. Imagine if Moses had left the Israelites stuck in the middle of the desert? Same thing. How would you like to be in my position?"

"I wouldn't," Anson admitted. "At all."

"God will say, *'Red Devlin, I gave you more talent than a hundred realtors. I made you the greatest realtor in a thousand years. What have you done with your talent?'*"

Anson gulped.

"I don't want Saint Peter nudging God and shaking his head," Devlin drew his finger across his throat. "I don't want him reaching for that lever to pull that trap door. I want to be able to say, 'God, your honor, I took the great talent you gave me as a realtor and with the help of my good friend Anson Dobell I did the biggest deal in history. I sold the White House. Because the White House needed to be sold. Because it was time. Because it was good for America.' Then I'll look Saint Peter in the eye and say *beat that.* Then I'll tell them both they'd better send out the red carpet for dry cleaning because sooner or later my good friend Anson Dobell will be showing up. *And he's coming in first class.*"

Anson was deeply moved. "Are you saying I'll get..."?

"Into heaven? Hell yes. With that kind of testimonial they can't say no," Devlin reached across and patted Anson's hand.

The bead of a tear formed in the corner of Anson's eye.

"*And* while you're here on this earth you'll get your asking price for the White House. That I guarantee. And it will be substantial. And you'll be doing a great thing for America. You said yourself America needs a new symbol. The White House is worn out as a symbol. People shoot at it. Fly airplanes at it. What more proof do you need?"

"There's one more thing."

"Name it."

"I want that store. To own it."

"Which store?"

DAVID JENNESON

"That little store where you went to buy cigarettes. The one with all the seafood specials. I want it thrown in."

Devlin winced at the thought of the murdered grocer Sheng. He'd been trying to put that ugly unfinished business out of his mind. *Real estate is a four-letter word.*

"Done," he looked Anson in the eye.

Anson still seemed to have cold feet. "Do we actually have to sell The White House right away? Couldn't we just sort of own it for a while first?"

"Anson, I'll tell you what we can do. We can give America the chance to get a new symbol; one they won't take potshots at. And who will they have to thank? Not me. I'm just the lowly agent. No. It'll be you. The owner. The only one with the courage to lead the nation through the next American century."

Devlin figured Anson was starting to truly believe his moment had come, but then his bureaucratic mind snapped back like a rubber band. "I'm sorry, but this will never work. By now the United States Government will have the White House property signed, sealed and delivered. I know. I've worked for them for thirty years. They'll have every kind of paperwork you can imagine proving they own the White House ten times over."

"All that really matters in real estate," said Devlin, slipping an envelope from his jacket pocket, "is the deed. I stopped by the National Archives this afternoon. I have a copy of the White House deed here. It must be an ancient document; full of loop-holes so big you can drive a truck through them. I'll bet in ten minutes we can find something in it that opens doors for us."

"I don't believe it," said Anson Dobell. He was a lifelong bureau-crat. "For documents as important as this, they leave nothing to chance. I guarantee you the deed for the White House is rock solid. Tighter than a drum."

"Tighter than a bull's ass at fly season, huh?"

"Tighter."

"You have a legal claim to the goddam property. Aren't you even interested in seeing how they stole it from you?"

Anson admitted he was. He lit his pipe thoughtfully and stood over Devlin as he pulled the copy of the deed from the envelope.

"What? Shit! This is no deed!" cried Devlin. "Goddammit, this is nothing but a stinking letter." They read it together:

> Dear Mr. Devlin
>
> This is in reply to your January 29 request for a copy of the deed to the White House.
>
> We examined the records of the Office of Public Buildings and Public Grounds and the record of the Government of the District of Columbia but could not locate a deed for the White House.
>
> Sincerely,
>
> Kenneth Batter, Archivist
>
> Archives I Reference Branch

So it was that finally the Dobell household rang with shouts and laughter, as Red Devlin and Anson Dobell danced arm in arm around the dining room table in the snowy Foggy Bottom night.

DAVID JENNESON

CHAPTER 15

$\mathcal{M}$oney had never come easily to Ray Seawee. When it came at all it has usually been from someone else's wallet.

The morning of Red Devlin's hasty departure for Washington, Seawee sat in his bed and stared at his ten thousand-dollar check for a good long while. He had never seen so many zeroes next to his name in his life. The harder he stared at them the more they shimmered and vibrated, as if wanting to multiply themselves further.

He tried to keep Devlin's complex list of instructions clear in his head. So many things to remember. Devlin had said to be businesslike. Waste no money. Keep all ducks in a row. To act professional, the way a Director for Open Homes International ought to act. He had even touched on commissions, hadn't he? Seawee wished he had written it down. He wondered what he should do first. He lit a cigarette and studied the check harder, hoping all those zeroes would add up to an answer.

They did. He had an inspiration. He hoped it was as powerful as the inspirations Red Devlin had. Ray Seawee gathered up his things, called a taxi and decamped to The Carriage House.

He walked through the main front doors. In the lobby sat the Carriage House namesake - a strange looking carriage. Yet it did not look like any carriage Seawee had ever seen. It wasn't. In truth it was a dull workaday artifact, a dusty Ford rural postal wagon from the 1890's. On either side of the white postal wagon, curving staircases with wrought-iron railings swept up to the second floor mezzanine balcony. Off the balcony, to the right, were hidden the lounge and restaurant.

From the mezzanine, customers who had dined in the restaurant could hang over the rail. From there they could view the goings-on in the lobby below - usually less than nothing. No one in his right mind except a businessman on a cheap expense account had any good reason to stay at the Carriage House in January. Occasionally a party of poorly informed tourists blundered in. There were three features: an empty swimming pool, complimentary indigestion, and of course the Carriage House bar with its peelers, tobacco smoke, noise and Neanderthal audience. Normal people stayed one night and fled.

One bright note was the round yellow illuminated Carriage House sign at the entrance to the parking lot. It hadn't changed in thirty years. In red letters it cheerfully promised things that no longer existed, like fine dining, live music and dancing. Tall prison yard lights stood on poles and bathed the parking lot in harsh, wet light. Everything was usually dripping with rain.

Nevertheless, it was a leg up on Seawee's last two addresses. First, it beat prison. Second, it beat the rooming house where he had previously lodged. That had been nothing more than a home for aging alcoholics and a layover for ragged Australian drifters who were heading that way themselves.

Although Devlin had not instructed Seawee to move to the Carriage House in so many words, Seawee was sure Devlin would want him to do this. Hadn't Devlin said he would stay in touch with him via the Carriage House front desk? Seawee figured that

DAVID JENNESON

if a person was going to be kept in touch with at a front desk, then that person ought to be there in the first place to be kept in touch with. Or something like that.

So Seawee asked for the monthly rate. He established his account at all Carriage House facilities - bar, restaurant, empty swimming pools, deserted lobbies, what have you - and set out to run Open Homes International in a style he hoped Red Devlin would applaud.

With no other tools at hand, Seawee unwittingly used inverse reasoning to determine what Red Devlin's unspoken wishes might be. Since Devlin had made him a Director of Open Homes International, he figured Devlin wanted to keep him happy. All Seawee had to do was figure out how to make himself happy and it followed that that is what Red Devlin would have wanted. So Ray Seawee's first act as a Director was to phone Tasha, Cutsie Wu and God and invite them all over for a huge dinner on the company tab so they could plan their strategy.

When they arrived, Seawee expected merriment. A party attitude. But it was eerie sitting down when they met again. It was as if they had all lived through some spectacular but unreal cosmic disaster and now the rattled survivors were reunited.

A dumpy, sour-tempered waitress came and took their orders.

"What happened to Devlin?" asked Tasha. "Where does he get off leaving us high and dry like he did last night? "

"Got called to Washington," said Seawee. "It must've been a big deal because he was in a big hurry. He said we have to carry the ball for a while."

"Meaning?"

"He said something about you two (he indicated Tasha and Cutsie Wu with a nod of his head) being God's gift to real estate. So tomorrow you'll both start selling Open House contracts. Door to door."

"Door-to-door?" Cutsie Wu narrowed her eyes. "I've never sold anything door to door in my life. That's lower than *peeling*."

"Gotta start somewhere I guess," Seawee shrugged.

"Not with door-to-door."

"Only for awhile. Until we get the franchises going. I figure that's where the real money is."

At the mention of money God piped up, "What about me?"

Seawee was momentarily stumped. Devlin had not mentioned God in any context, yet it didn't seem fair to leave him out.

"Can you sell door-to-door?" asked Seawee after a moment.

"Do anything I have to."

"Tell you what. You drive. Get these two where they have to go then go do some door-to-door yourself."

The waitress interrupted with plates of food. As they moodily settled down to dinner they found it hard to dispel the surreal air brought on by the whirlwind of events and Red Devlin's sudden disappearance.

True to her discipline, Tasha had ordered a seafood salad. As a result she was served the contents of one can of tuna, upturned, and still retaining its cylindrical shape. It sat on bed of pale lettuce with hard pink tomato garnish. It was a heartbreaking sight. A stunningly beautiful woman who carried herself like a queen was being forced to eat cat food. Even God couldn't look. This only increased the uneasy sense that they were living in some scammy fantasy that could not last.

"That does it," Tasha looked down at the cat food salad and pushed it aside. It was all too much. She wiped moisture from the corner of her eye. "I have bills coming out of my ears. How are we getting paid for all this? I haven't seen a cent. So far this has cost me nothing but money."

This created a moral dilemma for Ray Seawee. He was developing a sweet spot for Tasha. As most of his young life had been spent in prison, the only people he had a chance to feel affection for were other prisoners. Not. He could never figure out how his hairy fellow inmates managed to fall in love with each another. He was

DAVID JENNESON

not interested in getting to the bottom of it either. So he had long-suppressed feelings of affection. Still, his feelings for Tasha were much more potent than any he had felt before. It would be a struggle not to fall head over heels for her.

So Ray Seawee resorted to the one thing he knew that would see him through. Be honest, act in innocence and do the right thing, just like the prison shrink said.

He considered Tasha's request in this light. He concentrated hard, trying to do three things at once: keep Devlin's marching orders straight in his head, suppress his affection for Tasha, and obey the prison doctor's moral epithet. Finally he came up with what seemed like a fair compromise. His heart said give Tasha one hundred percent of everything she earned and keep nothing for Open Homes International, but he was sure this was wrong, so he decided to split the difference.

"Everyone gets fifty percent commission," he announced.

"On what?" Tasha asked suspiciously, "Spell it out."

"On everything."

"Everything?" she asked. "Are you serious?"

"Everything," confirmed Seawee, as if giving away half the gross revenue of a company were the most normal thing in the world. He looked around the table. "And that goes for *everyone*. I mean, why would one person get less than another?" he added to head off charges of favoritism.

"Including franchises?" asked God.

Seawee stuck with the fair play angle. It seemed to be working. "Sure. Why would anyone get less for selling one thing than another?"

Silence.

"Are you sure you have the money for this?" asked Cutsie Wu.

Seawee had been bending over backwards to be fair and now they did not believe him. This made him mad. He picked up a piece of bread.

"See? This is bread. It costs money. Are you eating? Yes. Are you drinking? Yes. Do you see any signs saying free dinners around here? So who's paying? Are *you* paying?" he shot a sharp look at God.

God shook his head rapidly from side to side.

"You?" he asked Cutsie Wu

"No, but I only meant . . ."

"*You?*" he asked Tasha.

She shook her head slowly, glanced at the other two and raised her eyebrows. *Maybe this is for real.*

"Does that answer your question?"

They nodded.

Seawee felt victorious. If Red Devlin wanted him to pay out commissions he'd pay them all right. In prison, being penniless had made Seawee feel curiously pure. He didn't mind staying that way. But if others wanted money, so be it.

Of course when Red Devlin had said commissions he was speaking as a realtor. Everyone knew a realtor's commission was never more than eight percent. Except Seawee. In going to fifty percent, Seawee had radically altered the financial engine driving Open Homes International, forcing it to run on far richer fuel.

The next morning Ray Seawee's employees were highly motivated. They went out and beat the bushes with a vengeance. For his part, Seawee went to one of the banks Devlin had diddled. He used Devlin's credit cards to withdraw two thousand dollars. He then remembered Devlin's warning to not spend a dime he didn't have to, so he took the Upper Lynn Vale bus to Dempsey Road to settle up with McGregor. It bothered him that as Director of Open Homes International he still had to ride the bus.

He hopped off at the bus stop opposite the closed and yellow "crime-scene" taped Upper Lynn Vale Grocery. He paced along

DAVID JENNESON

Dempsey Road and sniffed the air like a dog. The sky darkened. There was rain in the wind again. He dawdled up McGregor's front stairs and rang the doorbell. Nothing. He waited a respectable minute. He rang a second time. He wondered why the McGregors were always so slow in answering doors. Maybe because they were too old for the real estate revolution. He fretted about Mr. McGregor being under all this strain. Finally he heard footsteps.

"Sorry, I was on the phone," said a harassed-looking Mrs. McGregor. "If you want Rockefeller he's in the back yard. Sorry, there goes the phone again."

Seawee mooched down the side of the house to the back yard. He heard hammering. A brief silence, then an explosive cursing.

"GodDAMMIT!" roared Mr. McGregor as Seawee rounded the corner. McGregor hopped on one foot. He'd constructed a crude workbench in the back yard and appeared to be preparing for a massive construction project. A panel of heavy plywood had slid off the makeshift bench and its corner had caught him on his big toe.

"Hey there," Seawee waved to get his attention. "It's me. I've got your money."

"YOU?" roared McGregor. He limped around in a circle. For some reason his sore toe made him hold his jaw like he also had a toothache. Perhaps they were connected.

"Who else would it be?" asked Seawee.

"What happened to that Miss what's 'ername? The one in the suit?" He held out his hands in front of his chest to indicate not merely a suit, but one filled with assets. "I thought I was dealing with her."

"She's busy," said Seawee in a maudlin voice. "Meetings and stuff."

"Well then, just put it there," McGregor snapped, pointing to the bench. Seawee went over and counted out six hundred ten dollars and fifty cents and laid it on the workbench.

"And there better be more where that came from," said McGregor. "I'll let you know how much more you owe me. Soon as I finish this."

Seawee looked at the mess surrounding McGregor. Sharpened stakes lay among sheets of plywood sawed into five-foot squares. Some had been crudely nailed to the stakes. Seawee whistled to himself. McGregor was serious about this. There were cans of paint everywhere. "Building a rec room?" Seawee rubbed the back of his neck in puzzlement.

"No, you fool." McGregor limped off to the garage and produced one of the finished articles. It was a sturdy white sign with "OPEN HOUSE" painted in thick red house paint with the letters two feet high. The red paint had run, giving the sign a bloody, house-of-horrors look but this did not seem to bother McGregor.

Seawee stroked his chin, impressed my McGregor's industry.

"We'll need these," McGregor informed. "Or rather, *they'll* need these," he swept his arm grandly, indicating neighbors in all directions as far as the eye could see. "So I'm going to sell 'em. Twenty-five bucks each. Maybe more. Essential part of the package. You gotta buy the sign with the Open House contract or you don't get the contract. I'm trying to finish this batch before the rain hits."

At that moment a fat rain drop splatted on McGregor's OPEN HOUSE sign. It mixed with the still-wet red paint and ran down the white surface. It made it look as if McGregor had carved it from living flesh.

"Damn. Rain. Well, that's it. Back to the phones." He scooped up the money from the workbench. "And where are those franchise agreements you promised? And that extra money? Check with the missus for the exact amount."

It turned out Ray Seawee did owe McGregor more money for new contracts - over two hundred dollars. There was a threat of more bills to come. As a final blow it rained hard enough to give Seawee a good soaking as he waited for the Upper Lynn Vale bus to take him back to the Carriage House.

DAVID JENNESON

That evening Seawee's crew returned to the Carriage House. The results were predictable. They had fists full of contracts. Lists of clients demanding franchises. Seawee dutifully trekked to the disk jockey's booth in the Carriage House pub and used the direct withdrawal machine to get the cash payout. He paid them for the contracts plus their commission - all doled out in cash, cash, cash.

Then it struck him that this was impractical. It meant going back to the OPEN HOUSE clients a second time to pay them once they had signed. So he went back to the booth and withdrew much more money this time. In addition to all fees owed, he gave everyone an extra thousand-dollar cash float for the next day. Now his field workers would be able to supply immediate payment for OPEN HOUSE contracts, on the spot, and move on to fresh pickings the next day without missing a step.

Seawee had a funny feeling handing it out. Like he was going broke. Fast. The next day he rode the bus to a printer and had franchise agreements run off. He decided to sell the franchises for five hundred dollars each. He settled on the five hundred dollar figure because he was giving everyone a thousand dollar daily float, so it seemed a good way to balance things. He was proud of his financial dexterity. Now there would be money. Incoming.

Indeed there was. Tasha, Cutsie Wu and God came back the next day with nothing but franchise contracts and checks. Seawee happily deposited these after giving a tally to Cutsie Wu. He also paid out fifty percent commissions on the franchises to each of the three in cash. Then he retired to the Carriage House pub for a beer.

He watched the 5:45 Triple Sextravaganza. Three shapely dancers in black gowns swayed before a bent and brooding Seawee. Everyone seemed to be getting rich but him. He had not yet figured out how to pay himself. That would have to come later. Weighing on his mind now was the next wave of new OPEN HOUSE contracts at a hundred dollars a crack plus commission. He could expect these any time now generated by the newly signed franchisees.

He shuddered at what the total bill might be. He knew he couldn't pay it. He doubted he could even pay his hotel bill. The black veil of a dancer's dress swished above his head as she whirled around the brass pole in front of him. In the backwash of perfume he stared at his beer. Perhaps it was the last beer he would ever be able to afford. Suddenly he heard his name paged. Phone call. Seawee slouched to the lobby and was handed the desk phone.

"**Ramon**," came Devlin's voice. "It goes well?" He sounded jubilant.

"Good and bad," Seawee replied tentatively. "I mean, too good. Selling too fast. We're running out of money."

"Can't be," said Devlin. "There hasn't been time. You selling franchises?"

"Yes."

"And collecting?"

"Yes sir"

"Depositing?"

"Um. Yeah."

'Paying commissions like I told you."

"Oh yes," said Seawee gloomily, imagining Tasha and Cutsie Wu in mink and God in a Ferrari tow truck. He sighed and hoped he would not loose his front row seat in the pub. His last beer on earth sitting there. He waited for Devlin to launch into a more detailed line of questioning. He would probably discover some mistake Seawee made, then fire him right over the phone from Washington.

"Well then, we'll just have to send you more money," cried Devlin joyfully. The man seemed plugged in to a bliss machine.

Seawee perked up, gave him his credit card number and hurried back to his front row seat. His beer was still there, but now it looked a little stale. Why should he drink flat beer with everyone making so much money? He pulled out his about-to-be refilled bankcard, looked at it with something approaching love, and ordered a fresh pint.

DAVID JENNESON

Judge Mannheim took his morning coffee at the McDonald's across from the Zum-O-Zar Dry Cleaners. He was waiting for the Zum-O-Zar to open to recover his de-oysterized clothes. He looked forward to picking them up from that slim Iranian boy, Aziz, and getting his eyeful for the morning. Sitting in this McDonald's was also a good way for him to keep his ear to the ground. Those two beat cops came in here for morning coffee. Nothing wrong with a judge rolling up his sleeves and getting his hands dirty down inside the wheels of justice once in a while.

The Judge contemplatively chewed on his hash browns like he was working a cud. A young McWorker was cleaning up. Why did teenagers have such perfectly formed butts these days? The Judge exercised regularly to stop his own ass from dropping but it was a losing battle. The young girl bent low to pick up a discarded napkin. This gave Judge Mannheim warm and evil thoughts. He dropped one of his own napkins on the floor.

"Another one over here, miss," he said. He loved this girl's moves. She did not stoop. No, she turned and bent low from the waist. Perfect target. Soft warm valentine. *Booma-looma*, thought the Judge.

Judge Mannheim's appreciation of his little anal angel ceased abruptly as Needle-nose and Mustache came through the door. They were bickering and carping at one another. Needle-nose spied the Judge and approached. His dark blue trousers with their broad yellow stripe made him look all the more military and butch.

"May we, your honor?" he asked, pulling out a chair.

"By all means," Judge Mannheim liked the aggressive style of this slim officer.

"I noticed you boys seem to be having a difference of opinion over something," the Judge observed. "Some enforcement issue? Perhaps I can help."

"That would be most appreciated, your honor." replied Needle-nose humbly. "I'd like to share this with a good legal mind." He glanced over at Mustache. "By the way it's your turn to buy coffee."

Mustache marched off.

"What's the nature of the problem, exactly?" asked the Judge.

"The Sheng case," said Needle-nose.

"The grocer? Knifed?"

"We're on it full time. Both of us . . ."

" . . .and no leads," the Judge finished his thought. "It's still early," he leaned forward and patted Needle-nose on the knee. "Give yourself time, son."

"It's not so easy," said Needle-nose. "The descriptions the detectives got are useless. The first perpetrator fits any one of a hundred thousand Asian businessmen. The second one sounds like a cross between Colonel Sanders and Elvis. But I have a theory."

"Not this again," said Mustache as he brought back the coffee.

"Ignore him," sniped Needle-nose. "Consider this. The night before the murder there was an accident outside the store. Someone in an old dinosaur of a Merc cut off a bus and forced it to rear end another bus. We were looking for the car and found one matching the description outside The Carriage House. Questioned the owner, some old guy in a white suit. Like some sleazy Colonel Sanders."

"And?"

"He had an alibi. It was bullshit of course. He paid a couple of peelers to back him up."

The Judge leaned forward, suddenly interested. He found the concept of bribing strippers to do *anything* stimulating. What did you bribe them with, he wondered. And how much did it take? "Intriguing," he nodded. "How did you say this connects to the crime?"

"Well, I'm not sure. This case is dead in the water. No trace of either suspect. But doesn't it seem odd to you that the only person even remotely matching the description has an accident outside the murder scene exactly twenty-four hours before, then wriggles out of it?"

"Dressed in white, you say?" asked Judge Mannheim. Something in his memory twigged. Something hazy. A memory clouded by whisky, stained by oysters.

That realtor. The one who had stolen his wallet. When the Judge canceled his stolen MasterCard it had no extra charges on it. With all the security cameras around nowadays, why risk getting ID'd for some petty purchase?

But the realtor also had his address book. Damn. What was his name? Some kind of lipstick. Revlon? Damn, no. He had given him his business card, hadn't he? Yes. Where? The Judge's head snapped toward the Zum-O-Zar Cleaners. The realtor's card was in there. In his clean clothes.

"Yes sir." Needle-nose carried on. "White pants. White belt. White shoes. White shirt. White tie. Dressed in full Nanaimo."

"You boys finish your coffee and come with me," said the Judge. "I've got a present for you."

"See," said Needle-nose to Mustache. "*See?*"

Mustache seemed confused as he followed them across to the Zum-O-Zar. He hung back and whispered to Needle-nose. "This guy's a sitting Judge. He can't be buying this lame brain theory of yours. You can't build a case on coincidence. If it ever goes to trial this same Judge would have to throw it out of court. Even I know that much."

Needle-nose sniffed and ignored him. As they entered, the young Iranian clerk seemed to shrink back at the sight of the Judge flanked by two uniformed police.

"Aziz, fetch my things," said the Judge warmly, handing him his stub. "Bright lad," he said to Needle-nose as Aziz disappeared into back of the shop. He emerged with the clothes. The Judge tore off the plastic shroud. He rifled through one pocket, then the next. Aziz grew increasingly fidgety. The Judge's neck turned red.

"You are missing money?" asked Aziz nervously.

"No. A card. A business card. Where is it?"

Aziz relaxed. "Oh, card. No need to worry about cards and other garbage. We clean everything. Outside, inside. Throw all garbage away for you. Part of service, special for you."

"You WHAT?" hissed Judge Mannheim. He reddened to the color of nail polish.

"Throw away garbage. Our service to you ..." Aziz's voice petered out.

"That's private property," the Judge yelled. "You could be charged. Evidence tampering. I OUGHTA RING YOUR NECK!" He lunged as Aziz wailed and fled to the back of the shop. The two cops had to hold the Judge back.

"Calm down your honor." soothed Needle-nose as they led the furious Judge from the Zum-O-Zar. Mannheim was shaking.

"Find this guy fast," said Judge Mannheim through clenched teeth. "Hunt him down. Give him no rest. He's a realtor. That much I know." He stalked off to his car. "And keep me informed," he snarled as he slammed the door.

Needle-nose turned to Mustache in the wet McDonald's parking lot. "*See?*" he said.

*   *   *

Ray Seawee sat in his hotel room and watched the phone beside the bed. He reached into his pocket for cigarettes and felt something else in there too. He pulled out one of Red Devlin's business cards. He must have been carrying it around all week without knowing it. He was going to toss it in the wastebasket, but having nothing else to do, he studied it dejectedly. It was funny how Red Devlin had his home address printed on his business card. Maybe all realtors did.

Then it dawned on him that here was the answer to his worries. Red Devlin was out of town. But his car was not. Nor would Red Devlin need it. And what was to stop one enterprising realtor from borrowing another realtor's car? Even if he had no keys it did not matter. Ray Seawee had never needed keys before.

A mobile Seawee would be a profitable Seawee. A profitable Seawee could afford to take a certain beautiful woman out riding in his car. It opened up all sorts of possibilities.

The telephone beside the bed gave a soft, purring ring. He picked it up. It was God calling from the lobby. Seawee said he was ready for them, and they should come up and get paid.

He was not enjoying his first dip into the lacquer of high finance. The big bucks gave him melancholia. Devlin's second infusion of cash had come in and would soon be eaten up.

While the others were out making money hand over fist, Seawee had been forced to take the bus back down to the four banks and open more accounts. He put twenty-five dollars in a checking account in each bank, and then wrote five hundred dollars on each and cashed them in the bank machines. Seawee hoped Devlin would send more funds in a day or so. The transfer would then be deposited into the accounts he had just opened. Money chasing checks. In the meantime there were bills to pay. Seawee had never been in business before. But he was sure that if all businesses ran this way, the streets would be pinstripe blue with bankrupt businessmen.

The way Red Devlin had originally conceived it, Open Homes International was only designed to break even. Yet due to Seawee's haphazard administration and attempts to do the right thing, Open Homes International was now set up to run like an upside down pyramid scam. Conventional pyramid sales, illegal almost everywhere, are calculated to make those who created them rich. Open Homes International now worked in the exact opposite manner. It thrust those powerful forces into reverse, sucking up enormous amounts of cash from those who had gotten in on the ground floor. It was a unique concept. Ironically it was legal. No government in the world would pass a law against con men making themselves poor.

There was a soft rap at the door. Seawee got up off the bed and opened it. Tasha came in first. She was wearing the same tweed suit jacket, minus the blouse, that had driven McGregor to distraction. She was followed by God and Cutsie Wu.. They dumped their contracts on the bed. Seawee counted out five hundred sixty dollars in cash and handed it to God and Cutsie.and they happily departed. Then he and Tasha were alone. He handed her a wad of bills.

"Thanks," she said brightly. "Gee, this is the best job I ever had." She paused, and then pecked him on the cheek.

'Do you think we could go out sometime?" he asked suddenly. "I mean, for dinner or something?"

"Sure, why not?"

"Good. How about tonight? I'll pick you up at eight."

"I'll be waiting," Tasha gave him her address on a piece of paper and a little wink and was gone.

Seawee couldn't believe how easy it had been. All he had to do was get up to Red Devlin's place, hot-wire the Turnpike Cruiser and he was in business. "WOO!" cried Ray Seawee joyously.

CHAPTER 16

*W*hen he left Anson Dobell's, the sipping whiskey and the crisp Foggy Bottom night made Red Devlin think he should walk. Clear the head a bit.

One sniff of the brisk air put him in the mood for singing. A man had a right to sing after this, he thought. The lights of The Promised Land danced on the horizon. He was on his way to closing the deal of the century.

No. That was wrong. Deals of the century came along once every hundred years. A realtor did not sell the official residence of the leader of the most powerful nation on earth once every hundred years. No one had ever sold 24 Sussex Drive out from under a sitting Canadian Prime Minister. Nor had anyone sold No. 10 Downing Street out from under a British Prime Minister. Nowhere in history had an agent of any kind sold Windsor Castle out from under the Queen or King of England. Oh, it might have changed hands a few times through the centuries but the transfer of royal property in medieval times had been *unprofessional* as

Devlin recalled. Real estate was a dangerous game in those days. There was bloody-mindedness between parties, and the vendor got beheaded the day the deal closed.

And no one had sold 1600 Pennsylvania Avenue. Ever.

But this deal was clean. Elegant. And in his opinion, legal. He took a slug of sipping whiskey from his flask as he trudged down the snowy hill. He wanted to clear his head, but not too quickly. A too-rapid clearing of the head might interrupt the free flow of ideas. *Real estate is inflicting creativity on other people's property.* He broke into song. Actually, he broke into two songs. One was a Canadian fishing ballad and the other was a World War II drinking song. Their melodies were close enough and Red Devlin was a happy man, so he ran one into the other. His voice rang out in a gravelly baritone:

> *Ho, ay's the b'y what builds the boat*
> *And ay's the b'y what sails her*
> *Ay's the b'y what catches the fish*
> *And brings 'em home to Dinah*
> *H"way h'way with the fife and drum*
> *Here we come*
> *Full 'o rum*
> *Lookin' for women to peddle their bum*
> *Inna North Atlantic Squadron!*

At the bottom of the hill, the hoods mooching around the Uganda stirred like a pack of shivering wolves.

"Wha's that noise?" asked one.

"Someone gettin' theirs up the hill?" asked another. "Shit man, this be our territory."

They all listened. A strange lyric drifted down through the cold air.

> *Ho! Ay's the b'y what builds the boat,*
> *An' ay's the b'y what sails her.*

"Naw," said the leader. "I heard that shit before. It's a Russian. Fuckin' drunk Russian diplomat. We'd best get our *dip*-lomacy together." They all laughed.

DAVID JENNESON

Red Devlin took another slash of sipping whisky. He swung his red tartan bag. He thought about Anson Dobell, who he had tucked safely into bed before he left. The man couldn't take his drink. Clearly he hadn't been practicing. Nonetheless Devlin was elated that things had gone so well, especially the part about how the Good Lord had given him a divine mission to sell the White House. On reflection, he wished he had been more precise. It was not so much that God wanted *him* to sell the White House. It was more that God wanted the White House sold. Period. God had placed Red Devlin on the Earth as the specific instrument by which He meant to achieve it. The concept impressed the shit out of Anson Dobell.

Yet when Red Devlin thought it over now, trudging down the hill, the proposition seemed to put him on a more shaky celestial footing than ever. Going to heaven after having tried to sell the White House was one thing. But who wanted to face them having tried and failed? He could imagine Saint Peter whispering in God's ear: *'Red Devlin? Him? Defective tool, Sir. Better to melt him down and try again. No, Sir, back down to the foundry for Devlin.'*

Red Devlin had a fair idea where the foundry was located and was not interested in finding out more.

As he approached the bottom of the hill he noticed what appeared to be a fortified grocery store. A retail bunker. Silhouettes of tall, husky figures fanned out as he drew closer.

"Hey Ivan," came a voice. Laughter.

Ivan? thought Devlin as he peered into the murky light. *Must be looking for someone else. These are probably Russian tourists, drunk and lost and looking for their friends. Poor fools must think they are on Embassy Row*, he nodded smugly, like some know-it-all Washington tourist. He glanced over his shoulder to see if they were shouting at someone behind him. Nope. Then they were drunken Russians mistaking him for sure. They would see soon enough. He was relieved. He shrugged and trudged on across the snowy tableau approaching the Uganda with an open spirit.

Ho, ay's the b'y what builds the boat,
And ay's the b'y what sails her -

"Hey! Spud!" came a voice, followed by a cackle of laughter.

This stopped Devlin cold in his tracks. He hated being referred to as a potato. His impoverished boyhood had forced him to survive on a potato-rich diet. If his body now looked like a potato more than it should, it wasn't his fault.

The hoods stepped, one at a time, into the glare of the M Street streetlights. They now looked un-Russian in the extreme. Suddenly Devlin's red tartan bag stuffed with $10,000 cash felt like hot kryptonite in his left hand.

"Gimme a smoke, spud," threatened the gang leader.

"Jaysus, do I got a smoke, b'y?" replied Red Devlin with a lunatic Newfoundland lilt to his voice. He spoke in the same Newfie accent in which he had been singing. He hoped the friendly dialect would protect him. He pulled out his of pack cigarettes and offered the gang leader a couple.

"See?" the gang leader gestured to the rest. "Some Fuckrussian. Dude can't even talk right." He slowly pulled a long Pall Mall plain end from Devlin's pack. Enjoying this.

Devlin put them back in his pocket with a cheerful nod. "Be seein'ya 'den b'ys."

"Hey Spud!" shouted the gang leader, grabbing the furry lapel of Devlin's overcoat. "You forgettin' your manners." He motioned toward the rest, their hands outstretched. Devlin smiled. Humming and bobbing his head like the village idiot he passed out more cigarettes.

"Now gimme the pack."

Devlin did this. His asshole puckered up by the second. He turned to go.

"HOLD IT," he grabbed Devlin by the back of the collar. "You gotta pay the toll."

DAVID JENNESON

"Yeah, pay the toll," they yelled.

"What's in the suitcase, Spud? Gimme it over."

He grabbed for it.

Devlin leapt back. The gang leader made another lunge. He leapt back again. Another gang member swiped at the tartan suitcase. The pack circled him completely now, laughing and grinning like jackals. He was surrounded.

Terrible images flashed through Red Devlin's mind. *My money, gone*, he thought. *Spent. Priceless documents ripped to shreds and lost forever in a back alley dumpster. The Promised Land. Never Reached.* His mind recoiled at the thought of the White House never having a huge FOR SALE/OPEN HOUSE sign in front of it. And the face of The Almighty, sadly agreeing with Saint Peter. "Yes, best send him back down to the foundry. Melt him and try again." Saint Peter rubbing his palms together and reaching for the lever that opened the trap door.

It was too much.

Devlin reached into his overcoat pockets for a weapon and felt a small cold lump. A miserable little can of Bumblebee flaked light tuna, left over from his shopping spree. That and a flask of sipping whisky. Useless as weapons. He had nothing left but the force of his spirit. In a moment of epiphany he knew what Moses would have done when confronted by thugs in the desert.

He shuffled back a few feet further from the gang leader. He needed a run at the bastard. He lowered his center of gravity. Suddenly Devlin looked like a bull that had swallowed a red-hot bowling ball.

Then he charged. Roaring. Devlin was quick on his feet for such a big man. The gang leader, tall and gangly, backpedaled a few steps trying to meet the attack. Suddenly, as if impelled by a divine force, Devlin leapt into the air like a paunchy lineman from the 1948 Washington Redskins.

"Hut!" Devlin cried, as he became airborne.

The gang leader scrambled to get out of the way. At the last moment he slipped in the snow. He fell on his ass.

A split-second later the full mass of an enraged realtor landed on top of him. Spread-eagled. There was a sickening crunch. Then snow-softened silence and moaning, like a light plane had crashed.

Another low groan.

Suddenly Devlin felt unwell. His head had cracked his nose on the gang leader's skull as they went down and a sharp knee had caught Devlin below the ribs. It sent a wave of nausea through him. All that rich food. All that stress. All that sipping whiskey. Red Devlin had a strong stomach, which in this situation meant he could throw up at least ten feet. His mouth snapped open like a steaming trap door from hell.

"I got bad news for you," he choked. Slobber drooled from his mouth as he stared down at the pinned gang leader. "I'm not calling the cops."

"Nooooo!"

Strictly speaking, the gang leader got a better deal this time than with Anson Dobell. Dobell had merely sprayed him with semi-digested martini. The contents of Red Devlin's stomach contained far more expensive fare: oysters, mussels, the finest white cheeses. Pound for pound it was worth more on the dollar.

It hit the gang leader's face with the force of a fire hose. Then Devlin sprang up and spun around to face the others. There was blood on Devlin's face where he had cracked his nose. It made him look even more berserk.

"Which one a' you buggers wants it next!" he spat blood.

They stared at him, not knowing what to do.

"That was breakfast," snarled Devlin, pointing at the mask of steaming puke on the gang leader. "Who wants lunch?"

The gang members slowly backed away. No one seemed to want any part of this. It had already been a bad week for them and their leader. Privately, some had been thinking about holding a leadership convention. There did not seem to be much left of the current leader any more. He looked two-dimensional squashed down into the snow like that.

Red Devlin huffed and wheezed as he departed. He snorted menacingly over his shoulder like a cave bear. Spat on the ground a couple of times. Some primeval realtor's instinct told him to not run, but to keep a steady, hostile retreat. This would keep them at bay.

But he was hurt. He felt a twang of pain in his side as he breathed hard on his way back up the hill. The tartan bag was torn open along the zipper and now pink Canadian hundred dollar bills poked through the rip.

He fought his way up the slippery hill until he saw the fuzzy lights of the Tax n' Spend through the falling snow. And a phone. For a cab. He wanted to go back to Gloris Dilt's and lick his wounds.

Devlin walked into the smug, elite little bar and got curious stares from the assembled Washington bureaucrats. He could see why: a foreign-looking realtor, covered in blood, pink hundred dollar bills sticking out of a tartan bag, just back from making the deal of all time. *Well that's how we close 'em up north*, Devlin thought. He asked for the bar phone and the number of Diamond Cabs.

"You okay, Pops?" the tough old bartender slid the phone across the bar.

"Sure I am," said Devlin. "Just a hard day's sell is all." He winked and laughed. He dialed the phone. A moment passed. Then he frowned. "Line's goddam busy. Gimme the Yellow Cab number."

The bartender did. "Looks like you got mugged," he said, then glanced down at the tartan bag with the bills sticking out of it. "Or maybe you mugged someone else," he stroked his chin.

"That's real estate," shrugged Devlin. "Goddam it, Yellow's busy too. Gimme the Diamond again."

When the Diamond Cab finally arrived at the Tax 'n Spend, the driver made the bloodied-up Devlin pay in advance.

They pulled up in front of the turreted Dilt townhouse. It was late, but Devlin thought he saw a light peeping from a back room. He cried out as a ribbon of pain shot up his side from his rib.

"All right old timer?" the driver asked.

"Yes sir," Devlin said proudly. If there was anything he hated more than being called a potato, it was old timer. "I'm a hundred percent."

Devlin gazed up at the looming tower where his rooms awaited. He considered his best strategy. The stairs of the ancient fire escape wrapped up and around to the second story of the tower. From there he could quietly slip through his unlocked window.

He fretted about the pain in his side that the steep climb up the fire escape would cause, but compared to the gale of questions his arrival would unleash if he went in through the front door, and woke up Gloris Dilt, it was a no-brainer.

He clutched the tartan bag and placed his foot on the first step of the fire escape. It was so narrow he had to twist sideways to squeeze up between the rails. It groaned. So did he. He inched his way painfully up, moaning like a round and wounded mountaineer caught in a tight crevasse. The device creaked and struggled to support him. This was Devlin's first encounter with heritage fire escapes. People must have been a lot smaller, or at least narrower a hundred years ago, he thought ruefully. Hadn't he read that somewhere? He worked his way sideways as another ribbon of pain shot up his side.

He gained the summit with relief and now teetered along the narrow walkway toward his second story window. He saw it was open a crack. He bent low slowly and pulled it up a bit. Another jolt of pain shot up his side. The railings on this narrow metal walkway barely reached up past his knees. Maybe this had been a mistake. What if he fainted? The notion made him dizzy.

He realized he needed to get inside fast before the situation deteriorated further. He gave one more tug on the window. The pain made him see bright lights. The window grudgingly yielded another foot. It would have to do. *Can't wait another minute,*

DAVID JENNESON

Devlin's mind raced. He lowered his bulk, put one leg through and tried to squeeze himself through the two-foot space.

Naked he might have made it. But not like this. His thick overcoat wedged him in tightly. He struggled to undo the buttons and succeeded only in releasing his ample gut, which flopped down. Now his belt buckle firmly wedged itself into the outside of the sill like a plowshare. He arched up with his back and pushed with his legs to open the window more. Rock solid. The effort made him cry out in pain.

Inside the office door suddenly slammed open and the lights blazed on.

"Freeze!"

It was Gloris Dilt. She was hard set in a shoot-to-kill stance holding a black Thompson submachine gun, the kind favored by Capone's people in the 1930's. Its drum magazine was filled with heavy .45 cal. bullets. "I've got you covered. And this ain't no goddam replica," she warned, fumbling for her glasses in the pocket of her dressing gown.

From his wedged-in position, Devlin viewed the order to freeze as redundant. Sighing, one foot in, one foot out, he waited.

"Jesus Christ, I thought it was a goddam moose trying to second-story the place," cried Gloris Dilt, focusing. "Hold on a minute," she removed the lead pipe securing the window and it popped open. Devlin tumbled through and fell on top of the tartan suitcase. Now it burst altogether and split even wider. Hundred dollar bills floated into the air and down like snowflakes. Devlin rose painfully to his feet, covered in blood.

Gloris Dilt frowned. She did not lower the Tommy gun's snout. To any normal person Devlin looked like a mass murderer back from a night of butchery and theft.

"You just hold it right there, Mr. Realtor," she said grimly. "You march downstairs right now. You've got a lot of explaining to do."

He bent low to scoop up the money and groaned in pain. Gloris Dilt seemed unmoved.

"C'mon, move it. Hup two."

Thus, on his second night in Washington, DC, Red Devlin was marched downstairs at the point of a genuine Thompson submachine gun held by his landlady. It had been given to Husband Number Two by a grateful J. Edgar Hoover many years ago. In his long coat with its fur lapels Devlin looked like Hermann Goring caught with a bag of Nazi loot.

"It's not at all that it seems," huffed Devlin as he sank into a kitchen chair. He clutched his side. His breathing was labored.

"Never is in this town," said Gloris Dilt.

Devlin's shoulder's sagged. He felt like Moses, in sight of the Promised Land, suddenly being hauled back to Egypt and put in front of some bloodthirsty old Pharaoh.

"You come clean or I'll call 911. Talk."

Devlin considered the threat. Ordinarily he would have said *go ahead. Call 911. Call the goddam President if you want.* But now he would have to explain being in possession of his own money to the police. Not so easy without that stupid permit she had mentioned - Form 4790, which he'd innocently neglected to fill out at the airport, and without which he was liable for a half-million dollar fine and five years in some stinking American prison. He decided to strike out in the general direction of the truth.

"I was at a meeting. Making a deal."

"Must've been a hell of a meeting," said Gloris Dilt suspiciously.

"Well, yes, it was actually," Devlin admitted on reflection.

"Looks like you beat someone bloody and ran off with their money. Some meeting. Down here we call it robbery with malicious intent. Or attempted murder."

"No no no, you don't understand. This is *my* money."

"Guess that depends on who you ask. Prove it."

Devlin sagged. People were always wanting him to *prove* things down here. In his rush he had not bothered to keep the receipts

DAVID JENNESON

from his complex duel with the bank machines. Just the dough.

"I can't. Not really," he admitted. "But I was the one who was mugged. I swear it."

Her eyes narrowed. "You're saying you duked it out with a dope-fiend punk and walked away with this bag of cash? What'd you do, hit him with your wallet? "Actually there were five," Devlin sniffed, correcting her.

"At the meeting?"

"No. The mugging. One at the meeting. Five at the mugging."

"I see. So you met with someone, beat him bloody and ran off with his money. That makes one at the meeting. Then he gets four friends and comes after you to get it back. That makes five at the mugging," she said with prickly sarcasm.

"No, no, you're missing the point. I brought this money with me *from the start.*"

"To the meeting. Or to the mugging?"

Devlin thought about this. He felt safer sticking to short answers. "Both."

"Ah, but no one wanted it."

"Well, it turned out not to be necessary at the meeting. And I certainly wished I didn't have it at the mugging. God, who wants a bag of cash at a mugging?"

"This ain't addin' up, Mr. Realtor," said Gloris Dilt, struggling to follow him. She leaned forward to make her point. She fingered the safety catch on the dull black Tommy gun. "It ain't addin' up to *Tomasso* here either," she patted the weapon. "Then why in hell did you have all that damn loot with you *in the first place?*"

"In case I needed it," Devlin pleaded woefully.

This was exhausting him. His side hurt. His nose throbbed. He was attempting to parcel out tiny snippets of the truth to Gloris Dilt as before. Whereas previously she had been content to take each morsel and chew it calmly like a feeding crab, this cross-examination was more bloodthirsty. She wanted bigger hunks. In his painful angst he felt like an American tourist being pursued through the Canadian woods by a sow grizzly as he frantically shed articles of his clothing to throw her off the trail. But it was not working. She would sniff, shake it in her teeth with a growl, toss it aside and continue the chase.

"If the person at the meeting didn't want money, what did he want?" asked Gloris Dilt.

"Why, the deal."

"So he had a choice. Take the cash or the deal. In his wisdom he took the deal."

"Exactly!" cried Red Devlin, relieved she had finally grasped the nub.

"I see," said Gloris Dilt. She clicked off the safety catch. "You don't move a muscle, Mr. Realtor. "I'm calling the cops. Here and now. Maybe they'll believe you. That's the biggest bullshit story I ever heard." She reached for the phone. "What were you selling, the Brooklyn Bridge?"

"No," Devlin sobbed, holding his head in his hands. "The White House."

"I shoulda known. Just one more goddam scam artist. I knew you were too good to be true." She picked up the receiver and regarded him with loathing.

I'm a dead man, Devlin thought. His mouth moved but nothing came out.

"Some realtor," she snorted.

"No, please stop. You must listen to me. I'm not selling the White House yet. I'm just listing it. You have to list it first. Then you can sell it."

Gloris Dilt eyed him but paused, clearly incredulous at the lengths to which this song and dance was going.

"Now you're saying you had a meeting with the President tonight,

DAVID JENNESON

huh?" she sneered. She shook her head slowly from side to side. "Got him all signed up I bet." She laughed to herself then frowned. "Jesus, maybe I oughta phone the nut house first," she picked up the phone. "You're probably some new kind of criminal. A serial realtor."

"The President doesn't own the White House," Devlin confessed. He felt sick throwing out huge hunks of the truth to Gloris Dilt like this. "There's no deed. None exists. I've found the person with the next best thing. Please. Put down the phone. I'll tell you everything."

To Gloris Dilt, weary veteran of every Washington screw-up, intrigue and cover-up since '47 and the glory days when the DC 3,'s circled high above Washington in the cold Canadian night air, and the *East Coast Champion* connected New York and Washington along miles of dead straight airline track, Devlin's words appeared to have finally acquired the ring of truth. It was enough to stop her from calling 911.

She paused. The receiver was halfway to her ear. "You're serious, aren't you?"

Devlin sagged with relief; "Do you mind if I have a snort? It's been an awfully long day." He reached for the sipping whiskey in his pocket.

"Easy does it," Gloris Dilt stabbed with the muzzle.

Devlin edged the flask carefully out of his Hermann Goring coat. He sensed that Gloris Dilt was not going to just burn him for what he was about to tell her. She was going to bake him. The very concept of selling the White House was a direct assault on everything she stood for. So his crime might call for the far more painful punishment of baking, which was slow, as opposed to burning, which at least had a humanitarian quickness to it.

"Talk," snapped Gloris Dilt. She lit a butt and motioned for Devlin to slide the flask over.

Red Devlin did talk. Instead of snippets of truth he now produced great bleeding chunks of it in long raw passages. He started with

George Washington being the Father of All Realtors. He went on to recount the tragic case of the ill-fated Dobson Dobell, screwed out of his land by the tobacco farmer David Burnes. The more he talked, the more he felt the deal slipping away.

Gloris Dilt fell silent. She reached again for his flask of sipping whisky.

Soon the only sound, other than Red Devlins voice, was the sipping whiskey being slid back and forth across the turquoise blue arborite kitchen table. Occasionally the snick of a Ronson lighter. Pall Mall plain ends were lit. As he talked, Red Devlin felt relief in spilling the beans. He imagined this was how Communist spies must have felt when the FBI captured them in the early 1950's. Long isolated by their secret lives, once they started babbling there was no stopping them.

So it was with Red Devlin. He told of Anson Dobell, heir apparent to the White House. He described Open Homes International, and how its role as a grand diversion would misdirect the government into jumping on the bandwagon.

He puffed on his smoke and talked and sweated.

Still Gloris Dilt said nothing.

He added more truth: how Open Homes International had already skyrocketed in Canada, and that he had a staff working full time on it.

Gloris Dilt watched him like a lizard watches an insect.

Devlin plunged on.

At key turning points in the story he produced documents from the tartan bag that proved every word. He even managed to fit in the part about the Good Lord and Saint Peter, and how they wanted the White House sold, no questions asked. And how he, Red Devlin, was merely the instrument to that end, which in context with the rest of the story did not sound all that crazy.

Gloris Dilt rubbed the side of her jaw. Her cigarette stuck out from her fingers.

Devlin talked more. He waded into the tale of how the incident in front of the Uganda had ruined his moment of triumph. In an inspired stroke he claimed he had bought groceries for her but they had been lost in battle. He told that part of the story as modestly as he could, although it was plain to anyone listening that the episode was shot through with heroism.

Devlin finished. His story was over. His confession was complete. The bottle was half empty, the ashtray half full.

Gloris Dilt had not uttered a word. She rolled *Tomasso* from side to side in her lap.

Like any foreigner who has confessed to something of this enormity while on American soil, Red Devlin expected to be machine-gunned. Gloris Dilt did not seem amused by any of this. He looked up at the ceiling, through which God and Saint Peter were hopefully peering. He wanted them to see this. *Here I come, you bastards*, he thought.

"It's okay," Devlin held up his hand in the silence that followed. "Do what you want." He pulled his coat off his shoulders and thrust out his chest to give her a good target. "I only ask for one more cigarette, and a moment to figure out how I'm going to deal with Saint Peter. I think I may need a note from you before I go." Devlin's final words were spoken with the dignity of a condemned man wrongly accused, but condemned nonetheless.

He reached for the lighter.

She raised *Thomason's* muzzle and pointed it.

Then wavered.

Then dropped it.

"Oh you poor *poor* man!" Gloris Dilt wailed. She leapt into his lap and stroked his face. "How could I have misjudged you? And you fought off those brutes. All alone?"

"Well, it wasn't a total victory," Devlin reminded her. "After all I had to leave all those expensive groceries behind in the snow. The ones I bought for you."

This produced another round of wailing and cheek stroking. "And you're hurt. Here, off with that shirt. I've got my First Aid."

Gloris Dilt undressed Red Devlin. Slowly at first. Off came the Hermann Goring coat. Next the white suit jacket. Then the tie. As each garment was shed Red Devlin issued the appropriate number of painful moans, some of which were genuine, some maybe not so much. Then, button-by-button, off came his Triple Xtra large tall bloodstained white shirt. "You couldn't have picked a better time," she soothed.

"Eh?" Devlin drew back a little. "What, to get mugged?"

"No, you silly man. To sell the White House. I happen to know that McGeorge Lewis at RICO is about to unload a whole lot of government real estate."

"Hold it," Devlin held up a hand. "Translate for me here. What's RICO?"

"Stands for Racketeer Influenced and Corrupt Organizations. They seize properties from crooks."

"Like a proceeds from crime thing."

"Exactly. McGeorge Lewis has seized thousands. He's been threatening to dump them onto the market for months, but keeps putting it off. All of Washington is tired of waiting. I could make him to put his ass in gear, but quick."

"How?" he asked. He felt as if he were Moses beginning to see the Red Sea part.

"I can screw down enough pressure to make him act. In fact, I can make it irresistible. I happen to know the President is going to sign new legislation within a few days - Law HR 4568. Low- and middle-income Americans can get government mortgages. But agencies like The Department of Housing and Urban Development and the Government National Mortgage Association for Government Assistance are running out of money.

"And the President is getting involved?" Devlin seemed incredulous.

"Of course. Law HR 4568 gives supplemental funds to these agencies so they can keep lending mortgages. And he wants to see it used. It's one sure way to boost housing starts, and that means votes."

Red Devlin became so excited that a line of sweat formed along his hairline. "So there will suddenly be all these properties for sale on the market, and at the same time the country will be awash in cheap government money."

"Told you it was good timing, sweetie."

"It sounds like a sales event."

"It does."

"A government sponsored sales event."

"What a concept. Never before in history has this occurred to anyone in government. Trust me."

"If I could just tie it in …" Devlin coughed.

"You poor baby," she cooed and patted his chest. "You fought so bravely. One against five. Such manly conflict turns me on. Ooo, all this flesh. So much of it. I'll have to tape your ribs," she said in a throaty whisper, which considering it was Gloris Dilt, was throaty indeed, "but first, to be safe for taping, I'll have to shave you. I'll get the shaving cream."

Down inside, on some deep instinctive level, Red Devlin sensed he was about to be date-raped by a grandma alligator. Yet he was a realtor. Maybe there were worse things than horny old alligators. Different belief systems in his mind came seemed to collide.

His manhood begged for mercy. *No*, it pleaded. *Not this. Anything but this.*

Hold on, the realtor in him argued back. *This might be a gift from God in disguise.*

If I have to do this there IS no God, cried his manhood, close to tears.

Gloris Dilt's voice interrupted Devlin's tortured interior dialogue.

"That's a very novel idea, selling the White House," she said in a husky whisper.

"And we have all these government properties coming for sale, and all this mortgage money, and a President who wants to see the money used. My company, Open Homes International, will be holding a major promotional event called Open Homes for America Night. It'll get thousands of Americans mortgaged to their eyeballs. Do you think the President would cooperate?"

"Dreams come true for him, sweetie. That little twerp will do anything for votes."

"Would he actually hold the White House Open? I mean symbolically of course, to help things along."

"Don't see why not. It's about time we had some originality in this town." She slipped back into his lap and slowly lathered his chest.

"Maybe *you* could help?" Devlin fought to conceal his panic. His manhood now tried to manually override the realtor in him, a submarine that wanted to crash dive and flee into the cold deep beyond.

"I *could*," answered Gloris Dilt slowly, drawing hearts in the lather on Devlin's chest. "Of course, in this town, friends only help other friends. Special friends. Do you know what I mean by *special* friends?"

"I think you're a very special person," Devlin said hopefully.

"Thank you," she kissed him on the forehead. "I think you're a very special person too. And if we became special friends, I could help you and your Mr. Dobell get that claim through on a certain piece of property. Have to match the legal descriptions of the property. I know people who can. And get the right people to cooperate. All very hush hush, of course. Do you think you and I could become special friends?" she stroked his chest with a razor. "I could light a fire under McGeorge Lewis. I could even speak to the White House. They're afraid *not* to listen to me."

Red Devlin was so terrified he felt like bawling.

DAVID JENNESON

"But I mean, *special* special friends."

Somewhere in Devlin's interior his conscience crash-dived, a submarine with all hatches open. All hands were lost.

"I think we eventually could," he swallowed.

CHAPTER 17

$\mathcal{B}y$ the eleventh hour of the eleventh day of his campaign, Red Devlin had contacted the presidents of seven major Washington, DC real estate firms.

Gloris Dilt, that 75-year old walking database, had been invaluable. She'd given him a list of the personal direct line numbers to the mega real estate bosses. Then she gave him a file of which high-powered government names to drop in a way that was uncheckable. She made him promise not to drop her name, but Devlin said it didn't matter. He said he didn't much care if the list was checkable or not because realtors never checked anything. It worked. The big kahunas couldn't afford *not* to pay attention. They were helpless. Red Devlin started having fun.

By working the phone extra hard over the next hour he had representatives from five more national companies lined up.

By one in the afternoon he had them cloistered in a private meeting room off *The Club*, the exclusive lounge hidden inside the

Jefferson Hotel at 16th and M Streets. Devlin ordered lunch brought in for all one dozen of the real estate power brokers.

From the head table Devlin looked from face to face. These men and women were the cream of upper management. Coldwell Banker. Century 21. NRS. Together they controlled armies of realtors. The Joint Chiefs of Real Estate. At that moment he was keenly aware of the jaggedness of existence. This was all or nothing. Walk the walk on broken glass.

He cleared his throat to speak. At that moment his stomach knotted into a ball and sent up a wave of acid reflux. He swallowed dryly. He wondered if ever Moses got acid reflux when speaking to an organized gathering of Israelites in the desert. Perhaps these were not Israelites, but the Pharisees, the infamous high priests. Damn, he'd meant to check the scriptures about this too. How would Moses handle it?

The truth, Devlin thought. *The truth will settle your stomach.*

He gave them a deeply conspiratorial smile, like they were in the loop on such inside insider information that it would burn the ass of your pants if you got any closer.

The realtors relaxed immediately.

There was plenty of coffee and bone china service, but in keeping with his *pot valiant* personality Red Devlin had a small crystal tumbler of Coke and ice. The Alberta Sipping Whiskey was inside.

"Thank you for coming on such short notice," he began. "I have some information to share with you that opens up certain opportunities. Very soon the United States Government - RICO in particular -"

"Not that crap again," muttered a realtor from the back.

Red Devlin drummed his fingers on the table. "Who said that?" His voice was short and sharp, like the minister of a high church who had been interrupted at the beginning of a key sermon.

"I did," the Manager of Coldwell Banker's South East Region crossed his arms smugly.

"Your name?"

"Jones."

"Yeah. Erogenous Jones," another realtor cut in. "He'll screw anything." This produced a ripple of good ole boy laughter.

"Excuse me, sir," Devlin politely ignored the remark. He placed his coffee cup and saucer down. He addressed the man in a courteous, controlled manner. "Have you been in business in the Washington area long?"

'Yeah. Sure. Everyone knows who I am."

"Excellent. So am I right in thinking I am speaking to an industry leader?"

"Yeah," the realtor shrugged a little self-consciously. "You could say that."

"By industry leader I mean not only the capitol area, you understand, but nationally. You are an industry leader on a *national* level."

The realtor nodded again, less sure of himself.

The other big shot realtors with their bloated egos bridled at this but said nothing.

"Excellent again," Devlin licked his lips. "Then I have the right man. I can assume you are well connected and know the necessary people. You understand the shorthand of Washington power politics. People. Names. Surely with a recognized national leader of the real estate business such as yourself, we can all consider you an industry spokesman."

"Get to the point."

"Do you have a card?

The realtor pulled one out. Devlin walked over and took it. He stood next to the man while he read it carefully and then placed it in his pocket. "Mr. Jones, you do understand what RICO is?" he asked finally.

"Good place to stay away from."

A relieved laugh rippled through the realtors at this inside joke. Devlin was pleased at how Jones had broken the ice.

"Ah good," Devlin placed his fingertips together. "So Mr. Jones, I'd like to pass on some information to you, just between you and I, and you can choose to act on it or not."

"Shoot," the Coldwell Banker man crossed his arms.

Red Devlin walked over to the small full host bar and picked up an empty whiskey tumbler. He dumped fresh cubes in it, returned to the offending realtor and leaned low. He rattled the ice cubes in his ear like cold, ancient runic bones.

"*Dilt.*" He whispered.

"What?"

"Yeah. You heard right," Devlin nodded. "Gloris Dilt," he rattled the cubes in his ear again. "Know her?"

"Of course," the realtor said softly. "Everyone does."

"My friend," Devlin leaned lower, "Gloris Dilt has thrown her full support behind this. She's making calls to her high level contacts as we speak. So what I am about to tell you is absolutely true. This is very inside. It is about to break. I am doing you a big favor by even tipping you off. Now if you don't believe me, feel free to phone her yourself and verify. *If you have the courage.*"

The man looked up. Devlin saw his face was a mixture of guilt and fear. "No, that's not necessary," the man's voice wavered.

Red Devlin knew realtors inside out, and his instinct told him this one was hiding something. Suddenly it hit him. It was unmistakable. "God, you didn't …." he whispered.

"What?" the realtor looked up wretchedly.

"… not like, have sex with her? Did you?"

"For God's sake keep your voice down," the realtor hissed. "It was a long time ago. I was drunk."

"If you know her intimately you know her power. What more can I add?"

"You've got my cooperation, okay?" Jones whispered. "Go ahead and make your pitch."

Red Devlin walked deliberately back to the head table. He nodded ever so slightly in the direction of the Coldwell Banker man, who nodded back.

"RICO," Red Devlin continued, "is going to divest itself of thousands of proceeds-from-crime properties. To achieve that, I will launch an event, Open Homes for America Night, in the near future. I fully expect that Open Homes International will be the agent for those transactions."

The assembled realtors raised their eyebrows and nudged one another. They all knew about RICO. McGeorge Lewis had a reputation in real estate circles as a temperamental nut case.

Red Devlin sensed their disbelief and glanced toward Mr. Jones again.

"Listen up. He's on the level," the Coldwell Banker man said.

"Furthermore, in order to include the private sector," Devlin continued, "Open Homes International has a promotional program where we will pay homeowners one hundred dollars to hold their home open. It's called Open Homes for America. This will be on the same night the government properties are held open, on a date in the very near future to be determined by me. Personally. The homes do not have to be for sale. We'll also pay a hundred dollars for any reasonable offers that are written, whether or not they are accepted. Nevertheless, there should be a realtor present in case a sale should result. You provide the realtors, we provide the cash, and we split the commission of any sales. Any questions so far?"

The man from NRS grimaced with skepticism. "How do you expect to make any money?"

"We expect to make a considerable amount."

"I didn't ask how *much* you expect to make. I asked how you expect to make it in the first place."

"We make it from the commissions. What else?"

The realtor shook his head. "There's a margin for us, maybe. But not for whoever's shelling out the a hundred bucks for every open house."

"We've done our research. The margins are there. Count on it."

"Never in a million years," he shook his head. "What's this all in aid of? I think there's something else going on here."

Throats cleared nervously. Chairs scraped.

"Yeah, there is," said Devlin. "It's called open house fever. I plan to cause an outbreak. Then a national epidemic."

The man from NRS rolled his eyes. "Have you got the money in advance? This won't go up the river unless someone's rowing hard."

"I am. We have deep oars.. There are also franchise opportunities, which I will discuss later. I might add the entire promotion has already been test-marketed, with great success."

There was a low rumble as the powerful realtors exchanged surprised comments.

"This is going to cost someone a mighty big chunk up front," whistled the man from Coldwell Banker.

"The funds are in place," Devlin assured them. "Now, to create awareness and build consumer confidence and pro-action, on Open Homes for America Night the United States Government will be symbolically holding an Open House in many of its own properties."

"You just said that," said the man from NRS.

"No. You miss the point. Within a few days the President of the United States will sign a law that will have America swimming in cheap government mortgage money. And I happen to know the President wants this money used. So we, that is, the President and I, are working toward a common goal here. I expect that top

Federal officials will be holding Open Houses in their own buildings and institutions. The very symbols of government power."

"Like what?"

"The Capitol Building."

Babble broke out.

"The Senate."

It grew louder.

"The White House."

It fell silent.

"I invite you to participate," said Devlin with open arms. I have the agreements at this table, all drawn up. I even have pens."

In the stampede to sign up, the man from Coldwell Banker knocked over the platter of spicy, pan-fried Chincoteague oysters.

After it was over, Devlin thanked the realtors, took each of their cards, and gave them Gloris Dilt's phone number as the main contact point. Then he hurried down to the lobby and left a long distance message at Miatma Matsumoto's office. It was time to pay the piper.

*   *   *

"Kangtaze okimausu!"

Miamata Matsumoto spat out the words to his secretary then slammed down the receiver.

In Japanese it meant, "I'll give it some thought."

"Give it some thought, give it some thought," Matsumoto muttered to himself. An edge of impatience crept into his voice. "That's all I do these days." He looked angrily out of the window. His gaze swept up Vancouver's long gray harbor. A big shot like him and he couldn't make the smallest decision.

This is an embarrassment he thought bluntly. *Every time this new secretary asks a question, she gets no answer from me. I can't make decisions anymore, can't concentrate, my feet aren't on the ground...*

He stared at the phone and drummed his fingers on the desk. He quickly flicked through his unanswered telephone messages. In no time he sorted them into two piles. One pile was for regular business people, the other for the realtor-*eta*, Devlin. When he was finished sorting he counted seven regular messages versus eleven Devlins.

He hated even touching the Devlin messages. Those eleven pink slips were contaminated with a virus of risk. And there was no one here for him to consult with about how to deal with Devlin. Unlike back home in Japan, he had no group to share his problem with and gain consensus. Here in the land of the white barbarian, belonging to groups was out of fashion. It had never been in. The only thing he knew for sure was he was honor-bound to handle this deal on behalf of his father.

"Mako." he cried. "Mako Mako MAKO!" he slapped his hand on the desk.

She darted in.

"Get rid of these." he indicated the pile of Devlin messages as if someone had shit on his desk. "Take them away. Take away all this harassment. Take away everything. Then bring me his most recent message."

Mako whipped through the messages like a card shark then handed him one. She giggled with quick energy. The phone burbled in the outer office.

"It's probably him again," she glanced at her watch. "He said he'd keep calling, no matter what. Are you ready?"

"Give me a minute. Put him on hold."

He fought to compose himself. Once again Devlin was trying to throw him off balance again by making him angry. Matsumoto had distinctly instructed him not to call for at least eight weeks. Now here Devlin was pestering him in less than two.

He wondered how this white barbarian had ever gotten through to his father, a high executive protected by ranks of middlemen. And how his father had ever fallen for Devlin's wild proposition. The realtor-*eta* had literally promised to sell him the White House. And do it on national television. He claimed to have found the real owner, who would be happy to sell it for the right price.

It was not possible.

But it was *how* Devlin proposed to do it that left Miamata incredulous. He would use Open Homes International to create a grand diversion. Bribe thousands of the American working class *gagin* to hold an Open House in their own homes, then get the American politicians swept up in the fever and want to take the spotlight. They would be so busy basking in the glory that they would not notice what was really going on. He could not believe how greedy these people were. And the whole thing was based on a stinking hundred-dollar bribe to the homeowner.

This made him slow down and think hard about Devlin. As he stared at the receiver in its cradle, he admitted to himself that it was an extraordinary plan, worthy of the *Bing-Fa* masters. If it was true, this Devlin was either a brilliant general or a master of deception. Either way, Matsumoto would have to exercise extreme caution. To straightforwardly comply with Devlin's requests risked giving him an even greater edge. No. This would be a duel. Matsumoto was up to it now. He punched the button for Line 8. "Matsumoto here," he said flatly into the receiver.

"Ah. Matsumoto-san. *Salute*," came the voice from the other end.

"You were not to contact me for eight weeks," Matsumoto clipped his words, getting straight to the point.

"Yes, I realize that. But you don't understand. Things have gone much better than expected. I need money immediately. You must send funds."

Matsumoto's teeth grated. The man was already being offensive. Presuming to tell him he didn't understand things. He was pushy. There was too much lye in his bones. Very well. Two could play at this game.

"If you say this is important," countered Matsumoto, "then it must be so. Important matters require a face-to-face meeting."

There was a sickened moan from the other end. "I'm in Washington, DC for God's sake."

"I am aware of that. I noted the area code on your phone messages."

"Why on earth do we have to meet? It's just money."

Matsumoto paused, "You may wish to study my proposal for a meeting and call me back at some later time," he said curtly, "I will wait for your call."

"No. Wait. Don't hang up."

Matsumoto waited.

"I'll be there in twenty-four hours," Devlin sighed grimly.

"Very well. And where shall we meet?"

"What's wrong with your office?"

"Not appropriate," replied Matsumoto. He had no intention of allowing this risk-tainted barbarian anywhere near his office.

"The Carriage House in North Vancouver then," muttered Devlin. "It's safe there. We'll blend in."

Matsumoto decided to leave Devlin with a little good old-fashioned Japanese wisdom. He might actually benefit from it. "Blending in is good," Matsumoto informed Devlin. "The nail that sticks up will be pounded down."

*   *   *

Seawee and Tasha sat alone by a window in the Carriage House Bar. Beer fumes and tobacco smoke filled the air.

This was the first time they had seen each other since he failed to show up for his date with her the previous night.

Indeed, that evening had not gone well for Ray Seawee either. He got the Turnpike Cruiser all right. He gassed up at the 7-Eleven and was pulling out when the hardworking Needle-nose cruised by and spotted the car instantly. Without a driver's licence Seawee knew he was dead meat anyway so he took off up Lynn Vale Road for the mountain side-roads, where he knew he could lose the cop. But Needle-nose gave a Thunder Road-style pursuit, and in a panic Seawee ditched the Turnpike Cruiser over the steep bank. Needle-nose nabbed Seawee strolling back down the gravel road and took him for an informal visit to Judge Mannheim.

There, things got much worse. The Judge scared the shit out of Ray Seawee by telling him Red Devlin was mixed up in Sheng's murder, and that he, Ray Seawee, was an accessory after the fact. Then he kicked Seawee out on the street to let him think about it. He had to hitch hike back to the Carriage House.

Now Seawee sat next to Tasha and realized he still needed to a pologize to her, let alone offer an explanation. "How come you're not saying anything?" he asked after a cold slice of silence had passed between them.

"You really know how to show a girl good time," she said with edgy sarcasm. She bit off the words one at a time.

Seawee was momentarily tongue-tied. He wanted to forget last night, and hadn't counted on having to actually explain it to her. "There was this police incident," Seawee blurted before he knew what he was saying.

"They're after you now?"

"It had something to do with Devlin's car and me driving it," Seawee waffled.

"God, now it's both of you," Tasha rolled her eyes. "Hey, I don't know what you've done, but I've never done anything wrong in my life. I just want to get by, okay? Things have been hard enough without this crap. What have you done anyway?"

Seawee felt uncomfortable. "Jesus you ask a lot of questions."

"Listen sweetheart, I don't know about you but I'm at the peak of my career as a dancer. After this it's downhill. I have to be careful what choices I make. I don't want to hook up with a bunch of

DAVID JENNESON

petty con artists."

"You're at the peak of your career?" asked Seawee in wonderment. "Like, the precipice?"

Tasha shook her head dismissively. "While I was waiting for your call last night I had time to do some thinking," she said. "If this real estate thing works out I'd like to start a business. Maybe a boutique to teach housewives how to dress sexy. But that takes money."

"I'm sorry for standing you up last night. I didn't have a choice."

"Look, level with me," Tasha said. "Have you done anything that the cops are after you for? I have to know. I don't want to get mixed up in any more shit. This real estate thing is weird enough."

Seawee was careful how he answered her question. He knew if he mentioned his little meeting with Judge Mannheim, and the Judge's suspicion that Devlin might be involved in a murder, Tasha would be gone in an instant. For him that was unthinkable. His reply was very artful for a Seawee. "I don't know of anything I've done myself," he answered truthfully. "I think it was a case of mistaken identity. I didn't get charged or put in jail or anything. I mean, I'm here, aren't I?"

"Did you tell Saunders and Cutsie about the meeting?"

"I called Cutsie on her cell last night, and she was up at Saunders' eating pizza on his couch with him. I think she's staying with him. They were watching some bizarre show called '*From Roswell to the Rotunda - Aliens in Congress.*'"

"Living together, huh?" Seawee rested his chin on his hands dreamily.

"Don't sound so surprised. It doesn't take much to keep most women happy. A little place with someone warm on the couch. Money coming in. You're a hard worker. You'd probably be a good provider, even if you do bend the rules a little."

"I would?" Seawee asked, stupefied.

"You know what your problem is? You see me as some impossibly beautiful woman. So you think my expectations are impossible too. As soon as most guys see me they think they could never satisfy my expectations so they just want to fuck me."

"But you're so *fuckable*," said Seawee as tenderly as he could.

"Or they're like you. They want to fuck me but can only make cow eyes."

Seawee looked at the table and said nothing. His face reddened.

"Get over it, will you? A few more months of this Open Homes International thing and I'll have enough to start my own business. Maybe we could work something out together. You could do something. Sales. Real estate. Who knows?"

Seawee felt the earth move beneath his feet. He was so excited he thought he was going to faint.

A gap-toothed waitress with sagging breasts and a short skirt passed by and missed taking their order.

"Whatever happens, I refuse to end up doing *that*," Tasha nodded in the direction of the waitress. "Man, talk about bottoming out. But that's what's waiting unless I do something now."

Seawee looked at the bar clock, then stood and peered anxiously toward the door.

"Where are you going?"

"Outside."

"What about the meeting? Why are we here anyway?"

Seawee waved at the waitress. "Order some drinks when she comes back. Devlin's on his way. From Washington. And our money guy. Everyone's late. I'm going outside for a minute."

As Seawee paced the packed, rain-slicked parking lot, he gathered his thoughts. Devlin had surprised him the night before by leaving a message at the Carriage House announcing a whirlwind visit to Vancouver. Tasha's idea of settling down and starting a business together stuck in his mind. He'd never dreamed of such a possibility. But there was a problem. For all of his work on Open

DAVID JENNESON

Homes International he was still broke. He was furious at Devlin for allowing such a thing to happen. He wouldn't let it go on a minute longer. Without money, he figured he had no hope with Tasha, now or ever.

A ragged tear opened in the low overcast. The setting sun cracked through the clouds from the North Pacific. It blazed as if a gray envelope been torn open and spilled out heavenly orange light. Its intense rays coppered the slate-colored clouds above the Carriage House and away to the east. To Seawee it seemed otherworldly, like standing on a moon of Jupiter and gazing up at the Great Red Spot. Against the backdrop of dark clouds he could still see the winking lights of jet liners streaming in from points around the world.

He hoped that Red Devlin was on one of those inbound jets - a twinkling, moving source of light and money.

*   *   *

The truth was Red Devlin never had any intention of re-entering Canada by a dorky method like a scheduled flight through the closely watched Vancouver International Airport. Instead he had flown to Seattle, rented a car, then quietly sneaked his way the sixty miles northeast and across at the sleepy international border post of Sumas, Washington.

Seawee watched in surprise as Devlin now roared in behind the wheel of a big white rented Chrysler. He drove right past, found a parking space behind the hotel and moments later he emerged, walking, from around the corner of the building.

"*Ramon,*" he came striding across and extended a hand. "You've lost weight."

Seawee was tired. Worried. Mad. He had pressing questions. "I need money," he said, "and then you and I need to talk."

"So we shall," Devlin clasped Seawee's hands gregariously, "so we shall."

God's tow truck gurgled past. Cutsie Wu sat beside him. They disappeared around the back of the hotel, looking for a spot.

"What are *they* doing here?" Devlin hooked a thumb at the noisy, grubby truck.

"You called a meeting," said Seawee defensively.

"I didn't call the damn meeting. Matsumoto did."

"Well I thought you'd want everybody in the company brought up to speed. All at once."

This got him a scowl from Devlin.

"Besides," he added, "everyone needs money. Every account is empty. I haven't paid them for a couple of days now."

Devlin scratched his head. "Why not? I worked it out beforehand. The franchise fees are five thousand dollars. The commissions are five percent. They balance out."

The setting sun shot through the cloud cover more intensely and cast a sheet of gold across the dirty puddles and wet asphalt.

Seawee shook his head. "No. You've got it mixed up. I've sold the franchises for five hundred dollars and the commissions to the salespeople are fifty percent."

"You've WHAT?' Devlin cried.

"And I haven't even paid myself yet."

Devlin rubbed his jaw in disbelief, "Tell me you're joking."

"You see anyone laughing?" asked Seawee irritably. "This is the hardest thing I've ever done. It's got me so worried I feel kind of sick."

"I told you how to do the money. Didn't I tell you how?" hissed Devlin out of the side of his mouth. He jammed his hands into his back pockets.

"You said, use my best judgment. Open Homes International is the best company I've ever worked for. So our employees deserve the best. You said it yourself. That's what I went by."

Devlin looked at Seawee like he was about to be ill. "Fifty percent. Christ. They must be wealthy by now. How much have you

DAVID JENNESON

paid out?"

"Plenty. In cash. They deserve it too. They work hard. Thousands of people are ready to hold an Open House now. We just have to give the word. We've spread into Vancouver now. We'll be expanding up into the Interior soon. Setting up in Kamloops, Prince George…the whole North."

Devlin wilted under the enormity of this new information. He steadied himself on a parked car as a showroom-new, gun-gray Acura drew carefully in to the lot. Matsumoto had just bought the car to further hide his identity.

Back inside, the Carriage House was celebrating its annual Jugs and Mugs Festival. It had drawn a considerable crowd, hence the packed lot. Devlin watched Matsumoto tool circumspectly around the lot, then slowly head toward them. They stood beside the Carriage House bar's double door entrance. In the parking space next to them a single Harley Davidson sat on its own like a fat bumblebee. In the space next to that, three more were parked together. Tiny black suicide helmets strapped to the seats.

Just then God and Cutsie Wu joined Seawee and Devlin.

Devlin now watched Matsumoto's car approach with growing alarm. The gray Japanese luxury car drew up before the parking space and beeped sharply. Matsumoto impatiently waved them out of his way.

"Check out the asshole," said God.

Matsumoto honked again, pointed at them and made an unmistakable gesture at the lone Harley: *Move that thing to the next space.*

"Er … Mr. Saunders," Devlin turned to God, "would you be so kind as to just sort of slip that motorcycle over in the next space with the others?"

"No way I'm touching that hog."

Another pair of bikes rumbled into the parking lot. The riders dismounted, shook the water off their leathers and regarded the group with baleful looks.

"Me neither," said Seawee.

Matsumoto now honked furiously. They stood like statues and watched him. He was having a fit; being forced to wait while a single motorcycle took up all that valuable parking space. He looked ready to run it over. The two bikers gave Matsumoto a final malevolent look before going inside, obviously to inform the bike's owner.

A moment later the doors to the Carriage House slammed open. A large person emerged. He had a tremendous belly. His hair was parted into greasy braids. His thick arms were solid tattoo-blue from the wrist up. *Kid Bombast* was emblazoned across the front of his black t-shirt. He sized things up. Walked over and drew a tire iron from the Harley's saddlebag. Without a word he stepped forward and cracked Matsumoto's Acura a shattering blow, demolishing the right headlight. Kid Bombast then carefully replaced the tire iron and went back inside.

Devlin rushed to Matsumoto's window. "Well, now that we have that little misunderstanding cleared up, why don't we just go inside? Mr. Saunders will park this for you around back."

Looking stunned, Matsumoto got out and allowed himself to be guided inside. The Carriage House ambiance seemed to strike Matsumoto in the chest like a large rubber bullet. The music sounded like a thousand electric guitars all clawing at one note and missing it. To the left a tall, robust woman rumbled about the stage. She reached behind her and removed a black leather-studded clasp on the bra that stretched across her back. It released with a loud snap like an inner tube. Huge breasts exploded out. The crowd gave a roar that hurt the ears. Like Happy Hour for Attila the Hun.

"This way, *Monsieur*" Devlin schmoozed, calmly guiding Matsumoto by the elbow. He seated him in the corner window table where Tasha waited. Seawee slipped in beside her, next to the window and leaned back in his chair.

Matsumoto looked preoccupied. His mind whipped through the 36 *Beng Fu* Strategies like a Rolodex. He had no idea what Devlin

DAVID JENNESON

was trying to do to him here. First a sub-human giant had attacked his car, then he was led into a fleshpot, and was now seated at a table full of strangers.

Matsumoto needed to buy time. To think. He decided to employ the *Beng Fu* strategy known as *The Guest Becomes the Host*. He would manipulate the agenda by prevailing on Devlin's hospitality. As host, Devlin could refuse no reasonable request. This would give Matsumoto time to suss things out.

Devlin's face showed the strain too. "These are my staff," began expansively, "and this is Mr. Matsumoto, our very important but silent partner. Mr. Matsumoto is our financial muscle," Devlin good-naturedly squeezed Matsumoto's bicep.

"Excuse me," Matsumoto ignored him. "Do they have drinks here? I would like one. What do you recommend?"

"Try beer," Devlin grinned. "It's a specialty here."

'Ah, so," nodded Matsumoto. "And how many kinds of beer do they have?"

"Two," Seawee picked his nails impatiently. "Bottled and draft,"

"I think what our guest means is which *brands*," explained Devlin. He shot a black look at Seawee.

"Very well. I will try the draft."

Devlin poked an arm in the air and waggled two fingers at a waitress. "Now as I was saying, Mr. Matsumoto will be providing more venture capital as we expand -"

"And food. Do they have food here?" interrupted Matsumoto.

"Why yes. All kinds. Would you like a menu?" Devlin pressed his fingertips together solicitously and handed him one. Although it only contained about five items, Matsumoto made a show of studying it and was still at it when God walked in from parking the car.

Devlin cleared his throat. He placed his hands on the table. His fingers splayed as he leaned forward. "We now approach our launch date," he said with gravity. "As every house in America becomes be an Open House our financial needs will grow. Our friend Mr. Matsumoto will support -'

Matsumoto coughed. He appeared not to be listening. Instead, he looked up from the menu and around the bar. Up on stage the 5:45 Triple MUGS & JUGS Sextravaganza was just getting under way. "Excuse me," he cut Devlin off. "I notice you have many beautiful women here. Are they available for . . . private sessions? You know. *Mizu Shobai*," he waggled his hand, clearly meaning a private fuck.

This silenced everyone.

In Japan it was a normal request in this type of venue. *Mizu Shobai*, or *the water business*, was a Japanese euphemism for the pleasure trades.. The widely recognized network of sex-oriented geisha houses, bathhouses, bars, inns, restaurants, cabarets and love hotels was one of the country's biggest industries. And in Japan, adultery was socially acceptable.

"These are professional dancers," said Devlin uncomfortably. "For public see-see only," he lapsed into pidgin. "Not for sale."

Matsumoto laughed with genuine amusement. "What kind of dancer is not for sale? Dance is only to show wares. The real performance is upstairs," he jerked a thumb. "There are rooms here for that? I'll take two young ones."

That did it for Tasha.

"I have a question," she announced calmly.

"Not you too," said Devlin, already off balance.

"Yes. I want to know why the police chased your friend here when they spotted him driving your car."

"What?' Devlin leaned forward. 'My car?'

Tasha shrugged and pointed politely at Seawee. If she'd ever wanted revenge for him standing her up, she had it. For his part Seawee leaned back in his chair and ran his hand down his face.

DAVID JENNESON

"How the HELL did you get my car?" demanded Devlin. He looked quickly over at Matsumoto, who was suddenly looking troubled.

"Borrowed it," Seawee replied simply. "But don't worry. They'll never find it now." He leaned further back in his chair and looked out the bar window not as if he was guilty of stealing Devlin's car, but simply disappointed with the outcome. When he did this he looked straight into the eyes of Needle-nose. The policeman had pulled his patrol car up just outside the bar window. Needle-nose regularly patrolled the Carriage House nowadays. He wanted to show Judge Mannheim progress in the Sheng case. For the moment only Seawee could see him.

Meanwhile, Devlin let out his breath in jitters, fighting to calm himself from the last bombshell.

"I have some more news," added Seawee. "The cop who chased me before is sitting right outside now."

"Lord God," whispered Devlin. "Can he see us?"

"I don't know if he can see all of us, but he sure as shit can see me. Now he's parking."

"You two get out through the back exit and into my rental car," Devlin pointed at Seawee and Tasha "White Chrysler rental behind the hotel. Move it. NOW." He turned to God and Cutsie Wu. "You," he said, "stay in Canada. You are in charge here. I will call you at your home and arrange things. Give me your number. Hurry!'

God rattled it off.

Devlin was scribbling it down when he looked over his shoulder. Matsumoto was already moving low and fast toward the front exit. Devlin caught up with him. "I need money," he said. 'Now. This instant. Or everything will collapse.'

"I have no money here,' Matsumoto sped up.

"Take these," Devlin thrust two credit cards at him. "I have duplicates. Put a hundred thousand on each. Here are the PIN numbers. Even that will barely see us through for now."

Matsumoto pushed the cards away. He broke into a dead run.

Devlin snagged him by the lapel.

"You cannot break your obligations to your father," he shouted over the music into Matsumoto's ear. "It is the ultimate shame," he stuffed the cards in Matsumoto's suit pocket.

Then Devlin turned and hurried toward the back exit and rear parking lot. He moved quickly for a big man in such bad shape.

CHAPTER 18

Gloris Dilt was surprised to see a Diamond Cab pull up in the snow in front of her turreted townhouse. The hour was late.

"*Ssssst*," she clicked her tongue. This new breed of foreign cab drivers were always getting lost and coming to the wrong house.

Back in The Day, when the streets of America shook and cooked with energy, nothing gave Gloris Dilt more of a thrill than to see a torpedo-back 1949 Plymouth taxi pull up. Its bright yellow livery with those big black hand-polished fenders were a real sight. Then Gloris found late night cab-watching a relaxing pastime. Jack Benny's face would deadpan from the black and white porthole of a Philco television in her front parlor while she read through the minutiae of arcane Federal legislation. She would make her marginal notes, light a smoke here, have a nip there. Get herself in the mood. Fifty years experience had taught her that if she stayed up late enough a cab delivered a husband, or at least a likely candidate.

Even tonight, seeing this cab pull up brought back fond memories. In her state of bureaucratic tobacco and whisky Zen she had been quietly reviewing her growing Open Homes International file. Its documents revealed the startling authenticity of Anson Dobell's legal claim to the White House. She was trying to keep everything quiet, off-line and under wraps, including her own considerable activity and influence in organizing things.

As far as she knew, and certainly in her imagination, Red Devlin was still up in his rooms, dressed in a burgundy velvet smoking jacket with silk lapels and a tasseled belt, pacing slowly about, deep in thought, like Sherlock Holmes' smarter brother. Gloris mused that Devlin had been especially silent over the past forty-eight hours. That was as it should be. Red Devlin had made a commitment to her. She pictured him at this moment moving quietly about his quarters in a contemplative manner of a great thinker, be-robed, brandy and soda in hand, spinning the antique ochre globe, weighing things out in his mind. How he should best satisfy his end of their firm agreement in a gentle and loving way.

As far as Gloris Dilt was concerned, she had fulfilled her part in their mutual and caring bargain. Big time. Now she was bursting with good news for Red Devlin. She'd matched legal descriptions between Dobell's documents and the White House grounds. Then she'd retained a certain politically incorrect lawyer who had ties to a network of equally politically incorrect civil servants, all of whom had a serious difference of opinion with the current President, his policies and his party. These people could oil and silence the procedural wheels when called upon once the Dobell application was filed.

In Gloris Dilt's opinion the real wild card was Anson Dobell himself. She questioned his commitment. Tonight he'd been a pushover. She'd called him over to sign the documents and he'd meekly complied. The only problem was that he was at this moment flaked out on the front parlor couch, curled up like a caterpillar in his tan duffel coat, an immobile, bespectacled presto log. The man couldn't take his drink.

She eyed the taxi sleepily. It sat there stupidly in the snow. Next thing the driver would be coming up with a cold pizza asking for an address three miles away. The driver actually appeared to be resting on the steering wheel. Probably taking a nap. Typical. Gloris Dilt's eyes slowly hooded over and closed like a lizard dozing in moonlight.

Down in the taxi it was a different story. Things were animated. Everyone was very much awake, except for Mohan, who slumped over the steering wheel in worn-out disbelief.

"But you must be having money to pay," his voice broke, "otherwise you would not be hiring me."

"Oh and we do, we *do*," soothed Devlin. "It's just that the money we have tonight is behind in time. We're spending it tonight, but it won't be in our accounts until tomorrow. It's still catching up."

"Then you must be giving me other money that is catching up now."

Devlin had no money that was catching up now. Paying for the plane fares out of Seattle had required stickhandling funds from Seawee's perilously thin credit cards to Devlin's. Devlin's Visa and MasterCard were so anemic by now as to be practically transparent, like corpses drained of blood. It had been an embarrassing scene at the ticket counter, laying out all that near-worthless plastic like a fortuneteller's deck on the counter.

Their lateness in booking seats caused them to be placed willynilly throughout the aircraft. Seawee was stuck beside a mother and child and amused himself by playing with the tot. Tasha's seating placement next to a computer salesman caused the young man to start drinking rapidly, but his drunken machismo came to nothing. The best he could do was bore her senseless by showing off his laptop computer which he claimed was so tough it had been used on the space shuttle.

Devlin ended up beside the business editor for the Seattle Post Intelligencer. He plied him with hype about Open Homes International, the upcoming Open Homes for America Night, and the glittering spectacle of an open house at the White House. Soon the editor was taking notes. After several drinks Devlin gave the man one of his new cards. He'd had a new business line connected to the office in the turret, with a brand new Washington phone number.

Nevertheless they arrived in Washington broke. Devlin pulled Mohan's card out of his wallet. He called Diamond Cabs and personally requested Mohan's services. Cab drivers dreaded getting personal calls. They usually meant a non-paying trip for a relative or a deadbeat friend. This was no different.

Now, as they sat outside Gloris Dilt's townhouse, Devlin touched his fingertips together solicitously. "Could you slip by and collect tomorrow?" he leaned forward from the back seat.

"Tomorrow I am having day off," said Mohan tiredly. "First in two weeks. It is for the religion."

'Then we'll start an account," Devlin brightened. "Monthly. That way, you can become our regular driver," he added, pointing out an extra benefit Mohan may have overlooked.

"No accounts or charges can be set up except at office," said Mohan miserably. "It is the way."

Tasha sighed. It looked like she was going to have to bail out Open Homes International one more time, but she was past caring. All she wanted was sleep.

"I have some cash," she reached into her purse, withdrew a Canadian fifty and passed it over the seat.

Mohan scrutinized the pinkish-orange bill like it was moon money.

"Not taking pesos," he announced. "It is not allowed."

'Not pesos,' said Devlin. "Canadian money. Coin of the realm."

"Canadian money? Then you are British Commonwealth. Like India. Where is picture of English Queen?"

"No English Queen," Devlin scoffed. "We've gone beyond that. No sir, that's McKenzie King on that bill. The Canadian FDR. Got us through the war. And see here, on the other side. An owl. This could be nowhere else but Canada."

Mohan examined the bill for a long time beneath the shadowy interior light. "Mexican owl," he countered.

"This owl's white for God's sake" cried Devlin. "It's a snowy owl. They don't have snow in Mexico. Ever seen a Mexican in a parka?"

Mohan had to admit Devlin had a point there. And the bill did say Bank of Canada. Still, Mohan seemed to enjoy a good financial argument.

"Even better for you," continued Devlin. "The Canadian dollar is worth sixty-five cents American, so you can keep the whole fifty for a thirty dollar fare. Sort of a tip."

Perversely, Mohan's prior episode with Devlin, where they'd gone the distance together on his Howard Hughes-style food-shopping trip, had within the context of Mohan's religion, elevated Devlin above client status and qualified him as an actual friend. The religion demanded that Mohan give shelter to a friend in distress. Devlin now fell into that category.

"Sadly, the religion demands I grant your wish," he said with irony in his voice. "I am catching hell for this. Sometimes I wonder about the religion," he sighed.

"I'm sure we'll clear up any problems in the morning."

"As you wish," he said with resignation and pocketed the pinkish Canadian fifty.

"Remember," Devlin cautioned him, "we'll be needing your services regularly now so stay on your toes."

Mohan bowed his head and placed his hand over his heart.

Snow crunched as they disembarked from the taxi. Being as he was broke, Devlin realized he'd be poorly advised to wake Gloris Dilt with the thumping feet of uninvited guests on the hallway's wooden floor.

"Shhhh ..." he warned Seawee and Tasha. "The landlady is a very light sleeper. Insomniac. Hates to be awakened. I have a strategy. I'll just kind of slip through the front door and let you in. Up there," he pointed to the turret.

"Why?" asked Seawee tiredly.

"I've negotiated your room rates. All that's done. But I still have to settle up, so we'll just keep this under our hats for now. Better for us in the long run."

"Up that thing?" Seawee pointed to the squeaky, archaic fire escape.

"Oh yes. Done it a hundred times myself. BUT," Devlin cautioned, thinking of his own ghastly experience, "you must be very, *very* quiet."

Muttering, Seawee took Tasha's hand and led her across the snowy yard. Their feet crunched underfoot and poked holes in the stiff snowy crust. Then he did his sweet and level best to assist her onto the ancient fire escape. He felt it proper that she should go up first so he could catch her if she slipped. Tasha had also won the *Miss Best Buns in BC* title while she was stripping. Seawee moaned immoderately while climbing the steep metal stairs behind her.

Down on the main floor Devlin cracked open the front door. Slowly. Quietly. He noted a dim light coming from beneath the parlor door. White-shoed, he padded down the hallway. It smelled of old wood-oil and long-standing authority. He wished he'd paid extra for the softer-soled models of the white shoes he'd just bought. He crept down Gloris Dilt's main hallway. It was hung darkly with portraits of presidents and immensely powerful directors of huge American institutions. On his left, J. Edgar Hoover scowled down in formal men's clothes. On his right, an oil rendering of FDR, pince-nez glinting. Next a 1953 photo portrait of Mamie Eisenhower dolled up like the young Queen Elizabeth, but in this case it was signed by Mrs. President herself.

Devlin tip-toed past the scowling faces and nervously tipped his hat to them all. He probed his way up the dark stairs to second floor of the turret and quietly pried open the window. *Shooshing* loudly, he assisted Tasha through in her tight skirt. Then Seawee.

"Excellent," whispered Devlin. "There's a bed for you upstairs," he nodded to Tasha. "And you," he nodded to Seawee, "can sleep on the office couch in this room. I know you're both tired. So have a good long sleep. In fact, don't get out of bed in the morning until I come and get you. Better that way for the moment."

Tasha and Seawee were too worn down to question Devlin's odd household rules. They both just wanted to sleep and wake to a better real estate world in the morning.

For his part, Devlin had to become a martyr to the spring-shot couch in the main floor parlor. If Gloris Dilt caught him there in the morning, he decided he'd claim to have fallen asleep at his real estate work. That, or some other ennobling excuse.

As he crept back down toward the parlor, Devlin silently congratulated himself on his long range housing strategy. Gloris Dilt was early-to-bed, early-to-rise. Until Matsumoto's money came through, he could quietly shuffle Tasha and Seawee into the household routine like extra cards in the deck without her noticing. When the money arrived he could then negotiate for their lodgings or stick them in a hotel. He'd be so flush it wouldn't matter by then anyway. But the last thing he wanted to do was explain about two more unpaid-for persons when he hadn't paid a dime of rent for even his own body, tight black jockey shorts or not.

He cut down the hall, around the corner and pulled back the sliding parlor door. Stepping inside he drew his breath. There was Gloris Dilt, asleep at the parlor table, a half-glass of whiskey before her, an Old Gold still smoldering in the ashtray. For some reason he thought, *Still Life with Buzzard.* His eyes zipped over to the couch. The passed-out, duffel-coated form of Anson Dobell lay doggo.

Red Devlin instinctively shrank from the scene. He had no desire to disturb its artistic integrity. He took one large, careful step backward, as silently as his white shoes would allow.

Gloris Dilt cracked open an eyelid.

Devlin froze. Grinned like a cat.

Gloris Dilt's eyes brightened. Became they briefly full, like a young woman's. She wisped away a stalk of coarse gray hair from her forehead.

"I didn't hear you come in, honey," she said sleepily. Her voice was throaty and low from sleep and whiskey.

"Yes ma'am," answered Devlin. A smile was pasted to his face. "Late meeting. Realtors, you know. They love meetings."

"Was it a good meeting," asked Gloris softly, still ninety-nine percent asleep. .

"Er ... why yes," answered Devlin. He was rooted to the spot. The woman seemed to be in a trance.

"Oh *good*," replied Gloris. "Why don't you just take your clothes off and come to bed?"

"Eh?" Devlin grinned. "Bed you say?" He looked nervously over at the couch occupied by Anson Dobell. "What bed are you talking about?"

"You know," she rose and came to him. She wore a sheer nightie with thin straps. She placed her arms around his neck and kissed him deeply in the mouth.

Red Devlin's eyes bulged in panic.

She dreamily took him by the hand. "It's late."

Suddenly Anson Dobell thrashed violently on the couch. He uttered a cry in his sleep and hurled a pillow across the room like someone suffering from a childhood trauma. The pillow struck Gloris' whisky glass and sent it spinning off the table. It shattered on the floor. Devlin watched in astonishment. He'd heard of throw rugs. He guessed these were throw cushions. Anson flopped over, popped his head up and blinked like a mole.

The noise seemed to dislodge Gloris Dilt from her time warp stuck in 1949. It propelled her forward through to the present again. She shook her head. Rubbed her eyes.

"What the hell's going on here?" she demanded, looking around the room.

"I think you were sleepwalking," Devlin said, trying to accommodate her state.

DAVID JENNESON

She looked down at her hand, still holding Devlin's. "What? With you?"

"You thought I was your husband. You were taking me to bed."

"I was? Hmmmm. Maybe that's not a bad idea."

'I want to go home," moaned Anson.

In a panicky instant Devlin realized that without Anson here, the way was clear for Gloris to demand her end of their bargain. The sex end. With no witnesses. Hell, hadn't he promised her that? Made a verbal agreement. They were binding, weren't they? What had he been thinking?

"Home?" Devlin turned to Anson. "Out of the question. I must be brought up to speed on absolutely everything. Now. Every detail. Vital that I know."

"My head hurts," Anson whined. He sat up and adjusted his glasses.

"Easy to fix." Devlin walked over, pulled Anson to his feet and hustled him to the table. "You'll feel right with a little of this," he twirled the cap off the whiskey bottle.

"Forget it," said Gloris. "Look at him. Man can't drink."

"Well I can." Devlin poured himself one. "Now fill me in here. I need a total update."

"Business before pleasure," Gloris Dilt shrugged. She sat down and poured herself a nightcap.

Anson looked more wretched as he watched these developments. He seemed alarmed to see Devlin sluice down a great draught of sipping whisky, light a cigar and settle in.

"I don't like the way things are going here," Anson complained.

He looked over at the table. There was a vast stack of documents. Affidavits and blindingly complex legal descriptions of property. "I feel like I'm in over my head. I'm a detail person but I've never seen anything like this." He looked at Gloris Dilt with a mixture of awe and suspicion. "Did I sign anything? I only remember fuzzy patches."

"Signed, sealed and delivered," said Gloris. "Close enough, anyway."

"I want coffee," he said peevishly.

Gloris Dilt hissed a frustrated sigh. This man didn't measure up to anything. Couldn't drink. Couldn't even stay up late. She was glad the country hadn't depended on an army of Anson Dobells to fight the Germans in World War II. America's only hope would've been to bore the Nazis into surrendering. Otherwise Americans today might well be goose-stepping down Pennsylvania Avenue to mass rallies at the Washington Monument hosted by Adolph Hitler's grandson.

"Here's what's going to happen," Gloris impatiently instructed Anson. "I'll get you coffee, and you'll finish signing these documents." She shuffled over and bent down to clean up the shattered whiskey glass. "And quit throwing pillows around my house or I'll bat you one."

Anson scowled. Now Devlin became alarmed. He knew from previous experience that this was not a good sign. When Anson scowled like this he was likely to shoot off in unpredictable directions. He might even up and leave. It could screw up the agenda.

"So we have some signing to do?" Devlin intervened solicitously. "Cause for a wee celebration then," he lifted his glass.

"One signature left" shot Gloris. "He signed most of it before he passed out. Five drinks worth. Now he's on his ass." She rolled her eyes as she clattered out to make coffee.

Waiting for his coffee, Anson peered at the documents. He closed one eye to focus better.

"I don't remember signing all *this*," he said. "This is what George Washington did to the tobacco farmers. I won't be party to it a second time." He turned away and stared out the parlor window in a snit.

Two floors up, in the cold darkness of the turret office, Ray Seawee

DAVID JENNESON

shifted uncomfortably on the leather couch. It was too short. Blankets too thin. He suffered from troubling thoughts.

He worried about Red Devlin being a murderer. Devlin didn't act like any murderer Seawee had ever encountered in jail. They were cold-eyed hardasses who bragged about their crimes, as if killing another human being were the only worthwhile thing they'd ever done. But there was that Judge. And the pointy-nosed cop who stuck to him like white on rice.

Seawee's thoughts rolled in and out like the dark waves of the night sea. Waving in and washing out, eroding his confidence. All that waving and washing made him realize he had to relieve himself. Then maybe he could sleep. He now faced another problem. Devlin had told him to remain confined to his room until he came down in the morning. Seawee sighed.

Rules.

Drowsily he got up and stumbled toward the office window. He opened it with a woody thump.

Downstairs preparing coffee, Gloris Dilt cocked her head like an alerted iguana.

Seawee sleepily unzipped his fly. Let go. The cold air made him want to empty his bladder completely. He watched, satisfied, as it arched gracefully down two stories past the front parlor window and made a silent impression on the smooth, snow-covered lawn. He tried to write his initials. He had enough in him to script a good RS.

"It's raining out," observed Anson as he stared moodily out the parlor window, waiting for coffee. "Just a little."

Devlin absently considered this. He came from the Pacific Northwest where you lived with rain. Rain ruled your world. You knew rain. He continued studying the documents and said absently. "Can't be raining. It's too cold. And if it rains tonight it won't rain just a little."

"Well if you don't believe me then look," Anson pouted.

Devlin looked up and beheld the stream curling down past the parlor window. *Real estate is helping clients see other realities.*

"No rain that I can see," he said distractedly.

"That." Anson pointed. A wind caught the urinary arc and gave it a spray-like aspect.

"Rain? Can't be raining." Gloris announced as she emerged from the kitchen carrying the coffee. "To damn cold for rain."

"See for yourself," said Anson peevishly, still pointing. People were always correcting him and doubting his word. A stiff little gust blew a final patter of droplets against the windowpane.

"What the?" cried Gloris. She made for the window. Devlin shot up and followed. They all peered out.

Anson poked his nose curiously between them. "I guess it's stopped," he said sadly.

"Odd," Devlin tried to dismiss it. He wished he could ring Seawee's neck.

"Someone just pissed on my lawn," said Gloris. In a flat voice. Sure enough, there was a dark swirl of evidence in the snow. Seawee's badly formed initials. Worse, the evidentiary trail led back and tapered off toward the turret. Her eyes followed it suspiciously. "Someone's pissing on my lawn from *up there*," she declared, pointing angrily.

Devlin's mind worked like a locomotive. "Probably some lazy cab driver relieving himself," he said off-handedly.

"Bullshit. Since when do cab drivers climb on the roof to piss? If you've got someone up in that room you'll all be out on your ass."

Devlin held his arms wide and shrugged in speechless innocence.

"Right." said Gloris. "Goddamn intruder then. A goddamn pervert pissing burglar."

She strode over and unlocked what looked like a liquor cabinet. When she lifted the door it revealed not booze, but her weapon of choice, the Thompson. She flipped off the safety. Cocked it. "We'll

258.

DAVID JENNESON

see what **Tomasso** can find out about this," she patted the brute.

Devlin felt wobbly with dread. His mind raced. "What if the burglar's armed?" he shouted after her as she started for the stairs.

"This is America. Everybody's armed. But there's armed," she patted the gleaming Tomasso again and winked, "then there's *armed*."

Devlin dashed up after her, waving his arms hysterically but no words came out. For once he was robbed of speech. He feared an admission of guilt here on the stairs while Gloris' blood was up might result in the sort of tragic firearms incident that you read about all the time in American newspapers. *Landlady Machine Guns Innocent Realtor Over Extra Renter.* Seawee would have to fend for himself. Anson Dobell followed up behind, his spirits improving.

They reached the door. Devlin prayed it would be locked to give Seawee time to escape.

It wasn't.

"Fa-REEEZE!" shouted Gloris Dilt as she kicked open the door. She caught a confused and sleepy Seawee half into his pants. Hair in a muss. He duly froze. The pants dropped to the floor.

"Who the hell are *you*?" She demanded.

"A realtor," Seawee shakily raised his hands. He'd never seen such a deadly looking weapon, not even in the hands of Canadian prison guards.

"So," she turned around and eyed Devlin. "Stuffing my house with realtors, are you?"

"I can explain -'

"Get dressed," she snapped at Seawee, ignoring Devlin. "We'll see about this."

At that moment two slender ankles appeared at the top of the spiral stairs leading upstairs to the turret bedroom. Next came long, firm, tanned legs. Smooth as satin and perfectly formed as any God's creation. They seemed to go on forever. By now everyone was staring. Next the frill of a short nightie. Milky soft hips. High waist, flat and narrow. Magnificently endowed. Tasha's face, her regal beauty. And her vulnerable eyes.

"What a beautiful girl," said Gloris Dilt, in awe.

"I couldn't sleep," said Tasha softly. "I heard shouting. Is someone in trouble?"

"This is my associate," whispered Devlin.

"Could I use the washroom?" asked Tasha sleepily, "I've been trying to wait 'til morning but I can't."

"Of course you can, dear," said Gloris. "Have they got you cooped upstairs? *Men.*" She shot Devlin a look. "And you," she poked *Tomasso's* black muzzle at Seawee. "Get yourself decent. There's a lady present."

Seawee hastily pulled up his pants and patted down his hair. In his entire career he'd never been so simultaneously guilty yet innocent.

"Have you eaten, dear?" Gloris asked Tasha as she marched the three men downstairs at gunpoint.

"A sandwich on the plane. I'm fine."

"These men know nothing. Pigs. How would they know to take care of a princess like you?"

"Honestly, I'm all right."

"Nonsense. You go and get yourself fixed up. I'll have something hot ready. Warm you up. Cold in that top room."

Tasha excused herself.

Gloris marched Devlin, Seawee and Anson into the parlor.

"You three park yourselves there," she pointed to the short couch with *Tomasso's* muzzle.

The three scrunched down together miserably, jailbirds on a prison bench.

"Now you," she poked Anson with the barrel, "finish signing these papers. I'm tired of screwing around." She dropped the sheaf into his lap. He dutifully scribbled away.

"You," she prodded Devlin, "better come up with some cash. When this deal goes through some high paid officials will lose their jobs. They expect the cash equivalent of their salaries to age sixty-five plus, ... shall we say their pensions. Up front. American dollars. That's the deal. Include me in that. The amount, I assure you, is considerable.

"Can you give me some idea?" asked Devlin meekly.

"Start at a million."

"How long?"

"A week. In return you will have this claim on the White House property duly authorized and registered. The historical data for your claim is impeccable. These documents clearly show that one David Burnes illegally sold property belonging to one Dobson Dobell to one George Washington. All quite straightforward if you know how to read it. Normally the people in charge of authorizing this new claim would immediately notify the White House so they could contest it. And contest they would. Stall till the end of time. Now they won't. Once the claim is registered, it will produce a deed for the property with Parcel Identifier 001-612-328, otherwise known as 1600 Pennsylvania Avenue. That deed will be issued in the name of one Anson Dobell."

Tasha entered, shyly clutching a robe around her. "I borrowed this. I hope you don't mind."

"I haven't worn that in years," said Gloris fondly. "Look at you. Reminds me of how I used to look. You just settle in at the table and we'll get something into you."

Ten minutes later when they were all down in the kitchen Tasha had finished a steaming bowl of bean soup and crusty bread. She smiled sleepily.

"That's better, isn't it," said Gloris kindly. "Now you get upstairs and get a good sleep. These dogs can fight for the leftovers."

Tasha thanked her and tranquilly withdrew.

With all this taking care of business Gloris had neglected to replace *Tomasso* in the cabinet. She absently kept the machine gun couched in the crook of her arm, where it continued to lend her a certain unarguable authority.

She yawned. "Okay. We'll sort this out in the morning. You," she nudged Anson, "call yourself a cab and beat it." Anson rose and happily scuttled over to the phone, finally having obtained permission to leave.

"You," she poked the tired, hungry Seawee. "Get back upstairs where you belong. And if you get restless, leave that girl alone." She poked him in the shoulder with Tomasso. "You follow me?"

"Yes ma'am," Seawee nodded. He left, unhappily climbing the stairs.

"And you," she poked Devlin in the gut, "you owe me rent. And you lied to me. I hate that. Do it again and I'm going to have a hunting accident with this thing. You can damn well sleep on the couch."

Devlin accepted the news with bowed head, trying his hardest to look like the disappointed and punished dog he was.

CHAPTER 19

$\mathcal{A}$s he lay in the darkness back upstairs in the turret office, Ray Seawee suffered from bad déjà vu.

The old leather office couch made for a short hard bed. It was bowed up, so it was like trying to slumber on the back of a skinny old cow. The blankets were short. He was hungry and felt picked on. The frigid air of the turret reached in and penetrated his bones like radio waves of old ice hockey broadcasts from chilly Canada. It felt like any one of a thousand nights he'd spent in jail. He shivered and hugged himself. He tossed and turned, half expecting a prison guard to pace by on his rounds.

Sleep evaded him. Every time he blinked open his eyes he came face to face with the large framed black and white photograph of Dwight and Mamie Eisenhower, frozen in black and white time, stepping off a Boeing Constellation at a wintry 1952 Washington airport. The image hovered in the dark above him. Seawee found Mamie Eisenhower scary. The woman had a face like a catcher's mitt.

He shivered again and saw puffs of his own breath in the turret's chilly air. Open Homes International was roaring ahead while his personal fortunes had advanced barely an inch. He was broke and hungry, still being ordered around and now sleeping rough on a hard old office couch. He might as well have stayed in prison, no better than a dog. He told himself that there were better days ahead but he was tired of surviving on faith alone. Something had to come of it all soon. He decided that in the morning he'd lay it out on the table with Red Devlin.

He was forming the thoughts in his mind, figuring out what he'd say, moving his lips in the dark, when the small hours took pity on him and he finally fell asleep. As the solitary occupant in the turret office at this hour, Ray Seawee was also by default the night desk clerk for Open Homes International. Two minutes later the phone issued a throaty metallic *brrring*.

He stumbled to his feet and bumped into the globe, sending it spinning. As he groped for the phone he fretted that the noise of the ringing would wake Tasha, one floor above, and that he'd be blamed. The old black Lucite receiver felt heavy in his grip. As he fumbled around in the dark it occurred to Seawee that his quality of life had truly gone into the dumper. You could say what you want about sleeping in a prison cell, but at least the phone didn't wake you up.

"Um," mumbled Seawee into the phone.

"Have I got Open Homes International?" inquired a twangy voice.

Seawee's eyes opened a notch, "Yup."

"This ar's Vernon Crouse. Callin' from Arkansas. Apologize for callin' so early but I gotta git a-movin'. Drive Ford truck parts back an' forth to Michigan. Wife left a note on the fridge with this number. Says we got a contract for a hunnert bucks to hold our house open for sale when it hain't for sale in at all, but we still get the hunnert. Some ree-lah-tor from Cold'ell Banker come by."

Seawee tried to follow, "Uh huh."

"So. What's the deal? This on the level? Hit don't sound on the

DAVID JENNESON

level. Sounds like one a' them 'ar scams where a feller looses his house an' home fer a hunnert bucks by signing something away without studyin' after it first."

Seawee had no idea why this phone call was coming to him from a remote spot like Arkansas. He sighed. "All I can tell you is I've given out so much money lately that I wish I had a bunch of my own houses to hold open. Everyone gets paid. I've seen it myself. That's all there is to it. I'm worn out from handing out money."

Silence from the Arkansas end of the line.

"Hello?… Arkansas?… talk or I'm hanging up," Seawee said impatiently.

"I dunno." Vernon Crouse cut in thoughtfully. "You know, you sound on the level to me. I'm a working feller. My wife done got ripped off by mail order once with shit lottery tickets from Canader. I'll personally track down anyone who tries something like that. I got guns and I got friends with guns and we're all movin' all over the country all the time. Screw me around and there'll soon be a new face in hell. Git me?"

"Yeah," shrugged Seawee. "So what's that got to do with me? I told you I've never seen so much money get paid out so fast in my life as here."

There was another pause. "You know, it sounds okay. When do we get paid?"

"Soon," said Seawee tiredly. "From your realtor though. Not from me, not face to face, like."

There was silence again.

"The ree-lah-tor'll pay me?"

"That's what I said."

"When?"

"On Open Homes For America Night, like everyone else"

"An' when's that?"

"Real soon. I'll be glad when it's over so I can get some sleep."

"I'll take your word on it," said Vernon Crouse after a moment. "What'd you say your name was again?"

"Ray Seawee."

Seawee heard the flick of a lighter. 'Well Ray," Vernon Crouse coughed into the phone. "Just so I got it straight in my mind, who exactly are you in this organization? So's I can write it down?"

"A realtor."

"That's it? Not some big shot manager or director?"

"They gave me some fancy title but all I do is work anyway."

"Well that's good. You're a workin' feller too then. Take some advice. From me to you pal, you oughten to get you some rest. You sound plumb tard out. But thanks for takin' the time. And I'll tell you something else. I go up through eight states today. Me an' my buddies will spread the word about Open Homes for America Night. Real good, like." He hung up.

Befuddled, Seawee made his way back to the couch. Arkansas. Where was that? Who came from there? Maybe the Wizard of Oz? Wasn't there a dog involved? These images faded in noddy speculation when the *brrring* of the phone cut through again. Seawee trudged woodenly over and picked it up.

"Hello," said a male voice. "Is this Open Homes International?"

"Uh huh," Seawee replied, still woolly-minded

"Do I have Red Devlin?"

"Nope. Still asleep. What do you want?"

"Bill Rawlinson, business reporter for the Seattle Post-Intelligencer. Sorry for the hour but I'm working on the early morning edition. My boss gave me a lead. Met this Devlin on a plane. Told him about something called Open Homes for America Night. People holding Open Houses all over the country. Government's involved. He said it's going to be spreading like wildfire. What can you tell me?"

DAVID JENNESON

"I just got a call from Arkansas," Seawee informed him.

"And?"

"They're on board."

"Who's *they*?"

"Truck driver signed a contract for an open house. Says now they're spreading the word through eight states."

"Eight states? How far has this gone?"

Seawee rubbed the back of his neck. Aside from Arkansas, he could only think of one other location. "Canada."

"It's crossed the border already?"

"Sure. Everyone knows that."

"*Everyone* knows?" came a choked voice.

Seawee yawned. "I gotta go."

"Hold on!" cried the reporter. "You'll be there for a while? At this number?"

"Probably."

"Good. I'll call you back in half an hour."

Like hell, thought Seawee. He disconnected, then let the receiver dangle off the hook. He was tired of this. Questions without end.

Two hours later while they had breakfast at Gloris Dilt's kitchen table, Red Devlin nearly swallowed his boiled egg whole when Seawee groggily mentioned getting a call from Arkansas because a Coldwell Banker realtor had been making cold calls. Devlin got so excited that Seawee failed to mention the Seattle reporter's call at all. Obviously Arkansas was more important to Devlin.

One hour after that, Devlin had Seawee and Tasha in downtown Washington, waiting on the sidewalk while he went into a bank. Seawee's eyes watered from the chill wind. Devlin dashed in, stood before a bank machine, said a silent prayer to St. Homobonus, and punched up the balance. He let out a small cry of joy. Matsumoto had deposited two hundred thousand dollars in his account.

Thus armed, Devlin hauled Seawee and Tasha up to the tenth floor of the bank building and marched into the regional offices of Coldwell Banker. He aimed to find out why he was suddenly getting phone calls from a distant spot like Arkansas.

The real estate office looked more like the floor of a small stock exchange. Realtors bolted in and out of offices and yelled into phones. Fax machines burbled and whined and spat paper. E-mail backed up. People stared with almost hysterical intensity into computer screens. The pile of freshly-minted open house signs stacked in one corner of the large, high-ceilinged sales room was quickly diminishing. Above all the chaos, through the tall office windows, the Washington monument dominated the horizon like a talisman and spiritual anchor. Secretaries dashed to and fro, their arms filled with contracts. There was so much fuss that everyone ignored the members of Open Homes International. They wandered freely about the floor until Devlin spied the open office door of Mr. Russell Jones, better known to his contemporaries as Erogenous Jones, Vice-President and southeastern Regional Manager of Coldwell Banker.

"Ah screw you!" Jones shouted into the phone. "I don't care how many more branches you've got in Newark than I do. I'm NOT trading New Jersey for Delaware. Ever hear that expression?"

There was a pause.

"N-O! I keep New Jersey, you live with Delaware. Luck of the draw, pal!" he slammed down the phone.

Devlin peeped into the office. "Sorry. Not interrupting I hope?"

"DEVLIN!" Jones swabbed his brow. "Where have you been? Is your phone off the hook? Been trying to reach you. This is crazy. I've never seen anything like it."

"Going well, is it?" Devlin inquired innocently.

Jones looked a little squirrelly from the stress. "I don't know how these other companies are coping but we're barely keeping up here. The bunch of us - I mean the main players - we all sat down after

DAVID JENNESON

that meeting and divvied things up state by state, in some cases county by county - but you as just heard," he left his sentence hanging and pointed dolefully at phone. "All professionalism has gone out the window. Pretty soon it's going to be every man for himself. I have good evidence," he lowered his voice, "that Century 21 is poaching my turf in the Texas panhandle." His eyes darted back and forth. "*Bastards.*"

"I'll deal with that," said Devlin quickly. "My associates are here to represent the interests of Open Homes International. Handle the franchises. Sounds like you need a little refereeing too," he added with a concerned look.

"Good," Jones gazed abjectly about his littered desk for a moment. He still seemed agitated. Then he spotted something. "Here, you can start by paying this," he tore a long ribbon of paper out of his desk calculator. "A hundred and fifty-thousand dollars in contract and commission expenses. And rising."

Devlin scrutinized the length of paper carefully, as if he were a forensic scientist examining a strip of DNA evidence. "These pre-payments won't be necessary now," he said announced thoughtfully. "That call from Wichita convinced me this morning."

"*Wichita?*" Jones gave an anguished cry. "Witchita's in Kansas and belongs to me. MY STATE. We haven't even started there yet. Who called from Wichita?"

"Not Wichita," Seawee corrected the word. He tried to remember. "Maybe Omaha?"

Devlin gave him an uncomprehending look. "Omaha. *Nebraska?*"

"No." Seawee corrected himself again. He shook his head and rubbed his eyes. "Not Omaha. Arkansas."

During this exchange, Erogenous Jones' head switched back and forth like he was watching a tennis match.

"We spoke to someone from Arkansas this morning," Devlin placed his hands deliberately down on the desk. "A homeowner contacted by one of your Arkansas agents. He seemed quite happy to wait for compensation until the day of their open house. Nevertheless," he sighed, "I will of course honor the terms of our agreement." He gravely unraveled the strip of calculator paper from out of his white jacket pocket. "The money for these trans- actions will be in your account in an hour."

He stuffed the strip of paper back into his pocket like a hundred and fifty thousand dollars meant no more to him than a strip of confetti. Devlin knew he probably owed this much again to all of the real estate companies. He also knew that Mr. Erogenous Jones, in that way realtors have, would brag that he'd been paid in full. The others would now sit on their hands for a bit, not wanting to jeopardize their piece of the action with a rudely premature request for money. They'd know Jones had been paid almost instantly. Could theirs be far behind? Plus interest?

Jones sank into his chair, relieved. "That's a load off my mind," he breathed. "It was mounting up."

"I want you to call the other realtors," said Devlin. "Tell them we've had a meeting. Tell them that from this point on, all open house contracts will be paid out on Open Homes for America Night. The night of the event. They'll understand." *Real estate means changing the rules.*

Erogenous Jones nodded in silent agreement. He and Red Devlin saw realtor-to-realtor on this. No one had expected Open Homes for America Night to take off like a Roman candle, but it had. In these frantic circumstances no reasonable realtor could expect the huge amount of cash required to be supplied up front. People would just have to wait for the wad to hit the fan.

"What about franchises?" asked Devlin suddenly.

"Here," Jones distractedly poked a pile of agreements and uncashed checks on his desk. "I just haven't had time."

"My Franchise Director will deal with these," Devlin scooped the checks and dumped them in Seawee's lap. "And my Corporate Relations Officer will mediate disputes," he nodded toward Tasha. "If my staff here need office space, give it to them. Bill me with- out delay."

DAVID JENNESON

Suddenly Jones' phone rang again. He shrugged and answered it. Devlin quietly guided Seawee and Tasha out of his office.

"You go around to every real estate head office in Washington and collect these franchise checks," he said quickly to Seawee. "They must be piling up everywhere. Open an account in the bank downstairs and deposit the works. Then go out and start pushing franchises. Organize meetings. Do what you have to. I don't care. We're letting money slip through our fingers here."

Seawee nodded grimly.

And *you*," he nodded toward Tasha, "go back in there and sort out these turf wars before they get out of hand. I don't want any hitches or lawsuits clogging things up now. He looked at Tasha pleadingly, "Keep these boys in line, will you? If two of 'em are butting heads over something, take care of it *in person*. Get together with them. I never saw two realtors yet who didn't turn into complete gentlemen with someone as pretty as you. Let them know you want things resolved on the spot. They'll fall over themselves patching things up. Believe me. I would."

Devlin turned to go. He stopped halfway to the elevator, turned back and pointed at Seawee. "And *Raymon*. Pay yourself this time. And pay the little lady. I'll see you tonight."

Devlin emerged from the elevator and entered the bank on the ground floor. He knew he had to make himself do this now or he'd never do it. His eyes were damp with grief at having to part with all this money so soon. He wrote a check for a hundred and fifty thousand dollars to the Coldwell Banker branch upstairs. It left him with only fifty thousand in his own account, but the whole real estate industry would know that Open Homes International paid its bills.

No one would hassle him for money for awhile. In his heart Devlin knew that St. Homobonus, patron saint of realtors, would approve of this gutsy move. Perhaps St. Homobonus, George Washington and Moses were gazing down on him from some lofty realtor's lounge in heaven right now, clinking glasses to this maneuver. The thought made him feel better.

He also consoled himself by withdrawing five thousand cash. The idea of St. Homobonus and George Washington and Moses with nothing better to do than hang out in some heavenly lounge where the drinks were free and the gorgeous cocktail waitresses were all in love with you made Devlin thirsty. He wanted to find its earthly counterpart. It was lunchtime. He needed a dram and a bite to catch his breath and think. Things were moving fast.

He saw a pay phone and, in his flush state, he briefly considered dialing up Mohan and hiring him for the day. Then he remembered it was Mohan's day off. So he flagged a taxi and requested a drive-by of the White House, which was impossible because the two blocks in front of it were permanently sealed to traffic. The driver did his best. This eventually put them onto lower Pennsylvania Avenue. He finally spied a bar that suited him - Jenkin's Hill. It was dark and clubby - not quite loungey enough for his taste but it did boast the longest bar in Washington, DC.

Devlin needed only a little space at that bar. A spot for an Alberta sipping whiskey, himself, and an ashtray. That was room enough to think.

He took a slug of his whiskey and felt the golden liquor slide down his throat. He lit a cigar. He liked America. He liked Washington. Cigar smoke and whiskey were part of the natural environment.

Congressional aides and lawyers now swarmed in for lunch. Devlin felt lucky to have a seat. He was excited to be here. It was just noon. The bartender turned on the TV. This was too close to Capitol Hill to be a sports bar. Here, CNN was king.

"This just in from Seattle," opened the anchorwoman. "The Seattle Post-Intelligencer reports that thousands of Americans are being paid a hundred dollars each to hold an Open House, whether their homes are for sale or not. The company is Open Homes International. The event is called Open Homes for America Night, and the catch is," the anchorwoman paused for dramatic effect, "that there is no catch. Home sales are reported to be climbing, which could well trigger new home starts. The plan has spread through at least eight states and into Canada and is being promoted, in some part at least, by America's long distance truck drivers."

Devlin watched in disbelief as the news broadcast went live on location. There was a shot of an appalling, rain-blasted strip of tarmac outside a sprawling Seattle truck stop. The reporter struggled to thrust her microphone up to a truck driver who was already halfway into his cab. She flashed her piano-teeth smile at the news camera.

"They say America's long distance truck drivers are giving a big push to Open Homes for America Night. Are you a supporter too?" she shouted up through the wind and rain and hiss of interstate traffic.

"I ain't heard of it yet," said the truck driver, "but if America's truck drivers support Open Homes for America Night, then so do I. Soon as I get on the road I'll be on the CB to get the info and promote it. And so will they," he gestured with his arm.

The camera pulled back and panned to reveal hundreds of eighteen-wheelers, parked neatly in rows, engines idling, while their owners crowded inside the huge truck stop restaurant fueling up on hamburgers and coffee. Lines of amber running lights winked in the morning twilight, receding off into the distance. Occasionally from somewhere deep within the ranks of trucks a driver would fire up his rig and an angry blast of black smoke would shoot from the stack. It looked like a vast and terrible army about to mount an advance.

The camera swung back to the driver and reporter.

"In the meantime, where do I sign up?" the driver shouted as he climbed inside.

The reporter struggled to finish her story as the truck behind her roared and snorted to life. "The force behind Open Homes for America Night is believed to be a company called Open Homes International, based in Washington, DC. They could not be reached for comment, although it's believed they may be working through your local real estate company."

Behind her the huge silver-fluted semi slowly rolled forward and moved off toward the interstate. Its engine snorted and bellowed like a grizzly as it revved. The wind whipped the reporter's blond hair across her forehead. "Whatever the case, Open Homes for America Night seems to be an idea that is definitely on the move."

Quite a crowd had gathered around the TV over the bar by the time the newscast was over. They edged and elbowed around Devlin as they watched.

"Seems like a damn good idea to me," said someone behind him. "I was thinking of selling my place and moving up. Now it'll be easy. I can test the water and make a c-note. What was the name of that company?"

"National Open Homes?" suggested another voice.

"It shows real creative thinking," remarked a third voice. "I'll bet a lot of houses will be bought and sold. Money will move. Just what the economy needs. Too bad it takes some private citizen to come up with the idea while the government sits on its thumb and does nothing to help."

There was a rumble of agreement.

"What's the name of that company again?" asked the first voice. "American Open House? "

"Naw, that's the event the company's sponsoring," someone else said. "I think."

"Maybe I'll phone CNN."

"Maybe I'll phone my realtor."

"I'm phoning my wife."

The entire crowd moved off toward the pay phones or wandered off for a quiet cell call like a herd of entrepreneurial sheep, leaving Devlin relatively alone at the bar.

"God almighty," he whispered to himself. "I've just seen a miracle." He licked the end of his cigar and looked around nervously, as if someone might recognize him. Then he took a slug of sipping whisky and shrugged. *God helps realtors who help themselves.* He needed to get to a phone himself. He spent an anxious half-hour waiting for the pay phone lineups to die down. Finally he got through to the main number of RICO.

"Racketeer Influenced and Corrupt Organizations," answered a female voice, making the mouthful sound sweet.

"McGeorge Lewis please."

"Mr. Lewis is in a meeting right now. I can have him call you. Who's calling?"

"This is Devlin."

"Oh," Her tone changed. "One moment please." There was a complicated series of clicks then a haze of static. The voice of McGeorge Lewis boomed hollowly from a speakerphone.

"Hello Devlin? In a meeting here. Gloris Dilt told me to expect your call. I'll make it quick. I've been in touch with a few people myself. Capitol Building. Congress. The White House. Very ingenious promotion. They're interested in getting on board but it's been slow. You know how government is. What's going on at your end?"

"The story's out on CNN," said Devlin as calmly as he could. "*Everyone* wants in. We must hold a press conference today so the public can get the facts straight. Maybe we can get on the evening news."

"Good God. How on earth?"

"I don't know. But we don't have a minute to waste," said Devlin breathlessly. "Can you manage it?"

"Can I manage it? There are two operative words here. Two magic words, Mr. Devlin."

"Eh? Magic words?" Devlin's mind raced. Had he forgotten something? He grabbed for anything. "Please and thank you?" he asked hopefully.

"No, my friend. Try again."

Devlin's mind went blank. "I'm stumped," he tried not to

sound panicky.

"Two magic words. Government Leadership. Ever hear of that?"

"Of course!" cried Devlin. "So you can do it?"

"Tell you what," said McGeorge Lewis expansively. "You just keep those two little words in mind. In the meantime I'll touch base with the White House Press Secretary. You be here at three o'clock."

Devlin went back to his spot at the longest bar in Washington, DC. He didn't have time to go back to Gloris Dilt's and clean up so he had another whiskey. He wished Mohan were here to take care of him and keep him calm. The top of the hour rolled around and the newscast was repeated, but this time it showed crowds gathered around several Seattle real estate offices. The reporter commented that Open Homes for America Night seemed to be a little disorganized at the moment, but perhaps the bugs were still being worked out.

Devlin suddenly realized he needed a list of which major real estate companies were handling which states. Vital information for the press conference. If Century 21 had California there'd be no use in Californians going to Coldwell Banker. He ran back to the pay phones but the news broadcast had caused longer lines than ever. Out of sheer anxiety he jumped in a cab and headed back toward the Coldwell Banker office to get the list himself, but found himself caught in blocks of gridlock.

Minutes ticked by. Devlin sat and cursed. Finally, nearly weeping with vexation he paid out the driver and fled the motionless taxi. He ran to a pay phone. He called the Coldwell Banker number. A harried receptionist answered immediately and put him on hold. Then it went dead. Finally he got a line in, only to be told that Mr. Jones was in an urgent meeting and could not be interrupted. In desperation Devlin asked for Tasha. When he finally got her he told her to get the list at all costs and fax it to RICO immediately. Then he tracked down another cab and fought his way through back traffic to the RICO office.

He burst through the door sweating. It was a quarter to three. Sure enough, CNN was there with hot television lights and micro-phones, but McGeorge Lewis was nowhere to be seen. A recep-tionist pointed Devlin toward his office. In his highly excited state Devlin was shocked to see McGeorge slumped at his desk, his face as long as a government mule's.

"Mr. Devlin I assume," Lewis looked up miserably.

"What is it? Something gone wrong? CNN's outside."

McGeorge looked up at him glumly. "I've been end-run," he fumed. "Those bastards from the White House. Never should have got them involved in the first place. Now they're taking over the whole thing. The White House Press Secretary will be here any minute. He's doing the press conference himself. Story of my life. All of the work. None of the glory."

"But your properties. All those government-seized houses. Are they still ...?"

"Ah, don't worry about them," said McGeorge sniffed. "Nothing's changed there. Nossir. Only thing different is the White House crowd saw a good thing and decided to take the credit themselves. They need it too. Election year. I should've known."

Just then McGeorge's office door opened. A man in sunglasses with a radio earpiece scanned the room briefly then stepped aside. The White House Press Secretary followed. He was young, bright, and crisply personable. He shook Devlin's hand warmly.

"Mr. Devlin? Crawford Jones," he introduced himself.

"Yes. I've seen you on TV before," Devlin was a little in awe.

"Mr. Devlin, we really do admire what you're doing here. Now, if there's anything we at the White House can provide, you just say it."

"There's just one thing,' said Devlin.

"Go ahead and name it.'

"Government leadership," said Devlin humbly.

McGeorge looked up from his desk and silently rolled his eyes.

"Ah," Crawford Jones led Devlin out of McGeorge's office by the elbow. "Yes, Mr. Lewis mentioned that. If we were to symbolically hold the White House OPEN for a night, and maybe a few other of our great institutions and buildings, would that would be helpful? Is that the kind of government leadership you're talking about?"

"Exactly the kind," Devlin nodded, just as humbly.

"Well Mr. Devlin, I think we can see our way clear to do that. Now why don't you brief me on this? Then we'll talk to the media."

Devlin quickly explained Open Homes for America Night and what it was meant to accomplish. The young Crawford Jones, eyes blazing with ambition and intelligence, grasped every detail.

"What an ingenious plan. Just what the economy needs. Now, for the media, how do Americans get in touch with Open Homes International?"

"They don't need to. We work through America's real estate companies. State-by state. There should be a list sitting on the fax machine."

"Fascinating. America's realtors will thank you I'm sure. Now just one more thing. What's all this business with truck drivers?"

"They support us," Devlin said simply. "They're America's most independent businessmen and they're behind us one hundred percent."

"Well that's a first. We can't get the teamsters to support anything." Crawford Jones looked at his watch. "Well, shall we?" he gestured toward the podium and blaze of television lights.

"You go ahead," Devlin held up his hand. "You're the professional. I'm just a simple realtor. I've got a lot to do between now and Open Homes for America Night."

"As you wish. By the way, when is Open Homes for America Night?"

Devlin had no idea. He looked at his watch. "Why, a week from tonight," he replied, as if it were common knowledge.

"Thank you sir." Crawford Jones extended his hand. "It's been a real pleasure, and I mean that. America needs more men like you, Mr. Devlin."

Crawford Jones opened the press conference with the smooth, masterful touch of a game show host. "I am pleased to announce a joint initiative between government and private industry to get America moving again. Now any American homeowner can earn a hundred-dollar payment for holding an Open House on Open Homes for America Night. Working with your local realtors, a bold, visionary organization called Open Homes International will provide the funding."

"Is it on the Internet?" asked a reporter.

"The government will provide a web site," Crawford Jones winged it, "at www.openhomesamerica.org. Any homeowner in America can register their Open House on this web site and will be instantly registered with the appropriate realtor."

"What about the hundred dollars?" asked a reporter. "Does the government guarantee that?"

From the sidelines Devlin looked over at Jones, suddenly intent.

"With this administration's policy toward the helping the average American achieve the American Dream, we applaud the hundred dollar bonus," Crawford Jones shrugged and smiled ambiguously.

Devlin silent punched his fist into his palm in victory.

Now Crawford Jones paused and looked sincerely into the camera. "But there is no obligation to you, the American homeowner. Your home does not need to be listed for sale. You may wish to entertain offers, and you certainly may wish to visit other Open Houses on that night. The President's hope is that this will get the housing and real estate market moving again in a way it never has before. It will create jobs and opportunities in the real estate, home building and financial industries.

The President is proud to announce that Open Homes for America Night will be held a week from tonight. To mark the occasion he will be holding the White House itself open to honored guests in government and industry alike, along with other great government buildings. A list of realtors in your state will be provided after this broadcast. Happy house hunting, America."

Devlin had slipped out before the press conference was over. He was exhausted. He called a cab and went to a bar to watch the broadcast, but was too worn out to drink much whiskey.

He finally took a taxi back to Gloris Dilt's house. It was blissfully empty and silent. Everyone was still at work. He had one more phone call to make and then he would sleep. He dialed Matsumoto's home number in Vancouver.

"Matsumoto-*san*," said Devlin tiredly. "There have been more developments."

"I know." Masumoto cut him off. "I have seen the broadcasts. My father has ordered more money put into your account."

"Need a million at least. By morning."

"As you wish. No matter anyway. My father is coming to Washington himself as soon as possible."

DAVID JENNESON

CHAPTER 20

Still wearing his suit, Red Devlin slumbered on the couch in the thin morning light. As he snuffled like a big, pink cherub he felt himself being prodded.

"Erf," he gurgled. His eyes popped open. As he struggled to sit up, he saw Gloris Dilt clutching the million-dollar check he'd left stuck on the refrigerator door.

"This for real?" she snapped it between her hands.

Devlin seemed sleepily offended. "Of course," he blinked through a cerebral mist. "Funds in the bank this morning."

"No phony-baloney." It wasn't a question.

Devlin's face dropped, like he'd never had a check questioned in his life. "Would I do something like that now?"

"It's not every day a lady finds a million dollar check under the fridge magnet with a note telling her to please take this month's rent out of it."

"Covers everything, doesn't it?" Devlin asserted self-righteously.

"Just making sure, Hon. This is for all the marbles. It's serious now."

"Haven't you seen the reports on CNN?" Devlin rubbed his eyes.

"No," Gloris Dilt coughed guiltily. "I was, ah, working late myself last night."

There was a reason for her guilt. After a long productive day she met up with some of her old cronies. They went to a male strip club to blow off steam. Ended up closing the joint. At that point she announced to her friends she was fed up with this look-but-don't-touch stuff at strip clubs. She said was going to get a real man. Swore to right it before the sun set tomorrow.

"I burned the midnight oil myself," Devlin yawned. "A realtor's work is never done."

"You poor man," she squeezed his shoulder. "You must have worked yourself to exhaustion then fallen sleep."

"What time is it?" Devlin suddenly looked around. "It feels like eight. Eight on the nose I'll bet. Must see the reports," he got up and flicked on the TV. Gloris Dilt eased down onto the couch beside him.

The lead news story was a press conference. There was Crawford Jones, holding this latest briefing from the White House press center itself. Again he seamlessly took credit for Open Homes for America Night on behalf of the President. Devlin marveled at the way Jones stickhandled his way through half-truths and inferences to make it sound like the whole thing was the President's idea in the first place.

Suddenly the broadcast cut live to the White House lawn. The President stepped from a gleaming olive-green Marine PAVE LOW helicopter. Reporters shouted questions at him. The President responded to the questions like they were not questions but friendly greetings. He was a big money patrician, America's Crown Son in a long expensive over coat. As such he returned their focused questions with enthusiastic waves.

"What about 'Open Homes for America Night?' shouted one. Do you support it?"

The President stopped dead. He faced the camera. It froze on him from the waist up. His face suddenly grew serious. "Home ownership is one of the foundations of the American dream," he said gravely. "Renewing and expanding that dream is one of my administration's highest priorities and deepest commitments."

The President wasn't kidding. At least that's what you would have thought if you were watching him now.

The screen flicked to a tight profile of the President. He now elevated his chin nobly as he spoke. "As more and more Americans participate in Open Homes for America Night and realize that home ownership is within their grasp, many of them will turn to the Department of Housing and Urban Development and the Government National Mortgage Association for Government Assistance. These programs have enabled millions of Americans to enjoy the pride and sense of accomplishment that come with owning your own home."

There was a flurry of whirring and clicking as automatic shutters cranked off film.

The President continued, "As new home purchases and refinancing are likely to increase at a rapid rate, there is a danger that Americans may no longer be able to do business with the Federal Housing Administration and its agencies. The increased demand for loans will exhaust their loan authority."

A final close-up caught the President dead tight. Just his face.

"Today I am taking swift action to replenish these funds. I am signing into law HR 4568. This new law provides supplemental appropriation to these agencies so they can continue their good work in helping all Americans own their share of the American dream. To draw attention to this great initiative, this government will also be holding its own properties and great institutions open, and these, I assure you, are considerable."

"Does this mean you'll hold an Open House at the White House?"

clamored two reporters at once.

"It is," said the President with quiet dignity, "the least I can do for the American dream."

To give depth to the story, the news report then cut back to the massive ranks of trucks at the Seattle truck stop. The announcer informed viewers that the Teamster's Union planned a drive-by of the White House so members could show support. The report then showed clips of people lining up at hundreds of real estate offices around the country. Finally it gave a toll-free number set up by the Administration so Americans could find out which real estate company to call in their state. The web site address flashed across the bottom of the screen.

Devlin's jaw hung open. He felt giddy.

To him it looked like the President had ambushed the media for once. He'd hung back and waited for the one question he wanted to answer, then scored a direct hit. Not only did he nail them with a prepared statement, but also the brand new law. Under normal circumstances the legislation would have been second page news, but in this context it had spectacular impact. Guaranteed to boost his popularity. The President, Devlin realized, had raised credit-taking to the highest art form.

Ah, Devlin thought, America.

"Lyin' little shit," hissed Gloris Dilt.

"The President?" Devlin looked at her in shock. "I can't believe you said that."

"Like I told you before, that law's been in the pipeline for months. And he's making like it's a rabbit out of a hat. All his idea and his alone. Can't trust the goddam Democrats. Can't trust the *government.*"

"But you work for them."

"That's how I know. I'll let you in on a little secret. My first husband, Ronald. Sweet man. *Moral* man. America was entering the war and he was against it. Man's entitled to his beliefs. He worked hard in government to fight FDR and keep us out of it. Then he drops dead on the *Sam Houston Zephyr* between Fort Worth and Dallas in 1940. They said it was food poisoning. Crap. I say it was *FDR poisoning.* So they took my Ronny. He was the first. The best. It's been downhill ever since then. Just marking time."

A quiet, rasping cry escaped from Gloris Dilt. Tears welled up from deep inside some pent-up, pre-war pocket of grief and rolled down her cheeks. Devlin reached over and gingerly comforted her. He hoped this wouldn't develop into something more serious.

"I just need to be held," she sobbed quietly. "By a man. Hold me. *Hold me,*" she clinched him to her.

"I've felt that way myself occasionally," Devlin smiled nervously.

"I *knew* you had." Gloris Dilt gripped him tighter and gave his ear a good nibble.

The nibble sent an involuntary shudder down Devlin's body like a jolt of electricity. He gave a helpless whimper.

At that moment Ray Seawee stepped though the door on his way to work at the Coldwell Banker office. Devlin could have kissed him.

"Oh. I'm really sorry," Seawee seemed caught flat-footed. "I didn't mean to butt in."

"*Not* an interruption, my son." Devlin smoothly disengaged himself from Gloris Dilt. "We're just having one of those fireside chats," he patted Gloris lightly on the knee. He needed time to let her cool down.

Seawee turned to leave.

"Hold on a minute. Come back here," Devlin hooked a finger at him.

"What?" Seawee was hangdog. He couldn't think of anything he'd done wrong in the past twenty-four hours except start a nation-wide rumor that America's unionized truck drivers were spearheading Open Homes for America Night.

"A meeting," Devlin said suddenly. "I knew there was something. I need you and Tasha here at five o'clock sharp. Critical."

"That's it?" Seawee seemed relieved.

"Don't forget. Very important. And here. Take this," Devlin extracted himself from Gloris Dilt and stood up. He withdrew an indeterminate mass of hundred dollar bills from his wallet. "Here's a thousand or so. Buy yourself a new suit. In fact, buy new suits for and your well-endowed lady friend. And make sure she shows off her assets. You get me?"

Seawee skipped out the door.

Devlin turned tentatively toward Gloris Dilt. "Bit better now?" He glanced around the room for some tissue.

"Sorry," she coughed. Her fingers dabbled over her make-up. "Guess I got carried away. Damn government. What's this big meeting?"

"The buyer. Coming into town to sign the purchase agreement with Dobell."

"Well count me out. And here," she handed back the check. "This is wrong anyway. Make it out to *this* law firm," she drew a card from her purse.

Devlin saw it was an odd card. It had the particulars of the law firm but the space for the lawyer's name was blank.

"Who is this guy? There's no name here."

"Very specialized law firm." Gloris Dilt tidied herself up. "All their lawyers are American Indians. So are their clients. Tribes. Band councils. Land claims. Rights for casinos. These days, if you want to get something back from the government, ask an Indian. I don't know the lawyer's name. He calls himself *Lean Bear*. Maybe that is his real name."

Devlin scribbled out the check.

"They'll pay all the disbursements. Our names won't show up. We'll need another half-million right away."

Devlin moaned.

"Listen you," Gloris jabbed her finger at him as she walked out the door. "Count yourself lucky. This guy's a heavy hitter. He normally won't even take a case from white bread trash like you. But when I told him what it was for there was no stopping him."

*   *   *

Devlin was about to discover that renting a stretch limousine in Washington that week was no picnic. The limousine shortage was his own fault although he didn't know it yet. All limos had been booked by government big shots so they could scuttle back and forth on the day of Open Homes for America Night and look important. The government had plenty of its own limousines, but the big shots were so busy trying to get into the limelight that they'd used up the government's limo supply and gone into rentals.

In the end, Red Devlin was only able to secure a limo by placing another personal call to Mohan at Diamond Cabs. Mohan then went to his boss, who put the arm on a friend at Congressional Limousines to pull a unit out of the maintenance shop and lease it to Diamond Cabs for a day. Congressional drivers were all booked as well, so Mohan came with the vehicle.

Consequently Mohan drew up before the turreted townhouse just before two that afternoon, a little unsteadily at first, in a massive gleaming boat of a black Chryco stretch limo. Its oversize tires crunched through the crust of the January snow.

"You are paying me today?" asked Mohan as Devlin clambered into the front seat beside him.

Because he was driving a limo, Mohan had been outfitted in the required formal black suit and tie. With his great black beard and tall scarlet turban he might have been the foreign minister of some newly emerging democracy.

"What's with the get-up?" asked Devlin.

"Oh, not to worry," Mohan fingered his lapel. "Congressional Limousines is lending me suit with car. No extra charge."

"No, *that*," Devlin pointed Mohan's extraordinary turban.

"Ah this. For the religion. It is a three-day festival but I am taking no days off. Still I must be wearing."

Devlin became concerned at how the elder Matsumoto might react to Mohan. As President, or *Sha Cho*, of a huge Japanese company, he no doubt would feel free to throw around his opinions on those races he considered less worthy than his own. These views held that anybody who wasn't purebred Japanese, even another Asian, was lower than a weevil. Although this racist prejudice was held by a small minority of aging right wing militaristic Japanese, it was a view strongly held in those quarters.

"Your employer lets you wear this headgear?" worried Devlin. "Even driving a limousine? You barely fit in the car."

"He must," Mohan assured him. "It is the right of all peoples in America for wearing of whatever the religion or culture is saying. You are also looking like you need new suit."

"Eh?" Devlin looked down. Sure enough, the ruffles down his shirtfront were squashed flat from sleeping on his stomach. There were crud and whiskey stains on his white jacket. Although he'd endeavored to keep himself tidy, no white suit on earth could stand up to twenty-four hours of Red Devlin in Washington, DC.

"Looking worse for wear," Mohan pointed at Devlin's soiled paunch.

"Hmmm," Devlin examined his suit front and flicked away bits of food. "What about this?" he tugged the fur lapel of his new Hermann Goring overcoat.

"This you may be keeping."

Devlin felt for his wallet and handed Mohan a hundred-dollar bill. "Tell me when this runs out. And take me to some fancy men's shop. I have to look my best. Today must be perfect."

Mohan may not have been the best advisor to let loose in a bridal and tuxedo rental shop with a man of Red Devlin's atavistic taste. Devlin gravitated toward the more formalized ruffles and frills that

DAVID JENNESON

brought to mind an overweight courtier of King Louis XIV. Mohan on the other hand was drawn to bold statements in big colors. He especially favored green, it being the color of his religion.

Some time passed before there was a meeting of the minds. Devlin constantly emerged from the changing room in white pomp and ruffles that made him look like some eccentric king with bad taste. Mohan, with his anti-ruffle sentiment, sent him back with a curt shake of the head and a click of the tongue. Finally a compromise was reached; a plain, cloud-white double-breasted silk suit with a lime green silk tie. When it came to the choice between a lime green or white belt, Devlin diplomatically chose the lime. In the end, Red Devlin looked like the King of the Realtors.

Thus attired, he entered Washington National Airport to greet the *Sha Cho*, the Emperor of Clients. Suddenly he realized he didn't have the first notion which flight to meet or which gate to watch. He would have to look for all incoming flights simultaneously. He dashed back to get Mohan to help him in the search.

"We will be looking for which persons?" Mohan asked solemnly

"A snowy-haired little Jap," Devlin indicated the Sha Cho's short-ness with his hand. "Matsumoto Corporation."

"And which gate they are coming?"

Devlin shrugged. All he knew was that Miamata Matsumoto would arrive at three o'clock. Devlin fretted and paced around the broad terminal floor. He wondered if he'd even recognize the elder Matsumoto.

In was only through realtor-like persistence Devlin had managed to meet the *Sha Cho* the first time. Once Devlin had identified the *Sha Cho* as the ideal candidate, it had taken months of negotia-tions and dogged phone calls to arrange a meeting. Finally, when the Sha Cho came to Vancouver on business, Devlin had practi-cally rented an entire restaurant for the meeting. It turned out that the old *Sha Cho*, filled with post-war, right wing bitterness and pride, was extremely interested in what he had to offer - revenge for America's humiliating defeat of Japan in World War II. Buying the White House out from under them in a single bold stroke on national television filled the bill.

That was a year ago.

Now, as Devlin paced the floor at Washington National Airport, ten minutes felt like a year. Devlin anxiously scanned the timetable screens for arrivals from Seattle, Vancouver or points west. Then he joined Mohan, who, he noticed with annoyance, was now, idly staring out of a row of large windows that faced the runways.

Devlin dashed over. "Don't be standing here," he said irritably. "We've got to split up. Start looking. They could be anywhere."

"I have found them," Mohan announced.

"Eh?" Devlin looked around.

Mohan pointed solemnly out the window.

Sure enough, there was a twin-engined, fifty-foot private jet with Matsumoto's corporate symbol on its tail. It whined in closer to the terminal.

Devlin and Mohan hurried to the International Arrivals Gate. In no time sullen-looking Miamata Matsumoto walked through, then the *Sha Cho* himself emerged. He was a small, handsome man with a full head of snowy hair. When he saw Devlin he smiled and rushed down the stairs. His striking brown eyes danced.

"Devlin-*san*," said the Sha Cho warmly, bowing. "You look colorful! White and green!" He laughed that violent Japanese laugh that sounds like exploding propane bottles.

Devlin executed his special East Indian style bow, hands prayer-like. Behind the *Sha Cho*, Miamata Matsumoto rolled his eyes.

"*Sha Cho* Matsumoto," said Devlin respectfully. "I see you have not lost your sense of humor."

"Nor you," the *Sha Cho* touched Devlin's lime green tie. Then he looked over. For the first time he noticed Mohan, who stood with deep formality in tux and tall scarlet turban next to the open limousine door.

"Oh," the *Sha Cho* frowned. "I see you have brought some-one . . . *different*. You could not get your regular driver?"

Devlin leaned close. "For your protection, *Sha Cho,*" he whispered. "The man's a human machete. These people make the best soldiers in the world."

"Ah, so. Yes. I should have thought," the *Sha Cho's* face hardened. "America is a dangerous place."

"Not with my man here. You're safe now."

Devlin bustled them to the limousine. As they entered, Mohan bowed deeply, hands at his sides. Devlin personally supervised the loading of luggage then issued directions to Mohan for a down-town destination. They swept past towering, massive monuments, now lit and reflecting light, making them seem all the more immense and imposing. It was like being in a land of giants.

"These Americans take themselves too seriously for what they are," remarked the *Sha Cho* as he gazed through the tinted window. "And, oh yes," he took a package from Miamata and handed it to Devlin. "I have brought a gift."

Damn, Devlin thought. The formal exchange of gifts. Part of the Japanese protocol. He'd totally forgotten. Too much on his mind. Inside the delicate wrapping paper was a beautiful white silk scarf.

"My gift to you still awaits," he accepted the package with a jerky seated bow. He hoped he would think of something.

He also hoped he hadn't screwed up in choosing their destination, where they'd now arrived. With all this formal Japanese protocol to remember it was like walking across a minefield.

Devlin relied on gut feel in choosing the meeting place. He knew that drinking made it permissible for Japanese to loosen up on their tightly wrapped etiquette. He already felt like he was in a straight jacket. Besides, Japanese men appreciated being taken to the fleshpots. Part of the tradition, wasn't it? He offered a silent prayer to St. Homobonus that everything was ready.

The Weasel Inn was much like The Carriage House, except about ten degrees upscale in class and sensuality. Here the waitresses were as beautiful as the dancers. They wore about as little, and sometimes put down their trays to get up and dance themselves. It had three circular stages, one of them the main stage, with plenty of front row seating. There was a faint aromatic scent of perfume edged with whisky and cigar smoke. *The bouquet of the Gods*, thought Devlin. He scanned the place and immediately picked out Tasha.

She shone. Hair piled up high. A simple, black, off-the shoulder dress held up by thin fragile straps, clung to her stunning figure. High-priced lawyers and gold-plated bureaucrats at the surrounding tables glanced in her direction like so many wishful dogs. Beside her sat Ray Seawee. He looked deceptively on the ball in a snappy new glen check suit. Every inch the realtor. Next to Seawee, Anson Dobell sat at the end of the table in his favorite tan duffel coat, fooling with his pipe.

Devlin led his guests to the table. He diplomatically placed himself between Seawee and his Japanese guests. He gestured for the other two to be seated.

"This is wrong," Miamata glanced up and down the table. "I won't permit it. It is an insult."

Devlin felt the first flutter of panic. His eyes swept about the room for unseen transgression he may have overlooked. The Weasel Inn was fashioned after a gentleman's club of the Edwardian era. Warm dark wood, big green baize pool tables, overstuffed chairs, soft couches, long tables, and beautiful women serving frosty mugs and steaming trays. Just short of heaven.

Miamata stood with crossed arms. His jaw worked.

Frantically Devlin glanced at the walls. He expected to see some WW II vintage poster of a Jap Zero being raked out of the sky by an American Hell Cat, plummeting down in oily flames over Midway. But all he saw were pictures of foxhunts and busty turn-of-the-century women tumbling out of lacy dresses.

"What is it, Matsumoto-*san*?" Devlin asked nervously.

"*Seki Ji!*" snapped Miamata. "We are not sitting in the right place."

Devlin scanned the room again nervously. Maybe Miamata wanted to be up front on the row of the main stage to get his eyeful right off the bat.

"If you'd rather be closer to the entertainment."

"Up! Everybody up!" Miamata huffed. He hastily rearranged the seating order to meet his standards. This involved moving his father to the head of the table so he faced the bar's entrance. Miamata then paced around the table, pulled out a chair for Devlin opposite the *Sha Cho* and motioned for him to sit. He stuffed Anson Dobell into a chair on Devlin's right, opposite his own seat. To Devlin's left, opposite no one, he placed Seawee, and beside him Tasha.

"My son, he's a real stickler," the *Sha Cho* coughed his explosive laugh again.

Devlin quickly ordered drinks and food before Miamata could get things bogged down with questions and requests. The waitress leaned low over the Sha Cho, giving him a ripe eyeful of cleavage. He seemed disinterested. However, he gave the nape of her neck a longing look as she walked away.

Seawee noticed this. A *neck man*, he thought.

Devlin put his faith in bottles. That is to say, instead of ordering individual drinks he ordered bottles of them: whiskey, vodka, gin, sake, red and white wine, beer and anything else he could think of. He didn't want to risk the vagaries of table service nor did he want curious waitresses hovering within earshot.

Ray Seawee wasn't big on meetings. He looked uncomfortable already from the tension in this one. Things hadn't started yet and he saw Red Devlin already had his hands full with the prickly Miamata.

Seawee decided to help Devlin out. Do his bit. Grease the skids. He took the whiskey bottle, uncapped it and poured a round for everyone. Raised his glass. He then realized he didn't have the first idea of what to say. He thought about, *'here's to good friends,'* which he'd heard somewhere, but it sounded canned.

The table waited. Glasses hovered.

Seawee's mind went blank. He stared down in embarrassment. There, on the table, he spied a Jack Daniels whiskey coaster. On it, as if written by a divine hand was a ready-made toast. The answer to his prayers.

"May today be your day to plow behind a willing mule," he raised his glass to the *Sha Cho*.

Miamata slammed his glass down, white with anger. Whiskey slopped onto the table.

"I will NOT drink to this! You say my ancestors plowed rice? You say we are like ignorant American farmers? You are the ignorant ones. You do not have the courtesy to bring gifts. You do not know how to seat a group for a meeting in a way that shows respect. You do not even know how civilized people with manners pay respect to one another. The host must pour the first round of drinks. The guest of honor, *my father*, makes the first toast. We are leaving."

Seawee sat down and scowled at the table.

Devlin shot out of his seat. "Miamata-*san*, you're tired. You've had a long flight. You understand we're new at this."

"And do NOT presume to tell me what I understand!"

In the uproar, Anson Dobell leaned over to a confused and angry Seawee. "I thought it was rather a good toast," he whispered. "It reminded me of the tobacco farmers. Did you know tobacco farmers originally owned the White House? Before I did."

Seawee gave Anson a look of anguished bewilderment. Maybe this little nerd was genuinely nuts. He sank deeper into his chair.

Meanwhile Miamata was on his feet. Devlin desperately tried to salvage the catastrophe.

"We'll start over," Devlin stammered, "anything you want."

The *Sha Cho* watched all this without apparent emotion. His knew that his son was a hotheaded traditionalist and that nothing to be done about that. *The Sha Cho* knew how this meeting would end. The greed of these white *gagin* made them predictable. That gave him great comfort, and a huge advantage.

"Yes, Devlin-*san*," the Sha Cho said calmly. "Starting over is a good solution. It will satisfy everybody." He raised his glass. "To keeping an eye on the big picture." He tilted his head back and drained his whiskey.

"The big picture," everyone repeated and drank.

"Thank you, *Sha Cho*," Devlin muttered with relief.

"Let us understand the big picture," said the *Sha Cho*. He rose from his chair and slowly circled the table, pouring another round of whisky. "Japan has a two thousand year history. In two thousand years we made one mistake. At the beginning of World War II our easy victories fooled us. We overestimated our powers. That was the mistake. I know. I was there. We were plunged into a war we had no chance of winning. We were defeated. Humiliated. Yet even in defeat we were victorious."

Tasha narrowed her eyes.

"You cannot argue with the postwar economic success of Singapore. Taiwan. Korea. All due to Japanese administration of those countries during World War II. Do you know that the people of the Philippines lamented our departure? They mourned the loss of our work ethic. And what did the Americans bring to replace it? Food and money. This promoted laziness. This is not the Asian way."

This did not jive with Seawee's recollection of high school history. He tried to imagine heartbroken Filipino slave workers languishing amid heaps of food and stacks of American dollar bills after World War II, weeping and wishing they were back in a Japanese labor camp.

"No," the *Sha Cho* raised his glass, "the East is Asian. The East is yellow."

"The east is yellow," everyone repeated, draining their glasses.

"Through force of will Japan has rebuilt herself," the *Sha Cho* picked up the bottle. He slowly walked about the table and poured another round. "Great physical hardship was inflicted on us by the Americans. We can endure that."

He placed the bottle down deliberately. There was silence.

"Even greater political hardship was imposed on us," he continued. "First the Americans publicly executed our greatest hero, General Tojo. Then the American General Macarthur required us to become a democracy. Millions of Japanese were forced to accept freedom of choice instead of absolute obedience of their leaders. We suffered a national . . . what is your expression, Devlin-*san*?" the Sha Cho held out his hands to Devlin for help.

"A national post-traumatic stress syndrome?" Devlin guessed.

"Thank you, Devlin-*san*. And freedom of choice creates disorder. The Japanese have always preferred injustice to disorder. Yet it was rammed down our throats. Freedom gives us indigestion. But we endured that as well. To this day."

The Sha Cho held up his glass as if he was going to drink, and then extended it at arm's length as if he were aiming a pistol.

"What we cannot suffer is humiliation," he said coldly. "You are too ignorant to understand how painful humiliation is to a true Japanese."

"A little embarrassment's okay," Seawee began, in an effort to smooth over decades of smoldering hatred. "You get red in the face for a minute. Then it goes away. Big deal, right?"

"Silence, *gagin*," Miamata hissed.

"How come he called me a Cajun?" Seawee leaned over to Tasha. This caused the Sha Cho to shoot Devlin a warning look. Devlin rolled his eyes helplessly.

"Quiet," Tasha whispered to Seawee, listening intently.

"But we have endured the humiliation regardless," the Sha Cho continued. "And we have waited. The Americans have let themselves grow weak. They are motivated only by personal interest.

DAVID JENNESON

They glorify selfishness. They continue to buy our products without a care, thinking only of short-term profits and gratification. They spend their time producing expensive goods and chasing their greed. Now they chase our money. Japan has pretended to be the pig in order to eat the tiger. Now the tiger is trapped. We are stronger than our oppressor. The past belonged to the white race. The future belongs to the yellow race. Soon we will own everything you own. We almost do now. You just don't know it yet. Then you will work for us. Then we will teach you our work ethic."

Seawee didn't like the sound of this. He pictured armed Japanese guards with stopwatches on every street corner, shooting at the heels of slow moving office workers.

"To the work ethic," the *Sha Cho* raised his glass.

"The work ethic," everyone repeated somewhat woodenly, and drank.

"Remember, we prefer injustice over disorder, so there will be injustice. What is that expression you have? Life isn't fair? The first thing we will do is institutionalize injustice. But that is for the future."

"Hear hear," Devlin cleared his throat nervously. "To the future."

"So tonight we begin." The *Sha Cho* rubbed his hands together. He seemed to enjoy pouring the slugs of whiskey now. "I am just one of a group of wealthy and powerful Japanese patriots. Many years ago we vowed to restore Japan to its place of greatness. In the meantime we have taken our fortunes from American pockets. Yet we have never forgotten our vow. On behalf of my group, I repeat my vow to avenge Japan's humiliation.

You, Devlin-*san*, have provided an elegant solution. You have taken the Americans' own greed and selfishness and used it against them. To deprive them of their own national symbol, no less. Together, you and I, we will cut off the tiger's head. Americans will be shocked and stunned. They will lose their will. They will realize how powerful Japan has become. But too late. We will come out of hiding. We will assert control over aspects of American life that you never dreamed of. Every American with a Japanese boss. And we can. Because we own it. America can not afford to buy itself back from us."

Devlin smiled and nodded. Seawee's look became more troubled.

Tasha narrowed her eyes and listened hard.

"We will build places like this," the *Sha Cho* gestured at the club, "American men will serve us. American women will dance for us alone. We will do what we please, as we have done for two thousand years. We will take our pleasure."

The *Sha Cho* returned and stood before his place of honor at the table. "You, of course, will be well rewarded. All of you. I am obligated to show you great gratitude for the opportunity you have given me. I humbly salute you. I propose a toast," he raised his glass, "to the new masters."

Around the table there was a battle between greed and repulsion. Hands struggled to raise glasses. Greed forced them up. Repulsion held them down.

"The new masters," they repeated in a low mumble.

All except Tasha. "I feel like I'm drinking away my own freedom," she whispered to Seawee. "I've been a sex object for the last ten years and now I need this asshole? That's so not going to happen. Someone's got to stop him." She dumped her whiskey under the table.

"I hear you."

The *Sha Cho* bowed. "Please take these as a symbol of my gratitude. These are Matsumoto corporate credit cards drawn on the Nippon Imperial Bank. They are for your personal use until this transaction is completed. He walked around the table and ceremoniously passed them out with stiff bows. "No spending limit," he winked, "like before the war."

Anson Dobell had gone a little heady with all those quick shots of whiskey. He clapped his hands with joy on receiving his.

He leaned over to Seawee and held up his card. The bright red

Imperial Japanese Rising Sun blazed over the Visa logo. "I'm going to use this to buy specialty items for when I own that grocery store," he winked.

"Grocery store?" Seawee gave him a perplexed look.

"Oh yes. I get the Upper Lynn Vale Grocery as part of the deal. It's all set up. First I'll find that beautiful native Indian dancer from the Carriage House, Sweet Serenity. I'll sweep her off her feet. It'll be easy. I've got money now. We'll settle down together and run the Upper Lynn Vale Grocery. We'll sell exquisite delicacies to the folk roundabout."

"Aren't you worried about what this guy here has is store for people like us?" Seawee jerked a thumb at the *Sha Cho*. "Japanese bosses making everyone work like slaves? American women dancing naked *only for them*? It'll be like they won the war."

"America has lost its way anyway," shrugged Anson. "The man's right. It makes perfect sense. How can America remain great when its own government ignores a person of destiny like me for thirty years?"

"But now it'll be worse," whispered Seawee desperately. "'*Way* worse."

Anson fingered his card again. "Who cares? I've got this. And by the time all that happens I'll be safe. In Canada."

"You're going to Canada?"

"Oh yes," Anson assured him. "As soon as this is done. It's the smart move. Only safe place. Go back to Canada immediately. Where all this started."

A light came on in Seawee's eyes. "Back to Canada," he repeated to himself. "Where all this started. *Yes.*"

The Sha Cho finished handing out the credit cards. "When the time comes," he smiled coldly, "your new Japanese masters will not forget your loyalty. You will get special treatment. Not," he gestured around the room full of rich lawyers and half-naked waitresses, "like the rest."

There was a long, uncomfortable silence.

What will happen to them?" Seawee finally asked.

Miamata's head angrily snapped in Seawee's direction but the Sha Cho held up his hand. "My young friend," he smiled beatifically. "You *gagin* refer to we Japanese as the Germans of Asia. The Germans are known for their cold brutality. Paradoxically you also describe us Japanese as giggling torturers. Very well. Have it your way. At last you will get both in one package. Somehow I see lines of American businessmen in long overcoats with heads bowed, waiting in the rain to board boxcars. Maybe Hitler wasn't so crazy" he laughed his explosive laugh. "But don't get me started."

Devlin cleared his throat. "Well, now that we've got that out of the way maybe we can just clear up little bit of paperwork." He shuffled the documents out on the table. "This is the listing. It shows the legal description of the property. Anson Dobell agrees to offer for sale 1600 Pennsylvania Avenue to Akio Matsumoto for the sum of fifty million dollars."

Anson leaned over and signed.

"And the deed?" asked the *Sha Cho*.

"Within days," Devlin promised.

"Ah, so." *The Sha Cho* signed. He then clapped his hands rapidly, performing the *te uchi*, the ceremonial clapping of hands to signify mutual commitment. He poured a round of sake, toasted, and clapped again. "In Japan, when we conclude a successful agreement, we clap."

"And here," Anson Dobell downing his sake, "we dance!"

"We do?" asked Devlin, caught off balance.

"Yes. We do. Remember? On stage," Anson motioned toward Tasha. "Like before. You said it yourself at the Carriage House. WE DANCE! We must have it," he clapped his hands excitedly.

Devlin saw where this was heading. "Oh yes, we *do* dance," he looked at Tasha pleadingly. "And *Sha Cho*, this is the gift I was saving for you. As a realtor."

The *Sha Cho* seemed to understand. His brown eyes brightened. "You do me great honor."

Tasha's eyes were cold as steel as she gave a curt bow in the *Sha Cho's* direction.

"This is *my* gift too," she smiled, "so you must sit close to the stage. At the seat of honor. In front of the pole."

It didn't take much more convincing to get the excited *Sha Cho* and everyone else to the seats at the edge of the circular stage. Tasha stood up and walked to the disk jockey's booth. When it became evident of what was about to happen, every lawyer and bureaucrat in the place abandoned his table and scrambled for seats around the stage.

She walked over to the sound booth. "I'm a professional dancer," she said to the disk jockey. Underneath, her tone of voice said, *and I'm not proud of it.*

"Why do I believe you?" he looked her up and down.

"I'm going to do a freebie." She reached into the bottom of her purse and found a tape, left over from when she'd been grinding it out six nights a week at the Carriage House. "Here. Play this. It's already rewound."

"I know a good thing when it's lookin' me in the face, Babe," he took the tape.

Tasha turned and walked toward the stage.

The deejay cut the music for extra effect. "Gentlemen, your attention please. We have a special guest performer. One show only. Feast your eyes. That's all I can say."

Tasha climbed the stairs onto the stage as the lilting, swinging beat of Chanson D'Amour cut in. Songs of Love. Her body swayed fluidly as she seemed to fill the words of the song with warm passion.

> Chanson d'amour-ay
> Ra ta da da da
> Chanson, chanson d'amour-a*aaay*

Men stopped drinking. Bartenders stood with glasses half full. Waitresses stopped where they were and watched. Hands holding cigarettes paused halfway to the mouth. Tasha danced, and the room filled with sensual magic. She shook a shoulder. Down slipped a strap. It drove them mad. The air filled with some invisible, erogenous gas. Suddenly she flung herself into a half-swing around the brass pole. The Sha Cho's hard eyes lit up. She effortlessly slipped out of her dress. There was a gasp. Silence. Then explosive applause.

The other dancers stepped out one by one to watch. They exchanged looks. It seemed clear that they knew they could expect only lukewarm response for the rest of night. Once the audience had seen this, nothing else could compare.

The *Sha Cho* leaned forward toward Tasha. Like he was powerless to resist.

Tasha glanced over at Seawee. He was trying to tell her something. He nodded in the *Sha Cho's* direction, shook his head and drew his fingers across his throat. The message was clear. *Not. No Way. Never.*

Tasha nodded back. She let the music carry her toward the Sha Cho. Suddenly she swung around the pole again. The momentum carried her bra away. She smiled down at the *Sha Cho*, who reached forward as if to touch her. She pulled away, then returned, grinding her hips as if to remove her panties. She looked at the *Sha Cho* like she wanted him to help her pull them down. He stretched further out of his chair.

Tasha reached high up the pole, sent herself whirling down, long legs extended as the *Sha Cho* strained forward for his promised opportunity. She spun downward. Her leg shot out. The spike of her high heel shoe grazed the *Sha Cho's* head. The impact sent him sprawling out of his chair onto the floor. A small cut opened on his temple. The sharp heel had come close, but not close enough.

Seawee's eyes widened. *Good thing he's not a shoe man,* he thought

"Jesus K. RIST!" cried Devlin, bending over.

Seawee dropped to one knee beside the *Sha Cho*. "Is he dead?"

Devlin wheezed and struggled to kneel and still breathe. He plopped down next to Seawee. Felt for a pulse. "Not yet."

"Give my father air," Miamata tried to fling back the gathering crowd. He was furious. "This is murder," he accused Devlin.

Tasha was crying. She looked like she was overcome with remorse, possibly because she'd missed delivering the Sha Cho a mortal blow.

Devlin thought frantically. What would Moses do when his main mark just received a spike heel in the head? "Call 911!" he hollered at the bartender. Suddenly they were buried in turmoil. Men in expensive suites ringed around them. Dancers stopped. So did business. A bouncer pushed people back to their seats while the manager knelt and made great efforts at lawsuit control.

Seawee saw his opportunity. He made his move. "I have to go back to Vancouver," he told Devlin suddenly.

"Shut up! Hang tight! We'll talk tomorrow!"

"No. Now. Tonight. I got a call from Saunders," Seawee lied. "They're in trouble. I'll use this," he held up his corporate credit card.

He was gone before Devlin could clamber to his feet and shout him back.

*   *   *

Twenty-four hours later Ray Seawee arrived in Vancouver. It was Sunday night. The trip had been a nightmare of weather delays, canceled flights and missed connections.

All the way back he'd wrestled with his thoughts. After the *Sha Cho's* speech, it seemed to Seawee that the North American way of life was in mortal danger. Only he could save it. On the other hand, he told himself he could be part of the most famous real estate deal of all time.

Do I want that? he asked himself.

Yes.

He looked down at his expensive suit. He reached into his inside pocket and slowly turned the Nippon Imperial Bank credit card, with its immense buying power over and over in his fingers. *Look at me*, he thought. *I'm a high roller. Thanks to Red Devlin. Do I want to be loyal to him?*

Yes to that too.

But at this price? Hard working people just like him enslaved by Japanese bosses. Everything from skyscrapers to baby bottles labeled with the Japanese Rising Sun. Could he live with himself?

He wasn't sure.

He knew that whatever he did, he'd never be able to stop the *Sha Cho* by staying in Washington. Ray Seawee didn't know a soul in Washington besides Red Devlin. Who would he tell? Who'd believe him? Seawee knew half the secret of getting people to believe you were telling them what they wanted to hear. At this frantic last minute stage in Open Homes for America Night, Seawee's story was the last thing anyone wanted to hear. It would be dismissed as paranoid fantasy. The only other person he knew who believed it was Tasha, and it seemed she'd given up trying to change the world a long time ago.

The jet touched down at Vancouver International Airport. Seawee felt better already. Back in Canada it was different. He figured his only hope of stopping Open Homes for America Night from its source, if stopping it was what he chose to do. Anson Dobell's words echoed in his ears. '*Only smart move. Go back to Canada. Where all this started.*' Maybe the little dipshit had finally got it right.

At least for once in Seawee's life, money was no object. At the Tilden counter at Vancouver International Airport he rented the biggest luxury car he could find. He used his old driver's license and the frazzled clerk never checked the date. When he got behind the wheel he decided he needed more time to think.

Since it was late Sunday night, all of the places to think - like good coffee shops, were closed. He drove idly through the city, angling vaguely across town toward the North Shore Mountains and the Carriage House. The night sky had been brooding and now a terrific storm dropped. Through the slanting rain he noticed a converted movie theater called the Metropole. It was a haunted looking place, but advertised non-stop dancers. Seeking a place to contemplate his next move he went inside.

They charged Seawee ten dollars to get in. This struck him as odd. He couldn't remember having to pay to get into a bar in his life. His eyes got used to the darkness. The seats of the musty old theater had been ripped out and replaced by rows of second hand couches. Barely clad girls lolled on them listlessly. Pounds of sexless dough. Then he discovered it wasn't a bar at all. That is, it didn't sell booze. He found a high, small, circular table close to the stage and he perched on the stool. A waitress asked him if he wanted a coffee, or a coke.

Suddenly a girl materialized beside him.

"Will you buy me a coffee?" She sounded mortally bored.

Seawee didn't want company. He made the mistake of shrugging. The waitress brought two coffees. Twenty bucks.

"Do you want me to dance for you?" asked the girl. She was thin and unpretty. "Twenty dollars, but no touching."

"Nope, thank you."

He looked around and realized he was the only customer in the place on this forlorn Sabbath eve. The poor girl didn't have any-where else to go. She sat next to him and said nothing. He felt more and more uncomfortable. He tried to watch the next dancer when she came out on stage but she was pale and overweight and went through the motions like a giant amoeba.

"You don't have to stay sitting here," Seawee said hopefully to the girl. "I mean, you can get up and look around for more customers if you want. I don't mind."

"I do," she looked at the table. "Those are the rules. Until I finish this coffee you bought me I have to stay here. Are you sure you don't want just one dance?" she begged. "I'll try hard."

Seawee finished his coffee in a gulp. These girls were hopeless slaves. It was horrible. He imagined Tasha being forced to work in a place like this under the *Sha Cho's* new world order. Being grabbed and abused by coarse Japanese bosses and soldiers. All trace of hope extinguished from her eyes.

The possibility of this happening to Tasha was too much for Seawee.

He had to act. Now. He fled the Metropole stumbling up the darkened aisle, bumping into waitresses and dancers.

When he got to the street he realized he only had one weapon left. The one he'd always used when things got too fucked up. The one the prison shrink had warned him never to use. Maybe it was time to trot out Victor, his twin brother. If he blew the whistle and things exploded in his face, he'd have someone to blame.

DAVID JENNESON

CHAPTER 21

The wind whipping off Dog Mountain made the tall cedars along Dempsey Road groan and sigh. Wet gusts scooped up under Ray Seawee's long black raincoat as he stepped out of the big Buick Roadmaster. He could smell distant rain.

He skipped across the puddles and picked his way up the McGregor stairs. A bug lamp swung, dripping and useless.

He knew he had to ring the doorbell. He wasn't sure what he'd say when the door opened. He still wanted more time to think. Standing alone on the porch, it crossed his mind that, even though he'd become a splashingly well-dressed realtor driving a brand new car, there was no telling what he could have accomplished in life by now if he had more time to think.

He gulped. His damp index finger touched the doorbell once.

It produced a distant *ring*, three rooms back.

He waited. Nothing. Rang again.

Ring.

Ring ring ring ring *riiiing*.

An ochre yellow light flicked on deep inside the house. He thought he saw a shadow pass before it. Through the rain pounding on the porch roof he detected a soft footfall. The wind slapped the screen door gently against the frame.

The door swung open. Mrs. McGregor looked at him in surprise. The warm aroma of a roast of beef drizzled out around her in a savory zephyr. Seawee nearly swooned. He'd forgotten to eat again. He smelled the faint, buttery scent of Yorkshire puddings, their crusts rising and crisping in the Sunday night oven.

"Is this the McGregor household?" he asked, seemingly unsure.

"Of course it is," Mrs. McGregor recognized him instantly.

"Has Ray Seawee been here?" he asked. "Oh, sorry. I haven't introduced myself. Victor Seawee," he gave a curt nod and shook her hand "Ray's twin brother. I'm a bit concerned. Could I step in for a minute?"

Mrs. McGregor stood aside, but the shock in her face was evident. Seawee shook the rain from his new black Burberry raincoat. It made him look broader. Taller. She stared as he passed into the house.

"Ray Seawee mentioned he had a twin brother," she closed the door with an audible click. "But I've never seen such a likeness. It's incredible. You're identical. *Clones.*" She couldn't seem to take her eyes off him.

"Yes ma'am." Seawee acknowledged tiredly, as if shouldering a great weight. "Identical twins. All our lives."

She reached out and touched his hair in frank wonderment. Seawee's original prison cut had grown out. Now it swept back a little over his ears. Mrs. McGregor touched it like she wanted to snip a piece off and put it between the pages of a big book as a souvenir. Like he was some biological freak. "Your hair is longer than his, but other than that..."

Seawee felt her hand brush behind his ear. "Well ma'am, poor Ray. He's been in jail for a long time so he's still bound to have the old buzz cut. Ray's hair," he added ruefully, "is short a lot of the time, if you know what I mean."

"Wait a minute. Didn't he say *you* were the one in jail? Yes! I'm certain he did."

"Did he, ma'am? Well that's what I'm worried about. It's why I've come. Maybe we'd better clear this up right now. Is the man of the house in?"

"In the yard," said Mrs. McGregor. "He's busy. Come, I'll take you back." She continued to marvel at Seawee as he passed. "Well," she said, "this is the best argument I've ever seen against cloning, I had no idea the human organism could duplicate itself so precisely. It's terrifying."

Seawee privately congratulated himself on his biological abilities. Mrs. McGregor lead him out into the back yard "Your brother told us you were a real bad egg, but obviously you've made something of yourself. At least someone in your family has," she yelled over her shoulder.

Mr. McGregor had expanded his Open House sign factory. He'd erected a small covered sawmill in his back yard and was now mass-producing Open House signs to meet market demand. At the moment he was busily sawing up sheets of heavy plywood to produce the raw signage. In one corner of the hut was a paint shop. Cans of paint and globs of red and white were everywhere on the lush green grass. Directly behind McGregor was the main assembly area, where he nailed painted posts to painted signs. There was a stack of the finished articles in the shipping area. He seemed to be in the middle of a production run.

Seawee followed Mrs. McGregor across the soggy lawn and inside. The sheets of corrugated iron McGregor had nailed down as a roof over his lean-to sawmill resonated with the rain like drumfire. It was like being downstairs from a cheap dance hall. Combined with the *wrang* of McGregor's buzz saw, it was nearly impossible to hear or be heard.

"Yoo hoo," yelled Mrs. McGregor in a housewifely falsetto. She pounded on the plywood roof. "HEY!"

McGregor looked up.

Despite the weather, the heat of his work required him to wear a khaki sleeveless undershirt. It showed dark patches of sweat. Gray tufts of hair shot through here and there. In his concentration on the job he had become unshaven. He looked up; a determined smile flashed beneath his mustache. Sawdust sprayed up and stuck in his teeth and gray stubble. He wore thick safety goggles. A khaki army surplus forage cap was jammed on his head.

To Seawee he looked for all the world like some aged and deranged Japanese Kamikaze pilot in a wounded Zero, about to make his death dive over the Coral Sea onto an American flat top, ready to sacrifice all for the emperor.

"Not now!" shouted McGregor.

"SHUT THE SAW OFF!" demanded Mrs. McGregor.

"COME BACK LATER!" Mr. McGregor screamed back.

Mrs. McGregor stood up to her full height, - hardly more than her regular height - and marched toward the jury-rigged switch box. She slapped down the main breaker. The scream of the saw blade died away.

McGregor glared at her, powerless and mad.

"This is Victor Seawee. Ray Seawee's twin brother. He says there's something wrong. You'd better hear him out."

The air was sweet with sawdust. The wind gusted the faint smell of wet pine off the mountain. It ruffled Seawee's hair. The wind swirled through again and sprayed them with rain. Mrs. McGregor hugged herself. Seawee stepped forward to introduce himself, sticking out his hand.

"Victor Seawee, sir," he kept his hand extended.

"So you say," McGregor eyed the outstretched hand.

"I don't know how to tell you this sir," Seawee began gravely, "but this is all a fake."

McGregor popped his goggles off. "Fake? Like hell. This is a legitimate business. I'm making good money!" He reached into his pocket, pulled out a wad of bills and shook it in Seawee's face. "Call this fake? There's a demand for what I'm doing here. People line up. I'm supposed to be retired and I'm working OVERTIME for Chrissake," he waved his hairy arms "So you tell me where you get off calling it fake?"

"No, you don't understand. Not you. Not just your operation here. I'm talking about everything. The whole deal. It's a scam."

"Yeah? Then how come we're gettin' paid?" McGregor shook the money at Seawee again. "Your brother Ray said you were in jail. In fact, from what he said I've kinda been expecting a visit from you."

"Well there's a sad comment right there."

"Yeah, real sad. And by the way, if you're his twin brother showing up at the last minute, how come you know so much about this deal in the first place?"

"Look, I don't want trouble," Seawee held up his hands. "I've got my own business now. In my own name, down in the states. But I have to keep an eye on Ray." Seawee leaned forward and lowered his voice. "For a variety of reasons. He's in and out of jail so much. He pulls these petty scams. Then the other morning I saw a news story about Open Homes for America Night on CNN. There was Ray, sneaking around in the background, looking like the cat who ate the canary."

"I saw that story," Mrs. McGregor interrupted. "The one with all the big trucks. But I didn't see your brother in it."

"There've been a lot of news stories, ma'am. You must have seen a different broadcast than me. But when the news announcer said this thing had crossed into Canada and I saw Ray standing there, the alarm bells went off in my head. Then CNN showed Dempsey Road and this house as the place where it all started. I knew there was only one thing to do. Get in my car, drive up here and get to the bottom of it. I warn you, this is not what it seems."

"What are you getting at?" McGregor's thick brows flattened into a line. "I saw the President of the United States himself on TV. He supports this whole deal. He's going to hold an Open House at the White House for God's sake. I felt proud. Where's our Prime Minister when you need him? On a goddam trade mission to the Caribbean, as usual."

"I'm not making this up," Seawee chose his words as carefully as he could. "The President is being set up. When he holds an open house at the White House, it really *will* be for sale. The US government doesn't have the deed. But they don't know it. Ray and his gang of realtors do. And they're going to sell it to a Japanese billionaire right under the President's nose. On national TV. He's called the *Sha Cho*. He wants to publicly humiliate the Americans as revenge for the loss of face they suffered when America beat them in World War II. This has been a long time coming. And once the Japanese own the White House, that will be the signal for the rest of them to take over. You. Me. Everything in North America. Everyone will have a Japanese boss. We'll be worked like animals. It will be a slave economy. For now and a thousand years to come."

McGregor cocked his head and peered at him. "How did you come by this information, exactly?"

"Believe me, I've been through this kind of thing before with Ray. I know where to dig. That's how I got your name. And Ray's up to his neck in this."

"And you say Ray's the one who's done the time in jail?"

"In and out like a revolving door. For just this sort of thing."

"What about you?" McGregor's frown deepened. "Have you spent time in any sort of institution?"

"Never," Seawee was disdainful. "Not a day in my life. Ray's caused trouble enough for both of us."

"Well maybe you oughta try it," said McGregor. "And I'm not talking about jail either."

"Huh?" Seawee blinked.

"I mean you oughta go book yourself into the booby hatch and tell your story to a shrink. That's the craziest thing I've ever heard. While you're at it, get your brother in there too. In the meantime I got work to do," he yanked down his goggles and slapped up the breaker switch.

The buzz saw screamed again. Mrs. McGregor gently led Seawee out by the arm and back through the house. "You really come from a remarkable family," she said in a comforting voice. "Identical twins, jailbirds, and now this. Paranoid delusions of Japanese fascists swarming over North America. You make it sound like we'll be working for Japanese prison guards carrying bullwhips. Your family should be studied," she said, "studied good and hard. For everyone's sake."

Seawee went on as if he hadn't heard her. "I don't know what to do next," he confessed in an anguished voice. "When Ray gets himself in a jam like this it's usually some penny ante hustle. I can usually put a stop to it before he gets himself in too much trouble. But this," he held out his hands, lost for words, "is huge. Too big for me. Too big for you. But we have to stop it."

Mrs. McGregor held open the front door and patted him on the arm. A sheet of rain spattered on the front steps.

"I'm sure you'll find a way," she gave him a slight, patronizing smile. "You know, everyone is making a lot of money on this although I don't understand how, because someone's got to be losing money too. So no one wants to hear stories like this. Maybe you'd better think it over."

Seawee turned. He leveled his eyes at her as he stood on the rain-drenched porch. His voice had a bleating desperation.

"Do you know the worst part? Do you know what scares me the most? It's what they're going to do to the women. They're going to build huge pleasure houses like," he reached to the depths of his descriptive powers, "like Masonic Halls. Only *these* pleasure houses will be filled with Japanese soldiers and their bosses. They'll make our women dance endlessly, like naked robots. And they're going to take their pleasure. That's what he said. *'We'll take our pleasure.'"*

A troubled look creased Mrs. McGregor's face. "Who said that?"

"Why, the *Sha Cho*. The man who's buying the White House," said Seawee, as if it were the most obvious thing in the world.

Mrs. McGregor stroked her cheek in alarm and confusion. "Then maybe you should go to the police," she said and closed the door.

Seawee slunk back through the rain to his car like a wet dog. He was confused. Tired. Hungry.

A few minutes later he tooled the big Buick down Dempsey Road. His mouth went dry as he passed the Devlin basement suite, still dark and undiscovered by the police.. He turned left down the hill at Mountain Highway. The 7-Eleven at the bottom of the hill was a red and white blurry spot through the rain. He drove down through the tall shadowy cedars, their tops waving in the wet wind, toward the Carriage House. He had to buy himself some thinking time. He booked the biggest room they had, stuffed a towel under the door, climbed into bed, pulled the blankets over his head and fell into an exhausted sleep.

*   *   *

Gloris Dilt had a present for Red Devlin. Several, actually. She'd long known the quickest way to a man's heart was through his dick, possibly passing through the stomach first. With this in mind she prepared her own special version of Oysters Rockefeller. The half shells rested on a bed of rock salt. Nested in the shells, soft oysters swam in a sauce that looked and smelled cheesy. It masked the real ingredients - pure Vitamin E, essence of ginseng and gotu kola. On top of the oysters was sprinkled a nutty mixture of deer antler and tiger bone. The final presentation was garnished with bear gall bladder, which was disguised to look like sliced mushroom from the deep, expensive forests of Provence.

One bite of this would make a normal man's balls explode.

Gloris Dilt and Red Devlin had the house to themselves. Tasha had jetted north of the Potomac to resolve a complex three-way dispute among realtors fighting over rural counties of the upper

DAVID JENNESON

Michigan Peninsula. Her near-decapitation of the *Sha Cho* had been explained away by Devlin as a slip of the foot and an error in timing, a double whammy of bad luck that could befall even the best dancer. Outwardly she had seemed suitably remorseful. This had soothed even Miamata's bruised ego. For her part Tasha had realized there was no way she and Seawee could stop the Sha Cho. She decided to take the money and run. For his part, the Sha Cho's injury looked a lot worse than it was. He had been stitched up and sent back to his hotel. In that curiously macho Japanese way, the Sha Cho was rather proud of the injury, like he'd received a war wound on the battlefield of sex.

Now the hinges of Gloris Dilt's front door whined, as if opened by a secret, ghostly hand. It was Red Devlin sneaking in again. Gloris Dilt knew that sound. She hurried across the rug to put a little Glen Miller on. Once inside, Devlin whistled quietly as he walked into the parlor. The tune died on his lips when he saw what was waiting for him.

"Oh. Are we celebrating?" he asked nervously.

"You just take your coat off and relax," Gloris Dilt soothed as she slid in behind and slipped it off him. "My hard working realtor needs a little relaxer." She poured him a massive jolt of sipping whiskey.

"Have I forgotten something?" Devlin's eyes darted about the room. Flowers. Candles. Wine. Jesus. He took a big swallow of sipping whiskey.

"Oh, I don't think you've forgotten a *thing*," cooed Gloris Dilt with a toothy smile. "I think you're a gentle, caring man who knows how to wait until a girl's ready for certain things."

"Ready? Oh yes I see. Ready. Of course," Devlin squirmed. "Well, that makes two of us who are ready then. Ready for dinner I'll bet," he glanced at his useless watch. "Eight o'clock? Dinner at eight. Right? Great movie I'm told. Ha ha. Boy, I'm famished," he rubbed his hands together.

"Girl has to keep her energy up these days," she winked. "For special occasions."

Devlin had by now caught her drift. He quickly scuttled to the table and placed himself in a defensive position behind an empty plate. He felt safer now. From here he could feed her some lines without getting hooked himself.

"Every night I've spent here has been a special occasion," he smarmed affably.

"Oh, I *knew* you felt that way," bubbled Gloris Dilt.

She vamped over, bent low and kissed him on the temple. Devlin noticed with dismay that Gloris' slinky dress tended to fall away from her body when she bent low, although he avoided getting his eyeful. It looked suspiciously like a dress Tasha might wear, with thin straps that tended to slip off the shoulder on their own. Maybe she'd borrowed it from Tasha. That carried alarming implications. Devlin's knowledge of women's clothing was scant. Nonetheless, the possibility existed in his mind that any dress borrowed from Tasha might be of a special construction allowing the wearer to shed the thing with a shake of the shoulder. The garment revealed the crepe-like skin on her neck and arms.

"Are you cold?" shivered Devlin suddenly. He nervously took another a large glug of his sipping whiskey. "Brrrr," he shook the cubes in the bottom of his empty glass. "*Brrrr*. Might need a sweater. These long hours must have given me iron-poor blood. You must be cold too."

"My poor over-worked realtor," soothed Gloris Dilt. She stroked his hair and poured him another big tumbler. "No, I'm *hot*," she gave him a little pelvic thrust. "But you must be hungry as a stud bull. Do you like oysters?"

"Oysters," Devlin raised his eyes heavenward with a smile. He felt on safer ground behind a plate of oysters. He vaguely wondered if Moses had been tempted like this in the desert. But by who? Samson and Delilah? Surely not. The Queen of Sheba? Some woman named Salami? Damn, he wished he knew. Confused biblical images riffed through his mind.

Gloris Dilt set down the Oysters Rockefeller. Instead of the regular six there were a dozen. They steamed and swam in the thick

DAVID JENNESON

cheesy vitamin E-gotu kola buttery sauce. There was more cheese, deer antler and tiger bone baked crisply on top. She sloshed Devlin a big glass full of cold white wine and set it beside his tumbler of sipping whiskey in case his thirst shifted in mid-meal. White wine would fuel his lust for seafood.

"These look fabulous," Devlin grinned.

Gloris Dilt took her seat opposite him. Then she stood up, and leaning low, offered Devlin another eyeful as she shunted the flowers off to one side of the table. "Blocking my view," she explained. "And I do so love watching a man eat. Go ahead."

"Down the hatch," Devlin cheerily swallowed one.

She eyed him like a loving buzzard.

Devlin felt a warm sensation pulse through him like a powerful single headlight. It ran through his whole body like the Union Pacific's swift and massive mountain locomotive, *The Big Boy*, then pulled into the station below his lime green belt, boiler hissing.

He blinked in surprise.

"Have another," smiled Gloris Dilt, downing one herself and chasing it with sipping whiskey.

"I must have been hungrier than I thought," Devlin rubbed the lower reaches of his stomach. He swallowed another, tore off a piece of French bread and soaked up the sauce.

Gloris Dilt did the same and gave an involuntary wriggle of excitement. A shoulder strap shook loose.

Devlin again sagged at the sight of this. In his experience, falling shoulder straps were followed by the total shedding of dresses. Nervously he downed a third oyster, followed by some bear bladder/mushroom, which he found chewy. He felt *The Big Boy* pull out of the station again, which was located somewhere below his stomach. It raced around his body on a cannonball run. It seemed to cover every foot of track in a matter of seconds. *The Big Boy* thudded in below his belt again, its tender packing twenty-five tons of coal, engine steaming, huge wheels hot, anxious to be off and away up the line again.

Devlin sat up straight and raised his head like he'd heard the howl of a distant wolf.

"I met with *Lean Bear* this afternoon," said Gloris Dilt coyly.

"Don't tell me he wants more money," Devlin eyed the oysters. He wanted another one. He felt feverish and hotheaded. "I've already paid him over a million. Can't he get by on that? Who does he think I am? Goddam George Washington? Tell him I'm a big supporter of the American Indian Movement. Canadian Indian Movement too, if there is one. Maybe that'll hold him."

"Oh *no*," cooed Gloris Dilt. "*Lean Bear's* well satisfied. That part of our bargain is paid in full. He even sends his respects."

"Well thank God for something," said Devlin headily. His eyes bulged as if from a drug rush. "Here"s to Lean Bear," he raised his sipping whisky sharply. "May his totem ever be tall and stiff." The moment he'd uttered these words it struck him as a suggestive and foolhardy thing to say. But it was too late. So he shrugged and drank.

"I'll drink to that too," Gloris Dilt winked. She splashed back some of her own.

Devlin thought he'd better get a handle on himself and quit shooting off his mouth. For some reason Gloris Dilt's bottle of sipping whiskey was making him giddy and light-headed. He put it down to overwork. . Best to get his feet back on the ground with some food. He downed oysters number four and five in quick succession.

Gloris Dilt watched fondly.

Devlin swallowed the oysters and was taking on the next. *The Big Boy* fired up again. It balled the jack though his system on sixteen driving wheels, hauling a hundred tons of freight. Steam blew from double locomotive chimneys. It slammed into the station below his belt, headlight burning. Devlin shuddered as a thrill ran though him. His eyes watered.

DAVID JENNESON

"Guess what I've got," asked Gloris, all coquettish.

"The clap?" Devlin asked hopefully.

"No, you naughty man. I've got the deed for the White House."

"You don't," Devlin's eyes blazed.

"*Lean Bear* gave it to me this afternoon."

Devlin was so excited he thought he was going fall out of his chair. He wiped his brow.

"Guess where it is?"

Devlin tried to think. He raised his eyebrows and pointed at the liquor cabinet. "Safe with *Tomasso*," his eyes glittered with a testosterone tao.

"Nope. Even safer." She pointed down the bodice of her low cut dress. "And only you have the key."

"Do I?" Devlin looked around the littered table.

"Oh yes. You do. Why don't you come and get it?"

In his wildly aroused state, this seemed perfectly reasonable to Red Devlin. Yes. Why not come and get it? Couldn't be hard. Maybe he'd just stick his nose down there and nip it out with his teeth. No reason why he couldn't. Unsteadily he stood up. Then, grinning like a lustful half-wit, he advanced.

*   *   *

At exactly 9 AM Pacific Standard Time Ray Seawee drew up in the puddles and gravel in front of God's bramble fortress.

The well-fed Buick Roadmaster looked out of place in this wild setting. Patches of bright, white cloud cut through the heavy overcast, giving the dark cedars and pines an eerie luminescence. Seawee got out and ducked into the tiny entrance hacked through the overgrown hedge that shielded God's home and property from the outside world. He expected to emerge onto the weedy ruins of a lawn, but no. Instead he stepped into a tunnel. A cathedral of brambles. They started at far side of the hedge and clawed their way upwards toward the house, reaching higher and higher, wanting to engulf it and pull it to the ground.

Seawee emerged to the bottom of the stairs. A big raven flapped down on the soft mossy roof. It eyed him. A watch bird? It gave a soft, throaty clacking of alarmed curiosity. He noticed a hemlock sapling had taken root in the fertile moss carpet on God's roof. Soon God would have a tree growing there. Off to the left, about a mile distant, he heard the muted rumble of Lynn Creek as it thundered through its deep gorge toward the sea. Clouds of spray rose up and drifted out of the forest as mist. They swept across God's house, making it appear ghost-like.

Seawee twisted his way out of the bramble tunnel and up the stairs. They were fat with rot. He noticed that off to the left God had constructed a plywood shed. There he apparently tinkered and made repairs to the bits of his life which seemed to be constantly falling down and needed fixing up. If God was such a handyman, Seawee wondered, why didn't he fix his own stairs? A visitor could fall right into lawsuit at any moment.

He climbed the stairs and finally gained a view above God's bramble sea. For the first time he noticed a big red and white *For Sale* sign stuck in the front window.

He leaned on the doorbell. No sound. Not even a dead buzz. For a time he contented himself with the sound of the far-off rumbling river rocks, and watched the ferns nod beneath the weight of the blowing mist. Finally, fed up, he thrust his fists in the pockets of the thousand-dollar Armani suit Devlin had bought him. The silk lining of the pockets felt cool and soothing on his skin. He turned slowly on God's lichened porch in his gleaming new shoes. From this elevated spot up on God's porch Seawee could see out over the brambles and mist. His gaze followed the washboard gravel road as it swept past the house and up into the forest. Then he noticed the tip of the boom of God's tow truck peeping out behind the side-shed.

Maybe someone *was* home.

He rapped on the door. There was a thump and a tumble within.

In a minute or so God opened the door. He wore a green flannel nightshirt and red woolly socks. With his slash of white beard, he looked like a trimmed down St. Nick resting up for Christmas.

"Has Ray Seawee been here?" Seawee asked in a halting voice.

God looked him up and down. "Whaddayou mean? *You're* Ray Seawee."

"No. I'm Victor. Ray's twin brother. I'm *very* concerned that Ray is in trouble again. Could I just sort of step in for a minute?"

God frowned and moved aside. Cutsie Wu emerged wearing a turquoise silk dressing gown adorned with tan-colored herons. It couldn't hide her tight little shape.

"Ray *Seawee*," she was caught off guard. "I thought you were in Washington. I'll make tea." She hurried off to fix herself up, which was totally unnecessary.

"Ray never said he had a twin brother," said God suspiciously. "He never said he had anybody."

"I don't doubt it," said Seawee. "For twins we're not exactly close."

The phone rang and cut Seawee off.

God picked it up. He immediately became embroiled in a complex argument over land rights involving Open Homes International.

From the gist of it Seawee gathered the caller had bought a major franchise in the Chilcotin district in British Columbia's sprawling Interior. The local Indians refused to honor it. They said they'd never signed a treaty to give up the land in the first place. So the Indians were setting up their own Open House scheme, cutting out the white man who'd bought the Open Homes franchise. Show us your title to the land and we'll talk, the Indians said.

God listened and stroked his beard. "Well then, show 'em the treaty," he told the franchisee.

"THERE IS NO TREATY!" screamed the frustrated voice over the phone.

God winced and held it away from his ear. "Then I'd say you're shit out of luck!" He banged the phone down so hard it gave a little traumatized ring afterward.

Cutsie Wu re-emerged with a tray of steaming Chinese tea and gently set it down. The delicate scent of green tea was edged with the sweet mildew of God's musty living room. They sat down on the damp overstuffed couch. The big For Sale sign in the window blocked the view.

"Ray. We thought you'd be in Washington," she carefully filled his cup. "With all the reports we've seen on TV you must be so busy."

"Says he's not Ray," God interjected. "Says he's Ray's twin brother. Says he's Victor."

The couple exchanged looks.

They let Seawee pour out his story. About the whole Open Homes International operation being a diversion to sell the White House from under the President. About the Japanese plan to invade North America with money and power and turn everyone into ant people. About the houses of pleasure they'd build, enslaving women to dance like robots for hours on end.

"The Japanese are like machines," Cutsie Wu frowned. "They're single-minded. We Chinese don't trust them."

"*YES!*" Seawee's voice shook, "And they said they'll *take their pleasure*. Can you imagine? Tasha? Dancing like a slave in front of them? I can't bear it. We have to stop them."

God and Cutsie Wu looked at each other doubtfully. Seawee, sensing he'd mis-stepped, suddenly shut up.

God cleared his throat in the embarrassed silence that followed. "Couple of things clear here," he said.

"*Finally* I'm getting through to someone," Seawee shook his fists in victory. He reached into his raincoat for cigarettes. "Do you smoke? Have a Marlboro? Fresh from the duty-free."

God put his hand out to stop him.

"First thing," said God, "is there's been something hinky with this deal all along."

Seawee nodded gravely. "More than you can imagine."

Second thing is you ain't no Victor Seawee. If you're Victor Seawee it's impossible for you to know who Tasha is, or care for her like you do. There ain't no Victor Seawee, Ray. Never was."

Seawee turned the pack of Marlboros in his hand. "What makes you such an expert?" he finally looked up. "What are you, some kind of swami? Some kind of head doctor?"

"What're you? Some kind of head case?"

Seawee didn't have an answer.

"What's the deal here?" demanded God. "You're just like Devlin. Full of shit."

Seawee paused for a painful moment, on the brink. Then he cracked.

"Okay I know. I'm sorry," he confessed. "It's just that I've used Victor before. He's smarter. People listen to him more. He gets Ray out of scrapes. It's always worked. Keeps me out of the slammer. The bigger the lie, the more people believe it. But this is too big. Devlin's lie is bigger than my lies could ever be. I can't fight his lie with mine. I need help. And there's more. Red Devlin's wanted for murder. That Chinese grocer. That's why the cops are always sniffing around."

God frowned. "That Red Devlin's done a lotta shit, but he's too smart to be a murderer."

"We've got to stop him," pleaded Seawee.

God sat back and stroked his white beard. He popped a sunflower seed into his mouth and cracked it contemplatively. "Tell you where we stand," he said finally. "We've managed to put away quite a bit of money from this Open House deal. And Devlin just funneled a lot more money into the main account yesterday. I paid McGregor off today. Figured I'd drive around and pay everyone else this morning."

Seawee nodded.

God downed his cup of clear tea. He pulled out an English Oval cigarette.

"Plus I got a pile of franchise fees sittin' in a bank account that no one's told me what to do with yet."

Seawee fingered the lapel of his thousand-dollar suit. He looked like a banker, bankrupt of hope.

"And," God added, "I've sold this dump. Just haven't taken down the sign. The little lady here has an idea to get a place on the Gulf Islands and grow herbs. Commercial. Sell to all those ritzy marinas and restaurants for the tourists. Got my eye on a place on Gabriola Island right now."

Seawee looked helplessly at Cutsie Wu.

"I go where he goes," she gripped God's arm. "And I'm never setting foot in another strip bar in my life. No more bending and spreading and standing on my head like a trained seal. Don't those guys have anything better to do night after night? Don't they get bored with it? How can they be so stupid? Those dolts make twenty bucks an hour. The dancer makes a hundred. They're just throwing their money away. Don't they *get it*? Guys can be such idiots. Present company excluded, of course."

Suddenly tears of relief and happiness welled up in her eyes. She held up a glossy real estate brochure showing the sun drenched sandstone cliffs of southern Gabriola Island. "This is all I want. It's all Tasha wants. It's enough for anyone."

God put his arm around her. "Excuse us," he coughed. "She gets a little emotional on the subject of peeling these days."

Seawee stood up to go. He felt a lump in his pocket and remembered. "I took this out of the bank this morning," he flopped down ten thousand dollars. "It was to pay the bills. Here. Take it. Run."

Cutsie Wu stood up on her tiptoes. She kissed Ray Seawee. Her tears brushed his cheek. "Thank you," she hugged him. "We'll always remember you for this."

DAVID JENNESON

Seawee sat outside in the Buick Roadmaster for a long time wondering what to do next. He pulled out the Rising Sun Matsumoto corporate card with unlimited credit and stared at it. Never had so much money looked so worthless to him in his life.

*   *   *

Crawford Jones fretted late at night in his White House office. He was starting to think the President didn't know the difference between a press secretary and a blueberry bush.

Jones had grabbed the *Open Homes for America Night* concept purely as an expedient political media opportunity. He'd seen his chance, moved swiftly, and stolen the spotlight. Now he'd taken the credit for it on behalf of the President. That was his job. The President desperately needed upward momentum in the polls for the fall election.

Now Crawford Jones had a different problem. As usual, he'd done his job too well. The President was so dazzled by Jones' dash and imagination he now didn't want anyone else touching the project. The Commander-in-Chief insisted that Jones personally micromanage the entire affair. After the first press conference, the job should have been shifted down to a White House special events flak. Someone who had time for this sort of detail work.

But no. Instead, last night the President had taken Crawford into the oval office to personally tell him how delighted he was with this little media coup. He was especially impressed with the recent 'spontaneous' White House lawn interview, also a Crawford Jones' tactic.

At one point during last night's Oval Office meeting the President leaned forward. "Confidentially, quick thinkers like you are in short supply these days in government," he informed Crawford Jones. "I wouldn't dream of passing on Open Homes for America Night to some hack at this critical stage. I want you to handle every detail."

"Every detail?" asked Crawford Jones in dismay.

"This thing has taken on a life of its own," the Presidential gaze was leveled at Jones. "An opportunity this big won't happen again before the election. This could cinch it. I want a quick thinker like you in charge."

Like some free enterprise voyeur, the President seemed oddly titillated by Open Homes for America Night. To Crawford Jones' great irritation, the President continually peppered him with questions about the complexities of the project, few of which he could answer. The Press Secretary now ground his teeth at the mention of Open Homes for America Night.

Tonight it was well past eight, but the White House was still a busy place. Crawford Jones had just polished off the final text for tomorrow's press briefing on the Middle East. He yawned and rubbed his eyes. Then he wearily opened the Open Homes for America Night file. He began to go over the guest list. He hoped he had invited the right people. But what about the president's speech? He didn't know how Open Homes International actually operated. He hadn't had time to even think about it. He fumed and drummed his fingers. Stared around his windowless office. Square gray cabinets. Heaps of sagging files everywhere. For all the glamour and television lights, here he was stuck in this basement bunker again burning the midnight oil.

Right, he thought. *If I have to work late tonight, so does that realtor Devlin.*

Suddenly the President slippered in. Typically he entered with no warning. Out of the blue. He had an annoying habit of roving around the White House basement like this after hours like it was his personal rec room. But no one could tell him to knock it off. That was the problem with Presidents. No one could tell them to do anything. Why couldn't he just go upstairs and loaf in front of the TV with the First Lady like a regular President? On the President's heels came his National Security Adviser, who seemed duty-bound to accompany him on these late night rounds.

Crawford Jones shot to attention out of his chair.

"How's our little project going?" asked the President.

"On track, sir," lied Crawford Jones.

"Got it down pat? The inner workings and so forth? Fascinating, you know. Very high political concept."

"I get a funny feeling about this," said the National Security Adviser. "Do we know these Open House people? Has anyone done a background check? Are we in control here? I think we should pass this on to our regular staff. Have them do a thorough work-up on it."

"So far Mr. Jones here has pitched a perfect game," said the President. "Why should I pull him now? I want him pitching *and* catching."

"Actually I was just about to call Mr. Devlin in and meet with him here tonight," Crawford Jones volunteered.

"Were you? Now that's quick thinking. Get right to the source. Do that. I'd like to meet the man. It's a little slow tonight." He wandered out.

Crawford Jones' staff had left long ago. He impatiently flipped through the Rolodex. Finally he dialed Devlin's number.

*   *   *

When the phone rang at Gloris Dilt's townhouse, Red Devlin's nose was down Gloris Dilt's bosom. His teeth snapped at the tip of the White House deed, which was stuffed deep inside. One more nip and he'd have it.

Devlin's head bobbed up. "Who'd be phoning now?" he looked dazedly around.

"Leave it!" shrieked Gloris Dilt in ecstasy.

"Gotcha!!" Devlin cried, diving deep. He emerged with the deed in his mouth like a joweley retriever with a helpless bird.

"Oooo!" Gloris Dilt whooped.

"Must get the phone," Devlin dashed toward it. He stuffed the deed in his pocket. "Could be anyone." He picked it up and listened briefly. His jaw dropped. He put down the receiver again.

"The President wants to see me," he said. His voice was subdued with genuine awe. "There's a limousine on its way as I speak."

"That little TWERP!" swore Gloris Dilt as Devlin dashed out the door.

Red Devlin entered the White House through the North Portico. With slightly bloodshot eyes he regarded the huge lantern hanging from the columned, two-story carriage entrance and wondered if it came with the house. *Of course*, he thought. *It's a fixture.* A Marine guard saluted him. Red Devlin tipped his hat with a flourish. Someone in a suit gave him a security tag and showed him in.

"Mr. *Devlin*," smiled Crawford Jones as Devlin entered the North Door. "Sorry for the short notice. Just a few details we have to clear up. But please. This way first."

Devlin had no idea where he was being led. He followed Crawford Jones through the corridors and hallways. As he walked through the White House, Devlin got the sense of being in an old and somewhat unsuccessful hotel. Still, he noted with satisfaction that there was plenty of square footage. A coat of paint. Pound a nail here and there. It had possibilities. In his mind the ad formed: *Executive Fixer-Upper.*

Before he knew it Devlin was ushered into the Oval Office itself.

Devlin had always imagined the Oval Office to be a little, *personal* -sized oval. He was surprised to see it was a much bigger oval than that.

Along the wall stood the bright flags of the armed forces, hung with streamers trumpeting heroic American battles. Before the President's desk lay a broad, royal blue carpet. It was emblazoned with the big, yellow *E Pluribus Unum* eagle surrounded by a ring of stars. Beyond that a pair of long couches faced across a coffee table. Behind them a pair of big wingback chairs. In truth the Oval Office was the size of a small ballroom.

This gave Devlin an idea. Perhaps the *Sha Cho* would want to turn it into a sushi bar. The oval shape naturally lent itself to a sweeping, curving counter. Where the rug eagle now lay, the chef and kitchen could go, in an open plan visible to all diners. Devlin made

DAVID JENNESON

a mental note to mention this to the *Sha Cho*.

Real estate is service after the sale.

The President looked up from his desk.

"*Mis*-ter Devlin," he said warmly and came around to greet him. Devlin extended his hand but to his surprise got a hug. He remembered seeing this President hug a lot of heads of state on the TV news. He supposed he was no different.

"Sit for a moment," the President led him to one of the wingback chairs. "You must be run off your feet. I understand you and young Crawford here are going to put your heads together and plan our little event."

"I have a few questions if you don't mind," said the National Security Adviser from one of the couches. He was a pill-headed, beetle-browed little man who wore a perpetually suspicious look.

"Eh?" Devlin blinked, still a bit groggy from Gloris Dilt's sipping whiskey.

"Are you working for any foreign government?" the National Security Adviser didn't change his expression.

"Good God no," laughed Devlin. "My only connection with the Canadian government is that I pay taxes to them. That's it," he shrugged.

"I didn't ask about taxes to the Canadian government. I said *working for any foreign government*. There's a difference."

Devlin tried to buy time. "Well, last time I looked Canada had its own seat in the UN and we had our own Prime Minister."

The National Security Advisor's face hardened. "Answer my question."

Devlin thought quickly. Although he couldn't be certain, he was pretty sure the Japanese government had no knowledge of what the *Sha Cho* was up to. Even they would balk at this. No, the *Sha Cho* was definitely in the private sector.

"No sir," Devlin answered truthfully. His smile was relaxed. "I'm no spy if that's what you mean. You know, in my younger days I was often mistaken for a cop. People came up and asked me if I was. I assure you, I'm the furthest thing from it," he laughed.

"What's wrong being a cop?" the National Security Adviser didn't share the joke.

"But I'm not a cop, you see," Devlin tried to explain. "That's the best part. I'm a realtor."

"That's exactly what concerns me. What's your motive for doing all this?"

"Profit," Devlin gave a look of bland innocence. "I hope to gain some sales. And if it benefits the US economy in the meantime, so much the better."

"How can you be sure it will?"

"If I'm not mistaken, I believe it already has," Devlin bowed his head humbly.

"He's right," agreed the President. "The figures are on my desk."

"Something's fishy," the National Security Adviser shook his head. "I say we go slow on this."

The President seemed indecisive. He gave Crawford Jones a questioning look.

"I say we use the East Room for the reception, Mr. President," Crawford Jones smoothly interjected. "And that we stay on schedule. The whole country is waiting. You can't let them down now. They *expect* it. It is too late to throw the mechanism into reverse."

Jones' words had the ring of pragmatic political truth.

The National Security Adviser sagged like a beaten man. He excused himself for a meeting and stalked out.

"The East Room," the President picked up Crawford Jones' thread. "Are you sure we want that? Isn't that where dead presidents lie in state?"

"Hey. Big event. Big room."

"Yes. Good thinking. We'll need a lot of guests to fill the East Room. I'm sure Mr. Devlin here will want his own people on hand. We'll also need the heads of the real estate companies. Bankers too. And union leaders for the building trades. That sort of thing."

"And the teamsters," added Crawford Jones. "They've taken to advertising Open Homes for America Night on the sides of their trucks. It's unheard of."

"Good thought," agreed the President. "This may snowball into teamster support for the fall election, and they don't support anything. Well, Mr. Devlin, you've really captured America's imagination with this. You embody the power of private initiative. America runs on her spirit, you know. Rev her up, give her something with good gut feel, and she'll go like a dream. Accomplish miracles for you. If we do this right, it could launch a surge of enterprise and prosperity. New lease on life. Another American century."

Devlin wiped his eye. "Excuse me, Mr. President. It's just the way you said that. Very moving"

"Oh, nonsense," the President patted Devlin warmly on the knee. "What we need are more people like you around. If America were full of enterprising individuals like Red Devlin, I could retire. Will you say a few words at the ceremony?"

"No, sir, but thank you. An associate of mine will speak, Mr. President. A Mr. Matsumoto. As a partner I believe he will want to express gratitude for the American entrepreneurial spirit."

"Well that's refreshing. About time the Japanese learned to appreciate us after all we've done for them. Now tell me, have we forgotten anything?"

"Just the sign, Mr. President."

"Now what sign might that be, Mr. Devlin?"

"Why, the sign for the front of the White House. It should be big.

It should look as authentic as possible. It should read, 'FOR SALE, OPEN HOUSE' in big red letters so you can see it a block away."

"Really? Now just why is that?" The President seemed genuinely interested, like he might learn a lick or two from this entrepreneurial wizard.

"Just another symbol of government leadership. A sign like that will get splashed all over the media. Could result in a million more people getting on board."

"Of *course.*" the President punched his fist into his palm. "How obvious! How do we miss these things, Crawford? Mr. Devlin, have no fear. Crawford here will personally see to it. He's one of the best men I have. Now, if you'll excuse me. You understand I have other matters of state."

The President rose. Devlin noticed for the first time that he was wearing carpet slippers. He gave Devlin a parting hug.

"Fine work," he whispered.

Devlin stood to go. He let Crawford Jones lead him out a side door.

"Oh, Mr. Devlin," the President called after him, "you dropped something." He walked over and picked the folded white sheet of paper off the blue carpet. "Here you go. Can't be losing important documents so close to the big day," handed Devlin back the deed to the White House.

CHAPTER 22

The main event was scheduled for the second Friday in February, a week later to the day, just as Red Devlin had confidently predicted. Yet to Devlin time went by in a blur. It seemed more like two days.

Even so *Open Homes for America Night* didn't fire up evenly on all cylinders across America. It coughed to life out of sequence, like the Turnpike Cruiser might have done on a cold January day. This was because some states tried to get the jump on others.

The misfiring was caused by the impatience of promotionally minded realtors. Under Devlin's ultra-simple system, a different major real estate company held the franchise for each state. Nevertheless, through radio talk shows and massive advertising, some realtors managed to link the number of signed Open House contracts to the emotional fires of State pride.

As the clock ticked down, it became critical for competing states to put on a good show. The first rally was organized in Cincinnati.

Signs were held aloft, 'Ohio - *The Buckeye State* - 120,000 Open Houses.' Next came Philly. 'Pennsylvania - *The Keystone State* - 180,000 Open Houses'. Local stations covered realtor-sponsored pep rallies. Then CNN picked up the story. TV coverage skipped like a stone over the water from state to state. It was like following a national election.

Wisconsin - *The Badger State*, bragged 200,000. Mississippi - *The Magnolia State*, topped that with 330,000. But everyone was caught off guard when South Dakota - the little *Coyote State*, weighed in with 502,000. It held the lead for some time until California - *The Golden State*, walked away with over a million Open Houses and rising. Computer projections were hastily cobbled together.

Not to be outdone, Nevada - *The Silver State*, staged a parade at dusk through the upscale suburbs of Las Vegas. Realtors uniformed in white suits and bright ties marched in formation, four abreast, carrying Open House signs. Their feet thundered in unison. The sound of their white shoes slamming into the pavement in lockstep was terrifying.

This upped the ante. Soon marches of white-clad realtors carrying Open House signs erupted spontaneously across North America.

The website recorded millions of hits.

CNN quickly gave up all pretense of regular programming. It followed the story full time from a special crisis center which was set up for the outbreak of war and national disasters. They labeled the story, 'American Enterprise'. The extra airtime gave reporters a chance to do background spots on Open Homes for America Night. They probed into its origins. Soon there were long shots down Dempsey Road, its tall cedars swaying in a rainy wind. Both sides of the street were lined with McGregor's red-lettered Open House signs. There was even a human-interest story featuring McGregor in his backyard sawmill, sawdust flying as he frantically filled last minute orders. Another example of free enterprise taking fresh root, the reporters said.

Other networks followed.

Restaurants and bars were packed. Many people took advantage of Open Homes for America Night to get out of their own houses for a bit, since they too were being held open. As events unfolded crowds of people became glued to television sets over bars across North America. This included most high government officials. Eager to follow the example of the Commander-in-Chief, they had signed their houses up too. Obviously the President wanted maximum impact. And no screw-ups.

Red Devlin couldn't have agreed more. Thus, on the morning of the main event he sweated the details. He fretted over forgotten invitations. At the last minute he decided to personally invite McGeorge Lewis as thanks for his government leadership. Devlin realized he might want *Lean Bear* on hand in case there was trouble, but was forced to send the lawyer's invitation through Gloris Dilt. She sneered at the idea of attending herself, refusing to be in the same room as the twerpish President. She informed Devlin that after tonight she was retiring and decamping to The Bahamas. Fast.

Devlin worried that Anson Dobell would lower the tone of the event by showing up at the White House in his tan duffel coat. This was no idle fear. Finally Devlin could take the tension no longer. He rented Mohan and the Chryco limo for the full day then picked up Anson from his office at noon. The three ferried themselves to the Congressional Bridal and Tuxedo Rental Center.

Anson stood in front of big mirrors trying on a badly fitting suit. Mohan clicked his tongue. He again assumed the role of fashion coordinator while Devlin stewed and paced.

"Everything is looking baggy," Mohan muttered to Devlin. He stroked his beard. "He is needing more fillings-up inside."

Now Anson became sulky and impatient. "No, no, none of these will do," he complained. "They don't *feel* right. I won't go if I'm not comfortable. You don't really need me there anyway. I'll sign the papers later." He scowled at his image in the mirror and stamped his foot. "Maybe I just won't go at all," he banged his pipe on his palm petulantly.

Mohan frowned. He hurried to the rear racks and rifled through them. After a moment he pointed something out to the salesman. Then he had a quiet word with the tailor. He coaxed the pouty Anson to the changing room one more time. A minute later Anson emerged in a tan mohair tuxedo. It looked as someone had magically transformed his tan duffel coat into formal wear. Although pinned back here and there, the suit fit his skinny frame perfectly. *Fred Astaire meets L.L. Bean.* Anson stared into the mirror for a long time without speaking then issued a sigh of long-tried patience. At last he smiled.

Red Devlin wilted with relief. He struggled into his own new suit, previously ordered. One tuxedo, totally, blindingly white.

Devlin dropped Anson at home, and then returned to Gloris Dilt's townhouse. It was now just after three in the afternoon. There he found Seawee mooching about the front room.

Since Seawee's return from Vancouver a day earlier he'd been acting moody and downhearted. Devlin was concerned that he might not show proper spirit on the big night.

Then Tasha came through the front door.

Devlin put two and two together, or thought he did. *Woman trouble.* As he looked at the miserable Seawee he felt fatherly. "I'm glad I caught you two together," said Devlin as Tasha walked into the living room. "Now what was it I wanted talk to you both about?" He pounded his forehead in an exaggerated gesture, pretending to think. "Oh. Yes. Yes. You'll both need formal wear for tonight. Take this," he handed them ten thousand dollars. Go out and get yourselves the best clothes money can buy. Get shoes. Watches and pens too. We must *glitter* tonight, *Ramon.* Believe that with every fiber of your body. The powers that be will be watching. But be back early. We're expected at six at the East Portico. Afterwards we'll celebrate. When you wake up tomorrow you'll be so rich you'll never have to work for the rest of your lives."

Tasha seemed to take this for what it was worth and went upstairs to change. Seawee watched her go and then stared at the floor.

"Aw, cheer up," Devlin gave him a paternal nudge. "Here. Take another five grand. And take some advice. Get yourself a grand hotel room for after the ceremony tonight and bed that broad of yours. And if she won't come across, sleep with the most beautiful woman you can find in the nation's capital."

"Huh?" Sea was troubled and confused.

"Spend this five thousand all in one place," he winked. "And remember. *Whoever* you wake up with in the morning, you'll be a rich man."

"Thanks," replied Seawee listlessly and looked away. He seemed to have something on his mind.

"*Ramon*, old son. Buck up for Christ sake," cried Devlin. He clapped him on the shoulder. "Here. Another two thousand. As a bonus. We're *there* man. We've done it! The Promised Land!"

Devlin knew they both had their own unlimited credit cards. Nevertheless he felt the personal laying-on of unlimited cash by the boss was the best way to ignite in Seawee the spirit of the deal that was about to go down.

And spirit was important. By the time the Chryco limo swept by the Jefferson Hotel to pick up the *Sha Cho* and Miamata, Devlin was positively ebullient. Everyone was on board. He scarcely worried about offending Miamata as he spoke.

"So, *Sha Cho*, have you chosen your words for your speech tonight?" Devlin inquired conversationally.

"Very carefully, Devlin-*san*," said the *Sha Cho*. He touched the patch above his ear where his wound from Tasha's shoe was still a purple gash. Even so, with his full head of snowy hair and erect posture he looked like a serene little monarch. "After all, I have planned fifty years to make this speech," he added as they glided down snowy Connecticut Avenue. Mohan carefully nosed the limo left around Layfayette Square. Devlin craned his neck to catch a glimpse of the White House. Sure enough, just as the President had promised, there was a huge FOR SALE sign out front on Pennsylvania Avenue. It was a fine sign. A grand sign. Best of all a big OPEN HOUSE was nailed across it, presumably by presidential decree. Curious crowds gathered around it flashing souvenir snapshots.

"No more beautiful sight on heaven or earth," Devlin confessed happily.

The rest of the party sat in the limo, elegantly dressed and silent. They watched the CNN coverage on the TV in the back of the Chryco. The reports showed that Utah - *The Beehive State*, had given up announcing Open Houses and gone directly to ringing up qualified offers. Utah bragged there would be five thousand sales resulting from Open Houses. They claimed this to be the more honest measurement. A big read-o-graph on a downtown Salt Lake City bank was racking up sales and compounding dollar value like a pinball machine. Mormons danced in the streets.

True to Devlin's prediction, people across North America couldn't resist snooping into one another's homes. In they went, peeking into bedrooms, nosing into cupboards, getting decorating ideas about this and that. *I could do wonders with this place*, the wife would think, and a deal would germinate.

The long wipers of the Chryco limo arced slowly and hypnotically across the windshield with a soft *thwup, thwup, thwup*. Big cottony snowflakes now gently drifted across their field of vision.

Devlin noted the *Sha Cho's* air of confidence. That meant the he thought he had Devlin where he wanted him. Which was exactly what Devlin wanted him to think, because that meant he had the *Sha Cho* where he wanted *him*.

Devlin prided himself on his understanding of the Asian mind. Years of spending the wee hours in cheap Chinese and Japanese restaurants drinking with the staff had given him major insight he thought, and it had been more than worth the sacrifice.

He turned around and gave a conspiratorial wink to the *Sha Cho*, who smiled and nodded back.

They drew into the East Portico. When they emerged from the limo, Devlin and his official Open Homes for America party were greeted by the multiple rifle slap of a full dress rank of Marine guards. They had fixed bayonets and a chillingly hard-edged salute. Devlin assumed himself to be a veteran of this saluting business. "Just nod your head like you know them," he whispered to Seawee as they passed.

Aides guided them through the Entrance Hall and down the red-carpeted Cross Hall. With Devlin leading the way they entered the East Room. There was a surge in the ambient buzz, then a sudden splattering applause. Devlin felt the sudden need to express his humility. He bowed slightly, hands folded, prayer-like in thanks. He hoped his followers would the good grace to do likewise.

Red rows of salmon sushi lined white buffet tables in front of the speaker's podium. Clearly Crawford Jones had paid attention to every detail, including the traditional Japanese lust for raw fish.

The Speaker of the House of Representatives stepped forward to greet Devlin. He was in his mid-fifties and wore formal black tie. His trophy wife, real beauty in her mid-twenties, cooed and oohed with big eyes over the Congressman's shoulder at Devlin as if he were a returning astronaut.

"I am proud to meet you, suh," the Speaker pumped Devlin's hand. "Master stroke, this Open Homes for America. I'm the first fella to admit I wish I'd thought of it myself. Folks are excited. The whole country's excited. I don't know who you are or what side of the house you sit on, friend, but this goes beyond politics. You're the Mahatmer Gandhee of real estate. I'm honored to meet you. I mean that."

At that moment McGeorge Lewis skipped in late. He gave Devlin a nod from across the room as he grabbed a white wine from a passing tray.

Then McGeorge spied *Lean Bear*. Dressed in a Brooks Brothers suit, his hair in tightly woven gray braids, he quietly stood with his back to the wall and wet his lips with a Jack Daniels. McGeorge knew *Lean Bear*. He'd butted heads with the American Indian lawyer in court. It was awful. *Lean Bear* always won. McGeorge had a kind of doggish respect for him, but there was no reason for him to be here tonight.

McGeorge shouldered up to *Lean Bear* through the crowd. He drained his white wine in one slug and swiped the excess off his mustache. He gave *Lean Bear* a cautious elbow. "Don't you think you oughta be home getting some sleep?"

Lean Bear gave him an arch look.

"So you can get up fresh and take more land off the government?" It was supposed to be a joke.

"Tonight you will wish you had ten thousand sleeps," nodded *Lean Bear* with a slow smile. He would not say more.

Then Devlin felt a nudge. A Presidential staffer edged him forward. Then a Secret Service agent guided him closer to the President. Devlin reached out and gripped the *Sha Cho's* arm.

"It's your party now," whispered Devlin as he drew the *Sha Cho* along with him toward the hot television lights and podium. "By the way, I had a thought. Don't you think the Oval Office would make a fabulous sushi bar? Ideally suited. Dinner in the round. Or in this case, in the oval."

"You may have something there, Devlin-*san*," the Sha Cho nodded confidently. "Later we will look at the space."

"Good luck," Devlin squeezed his arm and pushed him forward to the podium.

Right on cue a band struck up. In the background it sounded like fanfare for the nomination speech at a national political convention - 'Happy Days Are Here Again.' Somewhere else a drunken Congressmen started singing. Reporters wolfed fresh sushi. Yet to Devlin it seemed eerie. The East Room, with its twenty-foot ceilings and huge sparkling chandeliers, was traditionally where presidents who died in office lay in state. Somehow the East Room seemed like the last party in the ballroom of the Titanic, and in about two minutes this President would be on ice. Major ice.

For his small part, Anson Dobell filled himself with fresh seafood off flawless green and gold-rimmed Truman china. After he emptied his plate he carefully examined it, like maybe it came with the property and was already his. Devlin beckoned Anson, Seawee and Tasha toward the podium with an enthusiastic wave.

The President rose to the podium. As honored guests, Devlin and the rest of Open Homes International clustered around him. Behind them a gaggle of officials and politicians, not the least of whom was McGeorge Lewis, pressed forward to their fifteen minutes of fame. Seawee, Tasha and Miamata were edged aside.

The President began to speak. The heat from the television lights caused a trickle of sweat to run down Devlin's neck.

"Honored guests and fellow Americans, we are here tonight to mark the rebirth of private enterprise in America. As I speak to you now on Open Homes for America Night, millions of Americans will purchase their first home. Their piece of the American dream. This will cause new wealth to trickle down through the economy like never before. A transfusion into the American bloodstream. Prosperity will ripple across America. It will create jobs. Opportunities.

Americans everywhere will seize their chance to carve their own place. They'll increase their own worth and prosperity, and America's. But it takes government leadership. I'm honored to hold an Open House here at the White House tonight, for some of the hard working folks who helped make Open Homes for America Night possible. Now I believe *Sha Cho* Matsumoto of Open Homes International would like to share a few thoughts with you."

The *Sha Cho* stepped up beside the President. He was easily a head shorter. An aide slipped in to adjust the microphone. There was a chirp of feedback.

"Thank you, Mr. President," the *Sha Cho* gave a slight bow in the President's direction. "I am deeply honored to be here tonight, on behalf of my Japanese associates. There is much we have learned from American enterprise. You have taught us valuable lessons. We have taken them to heart. I congratulate you on your government leadership. Why, as I came in I noticed a big For Sale sign in front of the White House."

There was a trickle of laughter.

"The White House is a noble property. Maybe I will buy it," said the *Sha Cho*. He raised his eyebrows and glanced over at the President.

More laughter as everyone shared the joke. People were surprised to see the *Sha Cho* had a sense of humor. Everyone thought the Japanese never laughed.

"I could turn the Oval Office into a sushi bar," suggested the *Sha Cho*.

There was loud laughter now. This guy was funny. Even the President chuckled.

"I'm glad to see how easily you laugh. It was not so easy for the Japanese to laugh when you Americans defeated us in World War Two," said the *Sha Cho*. "You inflicted humiliation. But we learned. We worked hard. We made radios and televisions and cars and computers for you and in return you gave us all your money. Now, if I wanted to I could use your own money to buy your national symbol out from under you. Your own greed has allowed me to do this. Consider it the repayment of a debt of humiliation."

The East Room went dead. People couldn't believe their ears. The band trailed off.

"Thank you," the *Sha Cho* nodded. "After fifty years a Japanese person has finally got America's undivided attention.'

All sound died away completely now.

For a moment the Sha Cho savored the shocked silence and undivided focus of the crowd. "I want you to think of the next fifty years," his voice was strong and hard. "I want you to think, how for the rest of your lives, every time you look at the White House it will have the Imperial Japanese Rising Sun flying over it. What does this mean? It means you have lost the war your fathers and grandfathers fought and died for on those empty Pacific beaches. I was there. I can still hear the waves lapping. I can hear the flies."

Someone in the audience sobbed. The Secret Service could do nothing unless the President was in danger, and he wasn't. Just thunderstruck.

DAVID JENNESON

"Think of that tomorrow when I run up the Japanese flag over your national symbol. Ask yourself how you will explain away your greed and criminal stupidity to your children. You will look at America's symbol and say to your children that you sold it for a hundred-dollar realtor's bribe. A HUNDRED DOLLARS he pounded his fist on the podium. "While the bones of your fathers lie on the sands of some hostile and forgotten Iwo Jima."

There were more sobs now. The President instinctively stepped forward. "No, I have not yet finished!" the Sha Cho held up his hand. "This only begins your repayment. As you Americans are fond of saying, this is just for starters. We Japanese have ways and we have means. And we have mean ways."

The President stepped forward again. "Wait! I have one question to ask you, and God help you if you answer it wrong. Who *owns* the White House?" asked the *Sha Cho*.

A swell of bewilderment spread through the crowd. No one had ever asked the question.

"I do," piped up Anson Dobell. He stepped forward. His hand pulled the document from inside his mohair tuxedo. "This is the legal deed. In my name."

The President now seemed unsure of what was going on, or of what to do. He appeared to pause, then, typically, to err on the side of diplomacy, thinking this was perhaps part of some extended Japanese-style practical joke, like Sumo black humor.

Not so McGeorge Lewis. He clearly smelled trouble. He rushed forward and reached for the document. The pill-headed National Security Adviser was right behind him. There was a hush as he examined the deed.

"Anson, how *could* you?" he whispered.

"You guys ignored me," Anson sniffed back at him. "For all these years. You built your own little empires. Maybe you're all on top, but you're as stupid as oxen."

"How can I apologize?" muttered McGeorge helplessly. "The bosses liked our work."

"Currying favor with those idiots is like fighting over pig shit. And all *you've* ever done is lie and bully people. No one ever asked me what I thought."

"You always seemed too, er, preoccupied."

"Otherwise known as busy. Who do you think got the work done?"

"We all worked hard."

"You've never done a lick of work in your life," Anson said triumphantly, like he'd wanted to say it all his life. "You've just taken credit for what others have done. Do you know how hard it was to suppress my own talents for the sake of getting other people's work done? It took real strength. The weak lead, the strong follow."

"If that's so I'm sorry. Please accept my apology. Just don't follow through with this. I'll do anything." McGeorge begged.

"I'll tell you what."

"What?" McGeorge leaned close.

"Screw you. I'm not interested in joining your little insider's club anymore. I used to think I belonged in a Packard limousine with Mamie Eisenhower. But I was wrong. I belong here. In the White House. In my house. I've found *my* place at last."

"You can't *sell* the White House," McGeorge pleaded. "It's unsaleable. It's un-*American*."

"I told you. It's my house. I'll do what I want."

"What's the bottom line here?" the National Security Adviser craned through to see.

McGeorge ignored him. "The deed is real," he said flatly to the President, who went pale.

"Told you this real estate thing was fishy," the National Security Adviser said bitterly, shaking his head.

"That's impossible," the President's voice wavered. "America owns the White House. The deed is in the Archives, along with every-thing else."

"I'm sorry, Mr. President, but I'm afraid not," Devlin's voice was genuinely compassionate. He handed him the letter from the National Archives with its official seal on brown letterhead, terse-ly stating they had looked high and low for the White House deed but couldn't find it anywhere.

Lean Bear stepped forward. "I'm a real estate lawyer," he declared. "Whoever holds the legal deed owns the property. That's the law in America. This transaction may proceed."

"*Do* something," the President hissed at McGeorge.

McGeorge held out his hands, helpless.

The television cameras pushed in closer.

Devlin pulled out the *Sha Cho's* purchase offer from his white tuxedo. "Mr. Matsumoto makes an offer of fifty million dollars for this property, of which you are the legal owner," he addressed Anson Dobell, ignoring the President. "Do you accept?"

"I so do," said Anson.

"Good. Both of you sign here please"

Anson and the Sha Cho both leaned over to sign in front of the crowd, who had gone stupid with shock.

"The check?"

The *Sha Cho* handed Devlin a certified check for fifty million dollars US, drawn on the Imperial Nippon Bank. Devlin handed it to Anson, who put it in his pocket.

"Congratulations," Devlin warmly shook the Sha Cho's hand. "As the new owner of the White House, you've made a fine invest-ment. Now if you'll excuse me, I have one more thing to do."

All this was picked up by the expensive White House sound system and carried to the far corners of the room. The crowd, which had been rooted to the spot, erupted into pandemonium.

Devlin cut across the room toward the East Door and Mohan's parked limo. There he popped the trunk and pulled out a sign. Then, oddly for a man in such a hurry, he paused. The falling snow only increased the silence and the sense of intimacy with the Almighty. Devlin stood quietly for a moment and looked skyward, to where St. Homobonus, Moses, St. Peter and all the rest were no doubt gathered in that heavenly lounge, sipping whiskies in hand, watching his every move with keen professional interest. *Maybe now*, Devlin thought, *there's a chair up there for me.* "Dear Lord," he bowed his head and whispered, "you gave me the talent to be the greatest realtor in history. I pray I haven't disappointed you. It is with joy I now finish the work you gave me." He cocked an eye up at St. Peter, the one in charge of barring him from the Pearly Gates. "*That'll fix your little red wagon,*" he spat on the White House driveway.

Then he pelted down across the snowy White House lawn toward Pennsylvania Avenue.

Anguished Secret Service agents raced along with him. They didn't know what to do. They were trained to defend against physical threats to the President and the White House. They had no notion of how to deal with changes in legal ownership.

"You guys oughta relax," puffed Devlin as he ran. "This is private property now." The agents followed him helplessly.

Devlin found a gate and dashed around to the big For Sale, Open House sign on Pennsylvania Avenue. He nailed a huge SOLD across it.

"*MUCH* better," he informed the agonized agents as he stood back and admired his work.

         *   *   *

Judge Mannheim settled into the soft chair in *La Belles on His Toes*. He fingered the pink message slip in his pocket. He couldn't figure out why Ray Seawee had left a call for him to watch the Open Homes for America Night Ceremony broadcast on CNN. At least it gave him an excuse to get out of the house.

Beside him sat Needle-nose.

"You'll have to pardon the surroundings," said the Judge, "but I get an enormous amount of stuff here. Insight. It's a real den of information. And tonight I've got a tip. So you and I, we'll sit here and we'll watch. You ought to start coming down here more often," he suggested.

Judge Mannheim figured if Needle-nose hung out here enough he might get to like the action. The Judge lowered his head to speak in confidence. "You'd better show some gratitude for all the help I'm giving you," he growled and dug his fingers into Needle-nose's knee. He adored skinny dudes.

Now whatever else you might say about Judge Mannheim, he was a sophisticated man. He could wine and dine with the best of them. He calmly ordered a plate of mussels and oysters like he and Needle-nose were on a first date. Something for them to nibble on while they waited for the White House broadcast. It was hard to see the TV behind the bar because so many lawyers and Crown prosecutors were crowded around it.

"Probably the hockey game," observed the Judge. "The boys do so like sports. I like the action. Everything over and done in a couple of hours. I like fast results. You go in, you go out. Another way of saying progress. By the way, had any lately?"

"Any what?" Needle-nose asked nervously.

"Progress."

"Not much," Needle-nose glanced around. He looked a little nervous. A couple of these lawyers and Crown Councilors crowded up around the bar television had a hand on one anther's butt.

"Do you like piano music?" the Judge inquired. "I do. I like piano players. I think this fellow here is a real artist. Intimate on the keys. And boy, do I like intimate. Do you?"

"It's okay I guess," Needle-nose coughed. He looked like heaven and the legal system was shifting beneath his feet.

"Here. Have an oyster." the Judge smiled. "I'll pass one to you. Open wide."

Needle-nose closed his eyes and opened his mouth.

"Jesus Christ, that's HIM!" the Judge shouted. The half shell dropped with a crack on the glass tabletop.

"Huh?" Needle-nose opened his eyes.

"That's *him*. On TV. The realtor we've been looking for. DEVLIN! He's standing up there next to the President of the United States for Christ sake. Turn up the sound!" the Judge commanded.

A barman scurried to crank up the volume while the crowd of lawyers parted to give the Judge a clear view.

The TV cameras rolled mercilessly while the *Sha Cho* made his speech. Devlin first produced the deed, then the letter, then the offer and finally the check. The President looked gray. CNN's commentators were apparently speechless, because they just let the cameras roll, catching everything. The confusion. The anger. The tears.

"I don't believe what I'm seeing," said Needle-nose. "He just sold the White House. In front of the President of the United States. On national television."

"Like HELL he did," roared Judge Mannheim. "He's wanted for murder. You want a warrant? I've got a trunk full. I'll tell you what you do. You get on the phone. You phone the FBI. You get patched through to the White House. You fax them the warrant and tell them to hold Devlin. I want him arrested."

"Really?" asked Needle-nose. "Is that legal? I mean, don't we have to apply for extradition first?"

"Get MOVING!" the Judge roared. He aimed a furious kick at Needle-nose's butt as the cop raced toward the phone.

*   *   *

The President called together the White House staff on the second floor, including butlers, maids and kitchen staff.

"I'm sorry, but you may have to leave," his voice wavered. "I don't know what this *Sha Cho* plans to do. This is private property now."

There were sounds of weeping and muffled sobbing.

"You've made it very comfortable for me here through hard times. You know, maybe the White House isn't the biggest house for a world leader," the President's voice caught with emotion. "Others are finer. They have more art and expensive decorations. But this is the best house. It has a great heart, and that comes from you who serve in it. No, there is only one White House, and I'll never forget you."

The President passed down the line, shaking hands. People held handkerchiefs to their faces, clutched their arms, and clasped hands.

"Mr. President," McGeorge Lewis burst in the hallway. "This just arrived," he waved a fax. "From Canada. A warrant for Devlin's arrest. Signed by a Judge Mannheim. For murder."

There was a gasp from the staff.

"Where is he?" the President was suddenly furious.

"In the East Room. With a measuring tape."

"Then get down there with the FBI and execute this warrant."

There was still considerable confusion in the East Room. Although some guests had left, many stayed. Some wanted to be witness to history, while others still too stunned to believe this had happened.

Devlin paced off the East Room with the *Sha Cho*. "This is a big space. We could divide it here," he poked at a spot on the wall with his tape measure. "Maybe add an in-law suite."

"My son wants to turn this room into a video arcade," the *Sha Cho* looked around speculatively. "I find it quite impressive as it is." They both gazed about the huge room, which was decorated in classic off-white and gold. The large Gilbert Stuart portrait of George Washington stared down at them.

Devlin gestured toward the imposing painting. "The father of all realtors," he acknowledged with genuine respect.

McGeorge and the President burst into the room followed by a very upset-looking National Security Adviser, the Secret Service and FBI.

"Red Devlin?" McGeorge shouted at him as he strode up.

Devlin turned in surprise. "That's me," he had a triumphant gleam in his eye.

"Red Devlin, I have a warrant for your arrest. The charge is murder. I order you arrested and detained."

"On what evidence?" cried Devlin.

"I don't need evidence," McGeorge shot back. "I've got this." He waved the warrant in Devlin's face. I also inform you that DC law prohibits a person wanted on a felony charge to act as an agent in a real estate transaction. Do you even have a license?"

"I've got two. For Washington State and California."

"Whatever. I declare the sale of this property to be null and void. Take him away."

Devlin was handcuffed. Muddled in shock, he allowed himself to be led out.

McGeorge turned and collared Anson Dobell. "Anson, give me that check."

Anson stiffened. "Maybe Devlin has some problems but I'm still the owner of the White House. So no. You can't make me," he said resolutely. "It's mine."

McGeorge put an arm around Anson's shoulder. "Anson, Anson. My friend. The government will pay you ten times as much to settle this little misunderstanding. Now why don't you and I go upstairs and have a talk?" He led Anson to the elevator.

Ray Seawee tried hard to beige himself into the wallpaper. "We'd better beat it," he grabbed Tasha's hand. They slipped out and hurried down the red-carpeted Cross Hall, which was now filled with weeping and confused staff. They made it out through the

DAVID JENNESON

Entrance Hall and onto the North Portico.

Mohan's limousine was parked in the rank. They jumped in.

"Airport," said Seawee. "And boot it." He felt in his pocket. He still had some left over from the ten thousand in cash Red Devlin had given him. That would get them home. Just.

The *Sha Cho* was volcanic but he did not show it. He grabbed Miamata by the arm and quietly hustled him out and down the drive to the street. There he hailed a taxi and told the driver to take them to the airport. Then he picked up his cell phone, dialed his company's nearest office and barked instructions in his explosive Japanese staccato. All credit cards. Canceled. All contracts. Torn up. All demands for Open House payments left to rot.

He was white with anger. These Americans had humiliated him again. He vowed revenge there on the spot, but he wasn't sure if he had enough years left. He would work twice as hard. They pulled into the airport's VIP gate and climbed aboard his new one hundred-foot long Bombardier Global Express. It would get them back to Tokyo at over five hundred miles an hour.

Miamata flung himself down into a plush, padded armchair in the cabin as the jet warmed up.

"They have insulted us again!" he said petulantly. "I won't stand for it any longer!"

"Shut up you spoiled brat!" the *Sha Cho* slapped him across the face.

Miamata buried his head in shame.

CHAPTER 23

*R*ay Seawee sat guilty in the orange plastic chair. He squirmed. Candy bar wrappers and crushed pop cans littered the floor. He dreaded this confrontation. He'd been avoiding it since the spectacular collapse of Open Homes International. He'd moved in to Red Devlin's vacant basement suite when he got back from Washington and was paying rent to the new owner. Devlin wouldnt be needing it for a long time to come.

Seawee was out of work.

Lately he'd developed the habit of mumbling his most troubled thoughts aloud, like he was a kid reading a storybook. He felt he'd gone a little bit crazy and was trying to break the habit. Now that resolution failed him. "*My phone call did this,*" he moved his lips. "*I put him in here.*" Seawee looked up at the grim institutional decor. "*I was only trying to do the right thing.*"

"SHIT!" he slammed his fist down on his knee.

The collection of lowlifes eyed him from their seats. Near the door

DAVID JENNESON

a bony woman scrubbed her tot's face while he made mooing sounds. She stopped and stared at him weirdly.

Seawee realized he'd been caught talking to himself again. He didn't care. *I never meant Devlin to end up like this*, he thought.

"SEAWEE!" a fat tan uniformed guard poked his head through the door and yelled.

Seawee shot up as if an order has been barked at him. *Just like before*, he thought, adjusting his Armani suit. *At least I'll be on the right side of the glass for once.*

He stepped through the visitor's room door and looked for Devlin. For some reason Seawee expected to see him still attired in full realtor's trim - white jacket and pants, loud tie and belt, a fashion eyesore visible to the far horizon. The thud of a soft knuckle rapping on the glass panel of a visiting booth caught his attention. Devlin was waiting.

Seawee blinked and looked again. Devlin was hardly recognizable. He looked crumpled. Deflated. Unable to fill the orange prison jumpsuit.

As Seawee sat down Devlin's eyes lit up. He grabbed the phone. "*Ramon*! You look thinner."

"I came to see if you were making out okay," Seawee replied self-consciously. "This can be a hard place."

"I don't care much for their fashion sense," Devlin flicked an invisible mote of dust from the sleeve of his jumpsuit. "Other than that, life is good."

"Are they making you make license plates?"

"They were," Devlin confirmed. "For a while it was a nice change. No running around or worrying. I was actually getting to like it. You know me. Always a numbers man," he laughed and launched into a coughing fit.

It took Seawee some moments to digest the idea of license plates being fun.

"And you?" Devlin asked when his eyes stopped watering from coughing.

"Still looking for work," Seawee stared at the floor. "It's hard. I found out you need a permit to be a realtor. I mean a license. A real one."

"Take the course," Devlin wheezed. He spread his arms expansively. "You'll get in. Half the bozos with a license on the wall couldn't find their ass with both hands."

"It costs money."

"You're not broke already?"

"Pretty well."

"Got your rent paid?"

"First thing I do every month," Seawee said proudly. "By then I'm broke."

"Damn," coughed Devlin. "I wish I still owned that old dump up on Dempsey you're staying in. I'd give you that basement suite free. Still, it's probably cheaper than any other place you'll find. Didn't you hang onto any of that cash the *Sha Cho* was handing out?"

"I used it to fly Tasha and me back home. I tried to get more money out when we landed but the card was dead."

"How is she?"

"Back peeling," Seawee worked his jaw a little. "She did better than me with the real estate money. She's started a savings account to open up a business for sexy housewives or something."

"You see her?"

"Sometimes I see her dance. But it's a long way on the bus. She comes and sits with me after. It's still sort of pluto... monic."

"Platonic?"

"Yeah, one of those planets anyway. She says when I get on my feet maybe we'll do a gig together."

"Well I'd say you're halfway there," Devlin leaned forward enthusiastically. "Beautiful broad who gives a damn. All you need is something to keep you going."

Seawee fell quiet. "Why'd you do it," he asked after a moment.

"What? Take the tumble for Sheng's murder?"

Seawee rubbed the back of his neck. "Doesn't add up. There's no way I believe you killed that grocer. But you rolled over for it and went down for manslaughter."

"Manslaughter beats murder."

"But you didn't do it."

"What's your point?"

"It's not right you should end up like this. For something you didn't do. Where's the justice in that?"

"*Ramon,*" Devlin smiled. "When are you going to learn? There is no justice. The nearest thing is injustice and there's plenty of that."

Seawee tried to think about right and wrong again. He figured he'd done the right thing by blowing the whistle on Devlin to stop the *Sha Cho,* but now he was guilty of putting an innocent man in jail. *No favor should go unpunished,* Seawee thought bitterly. It seemed like he couldn't win. He wondered if he should tell Red Devlin it was his phone call that put him away. "This isn't how I wanted things to end up," was all he managed to say.

"I'll bet you didn't," Devlin wiped some spittle from the corner of his mouth. "And I'm sorry it turned out this way for you. You showed real ability. But all this," he wheezed and grandly waved a hand at the bleak visiting room. "Bars on windows. Armed guards. All this. It's got nothing to do with justice."

"How do you mean?" Seawee leaned forward.

"Oh no, my son. This is about *business.*"

Seawee gave a slow frown. He couldn't imagine any sort of business going on in the joint except funny business. "I don't get it."

"*Ramon*. You don't think I'm in here for my health, do you?"

"No, but you're in here. And you don't sound too healthy either. What else matters?"

"Oh, it matters," Devlin winked. "To someone else. It matters to them a whole lot when I'm doing their time."

"Who's someone?" Seawee's jaw set.

"Why, the *Sha Cho's* son. Miamata. There's your guilty party if you want one. Now I didn't say that and I'll deny I ever did."

"What's your piece?"

"Plenty."

Seawee gave him a concerned but disbelieving look.

"Look here," Devlin leaned forward, "you think it's cheap to rent the body of a high class realtor to spend three years in the slammer? Especially a body such as myself. Rent the body of the man who sold the White House? Oh no, there's a premium rate on bodies like mine. Payable when I get out."

"What if the *Sha Cho* stiffs you?"

"What if I get my memory back?"

"Where is he?" Seawee narrowed his eyes.

"The *Sha Cho*? Safe back in Japan sharpening his knives and signing checks to my trust account."

"What about the other one?"

"Who? The kid? Miamata? Don't worry about him. His father's found him a nice, safe place. Until I'm finished my time here, the only truly safe spot for Miamata-*san* is in a country with no extradition treaty with Canada or the U.S. In case I change my mind. Perfectly reasonable precaution. I'd do it myself if I had a kid like that."

"So where is the spoiled brat?"

Devlin got a sunny, satisfied look in his eyes. "Libya."

DAVID JENNESON

"Isn't that in the middle of the like … Mohammededan Desert?"

"No, much better. The Sahara," Devlin beamed. "Kalashnikovs and dirty water. Give me a choice between this joint and Libya, I'll take here any day."

Seawee smiled at this little bit of justice.

"And I'll tell you something. When I get out, you come and see me. Who knows? Old geezer like me with no previous record? They might go light on my time. Let me out early. Besides, I seem to have come down with a medical thing. They've got me in bed for observation. Maybe I'll get some sort of compassionate medical leave. The *Sha Cho's* paying top dollar for my time here. I plan to spread it around when I get out. Can't spend it all myself, can I? You worked hard. You deserve your chunk. Consider it an overdue payday."

Seawee's heart plunged into guilt. It made his eyes get damp around the edges. "Doesn't it bother you?" he asked after a moment. "I mean, in the end you didn't sell the White House."

"*Ramon*, but I *did*. The deal went down. Signed, sealed and delivered. On national television to boot. With legal witnesses. *Millions* of them. Who else can say that? If there's a few complications after the sale, it's not my affair."

"The President of the United States is the most powerful man on earth. Why did he believe your bullshit?"

"I was merely an instrument," Devlin's eyes sparkled. "It's how God teaches kings the law. I did my job. No one can take that away from me. I could die here on the spot and I'd die a happy man. Which reminds me, if I do, I've put you in my will in a big way, old son. You're kind of like my son, aren't you? Least I could do. You'd do the same for me. Right, *Ramon*?" he winked.

"But what about the Promised Land? You promised you'd lead us there. Like Moses."

"And so I did. The Lord's work is done. I'm there. So are you. You just don't know it yet. Trust me, you are exactly where you need to be. You'll discover that soon enough, *Ramon*."

Seawee was about to speak when Devlin dissolved in a helpless coughing fit. This time it didn't stop. A guard stepped up quickly and drew Devlin's chair back. For the first time Seawee saw he was in a wheelchair. For a moment the guard's eyes flicked to Seawee's. He wore no expression. Slow and grim, he shook his head back and forth. *This one's a goner.* Then he hurried Devlin's chair out. The last thing Seawee saw was Devlin's fist raised in victory.

*   *   *

Ray Seawee shivered beneath the covers.

The long bus ride back from the prison had given him time to think. When he thought about Devlin his mind became a snakes-and-ladders of innocence and guilt, right and wrong. He could make sense of none of it.

So he had thought about Tasha. As he did, he had traced frustrated X's and O's on the steamy bus window with his finger. *I have to get work,* he thought. He'd seen an ad in that new newspaper, the Poplar Press. They needed a salesman. *If nothing else, at least I know I can sell,* Ray Seawee thought.

His last bus connection, the Upper Lynn Vale, was typically late. He got soaked waiting for it at the stop. When it deposited him opposite the Upper Lynn Vale Grocery he paused a minute, wondering about Anson Dobell. The squirrelly little runt was now so rich he didn't need to buy his dream grocery store. He didn't need to do anything except sit back and count his money.

Ray Seawee on the other hand was forced to walk the whole length of Dempsey Road. Big drops spattered on him, soaking his already-damp clothes again. When he finally made it back to Red Devlin's old basement suite he was shaking with the wet and cold.

Now he lay in bed in the darkened bedroom. Then Seawee felt an impulse - he knew the great realtor's spirit had reached the Promised Land. He could see him clearly; a joy-crazed Moses, suit, belt and shoes blazing white in the bright sunlight of the divine upper atmosphere. He saw him poking OPEN HOUSE signs into all the clouds nearby for the pleasure of it. He skipped from cloud to cloud, quick on his feet for such a big man. Then Devlin poked his nose over a cloud. Thousands of miles below he saw the infinitely small contrails of jets, crossing and re-crossing the globe, filled with realtors trying to equal his feat. They never would. At last Ray Seawee saw Devlin enter the heavenly lounge. He schmoozed God and the assembled saints about his scheme to convert Heaven to strata title. He hollered up to an overworked St. Peter for a round of Alberta sipping whiskeys and Cohiba Esplendidos, the emperor Cuban cigars. Only the best for his new friends. All on the Devlin tab.

A slow smile crept across Ray Seawee's face. Through the basement suite window he heard the rain fall. The forecast was for rain all across the Pacific Northwest tonight. It fell on the mountains. It fell on the lighthouses down the coast. It fell on the sea. It fell on the tall firs and roaring creeks of Lynn Vale. It drummed and danced in the dark puddles of the deserted Carriage House parking lot.

Through its pounding beat he heard a distant night freight train start its journey from the waterfront, bound for a stormy night passage through the Rocky Mountains to the East Coast. As it gathered speed its whistle sounded like a sob caught in the throat of the world.

Ray Seawee drew the covers closer. It was good to be dry under this quilt with the storm raging outside. Slowly he drew his knees up toward his chest. At last he felt warm. The rain fell harder. He realized he had never felt happier in his life. He thanked God for his innocence, and for his guilt.

About the Author

David Jenneson
116 - 140 West 17th Street
North Vancouver, B.C.
V7M 1V4
604 985 4007
dmail@telus.net

David Jenneson has lived in North Vancouver all of his life and has been a published writer for the past 30 years. He has been employed in the newspaper industry since 1976 and most recently has worked freelance on marketing, advertising and writing assignments.

He finished his first novel at age 19, in 1968. *The Voyage of the Codfish Balls* was satirical science fiction, written at the height of the hippie movement, which accurately predicted the Yuppies social events that followed in the 1970's and 80's. The manuscript was sent to ACE Science Fiction and was about to be published when the manuscript was lost.

In 1966 - 68 he wrote a music column in called 'Record Stars' in Canadian High News.

In 1973 his novella, *The Helping Hands of Christmas*, was published in Vancouver by Pulp Press.

Between 1973 and 1986 he had numerous songs published and recorded by various artists, including Terry Jacks.

In 1989 he became a regular columnist for sixteen weekly

newspapers throughout British Columbia writing humorous columns under the title, *But Seriously*. His universally entertaining pieces now appear regularly in the Canada, the U.S, Great Britain, Africa, and translated into Chinese. They have also been broadcast on the Canadian Broadcasting Corporation's live national public radio show, First Person Singular.

In 1995 he began his second full length novel, *Night of the Realtors*, about a Realtor who sells the White House. This novel was short-listed for the Robertson Davies First Novel Prize.

In 1997 he finished his second novel, *Reps*, about a battle between two local newspapers.

In June 1999 he finished his third novel, *Direct Mail*, about a writer who gets mixed up in lottery scams and believes he can change bad luck to good.

In September 2002 he finished his fourth novel, *Moon Over Wal-Mart*, about a man who brings home the spirits of fallen soldiers from unknown graves of the Great War.

He has just finished a screenplay of *Night of the Realtors*. He is a regular feature writer and columnist appearing most recently in the North Shore Times news magazine. A collection of his observational wit is due to be published in March, 2005 by Hard Shell Word Factory under the title *But Seriously*. (ISBN Number 0-7599-4839-9)

His style has been described as visual, very entertaining and with solid cinematic potential. He is currently represented by *Mr. Stephen Ruwe*, Literary and Creative Artists, 3543 Albermarle Street, Washington, D.C. 20008-4213 Phone: (202) 362-4688, Fax (202) 362-8875 email lca9643@lcadc.com, website http://www.lcadc.com/

www.ingramcontent.com/pod-product-compliance
Lightning Source LLC
Chambersburg PA
CBHW031101030726
47496CB00002BA/320